"A contemporary Italian *In Cold Blood*…Provides a more complicated picture of crime and punishment than most crime novels, and the vivid depictions of the page." —Jon Jeffryes, *Library Journal*

"Compelling."—Miranda France, *Times Literary Supplement*

"Absorbing."—*Kirkus Reviews*

"Gripping…Startling."—Zachary Houle, *Medium*

"A magnificent panorama of Rome, dark and rotting…The world portrayed in Lagioia's book is deeply human: a world where parents don't know their children, where fresh young love is based on a lie, where dark passions unfold with cold, geometric precision."—Walter Siti, *Domani*

"A journey into the horrific murder of Luca Varani and into the decadence of Rome, 'a dead city, inhabited by the living.' A city from which Lagioia is on the run—psychologically and emotionally as well as literally."—*la Repubblica*

"Lagioia finds the words to tell the darkest of stories, and allows us to enter into the minds of the killers. Not to forgive them—that's not up to us—but to see them."
—Antonella Lattanzi, *La stampa*

"Will keep you up way past bedtime." *Durango Telegraph*

THE CITY
OF THE LIVING

ALSO BY

NICOLA LAGIOIA

Ferocity

Nicola Lagioia

THE CITY
OF THE LIVING

*Translated from the Italian
by Ann Goldstein*

Europa
editions

Europa Editions
27 Union Square West, Suite 302
New York NY 10003
www.europaeditions.com
info@europaeditions.com

*This book has been translated with the generous support
from the Italian Ministry of Foreign Affairs and International Cooperation.
Questo libro è stato tradotto grazie a un contributo per la traduzione assegnato
dal Ministero degli Affari Esteri e della Cooperazione Internazionale italiano.*

Translation by Ann Goldstein
Original title: *La città dei vivi*
Translation copyright © 2023 by Europa Editionss

Library of Congress Cataloging in Publication Data is available
ISBN 979-8-88966-041-5

Lagioia, Nicola
The City of the Living

Cover photo: Stormseeker/Unsplash

Insert photo by Pexels

Cover design by Ginevra Rapisardi

Prepress by Grafica Punto Print – Rome

Printed in the USA

CONTENTS

THE CITY
OF THE LIVING

Part I

Man's Dining Companions

Rome is the only Middle Eastern city that doesn't have
a European quarter.
—Francesco Saverio Nitti

Let's not attribute Rome's problems to overpopulation.
When there were only two Romans, one killed the other.
—Giulio Andreotti

March 1, 2016, a nearly cloudless Tuesday, and the gates of the Colosseum had just opened, letting the tourists in to admire the most famous ruins in the world. Thousands of bodies were walking toward the ticket booths. Some stumbled on the stones. Some rose on tiptoe to measure the distance from the Temple of Venus. The city, above, was stoking rage in its own traffic, in the buses that already at nine in the morning were having engine trouble. Forearms punctuated insults from open windows. On the edge of the street traffic cops wrote tickets that no one would ever pay.

"Yeah, sure . . . go tell it to the mayor!" The clerk at ticket window 4 burst into a mocking laugh, provoking hilarity among her colleagues.

The elderly Dutch tourist looked at her in bewilderment from the other side of the glass. In his fist he brandished two fake tickets that two fake employees of the archeological site had sold him shortly before.

The line about protesting to the mayor was among the most frequently repeated remarks of recent weeks. It had originated in the municipal offices, and had spread among taxi-drivers and hotel owners and garbage men and *grattachecca* sellers, from whom, in the absence of a more obvious authority, tourists asked for help amid the infinite number of civic malfunctions.

The Dutch tourist frowned. Was it possible that even the real authority, the one in official uniform, was making fun of him? Behind him the crowd got louder.

"Next!"

The Dutch tourist didn't move.

The clerk at the ticket window observed him, a cold smile painted on her face.

"*Next in line!*"

Many of those tourists had spent the night in cheap hotels in Monti, in seedy bed-and-breakfasts around Porta Maggiore. Looking up to admire an angel, they found themselves face down on the ground. They'd tripped on a bag of garbage, or the up-rooted pole of a traffic signal. Above, the white marble, on the street the rats. And the seagulls ate the rats. The ill-informed had waited in vain for a bus, then headed on foot to the Colosseum. Now they were there. They could have been angry at the slow-moving line, but the dead beauty loomed over all of them: the sky over the travertine arches, the two-thousand-year-old columns, the basilica of Massenzio. Threat echoed in the splendor, as if invisible powers had the ability to drag those who crossed them into the kingdom of the shadows. A danger the Romans couldn't care less about.

The ticket seller took care of another tourist. As did her colleague in the adjacent booth. The crowd before them was impressive, but they had seen worse. The Jubilee of Mercy had begun badly. A flop, wrote journalists hostile to the Pope. The year of remission of sins, of reconciliation, of sacramental penitence was not attracting any more celebrating pilgrims than the year of libations had, or the year of unpunished anarchy, or the year of shifting blame.

The elderly Dutch tourist abandoned the line. He walked toward Piazza dei Cinquecento. Next to him was a boy. They reached street level, disappeared among the oleanders.

"Hey, what's that stink?" the ticket seller burst out. Her eyes were fixed on the screen, her hand was on the mouse.

A Chinese tourist was waiting for his tickets.

The ticket seller pressed Print, then looked at her hand. And then she started. Next to the mouse pad were two reddish-brown spots. She barely had time to blink when there were three. And now on the desk there were four spots.

"*Madonna!*"

The Chinese tourist stepped back. The ticket seller jumped to her feet, frightened, in the grip of the worst sensation that an inhabitant of this city can possibly feel: a visitation of bad luck that spares everyone else. She looked up. Drops were dripping from the ceiling. So the ticket seller did what anyone in Rome would do when blood drips from the walls of a government office. She called her supervisor.

A few hours later, two of the four ticket windows at the Colosseum had been closed.

T he blood of a dead rat," said the superintendent of archeological sites.

"A rat?" said someone in the back rows. The crowd sniggered.

Wednesday, March 2. The press conference had been called to celebrate the end of the renovations around the Colosseum. But a reporter asked point blank why in the world two ticket windows had remained closed for the entire day preceding.

The superintendent was forced to get down to details. A large gray rat had been stuck in the air space above the ceiling of the ticket booth. It must have been impaled on a spike and had then struggled to get free, making the situation worse. "The woman working at the time saw blood dripping on her desk. The ticket windows were closed for extermination."

The rat emergency ended up on the front pages of the dailies. The rodents had been coming out of the sewers constantly in recent days. Rats in the area around Termini station. Rats in Via Cavour. Rats right outside the Teatro dell'Opera. They crossed the street heedless of the traffic. They entered the souvenir shops and scared off the tourists.

The papers noted that there were more than six million rats in Rome. Not that there was any shortage of rats in New York or London, but in Rome they'd become kings of the city.

"It's what happens after years of poor administration," said an urban planner.

"The main problem is the way garbage is managed," said one

of the exterminators. "Let's not forget that rats are man's dinner companions."

In Rome the sanitation department was going through dire times. Garbage was everywhere. The garbage trucks advanced slowly. Giant bags of garbage besieged the streets. The paramedics at Sant'Eugenio—there were rats cavorting even in the hospitals—told the press that that was the ultimate outrage, the slap in the face that would force the city to wake up. Many agreed. Right afterward, however, they were assaulted by the suspicion that they themselves were still asleep. The wing of a gigantic seagull shadowed the city. Again the Romans found themselves laughing.

"Yeah, sure . . . go tell it to the mayor!"

The remark was so successful because Rome, at the time, had no mayor. The city was being administered by a special commissioner. A judicial investigation, christened Mondo di Mezzo, or *world in between*, and signifying the nexus of politics and business with organized crime, had turned the city upside down. On trial were council members, consultants, prominent citizens, municipal administrators, public officials, fixers, entrepreneurs, an astonishing number of common criminals. Rarity of rarities: in Rome there were two Popes.

In moments of such confusion the inhabitants of Rome, faithful to ancient custom, scanned the sky in expectation of a sign. But even this—searching the clouds for a secret code—might sound, in 2016, like a fraudulent operation.

On Friday, March 4, the murder was committed.

The next day Rome was inundated with rain.

On Sunday, March 6, Mario Angelucci, who'd been working all week, was sprawled on his couch watching TV. He was a man of fifty-four, thin, and bald at the temples. He worked at a local radio station. The job had made him sensitive to the sound of voices. When he was in the studio, at the console, he didn't need to follow the speaker's argument: he could hear the "tail" of the radio speech, put his finger on the black button, and the cutoff would start half a second after the voice stopped speaking.

Mario changed the channel. He huffed. He tried to find a new position among the cushions. Something he'd heard a little earlier was making him restless. He hadn't given the words the proper attention, but he knew it was important. He switched to the news on RAI 1. The anchorwoman was saying that a twenty-year-old youth had been barbarically killed in an apartment on the outskirts of Rome.

The camera showed an orange apartment building that stood out among the late-winter trees. Mario Angelucci widened his eyes. The murder had been committed in Rome, and he was from Rome. It had been carried out between Collatino and Colli Aniene, which was where he was. But the TV was showing *from the outside* the same window that he could have opened *from the inside* if he had just stood up and walked over to it. Angelucci was seized by one of the strangest sensations of his life. It seemed to him that God was looking at him. And what usually happens when God opens his Eye wide upon you?

"Via Igino Giordani 2."

Proving that he wasn't going mad, the anchorwoman on

the news had just uttered the address of his building. Mario Angelucci jumped up. He headed rapidly into the hall. His heart was pounding. His son was twenty, he had last seen him the night before, he and his wife had said goodbye when he went out and hadn't heard him come home. *Saturday night*. The night of the week when kids get in trouble.

Mario Angelucci reached the end of the hall. He opened the door. An unpleasant odor of stale air hit him. Then the light illuminated the interior. Towels, comic books, balled-up socks, a roll of toilet paper. Mario Angelucci saw the covers flung every which way on a bed where anything could have happened, and, on the bed, a six-three beast, boorishly snoring.

A week later, when no one in Italy was talking about anything but the murder, Mario Angelucci discussed it with his colleagues.

"Guys, worse than a panic attack. My imagination just ran away with me."

His colleagues at the station asked him how he could have believed that his son was involved in such a story.

"What can I tell you, I can't even explain it myself."

The papers said the murder was committed in an apartment on the tenth floor.

"Did you know the owners?" one colleague asked Angelucci.

"Just to say hello to," he answered.

"But while you were panicking did you think your son was the dead kid or the killer?"

"As far as I'm concerned," he said, "it could have been either one. In this city anything can happen."

And at that point Angelucci, whose hollowed face and thin lips gave him a somewhat severe expression, brightened into a magnificent smile. Relief. Relief at having been spared, at having been *ignored*: no one knows in advance on whom the Eye will open, and although certain tragedies strike one person out of a hundred thousand, that unlucky one does have to exist. In him

the illusion that certain things will never happen to us is shattered—so that for others it can remain intact.

At one-thirty in the afternoon on Sunday, March 6, Mario
Angelucci knew that his family was safe.

A few hours later, on the other side of the city, a lawyer named
Andrea Florita received a phone call. Florita was forty-four years
old. He had a lean physique, an open and intelligent gaze, and,
like many of his fellow-lawyers, had opened an office in Prati.
Power and marvels were equally distributed on the two banks of
the Tiber. On the right the Imperial Forums, the Quirinale, the national government. On the other the courts, television, the Sistine
Chapel. That Sunday Florita had spent the day with his son: "My
son is young. When I'm with him I avoid turning on the television.
When I answered the phone I had no idea what had happened."

At the other end of the line the lawyer heard the voice of an
adult man.

"Good evening, my name is Giuseppe Varani. My son has
been murdered."

Not until late that evening did Florita understand that he had
become the lawyer for the plaintiff in one of the most sensational
criminal trials of recent years. On the way home after talking to
Giuseppe Varani, he met an acquaintance. This man asked what
he thought about the homicide even before the lawyer managed
to say who his new client was.

Everyone asked for opinions about the murder. But mainly
they wanted to have their own say. In a few hours the crime had
become the main topic of conversation in Rome. Taxi-drivers at
Termini discussed it, baristas in Piazza Bologna, kids in Monti
and Testaccio. Not to mention what was happening inside the
houses. Fathers who quarreled with children. Wives who warned
husbands about the consequences of an upbringing that was too
liberal or, on the contrary, too strict.

"Have you read?" "Have you heard?" "*Have you seen* what
happened?"

H orror on the outskirts of Rome. A twenty-three-year-old boy was killed in an apartment in Collatino after being tortured for hours. The crime has no apparent motive."

La Repubblica, March 6, 2016

On Saturday, March 5, Manuel Foffo left his apartment at a little after seven in the morning.

He was supposed to meet his mother, his brother Roberto, and his maternal grandparents. The day promised to be anything but fun. His uncle Rodolfo had died. They would have to make a stop at the Gemelli hospital, at the funeral chapel, and then they would go on to Bagnoli del Trigno, the town in Molise his uncle came from, and where the funeral was to be held.

Rodolfo was the brother of Daniela, Manuel and Roberto's mother. He had died of cancer at fifty-eight. Signora Daniela had stayed with him in the hospital during the night between Wednesday and Thursday. Roberto had gone to get her at three-thirty in the morning, and had driven her home. As soon as she came in, she sat down in the kitchen and remained there, in silence, surrounded by the solitude that that building conjured so well. Then she went to bed. A few hours later the phone started ringing. It was her son Roberto again. Uncle Rodolfo's condition had deteriorated, he said.

Signora Daniela then looked for her shoes, put on her coat, and left the house again. She headed over to see her elderly parents, who lived in the building opposite. They had to be prepared. But that very evening she would be forced to verify personally that, no matter how prepared a mother may be, there is no limit to the bad news that can be learned about her own children.

Manuel was outside the building. He was a tall, robust young man. He had a receding hairline, and his cheeks were edged by a fuzz that betrayed indecision: too thick for a goatee, too thin for a beard. He appeared older than twenty-nine, the age he'd reach at the end of the month, and although that morning he had a distraught look—his face was puffy, his eyes sunken—the first thing his mother noticed was his pants. A pair of torn, light-colored jeans. Not exactly the ideal clothing for a funeral. But the reasons that mothers find their children's choices inappropriate are always a bit startling.

"I told him to change because it's cold in Bagnoli," Manuel's mother told the police.

Manuel nodded, disappeared through the entryway of the building, returned a few minutes later in a different pair of pants. Also jeans, but not torn.

"I don't know if he had changed at his house or mine. That's where I keep his clean clothes."

Daniela's apartment was on the ninth floor, Manuel's on the tenth. Signora Pallotto had keys to her son's apartment, and she went up periodically to clean it, especially when Manuel was going to be there "with a girlfriend." Naturally Manuel also had male visitors. His mother was always around, ready to help out. Straighten the rooms. Polish the floors. These were activities Manuel detested. He didn't even have a washing machine; his mother also washed his clothes.

Signora Daniela checked her watch. Roberto would be there soon, and they would all get into his car, leaving behind the trees and the flowerbeds and the church and the imposing orange building that, Manuel alone knew, guarded what would change their lives forever.

At one time, the Foffo family had all lived together in the apartment on the ninth floor: mother, father, and two sons. When Roberto turned eighteen he had had the privilege of using the apartment upstairs. A few years later, the parents' marriage had collapsed. They separated. The father, Valter, left home. Then

Roberto left, and now was married and had two children. Manuel had moved upstairs.

Valter was the owner of several restaurants in Collatino. He also had a vehicle-licensing agency well known in the neighborhood. Roberto worked with him. It wasn't easy keeping up with everything. If you're not born rich, being an entrepreneur in Italy means living in a state of constant worry. You don't sleep at night. One wrong move is enough to go bust. But Valter Foffo hadn't gone bust. He and Roberto worked hard, they weren't frightened by difficulties, and when possible they didn't say no to the rewards. They dressed well. They drove nice cars.

At seven-thirty Roberto Foffo arrived in Via Igino Giordani. He parked the car. Signora Daniela and the grandparents sat in the back, Manuel got in next to his brother. The car started off again. Half an hour later they crossed the Tor di Quinto bridge, beneath which the waters of the Tiber run dark and slow.

Roberto drove with concentration. Manuel had to be careful not to fall asleep. Brothers. There's always something awkward about seeing them next to each other. Unless the age difference explains all the other differences, there's the risk of spotting, in the offspring of the same blood, the divergence between who wins the battle of life and who loses.

Roberto was four years older than Manuel and had graduated from the university with a degree in insurance management. He worked. He had a family. Manuel had studied law but never graduated, he had a messy romantic life, and it wasn't easy to figure out how he spent his days. Roberto was taking them all to say their last goodbye to a relative who had just died, and even in that banal occupation—gripping the steering wheel of a car—the brothers' roles couldn't have been reversed. Manuel had lost his license for drunk driving. In addition to excessive alcohol, traces of Xanax and Klonopin had been found in his blood. But who today doesn't take benzos?

The truly slippery terrain was work.

"What do you do, in life?"

Rome is a city that tolerates vagueness when it comes to such subjects. Past a certain point, however, forbearance becomes a sneer. Thus Manuel, asked about his professional life, might feel pressed to use the first person in an adventurous way.

"I manage some restaurants with my family. I'm also working on various digital projects. I'm developing a startup."

When the same question was put to his brother, the answer was: "Manuel comes to the restaurant to eat. He's a fan of marketing, he reads a lot, every so often he tries out an idea on us. But in fact he doesn't do any work."

Valter emphasized Manuel's character traits when he talked about his younger son. "He's a well-behaved, well-brought-up young man, very meek and reserved. At school he never got into fights." Also according to his father, Manuel was "very intelligent," lived a "regular" life, had a thirst for culture ("He can buy two books to read in one night"), but had never shown much interest in the vehicle-licensing agency, which would have guaranteed him a future ("I tried to get him involved, the way I did with Roberto. It was hopeless"). His son eagerly attended marketing and IT courses ("I give him the money for the courses"), and in recent months he had in fact worked intensely on a startup. It was a project for the Italian Olympic committee, thanks to which—Valter always said—"he could have turned things around." But the project, he added, "wasn't successful."

He could have turned things around. It wasn't successful.

When fathers speak of male children like this, it's never clear if their intention is to praise or denigrate them or subject them to that unpunishable exercise in humiliation that is excessive praise.

But the oddest statement regarding Manuel came from his mother: "Manuel doesn't tell me if he goes to the restaurant to work or not. I don't even know precisely what sort of relations he has with his father."

When they crossed Via della Pineta Sacchetti, the gigantic sil-houette of the Gemelli Polyclinic came into view.

Roberto parked. The five got out of the car and entered the hospital complex.

Manuel was now dragging his feet, feeling his brother's eyes on him. Two days before, at an hour that for Roberto was seven in the morning and for Manuel any point on a crazed time line, Roberto had received a text message that was ludicrous to say the least. In the text Manuel invited him to join him. As an incentive he promised a trans woman and cocaine.

"Ciao Roberto, want to join us? I met a trans. We've also got some *bamba*."

Apart from the content, the choice of words was strange. Roberto couldn't say that Manuel never snorted a line, but con-sidered it unlikely that he hung around with trans women, and was sure he would never have used the word *bamba* to refer to cocaine. Was it really he who'd written it? Maybe Manuel had spent the night with some lowlife and they'd decided to amuse themselves at the expense of people who had to get up early to go to work the next day. Were they making fun of him? Irritated, Roberto had called Manuel, yelled at him on the phone for a few seconds, and then told him to go to hell, without giving him a chance to explain.

Signora Daniela also reported a rather bizarre episode that had taken place the evening before. Around nine-thirty, Manuel had called her.

"Listen mamma, in about fifteen minutes I'm coming by with a friend to get the car keys."

The fact that Manuel wanted to make her complicit in a violation of the law had upset Signora Daniela. And then who was this friend? "I'm not giving you anything," she answered. Uncle Rodolfo had died, there were other things to think about. "Anyway," Daniela told the police, "my son's request seemed so absurd that the whole conversation went on between us as if it were some sort of harmless joke." Signora Daniela had stood her ground. Manuel hadn't insisted.

Manuel entered the funeral chapel under Roberto's severe scrutiny and his mother's forgiving gaze. To forgive, however, is to judge. Stooped shoulders bear witness to the struggle that at certain moments of life we endure in order not to let our identity—or what we consider our identity—be overwhelmed by the false image others have of us.

Manuel made his way between his relatives, reached his uncle's coffin. Pausing to observe the body, he promised himself to make a decision by evening. To know. To know while the others didn't. The sensation was new. Manuel knew when his mother had told him to change his pants, he knew in the car sitting next to his brother, he knew now in the funeral chapel. He knew what they couldn't even imagine. He was used to submitting to the decisions of others, and now he was the one who would decide. A few words. All he had to do was utter them to upend all their lives.

But as soon as they left the hospital, Manuel found that he had said nothing. He was tired, confused, he followed Roberto to the car. They waited for their mother and grandparents and the car started up again.

The funeral was scheduled for early afternoon. The car turned onto Via Flaminia. In a hundred kilometers they would stop. They were meeting Valter at the San Vittore exit. Things between him and Daniela were tense. There was an ongoing legal battle. In spite of that, Valter had decided to attend the funeral of his former brother-in-law.

Rain clouds thickened on the horizon. They passed Torre Spaccata, Cinecittà; the meadows of the Roman countryside rolled by. Manuel fell asleep.

"Give your place to grandpa, that way we'll have a little more room."

He was awakened by his brother an hour later. He heard birds chirping. They had stopped at a service station. In front of them was a snack bar. After a few minutes he arrived. They saw the car make a half circle before coming to a halt, then the man stood up on the asphalt. Valter Foffo had only to appear to focus the relatives' attention on himself. Manuel, giving his seat to his grandfather, got out of Roberto's car and headed toward his father's.

As soon as he got in, the young man felt an electric shock. Between certain fathers and sons storm clouds can gather even when nothing has happened: so imagine if one considers the other lacking in respect toward him. In this case it was Valter who was irritated. Manuel thought he knew why. Valter said nothing and started the car.

A few minutes later they were on the road. Every so often Valter observed his son, then his own head in the rearview mirror. He was a good-looking man of sixty. White hair, fleshy mouth, a nose that in ancient times could have been a consul's. That day he was wearing a black jacket over a white shirt, striped tie and dark pants. Looking at him, so well groomed and elegant, you'd find it hard to imagine how stressed he was. Work gave him no respite, the family wasn't any better. Finally he began.

"You want to tell me what happened?"

In public Valter spoke of his son as a shy young man, incapable of lying. But when he was with him, what in the eyes of outsiders were supposed to be fine moral qualities took on a different meaning. Sincerity could be a sign of weakness, reserve of secretiveness.

"Are you going to tell me what you were up to?"

He had tried to reach him all day the day before. He'd made phone call after phone call without getting the slightest response. As always he was reduced to chasing after his son in order to do him a favor: he had to pay an installment for one of the many courses Manuel took, he needed some information for the bank transfer.

Manuel, in the passenger seat, was silent. His eyes were swollen. This didn't escape his father; as soon as he saw him at the gas station he'd realized that something wasn't right. The young man was *strange*. The person who, according to Manuel, was more likely than anyone else in the world to misunderstand him was also the only one who had intuited that his son, that day, might cause more problems than the death of an uncle.

"So? I called you a bunch of times. Why didn't you answer?"

Manuel had promised himself to make a decision by evening, but when his father started with the interrogation he was capable of ripping the words out of him.

"So, what did you do? Were you drinking? Were you drunk? Manuel!"

"Dad, I was high on cocaine."

They passed a dairy, then an awning factory. A small group of poplars rose solitary amid the fields, caressed by the afternoon light. Valter came out of the stupor his son's words had thrust him into.

"What do you mean, cocaine!" His voice was angry. "How could you go so low?"

Stock phrases, in certain situations, are helpful.

"Dad, really I went even lower."

Now Valter was disoriented. He found on the tip of his tongue a question that was really too ingenuous: "What could be worse than cocaine?"

"We killed someone."

The car continued to travel along the state road. They passed a gas pump, a viaduct, a billboard inviting local entrepreneurs to buy advertising space.

"What does *we* killed mean?"

Valter was stunned, stupefied, incredulous, he felt something flare up in his stomach, but the blow didn't keep him, instinctively, from looking for a way out. The use of the plural. The presence of another person could reduce, if not exclude, his son's responsibility. Valter felt his heart race. Looking for something to grab on to in the confusion, the tangle, the absurdity into which he realized, second by second, he had been cast, he found himself aiming at a traffic death. Manuel had been drinking. He had done it before. Despite the loss of his license, he had been driving half drunk. That's what had happened. Manuel had really fucked up. Assuming that he had been the driver.

"Dad, there wasn't any traffic accident."

"Then how would this person have been killed?"

"I think stabbed. And hit with a hammer."

Valter looked carefully at the road to be sure he was still there, lucid, on the same planet where he had awakened that morning. He heard his own voice asking Manuel the name of his accomplice.

"Someone called Marco. I've seen him maybe a couple of times in my life."

"And when would this thing have happened?"

"I don't remember," Manuel answered. "Two, four, five days ago."

Two, four, five days ago?

How could he not know? Was there still the possibility that it was all a stupid joke? On the infinite scale of misunderstandings that link fathers to sons, and that lead certain sons to consider themselves offended, if not irreparably damaged, by the behavior of fathers whose goal is simply to make men of them, could this be an absurd type of revenge? Was it a story that Manuel had invented out of whole cloth to punish him for sins that even the psychologist Valter had once sent him to would have had a hard time attributing to him?

Valter asked his son the name of the victim.

Manuel said: "I don't know." He had tears in his eyes.

Then Valter asked *where* was the person his son claimed to have killed.

This Manuel knew. "At home," he said. The body was in his apartment on Via Igino Giordani.

R oberto Foffo heard his cell phone ring. He checked the name on the display, his father was calling him from the car in front. They were a few kilometers from Bagnoli del Trigno.

"Roberto, please, pull over."

His father's voice was very strange. After the call Roberto saw him slow down and stop on the side of the road.

"What's going on?" asked Signora Daniela.

In obedience to a code that he and his father had agreed on with no need for words, Roberto avoided explanations. He also stopped and got out.

He joined his father in the parking area.

Valter gestured with his hand, the two walked away. When he was sure no one could hear them, Valter said: "We have a dead man at home."

"*What*?" Roberto's eyes widened.

Trying to stay calm, Valter tried to summarize the situation. He presented the problem of the nameless corpse that might be in the apartment on Via Igino Giordani, saying they'd better return to Rome as soon as possible, then added that it was a possible murder. Finally he revealed the identity of the presumed murderer.

Roberto had his first moment of relief.

"But dad," he said, "Manuel always talks a load of bullshit!"

Manuel had gone to see a psychologist. He suffered from mood swings. Those details at the moment led Roberto to believe that his brother could be claiming responsibility for a murder he hadn't committed.

"You'll see it's not true. Who knows what actually happened."

Valter was increasingly anxious. If they had to bring up Manuel's peculiarities, he said, they needed to focus on the most unusual of all: "Remember that your brother always tells the truth." He pointed to the parked car. Manuel was standing near the guardrail, doing nothing.

"Go over and talk to him," said Valter.

When Roberto returned to his father, he wore a different expression. He was pale, drawn. "Dad," he said, "maybe something really did happen."

In a world that we consider to be constructed on concrete foundations, we struggle to believe that the word preserves its magical powers. And yet a few simple sentences, uttered by Manuel, had hurled them into a nightmare. They were two hundred kilometers from home, stopped in a roadside parking area. At any moment the hearse carrying the uncle's body might pass by. The cold wind lashed them. Manuel had just confessed to murder. And a few steps away, ignorant of everything, were the grandfather, grandmother, and mother of the presumed murderer.

From that moment on, Signora Daniela's memories became confused. On the one hand, stopped on the side of the road, she had understood that something alarming was happening. On the other, the truth—when, that evening, it was disclosed—began working in her in reverse, distorting details, corrupting her memory and the normal succession of events.

"When we got to the town, all I remember is going into the church," she told the police. "I don't know if they also came in. I mean Valter and my two sons. At a certain point Roberto said: *Mamma, we'll stay here for a bit. Then we have to go to Rome, I'm sorry.* I was dumbstruck. I didn't understand why they had to leave, I thought that at least they would come to the cemetery. But no."

Valter and Roberto left Daniela out of the management of the problem. When the Mass was over, Valter went up to his ex-wife's cousins and handed them the car keys, asking them to take her home. He mentioned a problem they had to deal with right away. Something unexpected. Then he, Manuel, and Roberto got in Roberto's car and left. They took the state road, an hour and a half later they were on the highway. Roberto's foot pressed down on the accelerator. Rome, beaten by the rain, was again before them.

When all is lost, there's always a lawyer to call.

Michele Andreano had three thriving law offices, one in Milan, one in Rome, a third in Ancona. He was fifty, born in Foggia, and had graduated from Bologna in bankruptcy law. His clients were mainly businesses, companies operating in the iron and steel and shoe industries. He also represented private individuals suing the tax authorities. Finally, he had clients accused of very serious crimes, the type who roused in people that feeling of revulsion mixed with curiosity which has always been reserved for fantastic creatures. The so-called monsters.

That Saturday Andreano was in Ancona, where he was working on the Boettcher case. In the early afternoon he received a phone call from Valter Foffo. The two knew each other.

"Hello, Valter, how are you?" he said, without taking his eyes off the trial documents.

Alexander Boettcher was a thirty-two-year-old property broker who worked in Milan. He had been accused, along with his lover, of throwing acid in the faces of several of her ex-boyfriends. The girl's name was Martina Levato; she was twenty-four and was getting a master's at the Bocconi University. According to the charge, the two had planned the attacks driven by "a cathartic urge." By eliminating the faces of those who had had sex with Martina in the past they would restore to her a sort of original purity.

"Alex wanted Martina to give him a list of all the men she'd been with," one witness had said.

The fact that two young people capable of maneuvering amid

investment funds and financial algorithms had behaved like medieval inquisitors kindled people's curiosity. Martina had had the
"A" of Alex etched on her cheek and his name tattooed on her
breast—a modern Hester Prynne whose scarlet letter, in a single
pyre, burned the ancient ghost of adultery with the twenty-first-
century need for the limelight. What type of people were defendants like that? Were they suffering from serious psychiatric
problems? Or were they *monsters*?

"Monsters don't exist," Andreano said to the reporters.
"We create monsters ourselves from time to time to clear our
conscience."

When the lawyer appeared on a television screen the first
thing you noticed was his physical build. He looked like a rugby
player. Tall, imposing, but not static. He began to speak and you
imagined him running toward the goal with a folder of appeals
for release from prison under his arm.

During that period Andreano was often on TV. He was capable of sustaining impressive hours of work. He worked at home.
He worked in the car or at the restaurant. He worked on vacation. You could imagine him fine-tuning details of a case even
while he slept.

"Michele, listen, I have a problem."

"What type of problem?"

"Something really serious has happened. You have to come to
Rome."

"To Rome? When?"

"Now. You have to come right away. We're in my office, in Via
Verdinois."

"What do you mean now?" Michele Andreano sighed. He
took his eyes off the trial documents. "Valter, listen, I'm working.
I'll try and see if maybe . . ."

"It's about Manuel."

"Manuel your son?" Andreano was surprised.

"Exactly."

"O.K., Valter, give me a moment. I'll try and see what I can do."

Andreano ended the call. He didn't know what to think. Should he drop everything and rush to Rome? After all, it was Saturday afternoon and the courts would be closed until Monday. Many clients insisted on the urgency of matters that invariably turned out to be manageable in a completely normal way. Andreano got up from his chair, calculated the time it would take to get to Rome, talk to Valter, and return to Ancona. He sighed. He thought a little more. Then, in his head, something clicked. He picked up the phone. Driving him now was not the fear of making a trip for nothing but an opposite sensation.

"Valter," he said as soon as he heard his friend's voice, "will you explain to me more clearly what the hell happened?"

"Miche', a lot worse than acid . . ."

"That's when I understood it was about murder."

That—the precise moment when he understood that something huge had happened—Andreano would recall at length in the following months, speaking with friends and acquaintances. You're defending Alex Boettcher, the person the press can't stop writing about, "the devil man," as Boettcher described himself, boasting to a woman friend, and a few days before the hearing another client phones you, an entrepreneur whom you could at worst imagine entangled in some sort of business problems, and who instead hands you the case of his son: a case that, in the space of a few hours, will turn out to be much more shocking, sensational, *monstrous* than the one you're working on, wedging itself in the public imagination with a force incomparable to anything you'd seen before.

For the second time Andreano ended the phone call with Valter Foffo. He called his driver (Andreano had a driver) and asked to be taken to Rome.

The driver didn't take his foot off the accelerator. As they approached the Mediterranean the air became cooler. The sky was dark. The first juniper bushes appeared on the side of the road. The change of scene, slow and constant, speeded up when they arrived in Rome. The immense city, bursting out beyond the ring road, was a black hole that could swallow up everything. Vegetation died or grew up frenetically according to whether your gaze met an urban folly or an abandoned area, two of the city's specialties. The seagulls, made mean and hungry, formed spirals that assaulted the garbage dumps. At night, attracted by the headlights that should have given a shine to the great monuments, they circled ghoulishly. Rome was a different story. In the rain it was the story of a madman that, as frequently happens, contained shreds of truth.

Andreano saw the buildings of Collatino. The stoplights testified to a giant traffic jam. The car slowed down, horns honked. Exhaust fumes rose slowly from mufflers. The rain, growing more intense, disfigured vehicles and houses.

Rain in London or Paris is the demonstration of how a modern city, if necessary, can assume the forms of a cruise ship: from within, drinking tea, sitting among sparkling brass, one can observe the stormy sea in tranquility. Rain in Rome reminds everyone that modernity is a blink of the eye in the infinite unfolding of time. When it rains in Rome the manhole covers jump, the traffic goes haywire, branches break and fall off the trees. On the Via Cassia a couple of old people are crushed by the collapse of a bus shelter. At that point a first appeal to the citizens comes from the Campidoglio: "Don't leave home!" But the Romans are all outside. From Ponte Milvio to Garbatella the streets become blackish streams that carry along with them parked scooters. Buses come to a halt or are detoured. Like the bulbs in a defective series, the metro stations stop functioning, one after another. The pumps depart from rusty garages and are quickly blocked amid the cars.

The city seems about to collapse on itself, revealing glimpses of an earlier city. Then another, even older. The old Portico degli Argonauti behind the Altare della Patria. The amphitheater of Caligula, vanished for centuries, in the place of Palazzo Borghese. If the rain continued, you can bet that the old gods would retake possession of the place. But the true message is different. All cities, sooner or later, will be destroyed by rain. London and Paris shouldn't be deluded. Call it rain. Call it war or want. Call it simply time. Everyone knows the end of the world will come. But knowledge, in man, is a fragile resource. The inhabitants of Rome have the awareness of last things in their blood, and it's so fully absorbed that it no longer produces any thought. For those who live here the end of the world has already come and gone, the rain has only the annoying effect of overturning the glass and spilling the wine that the citizens continuously drink.

It was dark when Michele Andreano arrived at the office on Via Verdinois. Valter and his two sons were there. The vehicle-licensing agency was reduced to a shelter in the middle of a cataclysm. Valter was agitated, and Roberto had the face of someone trying to come to terms with reality and not succeeding, but it was on Manuel that the lawyer's attention was focused.

"Manuel seemed stoned, really stoned, stoned out of his mind."

Was it possible that his relatives hadn't noticed anything? It had taken a suspicion of murder for reality, apparently contained behind a double-locked door—children expose themselves by lying shamelessly, parents look away from those poorly hidden lies—to come out into the open.

Valter summarized the situation for Andreano's benefit. The journey to Molise. Manuel's confession. The existence of this accomplice they knew nothing about. And then the most important thing: the body.

Manuel's apartment was nearby, it would take ten minutes to find out if his story was true. But they still couldn't do it, the lawyer said, first they had to call the police.

Andreano recalled having had dinner with the boy a couple of times. On those occasions Manuel had been mostly silent; he had kept up the conversation when to avoid it would have been rude, but otherwise he hadn't opened up. Hard to understand what sort of young man he was. For example, in spite of his passion for IT, he had no social media profile. Andreano had met him at dinner, in fact, for a consulting job connected to that interest: Manuel was working on an app he called My Player. In theory the app would enable professional soccer teams to find in real time the most promising young talents scattered throughout the world. Once that software was created, who would be able to give up using it? Reserved but determined, Manuel was convinced he'd had a brilliant intuition; he felt close to the next big step. As happens with such intuitions, he was afraid someone might steal the idea. That was why he had consulted Andreano.

When Valter stopped talking, Andreano looked at Manuel. "What do you say," he said, "shall we have a little chat, you and I?"

The young man gave a nod that could be interpreted as a surrender. At the same time he seemed relieved.

"Good," said the lawyer, "leave me alone with him."

Valter and Roberto left the room. Manuel asked for a cigarette. The lawyer handed him one. Manuel took a long drag, as if he were inhaling oxygen after the breath had been knocked out of him.

"You want to explain what happened?" said Andreano.

Manuel spread the hands that might have been for several hours now a murderer's, but in fact seemed only the hands of a young man who doesn't know how to make his bed.

"We messed up."

"Who, messed up?"

"Me and this friend of mine."

"A friend. What's his name?"

"Marco Prato. He's not really a friend."

"Then what is he?"

"Someone I met at New Year's."

A few seconds of silence passed.

"This person you killed. Who is he?"

"I don't know."

"You don't know?"

"I don't know."

"And why would you kill him?"

"I don't know. The reasons might be all and none."

Manuel had a stuffy nose, a congested voice. He seemed in a semi-confusional state: maybe he was trying to clear his thoughts in the so-called real dimension while a part of him was still trapped in the other dimension, which might have been the reality of the day before and now was the nightmare, making him suspect that this, the nightmare, and the other, the reality of the day before, were the same thing. He might be groping along the border like a shipwrecked man trying to return to the surface of the water, but he wasn't lying.

Manuel maintained firmly that he had killed someone, but at the same time he described himself as someone not in possession of himself, someone overwhelmed by superior forces.

"Listen, Manuel," said Andreano, "now you have to do me a favor. You have to tell me if you want to turn yourself in or not. Because if you want to turn yourself in, I will call the police. But if you don't want to turn yourself in, that means I have to get up and I have to leave, because otherwise I could be charged with aiding and abetting."

"I want to turn myself in."

Manuel said it as if he wished for nothing else.

On 03/05/2016, at 18:50, a telephone call arrived at our Headquarters in the Operations Center in Rome, in which we were informed that at Via Verdinois 6 there was a person, identifying himself as a lawyer, Andreano Michele, who requested our presence because a client of his, named Foffo Manuel, was responsible for a probable homicide.

Officers Andrea Zaino and Alessio Gisolfi
Headquarters Rome Prenestina

Andreano ended the phone call with the police. He looked at Manuel. All they could do was wait. The rain could be heard outside. They stayed still, listening. One sound became confused with another—up and down, Andreano found himself following Manuel's foot tapping on the floor. The young man was nervous. A quarter of an hour passed. No one arrived. In Rome, when it rains, people don't move even if they hear police sirens. More minutes passed.

A deeper sigh, then Manuel jumped to his feet.

Andreano frowned. The boy was looking at him with an expression that the lawyer couldn't decipher. "Would you give me another cigarette?" After lighting it, Manuel turned his back on the lawyer and, without a word, left the room, took a few steps, grabbed the handle of the front door, left the office, and went outside to smoke, in the rain and the wind. The lawyer followed him with a worried look, then lost sight of him.

And if he had tried to flee? If he had decided to flee *now*, after he had called the police, leaving them all in a sea of troubles?

N ow I'm going to give them a piece of my mind!" the man said, throwing off the covers.

"Rude," grumbled his wife with her head in the pillows.

On the fifth floor of the Hotel San Giusto the occupants of the room next to 65 were trying to sleep. A song was being played obsessively, and had been hammering them for hours. It ended and started again. The walls partly muffled the sound, but the voice of the singer came through clearly.

The man stood up. His wife rolled over under the covers. The man put on his slippers, turned on the light to look for his glasses, turned it off, and grabbed the door handle. He went out into the corridor in search of justice.

They had arrived in Rome from Treviso the day before. He was a doctor. Monday he was supposed to take part in a conference at EUR. He and his wife had decided to give themselves a weekend in the capital. No decision had ever seemed so mistaken. It was years since they'd been to Rome; they hadn't imagined finding it in such poor shape. People on the street were simply mad. The drivers all seemed like potential murderers, but the pedestrians didn't joke around, either. In Piazza della Madonna dei Monti they had witnessed a disgusting scene. Near the fountain a seagull was devouring a dead rat. It had pecked open its stomach and now was rummaging in the carcass. A little girl started tugging on her mother: "Mamma, mamma, the rat!" The child seemed very unhappy. The woman stopped, observed her daughter as if she didn't recognize her, then, using her free hand, gave her a loud slap that perhaps contained the city's philosophy: "What are you shrieking about, you moron, you're not dead!"

The man knocked on the door of Room 65. It was occupied by a young man named Marco Prato, but the man couldn't know that. He waited a few more seconds, but on the other side of the door, apart from the song, nothing happened. So the man decided to complain at the reception desk.

While he was in the elevator the title of the song came to him. *Ciao amore, ciao*, by Luigi Tenco, in the version by Dalida.

H ey, look here!"
The officers recognized the silhouette of a man in the rearview mirror. A figure distorted by the rain was running after the patrol car waving his arms. The patrol car slowed down. The man reached the car, one of the cops lowered his window.

"Good evening."

The man said his name was Valter Foffo. "You passed the office without realizing it." He was soaking wet. In the past few minutes the storm had reached maximum intensity. It wasn't easy to tell what was right under your nose, you certainly weren't going to see a building number.

"Follow me," the man said.

Escorted by Valter, the policemen entered the office. The lawyer, Andreano, came toward them holding out his hand. Then a very well dressed young man appeared. He introduced himself as Roberto Foffo. Finally the cops saw Manuel. He hadn't fled. He'd never had any intention of fleeing. Looking at him next to Roberto, you'd find it hard to understand what degree of relationship there was between the two. Roberto gave the impression that he hadn't neglected the slightest detail of his appearance. Manuel was completely unkempt. The cops asked if it was he who was responsible for the murder they had been called about. Manuel nodded. They asked if he had acted alone. Manuel replied that he had acted with a friend named Marco Prato. Then the cops asked the question that Manuel hadn't been able to answer when his father or the lawyer asked. For the third time he said: "I don't know his name, the person we murdered."

The policemen asked Manuel for his phone. He didn't have to be asked twice. They asked for his code. Manuel gave it to them. Then they asked him for the keys to the apartment, and Manuel gave them those, too. Then came the most difficult moment. One of the cops took out a pair of handcuffs. Manuel observed the small metal rings, then offered up his wrists obediently. The policemen said to the lawyer that the young man was in custody.

MF: Next Thursday if poss don't make plans. Will call u in the next day or 2.

MP: O.K. :)

MF: Perfect.

MP: How should I dress?

WhatsApp exchange between Manuel Foffo and Marco Prato, a little more than a month earlier.

No human being measures up to the tragedies that befall him. Human beings are imprecise. Tragedies, unique and perfect pieces, always seem to be carved by the hands of a god. The feeling of the comic originates in this incongruity.

The policemen parked in front of No. 2 Via Igino Giordani. The apartment block rose in the rain-battered darkness. Two identical buildings stood next to it. Looking at the scene from above, the spectator would have noted, a short distance away, a giant black rectangle. It was the beeches, the thorns, the wild flowers beneath which the biggest necropolis of Imperial Rome was buried. The area was supposed to become an archeological park, but the project was stuck in infinite bureaucratic problems. Not far from where columbaria and skeletons had been buried for millennia were playing fields, tobacconists, small businesses, and large apartment buildings.

The cops asked Valter to take them to Manuel's apartment. Andreano followed. Roberto waited on the ground floor. Manuel was in custody in the patrol car.

When they arrived on the tenth floor, Valter pointed to the door. "It's that one?" the cops asked. The man nodded. One of them inserted the key Manuel had given him into the lock. The door didn't open. "It's jammed." A shudder of worry—within which rested a secret hope—passed through some of those present. The fact that the door was locked from the inside contradicted Manuel's version. It was the first discrepancy, which meant that there could be others. The cops began to force the lock. "Wait." One of them had heard a noise on the other side. The men remained waiting. Nothing happened. They resumed fiddling with the lock.

"Stop! Stop!"

This time, they had all heard the noise. After a few seconds, *someone* clearly began to move *something* from the other side of the door. The cops started, Michele Andreano and Valter Foffo looked at each other with their hearts in their throats. They weren't dreaming. There was someone in the apartment and he was *alive!*

"We were about to hug each other, jump, shout for joy," Andreano recalled.

It's not clear what hypothesis led them to believe that on the other side of the door was the victim of the attack, still alive. A cool head would have reasoned that on the other side of the door there could have been anyone. For example, there could have been Manuel's accomplice, this Marco Prato of whom nothing was known. That hypothesis wasn't even considered. Wounded, maybe even seriously, but alive, the kid Manuel claimed to have killed had to be in there. That's what they all thought. That poor guy had managed to drag himself to the door, and now was trying desperately to get out.

"Hurry! Hurry up!"

Michele Andreano was sent to call an ambulance. The cops resumed trying to force the door. Valter hurried down to Roberto, ready to give him this most incredible news.

The scene lasted a few minutes, and no matter how you try you can't imagine that it wasn't controlled by the rhythm of an infernal farce.

It was Roberto Foffo who broke the spell. Although some hours earlier he had thought his brother was making it all up, the passing of time must have caused him to change his mind. Valter reported to him what was happening upstairs. Roberto said: "Papa, are you sure you told the police the right apartment?"

Crueler than the tragedy that strikes us is the tragedy we have the illusion of having escaped. When the door finally opened the surprise of the police was equal to that of the person on the other side. The old woman in the apartment, convinced that she was warding off an assault by thieves, found herself facing two young police officers.

"Hello, is this the house of Manuel Foffo?"

"No," answered the woman, "you have the wrong apartment."

Roberto refreshed his father's memory. The police changed stairways. A few minutes later they were standing in front of another closed door.

The last people to see him alive were a clerk for the city of Rome and a blond girl whose name no one knew.

The man's name was Fabio Guidi. He was forty-five years old and lived near Via Trionfale. He had read the news on the Internet (on the Internet and in the papers no one was talking about anything else) and had recognized the boy's face. He told the police he had met him by chance on Friday at ten of eight, shortly before he was killed.

That morning as usual Guidi had awakened early, left the house, and taken the train to go to work. These trains on the urban line were two-story vehicles that crisscrossed the city with the purpose of alleviating the street traffic—slow, dilapidated, like large wounded animals, they were the ideal target for fledgling graffiti writers.

"I settled myself on the upper level, next to the window. He was a little ways away. At a certain point he spoke to me."

Luca Varani was wearing light-colored jeans, sneakers, a dark jacket, on his head a baseball cap and over his shoulders a backpack.

"He asked me if the train stopped at Tiburtina. I said I didn't know, I take the train that gets to Ostiense at 7:48 or the one that gets there at 7:56, it doesn't matter. I advised him to look at the information on the platform signs at every stop."

If the scene had taken place in Milan, where people are too focused on work, or in Turin, where talking to strangers can seem inappropriate, the traveler wouldn't have had any way of memorizing the boy's features: the big black eyes, the shapely mouth, the harmonious and gentle face caught between light and shadow that, set by Caravaggio on the physical structure of an angel, wouldn't look unfamiliar to habitués of San Luigi dei Francesi. But in Rome complaining about your own affairs with the first person you see is a social duty. Not satisfied with the answer, the young man dashed off.

"He said he had to meet someone who owed him a thousand euros for a car. *He took the car, but he didn't give me the money*. It seemed that the person who owed him this money had suggested that he get off at Tiburtina and then take a taxi. *But how could I take a taxi if I don't have even a euro?*"

The train meanwhile was heading toward Primavalle, passing through broad fields, the outskirts, past crumbling apartment buildings, lots full of scrap metal and broken toilets.

"The boy asked if I could keep an eye on his backpack and the cell phone that was charging and he disappeared at the end of the car. A few minutes later he came back with the girl."

This girl might be between twenty and twenty-five. Blond, thin, in a dark jacket that came to her knees and tight pants. "I think the two knew each other already," said the man. "They sat next to each other and started talking."

If Rome weren't the city in which it's always permissible to pay attention to other people's business, the traveler wouldn't have pricked his ears and wouldn't have been able to report the conversation between the two young people.

"He asked her for a cigarette. The girl said she had only a few, but in the end she gave him one. At a certain point I think he said something like: *Usually I get thirty, but today I'm getting a thousand*. Then he also said: *If he reports me I'm going to report him. Let him, just let him go and report me!*" The passenger said to the police that Luca gave him the impression of being cocky but very naïve. In that naïveté you might also sense a sweetness that the apparent bravado made more intense and poignant.

After several stops, the girl got off the train.

"Before leaving she said: *Luca, please be careful.* He answered: *What can they do? I'm the one who has to get the money.* The girl had a serious expression."

At that point Luca again approached the passenger.

"He began to reason about the possible advantages he could get from the people he was supposed to meet. He said: *If I were to tell the address of this person who is supposed to give me the money to another person I know, that person would give me two thousand euros.* Then he said: *Sometimes there's money in being dishonest. What do you think?* I answered that I didn't think anything."

The young man began complaining about his phone. He said he needed to buy a new one, this one was always losing its charge. The man suggested that he just buy a battery, but the boy said he'd already found a buyer for his old phone: he would sell it for forty euros. Charger or no charger, he was intending to get a new phone.

"At that point he said he needed a metro ticket. From Tiburtina he had to go to Ponte Mammolo. *Do you have a ticket you could give me?* I told him I didn't have one, I have a monthly. In response he walked away. Just like that. Picked up his backpack and phone, turned his back on me, walked down the car, and disappeared among the other passengers. Didn't even say goodbye."

Here's a fine puzzle for the police criminal investigation department. Ponte Mammolo is one of the metro stops closest to Via Igino Giordani. Not, however, the absolute closest. One could hypothesize that Luca Varani had another appointment before the one that would be fatal. Or, more simply, one might think that he had never been to Via Igino Giordani before and had got off at the wrong stop.

Another dilemma: who was the person from whom Luca said he was supposed to get a thousand euros? And the second person who, informed of the address of the first, would give him twice the amount? Maybe the information was too confused to become a concrete theory. Or maybe the passenger didn't remember correctly. With a little imagination one might suppose that Luca felt the need to tell someone his troubles, but used a code. The "car," for example, could be not a real "car" but something else. It would be a touching hypothesis, because only in young men are shame and the need to externalize their own feelings one and the same. But young men trust only other young men. And then there's the blonde. Before getting off she'd told Luca to be careful. Be careful of whom? Maybe he had confided something to her that he hadn't said to anyone else?

"Do you remember any other details about the girl?" the policemen asked the passenger.

"She had straight hair, long, below her shoulders, a cute face, made up but not too much."

Soon the most outlandish conjectures about this girl began circulating. "Blonde Met on Train Sought" was the headline in the *Corriere della Sera*.

The most fanciful theorized that the blonde was an apparition, an imaginary friend whom Luca, feeling the approach of danger, had thought about so intensely that she materialized on the train to Ostiense. A benign spirit, or even an angel.

A few days later, the police listened to the statement of a twenty-four-year-old blonde who claimed she had traveled with Luca Varani on the commuter train to Tiburtina. The girl said she'd known Luca since school. That morning she'd met him by chance, they had talked about this and that until she got off the train. That's it: no allusion to an imminent danger, nothing especially strange.

One of the officers inserted the key in the lock and this time the door opened.

The police entered the apartment. They turned on the light, went down the hall, and looked around. The place was depressing and cramped, in the living room clothes, wastepaper, glasses, empty bottles were scattered randomly. The disorder was absolute, as if the owner of the apartment had ransacked it himself. Newspapers and magazines were scattered on the desk, including a copy of *Uomo & Fitness*, of *Millionaire*, documents, medical prescriptions, three A4 pages on which were printed the Wikipedia article on "Instigation to or help with suicide." On the shelf next to it were books, mostly legal texts, language courses, self-help manuals. The drawers were full of packets of Xanax and Haldol. On the TV stand was a kitchen knife with a black handle. There were no traces of blood on the blade.

On the dining table another mess—crumpled cigarette packs, a pizza box, advertising flyers, and, rather unusual, two pairs of shoes ("So as not to leave tracks on the floor: the two must have thought they could get away with it," said one cop). The shades were pulled three-quarters of the way down, imbuing the scene with an even grimmer and more claustrophobic atmosphere. You might suppose that in recent days the apartment hadn't received any sunlight.

The kitchen sink was full of dirty glasses. Then the bathroom. The cops noticed near the sink a pair of rolled-up socks. In the tub were two bags stuck one inside the other. In the bags was a pair of sweatpants. They were soiled with a dark substance.

"Don't touch them. Let's wait for Forensics."

Those who had the good luck to enter the apartment before it was sealed (or bad luck: some were haunted by the scene for weeks) recounted that the sensation of unease in there was tangible. Some said that all that disorder reflected the mental state of the person who lived there. Others, formulating an apparently more banal thought, maintained that it was like the apartment of a bunch of students who had thrown a wild party and decamped, leaving to the adults the job of cleaning up. One cop said that experiences like that convinced you definitively that evil wasn't an abstract concept but a palpable presence.

In the bedroom, the police found the dresser drawers open. In them were more drugs and a pack of condoms. On the floor a kitchen knife and a hammer of medium size. Then a pillow. The pillow was stained with blood. The walls were stained with blood. A plastic pail was full of paper towels, and that, too, was bloody. On the mattress a big orange quilt covered something. The policemen advanced and lifted it.

The boy's body was slender, athletic. Except for terrycloth socks, he was completely naked. A knife was stuck in his chest. He had been struck repeatedly on his head, his face, in his mouth, on his hands, between his teeth. There were deep wounds at chest height, broad gashes at the base of the neck. In addition to the deep wounds there were innumerable superficial cuts. The head was bent to the right. Half twisted around the neck, there was a rubber cord like an electrical cable. Maybe they had also tried to strangle him.

The policemen were used to criminals settling accounts. In those cases everything was reduced to gunshots or a couple of well-aimed knife thrusts. What they had before them bore witness to an explosion of violence of another type. Whoever had struck that kid had persisted in a shocking way, had unleashed on him a deranged, primitive fury. Still, besides the gashes and other injuries, the victim's body bore witness to something different: on his left arm, from the biceps almost to the elbow, the name MARTA GAIA was tattooed.

The police returned to the ground floor. Soon the men from Forensics, the medical examiner, and the public prosecutor would arrive.

Meanwhile the rain had stopped. Before Manuel was brought to the police station in Piazza Dante, the cops asked him some more questions: now that it had been established that he wasn't making it all up, a new game was beginning. Manuel said that the murdered kid had appeared at his house on Friday morning. He had never seen him before. He had been hanging out for a few months with Marco Prato, however. They asked where this Marco Prato had got to. Manuel said that after taking part in the murder he had left the apartment. He had ugly intentions.

"What do you mean?" asked one of the cops.

"He went to kill himself in a hotel near Piazza Bologna," Manuel answered.

MF: Want to move it up to tomorrow night? Can u?
MP: What do u want to do tomorrow night?
MF: Talk, then the stuff.
MP: O.K., where?
MF: I don't know, my house? Or you say.
MP: Your house is fine.

WhatsApp exchange between Manuel Foffo and Marco Prato a few days before the murder.

A ship in harbor is safe, but that is not what ships are built for."

The quotation, from John Augustus Shedd, was the last thing that Ledo Prato wrote in his blog before finding out that his son had been accused of murder. The phrase—Ledo had intelligently glossed it with a "these days, however, the harbor may be the least safe place"—alluded not to the relations between parents and children but to the challenges that small urban communities had to meet to survive the economic storms of the twenty-first century.

Ledo Prato was an arts administrator, among the most respected in his field. He was sixty-eight, with a wife and two grown children, male and female. He was born near Foggia, and after high school had moved to Rome, where he got his degree and started working. He was a man with a mild, serious look. Those who met him saw in him what today is sought, often in vain, in men who occupy positions of responsibility: equilibrium, strength of mind, absence of narcissism.

Ledo Prato worked as a consultant to the Ministry of Culture. He was the director of an association active in the effort to safeguard artistic treasures. In his circle were public administrators, judges and lawyers, academics who had taken government positions. Whether he was speaking to students (he gave highly regarded classes in various university departments) or writing in the newspapers, you felt his gentle strength and his cordiality. Never any gossip, never any misconduct; he was also a good Catholic, or at least tried to be, and despite the cruelty the world exhibited he believed that the capacity to work for the good was always able to prevail over destructive impulses.

"It's the challenge of every day," he repeated on his blog. "Sometimes we win, other times no, but we're in trouble if we give in to the worst!"

In the case of Ledo Prato, in short, only the side in the light was generally visible. It was difficult to picture him in the grip of anger, or overcome by rage. It was, as a rule, difficult to surprise him in any attitude that belied the image most people had of him. Thus when he learned, on the night of March 5, that his son was in trouble—serious trouble, trouble that surpassed every imagining—penetrating his thoughts must have been problematic even for those who knew him.

"Marco *my son*?"

What did Ledo Prato think in that moment and the following hours? Did he let the cautious optimism collapse under the weight of what was happening? Or did he use common sense and prudence as distorting lenses to escape the more brutal side of things?

The first phone call was from Ornella Martinelli. The police had found her number and those of other friends on Marco's cell phone. They had called, asking them to let the Pratos know that the police were looking for them.

This wasn't the first time Ledo had received worrying news of his son. It had happened when Marco was living in Paris and again, some time later, in Rome. Years had passed since then, however; things had improved; and it would have been ungenerous to be anxious until the arrival of phone calls like that. Ledo doted on Marco. He cherished his brilliance, his spirit of initiative, and although father and son seemed light years apart—an irreproachable administrator from the Catholic bourgeoisie, one of the most exuberant club promoters of the Roman gay scene—the bond that joined them was profound. Maybe what brought

them close was a secret melancholy that one hid behind composure and the other behind extreme vivacity.

"All right, Ornella, thanks."

After another round of phone calls, Ledo Prato managed
to talk to the police. They asked him to come to the Hotel San
Giusto, Piazza Bologna. They had found his son. "He's alive,"
they said. He had attempted suicide in a room in the hotel.

It took only a few minutes for Ledo Prato—Piazza Bologna
was very near his house—to be assured that Marco would make
it. But in this way he was also forced to learn that his son had
been involved in a horrendous murder. And he still had a few
days—despite his faith in human beings—before discovering the
magnitude of the cynicism, the meanness, the violence, the lack
of tact, the social hatred that had infected everyone out there.

"Now his daddy from the Roman bourgeoisie will get him out
of that mess by any possible means."

"A radical chic, snooty papa's boy: SCUMBAG."

These were the mildest among the comments that a tide of
strangers began to hurl furiously at Marco and his family. An en-
raged, unbridled crowd.

Ledo and his wife, Mariella, hurried to Piazza Bologna. The
ship had left the harbor, the storm had just begun.

O rnella Martinelli had called Federica Vitale. Both had talked to Lorenza Manfredi. The first details had begun to circulate within a narrow circle of friends. Then the news exploded, crashed through the dike. Admitted to the hospital after a suicide attempt? And in the middle of it there was *a murder*? The alarm was full of excitement, as when something incredible happens to a public figure. It wasn't so strange: Marco Prato was, in his way, a public figure.

Whether one knew him personally or followed him at a distance, Ledo Prato's son did not go unobserved. He was twenty-nine. He had fine dark eyes, wore his hair combed back. His lips were full, and the mustache accentuated his penetrating gaze: he rested his eyes on you and you couldn't tell if it was because you had aroused his interest or if he had just added you to the list of those he considered a waste of time.

"Just a pretty boy who thinks he's God's gift," said detractors.

"One of the most affectionate and intelligent people you'd ever meet," retorted those who liked him.

Marco Prato did PR, he worked in the club world. With two partners he ran a regular cocktail hour on Colle Oppio that was called A(h)però. He also organized other events. On New Year's Eve he had arranged a party at the Quirinetta that had gone very well. For many of the participants that type of entertainment, in Rome, wasn't the reward for a hard day's work but the most intense moment of a sleep that could last years. The lasers of the DJ sets licked the baths of Caracalla, intercepting, in the dead of night, the forces of the city below.

"We're looking for PERFORMERS, MALE and FEMALE DANCERS, ACTORS, ACTRESSES, SINGERS, DRAG QUEENS, BANDS, and ARTISTS of every sort. Auditions will take place the first week of March!"

At work Marco was brilliant and persuasive. He worried about making a good impression. Being disagreeable (denying entry to a club to those he deemed unfit) was also part of his job. He was endowed with an exceptional mastery of language, and this, on the other hand, had nothing to do with the PR guy's usual toolkit.

"He's a fantastic conversationalist."

"He uses all the right terms—when he talks he gradually surrounds you with these complex and elaborate speeches."

Surrounds you or *besieges you*? His rhetorical ability could get the listener in trouble, or—depending on the interlocutor, or his own mood—could make him feel welcome and loved.

"He's really skillful," they said, but it wasn't necessarily a compliment.

"Marco has a rare sensibility. He *sees you*. He recognizes in you what escapes others. You end up confiding secrets you've never shared with anyone before. And then he's sweet, caring."

Black liner around the eyes, polish on his nails: meeting him for the first time you might find him excessive (had he been a little over the top? had he hit on you shamelessly?), but isn't it usually for such reasons—the unpredictable, not the obvious—that people are remembered?

Marco hated homophobes. He defended the gay scene. He was at war with a certain kind of "right-wing Roman night life" that winked at the homosexual scene just to "have a place in contemporary life."

"But what does 'gay party' mean?" those outside the circle asked.

"It means a ghetto for those who feel it's confining and a place to feel free for those who find it comfortable," Marco answered.

His political passions were lukewarm but clear ("In the end politics can be reduced to a highway," he said. "Theoretically you should feel more secure on the right, but only those on the left can pass and go forward. And in any case . . . anyone who passes on the right is an asshole!"), but to the boredom of an electoral campaign he would always prefer the sparkle of the sequins on the gown of a successful singer.

It wasn't clear what his relations were with his family. Marco had had the guts to come out as a boy, when in Italy the expression "coming out" didn't exist. He had faced the derision of his schoolmates boldly. At first, said his friends, his parents didn't take it well. There had been misunderstandings with his mother. Ledo had been less rigid. Over the years tensions had diminished. Now Ledo followed Marco with unreserved pride: as with all parents you couldn't say that he grasped every aspect of his son's work, but he was busy, and that has to please a father. Marco publicly displayed his respect for his father, he wished Ledo happy birthday directly on Facebook: "Always supportive . . . even now. Best wishes, papa!" "What a kind thought," Ledo answered on Marco's profile. "In the end all fathers (and mothers) support their children and know that a day may come when the roles are reversed. But they aren't worried, because they know that, if they've given them the right support, they'll find strong and generous children who can always sustain them. And I'm really happy because I know that's how it will be with my children! I love you!"

Every so often a drop of sorrow seemed to leak out from Ledo's quiet obstinacy in the practice of good. In the son that sorrow acquired the dimensions of a shining mythology. Marco adored French music, he knew the songs of Dalida by heart, he had erected a cult of beauty around her voice and the tragedy of her life. He didn't confine himself to listening to Dalida; Marco *idolized her*, he knew everything about her, he would have *liked to be her*. He barreled across Rome in his Mini Cooper singing *Loin de moi* at the top of his lungs.

In a world that judges without giving you a second chance, Marco seemed to need to dispel any suspicion that he had not won a decisive battle. Opacity versus brilliance. Anonymity versus memorability. Isn't that everybody's problem?

Some said that Marco had changed recently: he seemed tense, irritable, if you met him at a club you might immediately regret going up to him. "You say hi and he disses you with a nasty comment. You don't understand why. And maybe he doesn't even know himself." "Work is going badly. He's always broke, asks everyone for money." "Look at his face. What do you see? It's coke that makes him smile like that."

Agreed, we all go through rough times, but how was it possible that the police were actually looking for him?

His friends would have reacted with a shrug to the news that Marco had spent two nights in a hotel half dead on cocaine. The most intimate wouldn't have been surprised even at the news of a suicide attempt: it had happened before. But a murder . . . Marco Prato who killed someone? One could imagine at most that he'd *come on to* someone, that amid the colored lights of a club he'd handed a cocktail to a guy he'd just met, leading him to do what, a few minutes earlier, the object of his attentions had denied wanting to do. But kill... *Kill, Marco*? Well, it was unthinkable, impossible, it was a real absurdity, surpassed only by the hypothesis (one detractor pointed out maliciously) that he could have done it in an ugly apartment in the neighborhood of Collatino.

Mamma, don't go to grandma and grandpa's—I have to talk to you."

Daniela Pallotto returned to Rome that evening. Her cousins had given her a ride from Molise. She couldn't believe the way her former husband and her sons had abandoned her at the funeral. It had been a painful day, but worse was to come. When she saw an ambulance outside the building, and on the street her former husband, her older son, and a large man who seemed to be watching over both, she understood that something had happened. *Something else* had happened.

As soon as the car stopped, Roberto came to meet her. He told her to let the grandparents go home. He had to talk to her. Right afterward the large man arrived. He introduced himself as Manuel's lawyer. *Manuel's lawyer?* She didn't understand. So Roberto said that Manuel had confessed to murder. The body of a young man had been found in his apartment. He must have been killed a few meters above her head, probably while she was home.

"At this point I recall that I felt an enormous disorientation," she told the police. She had buried her brother that same day, she had just taken home her aged parents, whose son had died, and now, all in the space of a few hours, they were saying that hers, her son, had committed a murder.

Signora Pallotto was brought to the police station with the other members of the family.

The policemen who had stayed in Via Igino Giordani meanwhile began to knock on the doors of the neighbors. They had
some questions for the residents of the building. What sort of
person was this Manuel Foffo? Had there been suspicious noises
in recent days? People shouting? Asking for help?

Those interrogated described Manuel as a "very normal"
young man, "very placid," "very good." Hearing the ordinary described in superlatives is always an interesting experience. To the
question of whether Manuel had a job some tenants answered
indignantly—"Of course he had a job!"—as evidence of how
well informed they were about one another. But no one claimed
to have heard or seen anything suspicious.

"And yet in these apartments you hear *everything*, even the
sound of a fork falling on the floor, even the footsteps of people
going in and out of their house." The person who uttered this
sentence was not an investigator making trouble for one of the
residents of the building but the person who might have felt the
greatest embarrassment, speaking to the investigators.

Manuel's mother repeated to the police that even she had heard
nothing strange, and it was this, if they thought carefully, that
should have made them suspicious. She asked them to assess that
apparent illogicality as a sign, she said that her son was "reserved,"
"very well brought up," absolutely "pacific": it was impossible that
he had murdered someone. It was he who had accused himself?
Well, he might be assuming a guilt that wasn't his.

In the next days she persisted. "Everything I'm hearing seems
to me anomalous, impossible." When she was reminded that, in
spite of every anomaly, the body of a twenty-three-year-old had
actually been found in her son's apartment, she was quick to
respond. "That kid wasn't in Manuel's usual group of friends.
And then I wonder: what was a boy of twenty-three doing in his
apartment? My son is twenty-nine and only spends time with
people his age." There are a lot of strange people around in that
enormous building, she added, in fact *very* strange people—is

it possible that no one noticed the *strangeness* of the whole situation?

In the hours that follow a homicide there is no hypothesis that the investigators can discard. There are people to question, evidence to analyze, statements to compare. Anyone can lie. Anyone can tell the truth. The cops listened to Daniela Pallotto's story all the way to the end. With an energy that was the inverse of what one might have expected from her, Manuel's mother tried to convince them that they were on the wrong track, she went so far as to almost suggest that the body had been brought into the apartment without her son knowing. The investigators considered every word carefully. Then, however, given that an exaggerated emphasis on the part of the speaker can become the main cause for doubt in the listener, they started to think that the woman was only trying to project outward an excruciating feeling of disbelief.

It's to settle these questions that Forensics exists.

The officers from the Seventh Precinct entered the barracks late in the evening. They greeted the other police. They asked where the young man was being held. They introduced themselves to Manuel, exchanged some polite remarks. They were very kind. Then they asked him to pull down his pants, take off his shoes, remove his socks, so that they could collect some samples with a laboratory swab.

"It's something that cops with even a minimum of experience try to do as soon as possible," one of them explained. "Someone who's suspected of murder, or even someone who comes to confess a murder, tends to tell the truth in the first hours. Then a few days go by, he consults with his lawyer, and maybe he persuades him to declare that we extorted the confession with threats of some sort. The accused's versions can change. Scientific proofs are more difficult to argue with."

Manuel undressed. Between his toes were some small dark

spots that the agents noticed immediately. They also noticed the tattoo on his ankle. How odd. Luca Varani had had the name of his girlfriend tattooed on his arm. Manuel Foffo, instead, had had tattooed the logo of one of his family's restaurants, Dar Bottarolo, a rather bizarre choice. A policeman ran the swab over the soles of his feet and his knees. The samples were sealed with a pressurized stopper and sent to the laboratory. The results of the analyses would categorically rule out the possibility that Manuel had found the body in his apartment without knowing about it.

Nothing is more difficult than to change the ideas that parents have about their own children. Parents can be convinced that their children are irredeemable losers, others believe they've brought geniuses into the world, or, more modestly, creatures incapable of making a mistake. This type of blindness can be exasperating, but in extreme cases it moves us to pity. Whether true or false, the rumor began to spread that Manuel's mother spent the months following his arrest looking out the window, waiting for her son to return. There had been a judicial error. A gigantic mistake. Time was needed for the investigators to understand what she, listening to her mother's heart, had known very well from the start. Thus one morning—soon, very soon—the pale figure of her son would emerge at the end of Via Igino Giordani.

MF: Let's meet at 11.00 at my house? You'll get the stuff? I'll pay you back, obviously.

MP: I thought you'd take care of everything tonight. This time I can't spend and the other time it was 7 or 8 hundred.

MF: O.K., but I can't spend more than 150.

MP: Give me the address again.

MF: Via Igino Giordani 2. When you're there call me.

WhatsApp exchange between Manuel Foffo and Marco Prato three days before the murder.

Ciao amore, ciao is a song from 1967, and Marco Prato was mad about it.

The song, written by Luigi Tenco, had a rather complicated genesis, having gone through several versions. The definitive one described the apprehensions of a country boy who comes to the city, a theme that was still current in Italy at the time. Apparently, Tenco wasn't satisfied with the song. The French singer Dalida, however, with whom he had an affair, convinced him that the song could do well at the Sanremo Festival. What happened is almost too well known. *Ciao amore, ciao* couldn't get past the popular jury and wasn't even saved by the repechage committee, which preferred *The Revolution*, by Gianni Pettenati and Gene Pitney, a song that today is remembered for that reason alone.

Tenco was sleeping on a billiard table when he found out he'd been eliminated. He'd probably ended up there drunk. When he heard the news, he got off the billiard table, went back to his hotel room, and there, a few hours later, shot himself once in the temple. The body was found during the night. Next to the body, a suicide note was recovered, destined to become famous:

> I loved the Italian public and devoted five years of my life to it, in vain. I'm doing this not because I'm tired of life (I'm not) but as an act of protest against a public that sends *Io tu e le rose* to the finals and a committee that chooses *The Revolution*. I hope this will clear somebody's head. Ciao. Luigi.

Two days later, *Ciao amore, ciao* had sold eighty thousand copies.

However, it wasn't Luigi Tenco's version that Marco Prato listened to continuously but Dalida's. The story seems to have been written by a screenwriter indifferent to any obligation to verisimilitude: after making a statement to the police, Dalida returned to Paris. She sang *Ciao amore, ciao* in public. On February 27, exactly one month after Tenco's suicide, the singer pretended to leave for Italy. Instead she went to the Hotel Prince de Galles, and, under a false name, booked Room 404, the same room Tenco stayed in when he was in Paris. She locked herself in, wrote three farewell letters (one to her former husband, one to her mother, the last to her fans), and swallowed an excessive quantity of barbiturates. She was saved by a chambermaid. At that point *Ciao amore, ciao* had sold three hundred thousand copies.

Ten years later, in 1977, Dalida entered another period of depression. A few years before, her second husband, Lucien Morisse, had killed himself, and several years later her former partner Richard Chanfray killed himself. An epidemic. On May 3, 1987, Dalida barricaded herself in her villa on Rue d'Orchampt and swallowed a fatal cocktail of barbiturates. The attempt was successful. The suicide note said simply: "Forgive me, life is unbearable to me."

Thirty years later, on March 5, on the fifth floor of the Hotel San Giusto in Rome, a busy night was about to start.

The chambermaid on duty reported that the occupant of Room 65 had been listening to *Ciao amore, ciao* at high volume since the afternoon. The guests in the nearby rooms had begun to complain.

"Marco Prato appeared at the reception desk between midnight and twelve-thirty," the hotel's night clerk told the police. "He asked for a room for two nights. He gave me his passport. I gave him the room key. He said he wanted to pay in advance, so he took out the cash."

"What else do you remember?" the police asked.

"He was wearing a suède jacket, and had a canvas bag with him. I gave him the wi-fi password, and he said he wanted to sleep for a long time, so please no cleaning the next morning."

"Is that the last time you saw him?"

"To tell you the truth no," the night clerk answered. "He was at the reception desk a little before dawn. Despite the hour, he didn't seem tired. I asked if I could help him. He asked for a pen. I think I handed him a Bic. Half an hour later I left."

The police reached the Hotel San Giusto around 9:30 P.M. The precinct in Piazza Dante had sifted through the registrations of all the hotels in the area until the young man's name came up.

The officers asked the desk clerk for a master key and went up to the fifth floor. Halfway down the hall was the room where Marco Prato was staying.

"It's a Luigi Tenco song," said a cop approaching the door.

"In the Dalida version," specified a colleague. Then he knocked, no answer.

The first cop pulled out the master key. The door still wouldn't open, it must have been locked from the inside. The cops forced the lock.

The room was modest and pleasant. On the floor was the same red carpet as in the hall. The walls were painted a pale color, and a reproduction of a *Madonna with Child* stood out on the wall to the right, over the bed. Dalida's song was coming from an iPhone 5 charging on the night table. A young man was lying on the floor face down with his head under the bed. The cops approached. He was in a confusional state. Five bottles of benzodiazepines on the desk established the hypothesis of a suicide attempt. Next to the pill bottles was a bottle of Amaro del Capo, indicating that the sleeping pills had been mixed with alcohol to be more effective.

The cops picked up the young man. Two of them tried to hold a conversation. The third called the ambulance. After a brief exchange, during which the youth managed to pronounce his name and surname ("Marco Prato"), the cops dragged him out of the room. They led him to the elevator supporting him by the arms. The ambulance was waiting outside the hotel. A short distance away, in the street, were Marco's parents: they had arrived just before their son was taken to the hospital. As soon as Ledo Prato saw Marco, he ran toward him, father and son embraced, Ledo whispered something to Marco, then the young man was loaded into the ambulance, which headed for the Pertini hospital with sirens wailing.

The police examined the room that was now without its guest. On the suitcase stand against the wall they found a synthetic fur coat. On the floor was the canvas bag the night clerk had mentioned. In it they found a padded bra, a pair of shoes with floral ornaments in the heel, a leopard-skin sheath dress, lace underpants, and an electric-blue wig.

On the desk, next to the pill bottles and the Bic pen, were seven lined sheets of paper making up five farewell letters.

The first letter was addressed to his parents. On the pages, written in list form, were the last wishes of Marco Prato.

Wishes 4 mamma and papa
1) Have a party for my funeral. No church. I'd like a secular ceremony, flowers, Dalida songs, good memories. A party! You should have fun!
2) Call Private Friends, the hair center in Piazza Mazzini, to regenerate my hair before cremating me. Put on my red tie. Donate my organs. Leave the red polish on my nails. I would always have more fun being a woman!

3) Once a week/month, organize dinner or lunch with my true friends whom I loved so much, Lulli, Serena, Miriam, Doda, Ornella, Francesca, Fiore, Monica, Patrizio, Guido, Fabio, and many others.
4) Always have parties. Listen to Dalida :) every so often.
5) Play *Ciao amore, ciao* when the party for me is over and all of you together remember my loveliest smiles.
6) Throw away my phone and destroy it along with the 2 computers. They conceal my ugly sides.
7) Take care of Silvana and Loredana, who brought me up together with you.
8) Elena Maria Crinò, my shrink. Please, stay close to her because she's among the few who gave me some stable years.
9) Be proud of my name and memory in spite of what people say.
10) Don't look into my murky parts. They aren't pretty.
11) Write on my social media that there will be a party. Then try to delete them without intrusions or investigations.
   I LOVE YOU!

The second letter was also addressed to his parents. Here the tone became more sober. There were passages that enabled one to intuit the nature of a relationship about which the police, the prosecutor, the psychiatrists, criminologists, journalists, not to mention an immense crowd of the curious, wouldn't stop speculating in the following months.

Mamma and papa
I love you and I've always loved you! I have no bitterness or rage, only love for you. Mamma, I've loved you every day of my life and you mustn't think even for a second of our silences because for me they never existed. I'm sick or maybe I've always been. I discovered horrible things in myself and in the world. Life hurts too much: because of how I learned to understand it I find it insupportable. Try to love each other

and go on with your lives. Don't ever feel guilty for all this. Continue to support each other and look to the future, as you taught me. I LOVE YOU.

The third letter was addressed to Patrizio Archetti and Guido Bonazzi, Marco's partners in his work as an event organizer.

4 A(h)però
4 Patrizio
4 Guido

Carry on with my determination. Don't <u>ever</u> forget our child. Keep it alive and nourish it as much as you can!
Patrizio, take care of yourself. You were my best friend. Help yourself, and don't ever think that I can forget it.

The fourth letter was addressed to his girl friends, the magic circle of female presences that anyone who investigated the life of Marco Prato would keep running into.

4 Lulù
   My rock
4 Serena
   My certainty
4 Doda
   My smile
4 Lolla
   My brain
4 Miriam
   My history

I love you all. Take care of yourselves. Always remember me for the good things.

The last was a rather generic farewell letter, written in an increasingly disorderly handwriting, a sign that the author had written it while the sleeping pills were taking effect.

> For all persons, loves, and friends of mine whom I haven't mentioned. I love you just the same but I'm writing everything while I'm departing. I think of you and <u>ask your forgiveness</u>. To all the people whom I've hurt or forgotten to mention.
>
> Forgive me
I can't
I'm tired and a horrible person
Remember only the good part of me
I LOVE YOU

Let go, and impose order. Exercise control over what is abandoned forever. If there was a spirit that animated Marco's letters, it aimed at the impossible. But for the police other aspects were important. For example, the request to destroy the computers. "They conceal my ugly sides," Marco had written. And then, naturally, the iPhone. It was thanks to that telephone that the investigators, in the space of a few hours, had traced the identity of the victim.

Everyone in Rome knows the neighborhood of Piazza Bologna, where Marco Prato's family lived. Over time, an area destined for the upper middle class developed around the post office, an imposing rationalist building constructed under fascism. Not far away is Villa Torlonia, then Villa Mirafiori. The area has a lot of bars and *salumerie*. At night it's full of young people drinking and listening to music.

Similarly, everyone knows the area where the Foffos lived. Unlike Piazza Bologna, Collatino isn't a gathering place. The big apartment buildings on Via Bergamini are certainly not an attraction, nor are the shaded avenues where solitary men walk their dogs surrounded by silence. Those who pass through Collatino are always headed elsewhere, always concentrated on something else, and so the dense urban fabric insinuates itself into the mind like the images we transfer from waking to sleep before dropping off.

In Rome, however, there are places that are pure dream. Testa di Lepre. Grottarossa. La Storta. Many Romans know they exist but have never been there; the names fascinate them, but they wouldn't be able to place them on a blank map. The truth is that Rome doesn't have well-defined borders. Once past the Vatican, you travel on the Aurelia. After a few minutes the light becomes clearer, the houses more scattered, vegetation takes the upper hand over the works of man. And once you pass the ring road, there are foxes, hoopoes, wild boar. Many, at this point, believe that Rome has ended. And yet gradually the city re-forms. Now some isolated houses. Then the big apartment buildings. Again pines and untilled fields. Once you pass the intersection with Via

Boccea, the horizon lowers. The sky is vast. Flocks of sheep feed
in the fenced fields along the road. The first farmhouses appear.
Every so often a winery. Via della Storta. At the 248 there's an old
gas station. After half a kilometer, a red brick structure protected
by a gate sticks up. It's recognizable because out front, at night
and in the early morning, there's always a van parked there with
blue writing on the side: "Euro Dolciumi."

That was the house where Luca Varani lived with his parents.
His father, Giuseppe, was a traveling seller of sweets and dried
fruit. In the vehicle (he called it a "food truck") he went around
to fairs and saint's day festivals. He was a man of sixty-one, dark-
complexioned, not very tall, with short hair, a compact physique,
and small, hard eyes. A mustache was conspicuous on his un-
shaved face.

At ten o'clock at night on Friday, March 4, Signor Varani and
his wife, Silvana, were very worried. Luca had disappeared. He
was twenty-three and their only child. He worked in a car-repair
shop in Valle Aurelia and every so often helped his father with the
fairs. He had left home that morning and hadn't returned. Many
young people don't feel the need to inform their parents about
everything they do, but Luca almost always phoned his mother if
he wasn't coming home for dinner. The phone call hadn't arrived,
so she had called him. The phone had rung and rung. Then, after midnight, it went straight to voicemail. Giuseppe and Silvana
continued calling for hours, and finally went to bed, preparing to
spend an agitated night.

The next day Giuseppe telephoned Marta Gaia. His son's
girlfriend was twenty-two, and worked for a catering business.
"Hello? Marta?" The girl was asked the same question she
wanted to ask the man as soon as she heard his voice.

"But you didn't have a fight?"

"No," answered Marta Gaia.

"No," Giuseppe Varani declared when Marta asked him the
same thing.

Cutting off contact. Avoiding the world as a form of protest. Every so often Luca did that, and Marta Gaia couldn't bear it: tremendous fights had erupted because of the way he disappeared without explanation.

After Marta Gaia, Giuseppe Varani telephoned Mario Aceto, the owner of the body shop where Luca worked. The two men barely knew each other. Giuseppe explained the situation. Aceto said that the day before Luca hadn't showed up at the shop. He was sick, no?

"What do you mean sick?" Varani was surprised.

Well, the body-shop owner recounted, Luca had sent some unmistakable messages. In the first he wrote that he had a stomach ache. In the second he had entered into details: he was stuck to the toilet seat, and couldn't come to work. "O.K., Mario, thanks," said Varani.

At that point it was clear that something was happening.

As far as Giuseppe knew, his son hadn't been sick in the past few days, neither fever nor stomach ache nor cold, nothing at all. He went straight to the first police station. He waited his turn, and when the cop asked him to sit down he explained the situation calmly.

The police told Signor Varani to wait a little longer before getting alarmed. His son was of age, only one day had passed since he disappeared, he might have gone somewhere of his own free will. It was within his rights to do so. Of course, it was strange behavior.

Giuseppe Varani agreed with the police that they would talk later. He left the station shaking his head. Once he got home, he and Silvana waited. Midday fell into afternoon, the afternoon wore away rapidly. At nine in the evening Giuseppe Varani called the police. Was there news? They said there was no news, they would let him know as soon as there was. Outside the air was cool, the shadows had descended on the pines and the farmhouses.

MP: Appointment confirmed also for the stuff.
MF: O.K., later.
MP: I'm here, at the church and the pedestrian entrance.

WhatsApp exchange between Marco Prato and Manuel Foffo three days before the murder.

M arco Prato arrived at the emergency room of the Pertini hospital at 10:10 P.M. on Saturday March 5 and left at 2:15 P.M. the next day.

The health worker wrote in the clinical file: *Reported consumption of 5 bottles of benzodiazepines + one bottle of liquor. Patient partly cooperative. Police present on site.*

Despite the arrival with sirens wailing, Marco Prato's condition was not critical. His pressure was 130 systolic and 75 diastolic, his heart rate was 84, his oxygen saturation 96. According to the toxicological analysis he had taken sleeping pills and consumed cocaine and alcohol in elevated but not lethal quantities. There was no need for stomach pumping.

"From what I read in the file it wasn't a matter of a patient whose life was in danger," the head of the emergency room said a few days later, "and I have serious doubts about the simultaneous consumption of five bottles of benzodiazepines. Five bottles would have reduced the patient to a far worse condition."

After the first examination, Marco Prato was seen by two doctors who confirmed that he was in fairly good shape (normal breathing, no neurological impairment) and sent him to a psychiatrist. However clumsy, and perhaps feigned, it was still a suicide attempt carried out by a patient who had arrived at the hospital escorted by the police.

The psychiatrist immediately noticed two details that no stethoscope would have been able to capture. Marco Prato was wearing nail polish. His hair was fake. The fine head of black hair that the young man displayed in public—and which he did not remove perhaps even in intimate moments—was a toupee. That explained the reference to the regeneration of his hair in one of the farewell letters. Marco Prato was going bald.

The psychiatrist tried to start a conversation. Despite the persistence of a confusional state—not to mention the knowledge that he was in a lot of trouble—Marco Prato showed that he was perfectly capable of carrying on a conversation.

He asks me why they've sequestered his cell phone and why he can't see his parents, the psychiatrist wrote in her report, *he says he remembers that he was with a kid named Fabrizio. Then he corrects himself and says this kid's name is Manuel, an acquaintance with whom he had decided to spend a few days consuming cocaine.*

Marco told the psychiatrist that he had been using cocaine for years. He almost boasted of it, in a way that, given the situation, had to be disorienting. "I'm for excess," he said. "When you go beyond the limits, you have to do it well."

It didn't seem like a confession. Rather, it was the morbid and assertive tone in which Marco conveyed an image of himself that suited him first of all. He said to the psychiatrist that he was a habitual consumer of Ambien. He took Ambien for sleeping. With the lormetazepam he had tried, instead, to kill himself. A few minutes later, partly contradicting himself, he stated that he used lormetazepam to weaken or boost the effect of the coke, depending on the moment. He spoke about his psychiatrist, Dr. Crinò. He saw her two or three times a week. Then he went on to family life. He said he lived in an apartment that his parents had bought, thanks to which, however, they had him in "a yoke." He talked about his work. To be successful in PR, he said, you have to know how to take advantage of a talent he happened to have.

"Which is?" the psychiatrist asked.

"The power of seduction," Marco answered. Then he asked for something to eat: "I haven't eaten for six days."

When I ask him why not, he smiles, the psychiatrist noted.

Marco continued to talk: with a wealth of detail he constructed a character for the benefit of an audience reduced for the occasion to a single person. It has to be said that he succeeded in his intention. His efforts to capture attention were never pathetic or banal.

There is no evidence of a depressive orientation of the patient's mood, wrote the psychiatrist, *although he's not completely recovered, he appears lucid and well oriented.*

What struck the investigators was a further consideration of the psychiatrist. *No evidence of ideas of guilt or self-accusation, or of feelings of shame or despair. The patient maintains adequate self-esteem.*

Several hours later Marco Prato was released from the hospital.

T he low point came with the closing of two windows at the Colosseum ticket office. What happened at the monument that is the symbol of Rome confirmed the danger of rats in the capital at the start of the month. Yesterday the prosecutor's office opened two more investigations on the subject."

Francesco Salvatore, La Repubblica

"Alert in the neonatal unit of the San Camillo hospital in Rome: 16 children and 17 health workers have been infected with *Staphylococcus aureus*. Tests by the regional health services have confirmed the presence of the bacterium in children who showed symptoms like dermatitis, conjunctivitis, and otitis. Staff has been sent home and placed on antibiotics."

Camilla Mozzetti, Il Messaggero

"The streets of Rome continue to crack open, the asphalt is crumbling and gives way as soon as it rains. Gulleys large and small disfigure avenues and main arteries. Yesterday chaos erupted in Parioli. Traffic jams and disruptions shortly after 5 P.M., when Viale della Moschea was closed. Drivers looked for alternative routes to get past the traffic jam: some used sticks to knock down the orange netting that prevented access to the Viale."

Adelaide Pierucci, Il Messaggero

A little before midnight Francesco Scavo arrived at the police station. Fifty-eight years old, born in Rome, he was the public prosecutor assigned to head the investigation. He had just made a visit to Via Igino Giordani. He had seen the body. Now he had moved to the headquarters at Piazza Dante, where he was to meet Manuel Foffo.

Francesco Scavo was of medium height and had lively eyes and black hair with a small tuft that kept falling forward over his forehead. He was the rare example of a professional in whom intelligence and humanity were in harmony. From experience he knew that deduction is a dangerous instrument when not preceded by listening, and his inclination to listen was guaranteed by an undamaged curiosity about the people he encountered in the course of his job. Seeing him in action you'd think that to him the human race was not a mistake to be judged by the divine rod of justice but a bottomless well that the tools of justice sought to illuminate at least a little.

"Scavo arrived between eleven and eleven-thirty for the questioning," recalled Michele Andreano. "I looked him in the face, and he seemed to me drained. Well, not surprising: anyone would be after seeing what they'd done to that poor kid."

If you counted up the murders that are committed in Rome, you would say that it wasn't such a dangerous city. It was violent on the psychic level. Moving through its immense neighborhoods you breathed a tense, angry air that could inspire imprudent behavior in the most foolish and at the same time total surrender.

Even violations of the law seemed to aim not at subverting order but at repeating a grotesque stagnation. The crimes committed in criminal circles spread an atmosphere of generalized breakdown. Crimes between spouses oozed impotence. In murders of relatives (father kills son with a rifle, brother attacks sister with a hatchet) resentment and frustration boiled up. That night, however, on the tenth floor on Via Igino Giordani, it seemed that all the despair, bitterness, arrogance, brutality, sense of failure that filled the city were concentrated in a single point.

The public prosecutor took a brief tour of the station. He greeted the policemen, did the same with Manuel's relatives. He made sure that the presumed murderer was able to sustain an interrogation, which he foresaw as brief. Then he greeted Andreano, the lawyer.

"Cigarette?"

It had stopped raining. In spite of the light pollution, a few stars shone in the sky above the Esquiline. Garbage trucks broke the silence of Piazza Vittorio. The homeless—stuck for hours under the porticoes—had disappeared. The Chinese shops were closed. Africans and Bangladeshis had been swallowed up by the shadows of San Lorenzo. The dream of the multiethnic neighborhood, which had animated the preceding decade, had collapsed on itself, producing not racial conflict and not class struggle but sleep, dysfunction, a gentle dissolution where, amid vomit and garbage, all were slowly sinking together.

"It seems to me like the classic party that ended very badly," said Scavo.

The public prosecutor described to the lawyer what he had seen in the apartment. The mess. The lowered blinds. The naked body of the dead man. He held out a cigarette to Andreano. The lawyer lighted it, took the first drag. Scavo had also lighted one. He inhaled, then asked the question.

"What's he doing? Will he remain silent?"

It happened often. If Manuel exercised his right to remain silent, the interrogation would end in a few formal remarks, and the important revelations would come in the next days.

"No, he wants to talk."

Francesco Scavo started, put out his cigarette with a rapid gesture, and although it was the lawyer who gave the news (the kid wanted to talk, it wasn't his intention to hide behind article 64 of the procedural code) the gesture of the public prosecutor was so rapid and contagious that Andreano, too, put out his cigarette without finishing it.

"Let's go back inside."

Thus the interrogation began.

Besides Scavo and Andreano, in the room were Colonel Giuseppe Donnarumma, Captain Lorenzo Iacobone, and Lieutenant Mauro Fioravanti, from the police. Facing them, Manuel had a frightening aspect; he was very tired, but he was also able to answer the questions. In fact he seemed anxious to do it, as if having yielded to evil in such a radical way gave him a chance that so-called normality—what we mistake for the practice of good—had long denied him.

"The accusation made against you is conspiracy to commit aggravated murder, jointly with Marco Prato, in the span of time between the 4th and 5th of March, 2016, in Rome, in the apartment where you live," said Scavo. "Do you know the name of the young man who was killed?"

"No."

"Not even his first name?"

"No."

"You didn't introduce yourselves?"

"Probably, but anyway . . . look . . . I don't remember his name."

"His name could be Luca Varani, that young man."

"I don't know."

"All right, you don't know. Now, tell me if you want to answer my questions or not."

"I want to answer."

"First of all the crime," Scavo said then. "You admit you killed this young man?"

"Yes."

"By yourself or with this other person whose name is?"

"Marco Prato."

"And how would you have killed this young man?"

"Stabbing him. And hitting him with a hammer."

"Who did what precisely?"

"We both took part in the murder."

"How long did the whole thing last?"

"A long time. What hurts in this situation is that honestly . . . well, he suffered *so much*."

The questions had only to be asked and the answers arrived without resistance. Those present understood they were in a fairly unusual situation: this time it wasn't justice trying to shine light into the dark corners of human nature; it was the bottom of the well rising furiously toward those leaning over to look inside.

"Let's start from the beginning," said Scavo.

"Here's what happens first. Marco and I meet."

"You get in touch with Marco Prato or he gets in touch with you?"

"We messaged, we'd agreed to see each other again. I should say first that we met two months ago, at New Year's, and then we met briefly for a glass of wine."

"You haven't known each other long."

"Right. But, practically . . . we knew we both used cocaine. When we met we were at my house for three days, but not always just the two of us."

"Who else was there?"

"For instance, another sort of friend of mine came."

"When?"

"I think between Wednesday and Thursday."

"Do you remember who this *sort of friend* is?"

"His name is Alex, I only saw him once, too."

"Alex what?"

"I don't remember his last name. I saved him on my phone as Alex Tiburtina."

"Alex Tiburtina."

"Because I'd met him in a pizzeria on Via Tiburtina."

"O.K. So between Wednesday and Thursday he came, too."

"Yes, but Alex came in a circumstance when . . . practically . . . we were, yes, under the influence of drugs . . . but . . . we were still inside a logic of . . ."

"You still had some consciousness of yourselves."

"*Consciousness*, exactly. We could start a conversation."

Manuel spoke in a thin, wavering voice; it was hesitant, then it became fluent, after another couple of remarks he even seemed overwhelmed by boredom, it was all a "practically" and an "honestly" that are the background noise of Rome, this eternal disorder where you meet by chance in a pizzeria and then find yourself at the site of a massacre.

"This Alex came," said Manuel. "At a certain point also a friend of Marco's joined us . . . I don't remember his name . . . Damiano! His name is Damiano. But then, when Luca arrived . . ."

"What does *when he arrived* mean? The two of you were expecting Luca?"

"I didn't even know him. Marco sent him some WhatsApps."

"What quantity of drugs had you taken?"

"A lot. I wouldn't know how to quantify it."

"Then tell me how much you spent."

"So . . . I took out some money . . . then mainly there was the fact that Marco . . . let's say . . . had also taken some with this Damiano's bank card. In all we must have spent something like fifteen hundred euros. A lot. Anyway Marco in those three days did various things on his own initiative, for example he took my phone and called some of my contacts, or . . ."

"Marco is gay?"

In theory it was an irrelevant question, but the public prosecutor had sniffed something and followed the trail.

"Yes, he's gay," Manuel said. Right afterward he felt the need to clarify: "I mean, I'm straight . . . but, anyway . . . I hang out with Marco . . . well, *hang out* is a little strong . . . it's the second time I'd met him . . . the fact is that, for instance, I *don't know* if Marco's friends are gay or straight."

"Take Marco," said Scavo, "did he have an interest in you?"

"Yes."

"Did he show it in a clear way?"

"Yes."

"You were aware of it?"

"Yes," said Manuel in a very low voice.

"And you had responded in some way to his desires?"

"I met Marco through friends in common," said Manuel. "We spent New Year's together . . . then, what happens . . . Marco and I took drugs . . . he *wanted* to stay at my house with the excuse of offering me more cocaine . . . and at this point, what happens . . . it happens that . . . practically . . . Marco Prato gave me oral sex."

There was nothing strange in a sexual encounter between men. Yet Manuel's words suggested great uneasiness, and Scavo knew that certain nagging thoughts—unimportant in themselves, so important for those who let themselves be tormented—could play an important role in the complex mechanism that pushes men to perform the most foolish acts.

"When did it happen?"

"I honestly . . . I understand that maybe I'm not credible," said Manuel, "but the thing disgusted me. So I didn't want to talk to Marco anymore. But we had friends in common . . . so on the one hand I didn't want to see him, but on the other I *couldn't* not see him . . . because practically, you see, Mr. Scavo . . . there was this video . . ."

"There was a video?"

"Yes."

"And who made this video?"

"Together," the young man said. "We made it together. A video in which he gave me oral sex."

It was still cloudy the next day. It rained on and off continuously. A weak, distant sun brightened the fields of La Storta when the police car arrived.

Giuseppe Varani had been awake for a while. He didn't know if he had slept or not. Tension kept him in a state of lucidity difficult to describe. Tension and anguish. It had been tension and hope the first time he saw him. Twenty-three years earlier, when they adopted him. Luca knew it. Everyone knew it. His wife got pregnant and lost the baby; this had happened more than once. The doctors said it was becoming dangerous. He and Silvana then made inquiries. They knew of people who had gone to Brazil. Others told of couples who had simply gone to an orphanage in Emilia Romagna or just outside Lazio. If you're interested in this subject, you end up hearing all sort of things. Giuseppe and Silvana made many applications. If you play the game on several fronts, the probabilities increase.

Giuseppe took the first trip to the former Yugoslavia with a Macedonian who served as a guide. The country had been destroyed by war. They arrived in Bitola, near Lake Prespa. There was the orphanage. The sisters were very kind. They asked for his documents, registered him, had him fill out forms. If something came up, they said, they would get in touch. They said goodbye and he returned to Rome without knowing what to think.

In May of the next year, 1993, Giuseppe Varani received a phone call. The orphanage in Bitola. He and Silvana left immediately. Along the way they saw the blue helmets of the UN. The war was over. They were advised to hurry: risk of attacks.

At the orphanage a surprise awaited them. There were in fact three adoptable children, and they would have to choose one. They hadn't imagined that; they'd thought the assignment would be automatic based on documents and priorities, whereas it was entrusted instead to their free will. Three staff members arrived, each carrying a child. It was like a scene from a movie, but it was a dramatic moment. You choose one, you wrong the others, he thought. He looked nervously at his wife. Whichever of us first recognizes in one of those children our son steps forward, they said, and that will be fine with the other. But they had barely stopped talking when one of the three babies smiled. A magnificent smile, addressed directly to them. Giuseppe held him in his arms and there, they had chosen. The orphanage workers left the room, taking away the other babies. The sensation was incredible: you look for the last time at the one who could have been your son. If you had chosen differently, it would have been another. Another and not him. Him and not another.

They came to interview them. They wouldn't leave them in peace for the entire year that followed. Giuseppe wouldn't retreat. He would talk, and shout, and rage, and protest. He gained the reputation of being irascible and hotheaded. Everyone said: "Not surprising, his son was killed, I would have done worse." But then behind his back people were critical of him, they blamed his heated tones, his working-class background. Yet he was useful. There were pages to fill, television broadcasts that, minus an interview with him, lost half their value. The reporters returned to flattering him. At first he was always awkward in front of the camera, but after a few exchanges he relaxed, he spoke in Roman dialect, he reconstructed the event with a profound analytical spirit undermined by sudden changes of mood. At a certain point his voice broke. The vile way they had murdered him. They had done what they had done, and not content with that they had also slandered him. They came from well-off families, they had good lawyers, they would do all they could to get off. Life in prison! Life in prison! There, he was off. He shouted with his eyes staring at the camera. The reporter told the cameraman to stay on the closeup. Cynicism was the air everyone breathed, no one would reproach them.

Every so often an intelligent journalist asked a different question.

"Signor Varani, what did you feel when you returned to Italy with that child?"

"A sense of victory," he said proudly.

"And what was the precise moment when you felt you were *truly* Luca's father?"

"Right away, immediately. When I held him. Then I felt he was our son."

"Who chose the name?"

"My wife liked Luca. She liked that name. That was fine."

"What was Luca like as a child?"

"He was a lively child. A child everyone liked. He was loved, he bonded with everyone, open, sunny. You understand? That was Luca as a child."

The newspapers published dozens of photos of Luca. At fifteen, at eighteen, at twenty. He was very handsome. A sweet gaze, big eyes, high cheekbones. Bare-chested, holding a kitten. Posing as a rapper. Dressed up in black jacket and white shirt against the background of Piazza Colonna. Then the photos with Marta Gaia. Dozens of images in which the couple were embracing.

Luca and Marta Gaia had been together since they were fourteen. For some it was the height of romanticism. Others found it a bit suffocating. At that age it's good to gain experience, they said, you can't be with the same girl all the time.

Every so often Luca disappeared into a rabbit hole. There were moments of the day when no one knew where he was. Rome always allows you to hide if you want to go about your own business. He had been enrolled in a technical school. At a certain point he had failed, then had started going to night school. He had quit night school a step away from the diploma, and gone to work in the shop. But he would have gone back to school, the teachers said after the murder. He was an intelligent boy, good in mathematics, always curious about everything. He would have got his diploma, they said, certainly he would have done it.

The policemen rang the bell. Giuseppe Varani observed them. They were alone.

"Please, come in," he said.

There were two in civilian clothes, two in uniform. While he turned his back on them to let them in, Giuseppe reflected. Luca wasn't with them. With his son absent, if it had been good news it would have come on the phone.

"So, what happened?" he asked without waiting for them to reach the living room.

"Yes, well, we'll tell you," one of the policemen said.

"You know where Luca is?" he insisted.

"We've seen him," said another in a vague tone.

The atmosphere was so strange that speaking plainly became difficult. Signor Varani began to feel agitated. "Could you get us a coffee?" one of the policemen tried to break the tension. "Of course, why not. Let me make it," he said.

After the request for coffee, Signor Varani thought Luca was in trouble with the law. They had arrested him. That's what had happened. A fight. He had had a fight with someone.

"Boys can find themselves in ten thousand strange situations a night," he would say months later, reconstructing the sensations of that morning.

It was true, anything can happen to a boy. But what he could imagine was nothing compared with what they had to tell him. Reality is too brutal for a human mind to bear. The human mind is designed to hold reality in check. It reorganizes the terrible mystery of time. It hides the thought of death. It lends a name to naked things, then transforms them into symbols.

"Can we take a look through the house?"

The cops were proceeding by trial and error. There was no instruction manual. No protocol to adhere to. Things were left every time to the sensibility of those who had to deal with them. It was difficult, partly because those receiving the news often understood what was happening. They understood but preferred to wait. The cops then felt it was their duty to support them, and they all started circling around the subject together in such a way as to keep the *thing* from being true as long as possible.

"Go on, go on, am I going to say no?"

The cops scattered through the house. They disappeared behind a door. Then they returned. He was never left alone. "How is your relationship with your son?" "Good, good. I mean, normal." "Is it true that you adopted him?" "Yes, adopted," he confirmed. "What are Luca's habits?" The questions came from all directions. Giuseppe answered, trying to do his best. Luca is dead. One of the men said it suddenly. You have to first enter into an absurd situation for absurd news to be communicated.

"Dead? What do you mean, *he's dead*. What do you mean *dead!*"

"He was killed," said the cop.

At this point Giuseppe Varani could have fallen to the floor. Instead he was still standing, still upright before the police. There had been a quarrel and someone must have pulled out a knife, he thought. Like the sound of a body in motion, that reasoning came before the collapse that was producing it. "We've arrested them, they've confessed," another cop said quickly. "Where did they kill him?" asked Signor Varani. The more rapidly reality destroyed the margins of what was bearable, the more rapidly reasoning hastened to reconstruct them a few meters farther on. "In an apartment," said the cop, again breaking down the man's mental barriers.

"An apartment?"

It had to happen on the street in order for the thing to make any sense at all. A kid doesn't stop at a traffic light, a driver insults him. The two come to blows. Fall, fate. Or: you offend someone dangerous. The street is the ideal place to make you pay for it. But it wasn't even that.

Some hours later he was taken to the morgue to identify the body. "Here it is," said the attendants. They showed it to him behind a glass panel. "Now you can look." The request was unbearable, everything had been unbearable for several hours then, but he did what had to be done. The body was lying on a metal stretcher. The throat cut. The teeth smashed. They had put a tremendous frenzy into it. But what he saw afterward left him even more agitated. On his son's face and abdomen were various superficial cuts. "Some very fine marks," he said. There were all these squiggles, like embroidery, on his cheeks and forehead. Signor Varani was quiet for a few seconds. "Bastards," he said finally, "they wanted to have fun." They hadn't been content to kill him. It was a concept impossible to take in, but Giuseppe Varani in the end did that, too: managed to think the unthinkable. Only then was he sure of having understood. It wasn't those cuts that had caused the death of his son, but in those cuts was an explanation.

"They went to the other side," he said, "while I'm still here."

He meant that he was waiting for Luca's killers on the shore of the humanly comprehensible, where those who had perpetrated the carnage would sooner or later have to return. Maybe for that reason, during the television interviews, even when he was at the height of rage, and raised his voice, pounding the back of his right hand against the palm of the left, Varani rarely called the murderers "monsters." He said they had done a monstrous thing, they had behaved like monsters, but they were human beings, creatures who can't be corrected by the abstract pronouncement of a moral principle. "It takes prison," he thundered, "the right punishment for what they did."

They had tricked him. Then they had robbed him. But the view from the Gianicolo was stupendous. The Dutch tourist sat down on a concrete bollard. From there one contemplated one of the most beautiful urban panoramas in the world, but things happened down below, in the streets, the crowd, the stink. The person he was supposed to meet was late. Well, naturally he's late, he thought. Among the legends of recent times was the one according to which Rome was the only European capital that hadn't suffered terrorist attacks because of its eternal unreliability. Two terrorists agree to blow up the McDonald's in Piazza di Spagna. They synchronize their watches, but they don't meet: public transportation strike, the metro shutting down early, unauthorized demonstration on Via Nazionale.

At the Colosseum two fake tickets had been palmed off on him. Two days later, between Lepanto and Manzoni, his wallet had been lifted from his pocket. He had realized it at Colle Oppio. Luckily he kept documents and credit cards at the hotel. It was the fifth time he'd come to Rome in the past two years, he had learned the rules: what the city relieved you of was nothing compared with what it offered, but you had to be careful. He was staying at the Ariston. But then he'd taken a second room, ten minutes from Piazza dei Cinquecento, a room where you didn't have to register.

A message appeared on his cell phone. The Dutch tourist read it, and responded.

The cannon on the Gianicolo shot its usual round, giving way to the bells of all the nearby churches. A crowd of starlings rose from the trees.

He had been an engineer for Boeing, now he was retired. Tourists of his type—men of advanced age, substantial culture, good social position, widowers or no longer married—came to Rome to immerse themselves in the past. They contemplated Michelangelo's *Moses,* misunderstanding it, and were stunned by the mosaics of Santa Prassede. Convinced that they knew about art because they'd read a few books, they had the illusion that the short time they had left to live would bring them closer to the mystery of those immortal works. It wasn't true. Mortals for the mortals. What was extraordinary about Rome was not the call of transcendence, which only idiots could feel, but the omnipresent awareness that everything is human and everything decays. This was the lesson of the past. No present is ever more precious than that of someone who knows he has to die. A boy and girl laughing in a bar, a taxi-driver sleeping with his mouth open, the eyes of a child amid the stalls selling apples in a market. For that he was here. At Porta Portese a piece of junk had been passed off as a real Etruscan vase, but the arguments of the dealer were so refined and so openly deceptive that in the end, admiring, he had taken out his wallet. On the Lungotevere Marzio he had seen something whose logic he struggled to understand: a boy had thrown a brand-new bike off a bridge.

In Monti he advanced along the narrow neighborhood streets. Voices. Colors. Extremely elegant girls. At a certain point a terrific stink nearly made him faint. A black odor of death. The butcher shop on Via Panisperna. The highest officeholders in the government were regular customers. President Giorgio Napolitano, Carlo Azeglio Ciampi, before them Francesco Cossiga. Normal people also shopped there, people willing to pay a few euros more to have in their mouths the same taste as the head of state. "Or to shit the same shit," said the witty. Now the butcher shop had gone bankrupt. When the officials came to seal it, they had made sure to turn off the electricity, without realizing that there were still many pounds of meat in the refrigerator.

The Dutch tourist had turned the corner. The stink had lessened. Like a shipwrecked sailor in search of safety he turned onto Via Nazionale. He had seen the drivers who went speeding along break their backs because of the potholes.

"The reason for the holes lies in the fact that businesses, to win a contract, pay a bribe to a city official," the head of the anti-corruption agency had explained during a press conference held a few days before. "The entrepreneur makes back that extra money by doing the job badly, and so the job has to be redone soon, which leads to further bribes, further illegal earnings, new holes in the asphalt."

Into those holes everyone fell, honest and dishonest.

The Dutch tourist checked his phone again, looked up and saw the man. He left the concrete support, turned his back on the beauty of the churches, and went to meet life.

"Here, this one seems interesting," he said a few minutes later, indicating one of the photos the man was showing him.

"W hen Luca showed up it's like a tacit agreement went off between Marco and me," said Manuel.

"A tacit agreement to do what?"

"It was as if whatever there was between him and me . . . well, look, *it was still alive*."

It was one-forty in the morning.

"Let's recapitulate," Scavo took a step back. "Marco sends this WhatsApp to Luca, and when do you find out?"

"When Luca shows up at my house."

"And what did you think when Luca arrived? You didn't think *Now who is this kid?*"

"Yes, I thought it, but considering the life we were leading . . . between cocaine, alcohol, people coming and going . . . well, it wasn't very strange."

"All right," said Scavo, "then tell us what you remember about when Luca entered your apartment. Did you talk? Did you have some conversation?"

"Honestly the only thing I remember," Manuel said, "is that this kid was adopted. And that he was a rent boy."

"Rent boy?"

"He was a prostitute."

"And how did you know?"

"Marco had told me so."

"Where did Luca's phone end up?"

"We threw it in a trash bin. Actually he had two phones. I think Luca also sold drugs."

They continued for several more minutes. Then, without any

connection to the questions, Manuel felt the need to explain something.

"You see, Mr. Scavo, in my circle of friends we're all guys who . . . well, it's not that we can't fall in love, but we tend to give . . . we think about sex more than anything else . . . sometimes we pay for it. And then," he continued, struggling, "I wouldn't want you to think that, because I don't have a steady relationship on the romantic level . . . I wouldn't want you to think that I might be one of those types who can't . . ."

He wasn't an Anders Breivik, he wasn't a Charles Manson. Here's what he was trying to explain to those he was facing. Although the facts seemed to demonstrate the contrary, he was *human*. Manuel seemed to be asking his accusers to shed light on what had happened—explain to me what I did, help me to understand. The crimes that filled the pages of newspapers had as protagonists individuals who were self-determined in their criminal acts. Here, on the contrary, it seemed that a very violent murder—preceded by hours of torture—had been carried out apart from the will of those who had committed it. There didn't seem to be a motive. There didn't seem to be an emotional bond with the victim.

"Look, we're not making ethical judgments," said Scavo.

"We're not here to make moral judgments." Colonel Donnarumma reiterated the concept.

"Listen, Manuel," said the defense lawyer, "do you remember if maybe Marco incited you or instigated you to do violence to that young man?"

"Yes," Manuel answered, "that also happened. But it's not that now Marco is the bad guy and I'm the good guy. I'm responsible."

Scavo got up from the desk at two-fifty-five in the morning. The interrogation was over. He gave the order to turn off the tape recorder. He said goodbye to Manuel and left the room. Then he asked an officer to write to the director of the district penitentiary of Regina Coeli.

Just as dawn was breaking, Manuel Foffo entered prison for the first time in his life.

Marco Prato was released from the hospital a few hours later. He was escorted by the police to the precinct at Piazza Dante. Here two officers confiscated a rather singular item. "On 6 March 2016 at 19:20," the report said, "confiscation proceeded of specimen no. 1 of fake Hair (toupee) considered to be physical evidence." Then Marco, too, was transferred to Regina Coeli, with an absolute ban on seeing his family or Manuel Foffo.

To hear the gates of prison close behind you for the first time is an experience that no one forgets. At Regina Coeli this desolation is mixed with other sensations. The structure is situated in one of the most beautiful parts of the city. Not far is the Gianicolo with its views. On the eastern side flows the Tiber. That is the magical point where a blink of the eye would capture, on the surface of the water, the Synagogue, the airy spans of Ponte Garibaldi, the bell tower of San Bartolomeo. All the magnificence that one might ask of shapes is within reach of the gaze. But under the greenish surface the true river is blind and cold and populated on the muddy bottom by faceless creatures.

PART II

The Surface of the Water

If a single individual can know nothing, why should all individuals
taken together know any more?
—GUSTAVE FLAUBERT

The mass media first convinced us that the imaginary was real,
and now they are convincing us that the real is imaginary.
—UMBERTO ECO[1]

[1] Umberto Eco, *How to Travel with a Salmon & Other Essays,* translated from the
Italian by William Weaver (San Diego, CA: Harcourt Brace, 1995)

C ristina Guarinelli called me at two in the afternoon on Tuesday, March 8. She asked if I wanted to write a story on the murder of Luca Varani. I turned down the proposal. A few hours later I called her back saying I would accept.

Cristina Guarinelli worked at *Venerdì*. She was a woman who was both professional and capable of human warmth despite the crazy rhythms of journalism. Along with Attilio Giordano, the editor of the weekly, she had decided to assign an in-depth report on the case.

The preceding Sunday, when I heard the news, I had been hypnotized in front of the TV. Even though the elements of the story were still confusing, I immediately seemed to grasp something familiar. The sensation was similar to that of recognizing in a passerby on the street the features of a person you haven't seen for years. I hated myself for watching the report to the very end and turned off the TV.

I was enjoying a period of tranquility in my life, as I hadn't for a long time. Weeks followed one another without upheavals. I was working on a book. My marriage was going well. I was managing things with a certain mastery. We usually have mastery over what we've already grasped. I was immediately afraid, I mean, that the Varani case could cause the derailment of everything I was making an effort to protect. That's why I was irritated when I got the phone call from the paper: I had never written a crime story—what was the likelihood that I would be asked to follow precisely the case I was trying to stay away from?

I answered Cristina Guarinelli in a tone that must have sounded rude to her. I said I didn't have time for such a demanding job and hung up.

Once I'd put down the phone, I returned to the computer. I started to work in a good frame of mind, and there, sitting at the desk, I found myself staring aghast at the text to which I'd devoted every day of the past months crumbling page by page under my impotent gaze, undermined not by a brilliant idea for a new book but by a *force*—a rather obscure force—of which in fact I knew nothing. Obstinately I continued to work. The more I dug between the commas, the less I found.

When my wife came home that night, she immediately saw that I'd had a bad day. I told her what had happened, but before I could go into detail she said, "How lucky."

It was truly lucky that I had been asked to follow precisely the case that—"Confess it," said Chiara—I'd done nothing but think about for days. If you took into account certain incidents from my past, a case like that couldn't leave me indifferent. To be clear, a case like that was impossible for me to stay away from. What we've avoided is very often what we haven't had time to understand, and when, years later, *that thing* reappears in a new guise it's usually to let us question it as we couldn't do at the time.

"I'm trying to clear my schedule. Let's talk when you can."

With that text message, I, worried about keeping up appearances, got back in touch with Cristina Guarinelli.

When I accepted the job from *Venerdì* four days had passed since the murder and two since its appearance in the media. The news had piled up in a frenetic way, then the story had assumed the form in which public opinion would long cast it, the inevitably mistaken form that gives free rein to the most unrestrained impulses.

At first the case was presented as an outburst of incomprehensible horror. The arrested youths were two normal guys, the murder had no motive, it was hard to understand what had happened.

What sort of world do we live in?

Looks like that poor guy was killed because the murderers were bored.

This city is disgusting!

For a few hours the comments on social media were limited to relaying a generic dismay. Then Monday arrived, and some details began to emerge. The murder acquired a class dimension.

A poor kid killed barbarically by two disgusting stinking murdering good-for-nothing rich kids.

I hope justice condemns Marco Prato to life in prison, but since he's a radical-chic communist what do you bet it ends in farce?

A shady failed university student, son of a restaurateur with a brusque manner, strikes up a friendship with the uninhibited son of a cultural administrator, friend of friends of important people, and together they have fun torturing a twenty-year-old adopted by street peddlers from La Storta. Three social classes, three income levels, three different areas of the city, and, see, it adds up perfectly.

Drown them in acid, I'd like to see what that's like!

Burn them alive with the same indifference they had.
Death penalty with a lot of suffering! Junkie animals!

The possibility of invoking the law of retaliation excited the re-actionaries. But the progressives were just as bad. Various Twitter users took advantage of the murder to attack Matteo Salvini and the League: it wasn't immigrants who had killed Luca Varani but two rich, very Italian white kids, well brought up, sons of so-called respectable families, roared the commentators, in turn Italian, white, from respectable families.

The wave of indignation infected the first public figures. The television host Rita dalla Chiesa, daughter of the general killed by the Mafia, wrote on her Facebook profile: "If I asked for the death penalty for these evil monsters, the so-called intelligentsia would attack me. O.K., go ahead, all of you, because this time I'd ask for the death penalty. I'd ask for it as fervently as possible."

The discussion continued deep into the night. Then, with the new day, other elements emerged. It was learned that Marco Prato was gay. It was learned that although Manuel Foffo claimed to be heterosexual, he had had sexual relations with him. The murder "of class" was contaminated by sexual orientation.

Luca Varani killed by gay perverts.
Fucking fags #lucavarani.
Now let those motherfuckers also adopt children #lucavarani

Marco Prato's Facebook profile was full of posts in which his homosexuality emerged naturally, ironic and subtle messages and videos, essentially innocuous; nevertheless, that type of noncha-lance increased the irritation of many commentators.

If Marco Prato were a fascist they'd all make a big deal out of it.
Instead he's an LGBT activist, the classic radical chic intellectual, a slimy bourgeois spoiled since he was a kid.
@marcoprato I'll cut off your thumbs and kill you myself!

At first the hatred was focused on Prato. But as the hours passed Manuel Foffo's absence from the digital world began to arouse suspicions. Why was Manuel not on social media? Photos couldn't be found even if you looked on Google, and in the newspapers a faded passport picture appeared that couldn't even tell you what sort of face he had. Someone speculated that the truly powerful family was his: the Foffos had so many connections, it was said, they could make the boy disappear from the Internet in twenty-four hours.

Then came the post on Adam and Eve.

Anyone who took the trouble to examine Luca Varani's Facebook profile found something unexpected. At first sight it was the profile of a twenty-year-old: messages of love for his girlfriend ("I'd like to wake up next to you with your body in my arms and tell you an ultimate truth . . . I love you"), good intentions ("Every day that passes is an opportunity to improve oneself"), outbursts without a precise object ("You all suck!"), short videos in which Disney films were dubbed in Romanesco ("Snow White and the Horny Dwarfs").

Every so often, however, something different appeared.

It was mostly posts that Luca had shared from other users. In one there was a doctored photo of Cécile Kyenge, the first minister of African origin in the history of the Italian republic. "I am Italian," the author of the doctored version had her say. "And I am a cat," a dog responded in the cartoon underneath. In another post a dialogue between Cécile Kyenge and Benito Mussolini was imagined. "The Italian immigration laws are a disgrace," said the minister. And Mussolini: "The disgrace is to see people coming from the Congo to dictate laws to a people proud of their history."

Worse, in addition to these posts was a fairly homophobic one, which happened to be the last shared by Luca Varani before he was killed. A religious image with a caption underneath: "God created Adam and Eve, not Adam and Steve."

Did these posts say something final about the personality of Luca Varani and his opinions? Did they make him a fervent homophobe? A right-wing extremist? Wasn't it rash to elevate them to the manifesto of a twenty-year-old about whom nothing was known? And yet, in defiance of all caution, for a large crowd of commentators, Luca Varani instantly became a heterosexual murdered by two gays because of his support for traditional family values. Riding the new wave were precisely those from whom prudence and composure should be required by their role: politicians.

The first to come out into the open was Mario Adinolfi. A former member of Parliament in the Democratic Party, Adinolfi was an anti-abortion Catholic, a strenuous supporter of the traditional family. In that year of leaderless city councils, Adinolfi was preparing to run in the election for mayor of Rome. He wrote on his Facebook profile: "The last post of poor Luca Varani is a Biblical image with the caption: 'God created Adam and Eve, not Adam and Steve.' If I had published it, I would have been called homophobic for weeks. Luca Varani was brutally killed by two gays who knocked him out, drugged him, and tortured him. The *Repubblica* has this headline: 'Sex, Night Life, and Other Madness: the Ruin of Manuel and Marco.' To find the word 'gay' you have to get to the end of the article. I say that in the media world a homosexual lobby is at work that sweetens any news that might damage the image of the LGBT community. What would the headlines have been if the dead man were a gay killed by a pair from the Sentinelle, the guardians of family values? I hope that honest magistrates ask themselves why Luca Varani was chosen as the sacrificial victim. It's important for understanding if the filthy violence that is unleashed against us—only because we try to say that we are against gay marriage—is generating a persecutory frenzy of which this act is the culmination."

A part of the LGBTQ community also began to be heard from, and in this case as well it was representatives of the political

world who took the initiative. Vladimir Luxuria, the first trans-
gender member of the European Parliament, revealed that she
had known Marco Prato in the past. Luxuria posted on Twitter
the screenshot of an old message from Prato in which he invited
her to present her latest book during an evening at the Os Club.
Luxuria said she was upset by what had happened ("Monsters
can be lurking inside people you don't expect") and offered her
opinion on the conduct of the victim: "Often the biggest homophobes are repressed gays, so I would also investigate this aspect.
The victim was barely older than twenty, and had a girlfriend:
but what was he doing on a Friday night in an apartment on the
outskirts of Rome with two openly homosexual youths who loved
to get high, instead of with her? The answer is obvious."

Other activists stated that the problem was self-hatred. Non-
acceptance generated pain and frustration, pain and frustration
generated violence, and where do pain, frustration, and finally violence originate if not in the homophobic and patriarchal culture
that has historically dominated our life? Intolerance, introjected
despite one's own desires, generated disasters: it had been the
failure to accept their own homosexuality that had driven Foffo
and Prato to kill Varani.

There was no lack of interesting opinions from criminologists
and experts in sociology. Some even called on the devil.

*Those who use the instruments of the devil have the illusion of
acquiring powers that others don't have.*

Cursed, despicable beings, followers of Satan!

The Internet is sensitivity without restraint, I thought, after
reading these messages for hours. Nevertheless, I wondered if
there wasn't a partial truth in that lack of restraint: didn't the
tones of social media, which deformed everything into a con-
flagration of simplification and Manichaeism, touch on, in the
wrong way, some points that more civil routes would have arrived
at more slowly?

"Nicola!"

But what happens when precisely the people involved in cases like this decide *themselves* to jump into the simplifying machine of the public narrative?

"Nicola, hurry!"

It was my wife calling me from the living room. I joined her, finding her with her back to me, pointing to the television, the ageless device on whose screen the large face of Valter Foffo was now framed: four days after the crime and two after his son's confession, with Manuel thrown in jail and Luca Varani not yet buried, he had accepted the invitation of a talk show to relate, for the benefit of some millions of Italians, his unforgettable version of the facts.

W *hat was he thinking?*
That was the question that the most forgiving asked themselves while Valter Foffo spoke on TV, offering an enormous audience the opportunity for outrage, disdain, invective, all ascribable to two principal motives: what Valter Foffo succeeded in saying and what he succeeded in *not* saying.

"Let's forget it, we got bad advice."

Sometime later Valter Foffo acknowledged the mistake. He was less upset than in the first few days. The initial shock had been replaced by routine management of the state of alarm: strangers who insulted him on the street, business foundering, long discussions considering how to get out of it.

"The lawyer. He's the one who convinced us."

As he spoke Valter Foffo looked away, as if to get rid of a thought that risked making him lose control. But where could he look? No matter where he turned, problems rained down on him.

"It's true, I advised him to do it. But it was impossible to predict what would come out of his mouth. I don't know what got into him."

Andreano, the lawyer, reconstructed the episode from another point of view. The appearance of Valter Foffo on TV had been a disaster, agreed. But people can't imagine what's behind it. They don't know about the anxiety, the pressure, they're ignorant of the genuine madness that can be unleashed around the family of a confessed criminal when a case like that enters the public domain. Journalists, TV news producers—all at a certain point were hunting him. They wanted him to deliver the boy's father. They wanted the boy's mother. At worst even the boy's brother would do.

"I'm sorry, Manuel's relatives aren't releasing statements."

At first Andreano repulsed the attacks, refusing every request for an interview. But the situation changed from hour to hour, the blazing fire of contempt was starting to move toward his client: the Foffos' silence risked adding guilt to guilt, and judges aren't always insensitive to that. Manuel's family, besieged by journalists, asked for advice. Andreano began to think about it. An interview. A single public outing capable of changing, even only in part, the narrative that was being created around the case.

"All right, I'll go."

If it was necessary to play that card for the boy's good, let it at least be the best-known talk show in the country. On *Porta a Porta* things happened that weren't possible elsewhere. It was there that Silvio Berlusconi had signed his contract with the Italians. It was on *Porta a Porta* that the Pope in person—throwing off even his experienced host—had decided to appear live on the telephone. Relatives of the crime boss Vittorio Casamonica had also been guests, just as, within a few weeks, the son of Totò Riina would come to tell the story of the family.

Valter Foffo appeared in the television studio dressed up, dark jacket over white shirt, red tie, white hair carefully combed, cheeks perfectly shaved.

Before letting him speak, Bruno Vespa played the segment that summarized the crime.

While an offscreen voice recounted the murder, on the screen images began to appear of Marco Prato, Luca Varani, Manuel Foffo. Between one image and the next entire pages of Manuel's interrogation were shown, the words uttered by the offscreen voice highlighted in yellow ("We got out of the car, I remembered we wanted to hurt someone"; "We said to ourselves that we had to kill him"), and then other phrases that were shown briefly but not read by the voice ("Luca was a prostitute"; "On New Year's night I had oral sex with Marco"). For viewers it was difficult to cope with all that information. The segment disappeared quickly, the camera was again on Bruno Vespa.

"Valter Foffo is Manuel's father," the host began introducing the guest in the studio. "To him Manuel confessed that he killed Luca. Signor Foffo, so, how did he tell you?"

Valter Foffo sighed. He recognized the camera on him. A fraction of silence. Then he started talking. He told the story of the car trip. He said that before confessing to the murder, his son told him he'd taken cocaine.

The interviewer interrupted him: "Sorry, your son said he'd been taking cocaine from ten years . . ."

Signor Foffo leaped to the defensive: "Ten years? Look, not as far as I know."

"Well, your son said it, I don't know."

"No, listen," Foffo specified, "in the reports it's written that he was several years older."

Vespa realized the misunderstanding. "No, no, for goodness' sake!" he was quick to say. "Not from when he was ten years *old*; from when he was nineteen, *ten years ago*."

How could Valter Foffo think that he was asking him if his son had become a cokehead when he was a child of ten? Had he thought it because he was in a state of confusion? Because on television anything can happen? Because he was getting used to the idea that around him anything had now become possible? Yet again, the comic caressed the scene when the possibilities of the tragic had been exhausted.

"Yes," Valter Foffo said quickly, "in the reports it says that."

"And in all that time," asked the host, "you didn't notice anything?"

Valter Foffo was an entrepreneur with long experience, he was used to managing situations that would have disconcerted the majority of the men in show business. But he had never been in a television studio. And so, bewildered by the lights, by the movement of the cameras, wasted by the previous days, hounded by what on TV ("You know that your son takes drugs?") was still the mother of all questions, Valter Foffo launched himself into the void.

"No, look," he said, "I never noticed anything, since Manuel has always been a model boy. Against violence. Self-taught. A very good boy, maybe excessively good. And also reserved. A boy with an IQ above the norm."

"Look, I don't doubt that," the host inserted himself, choosing the moment perfectly, and, after conceding to the interviewee the possibility that his son was endowed with superior intelligence, asked him to return to the facts of the murder.

Valter Foffo recounted the little he knew. But it was what he presumed to know, yet again, that roused the surprise of viewers. He said that at first he hadn't believed Manuel's confession ("He was too calm, he had a *glacial* calm"), and so the suspicion had come to him that the cocaine had made him say things that hadn't happened. Vespa asked if it was true that his son had had problems with alcohol. "Yes, I myself had referred him to a psychologist" was the answer. "And what did the psychologist tell you?" "He didn't talk to me, there's confidentiality." "Yes, of course," said the interviewer, "but the psychologist at least told you that your son's situation was alarming?" "Absolutely not," said Valter Foffo, then repeated: "Manuel . . . a model boy." At that point the psychotherapist Vera Slepoj spoke. She was among the guests in the studio, and she asked Valter if he hadn't formed an idealized version of his son. Valter Foffo answered that more than anything else he had the idea of his son as a studious kid. The psychologist pointed out that a boy with alcohol and cocaine problems should have aroused some suspicions. Valter Foffo gave signs of impatience. Bruno Vespa arrived to help both: "So, in the end, how did you think your son was doing?" "I thought he was doing *very well*," answered Valter Foffo. "As far as the subject of alcohol is concerned, as I said, I intervened right away. But real alcoholism, doctor, is *something else*," he said addressing Slepoj in a resentful tone. "An alcoholic is someone who drinks every day, while Manuel could go months and months without drinking." The crime writer Maurizio de Giovanni was also in the studio. He said he was disconcerted by what had happened. The lawyer, Andreano, connected from Milan, said it was necessary to understand to what degree Manuel had been mentally incapacitated while he did what he had done. Valter Foffo hypothesized that, as a result of taking cocaine, his son and Marco Prato had lost the light of reason. "Probably they are also two people who manipulated each other in turn," the psychologist ventured. "*Very remote* hypothesis," Valter Foffo responded resolutely. De Giovanni asked if it was true that Manuel had had some medical tests to get his license back. "Yes, because one evening he came out of a club," Valter Foffo answered, "and the car went out of control and the traffic cops arrived." "Well, but they don't do those tests if there's not a toxicological or alcoholic reason," de Giovanni pointed out. "It happened a year and a half ago," Valter Foffo said defensively. "Since then Manuel hasn't touched alcohol, he's had the tests. He's repeated them. They turned out negative."

"Signor Foffo," Bruno Vespa put an end to the discussion. "As a father I feel for you. As a journalist I believe another show has gone on the air."

No one knew how the reports of the interrogation had ended up in the hands of the producers of the program. Showing them on TV could offer an advantage to Prato's lawyers, providing information that they might not otherwise get. Also, offering assurances of Manuel's prolonged sobriety with all that confidence might not have been a very happy idea. Difficult days were coming up. Television still had the power to bestow instantaneous fame on those who, good or bad, managed to have a presence on the screen. For Valter it became difficult to leave the house without someone insulting him. "Murderers!" people yelled at him on the street. And then the Internet. It was there that the condemnation became an avalanche.

If I were Manuel Foffo's father I wouldn't think of Vespa but of suicide.

10 years of cocaine and daddy didn't notice.

That is the upbringing he gave his son! He should hide rather than go on television! He brought up a monster, he shouldn't defend him!!

That man thinks only of protecting the image of his son and of himself as a father.

What disgusting people. The electric chair for him and the whole family.

Valter Foffo understood too late that he hadn't reflected on other aspects. For example, he seemed to have forgotten that watching TV that night would be Luca Varani's parents, his friends, his girlfriend Marta Gaia. Why hadn't he addressed them? That would have been a good move on the media front. He could have said he was terribly grieved for Luca, he could have given him a thought, he could have addressed the parents of the victim, apologized for the benefit of the camera, invoked some type of forgiveness. Why hadn't he done it?

No one is pursued by the compulsion to repeat like those who make serious mistakes. And so, in the next days, Valter Foffo managed to commit another, then yet another.

Overnight, Marta Gaia Sebastiani found her life devastated.

Marta was twenty-two, she'd been Luca's girlfriend since she was fourteen, and in the space of a day she had found out that her boyfriend was dead, that it wasn't an accident, that two guys she'd never heard of had tortured him in an apartment that Luca had entered of his own free will, and, as if that weren't enough, she had to consider the idea that he had a double life.

"He's a prostitute," they'd said.

A prostitute? *Luca a prostitute?*

And since there was no limit to the madness of the world right now, on RAI 1 a middle-aged man was saying, undisturbed, that his son, the confessed criminal, was a model boy.

Forty-eight hours earlier things had been proceeding with absolute normality. Now it was all razed to the ground.

Marta Gaia lived in Casalotti, on a street of low buildings and magnolias. She'd been working for a short time in a food-service company. She felt lucky to have found the job, but really any employer who came upon someone like her should consider himself fortunate. Marta Gaia was a reliable and conscientious girl, if she was capable of carrying out a task she did it with the greatest commitment, and when she realized she wasn't up to it she tried to learn. At the hospitality school she'd learned just the basics, she had no idea what it meant to work between tables and kitchen until she set foot there. What at first she lacked in experience she had made up for with persistence, a sense of loyalty, the capacity to work on a team. You realized it, that she was a good investment. And anyway Marta Gaia had *him*.

1. You're beautiful.
2. You're attractive whatever you're wearing.
3. Every look of yours excites me.
4. I'd leave my life to the devil for a smile from you.
5. You're sweet and caring.
6. When you laugh the sun reddens.
7. For me you're synonymous with life.
8. You know how to calm me down.
9. You know my biggest dreams.
10. You're the guardian of my heart.
11. We understand each other with a look.
12. You like making me part of your life.
13. Reading this letter you'll correct the mistakes. ·
14. You can touch me and make me shiver.
15. Whenever you give me a present it's perfect.
16. You endure my useless rages.
17. You've eaten what I cooked (brave).
18. When you sleep everything shines around you.
19. You're surprised when I give you a surprise you already know about.
20. I LOVE YOU.

Twenty reasons to tell her he loved her, written on two pieces of lined paper.

Twenty was a magic number for them. They had transformed it into a battle cry: "Marta Gaia + Luca forever against everything and everyone, from 20/10/2007 on!"

The first time they saw each other they were fourteen. After school they took the same bus. He was at the back, talking with Vincenzo Giunta. Marta Gaia knew Vincenzo, but she had never seen that tall, slender handsome dark boy.

"Hey! *Who was that*?"

Luca had tossed his backpack among the bus passengers. Marta had stumbled on it. "He'd been a little crude to attract attention," Vincenzo recalled, laughing. "Who was that?" Marta Gaia repeated. Luca looked at her in silence. To Marta his eyes seemed very beautiful. Meanwhile the bus was approaching one of the last stops, Marta was about to get off.

It was she who held out her hand before it was too late: "Nice to meet you, Marta Gaia."

He shook it. "I'm Luca."

Marta and Luca became inseparable. They saw each other whenever possible, and during the day they called each other constantly or exchanged messages. She was *mogliettina*, "little wife," he was *mascottino*, "little mascot." "A hundred euros they get married," said their friends. They went to different schools, had different groups of friends. Marta's friends were in Casalotti, and Luca knew them. Luca had some friends in Battistini, whom Marta Gaia had never met. She didn't meet them on purpose. She didn't like them at all.

"Do you love me?"

"Of course I love you."

"Would you exchange me for another girl?"

"No."

"And if that other girl were an improved version of me, without faults, thinner, and let you do everything you want?"

"Perfection can't be improved."

Marta Gaia had an energetic character, she was stubborn and strong-willed, and she also had common sense. Luca was elusive without being egotistical, restless without being bad, and he found peace and shelter in her arms. Every so often they talked about the future. They would go and live together, they would find better jobs, they would get married and have children. They knew that times were hard, that nothing would be given to them, they weren't rich, they didn't have important friends, they didn't enjoy any type of privilege, they were aware that staying together would require commitment, a capacity to overcome their own failings, a willingness to fight. All this excited them.

"You're the woman of my life. I love you, *mogliettina!*"

At the best moments, hearing him talk, Marta Gaia thought that Luca was the sweetest guy in the world. At other times he became impulsive, prickly, got angry for reasons that he alone understood. Then he'd disappear. It was as if in him deep life flowed with the impetuousness that children feel, whose inner world lets new lands emerge overnight and suffers violent reactions. When Luca went missing Marta Gaia got really angry, she bombarded him with messages until he responded, they quarreled furiously on WhatsApp—reproached one another, accused one another of everything—but they always made up in the end. The last stop of the 905 bus was their meeting place. They'd talk, then re-emerge from the evening shadows holding each other. They'd go have a pizza and he'd say: "You make people better."

After the murder the malicious said that Marta Gaia tried to keep him on a short leash. She had to do that if she didn't want him to disappear one fine day and never return: Luca was so handsome, they said, anyone would fall in love with him, and it was only her tenacity that had kept them together so long. Others said that it wasn't necessary to divide the world into those who knew things and those who didn't, but between those who had the strength to know and those who, in order not to see, went around with blinders. All the signs that would have allowed Marta Gaia to draw conclusions were available if only she'd had the courage to look.

He had come to see her Thursday. It might have been five in the afternoon. They had talked for a while. At a certain point Luca had said he needed a new phone charger. "I'm going to bum some cash off Cornelia."

He was chronically short of money. He scrounged money

for cigarettes or gas, some friends said. When he went out with Marta Gaia, she frequently paid. Every so often Luca asked her for a small loan, and Marta didn't refuse, so now he owed her almost a hundred euros. When Luca had money in his pocket, however, he had no trouble spending it on others. He was generous, showering Marta Gaia with presents, taking her to dinner, and the next day he was broke again. At the body shop he got a hundred and fifty euros a week. Too bad that Boccea was full of gambling arcades. Luca spent a lot of money on slot machines.

Luca reappeared before evening. He went with Marta Gaia to volleyball practice. When it was time for a friendly game, he acted as scorekeeper. It was fun. The practices finished at ten-thirty, just in time for the last 31 bus. At ten of eleven Luca and Marta kissed surrounded by the night of the Roman periphery.

The next day they began sending each other WhatsApp messages starting in the morning. ("Kitten, what are you doing?" "I just woke up, have to go to work.") He wrote that he was going to the body shop, but, as he had lied to his employer, now he was lying to her. (In the following days Marta Gaia calculated that he had written her the last messages when he was already at Manuel Foffo's apartment.) After a few minutes there was no more contact; Marta Gaia sent more WhatsApp messages, but Luca didn't answer. She tried calling him. The phone kept ringing. He had done it again, she thought. Disappeared into nothing. What an impossible guy! She guessed that he'd had a fight with his parents. And if he hadn't gone to work? Was he with those losers from Battistini? Marta began to send him furious messages, she called him again. What the fuck had happened to him? After several hours, Luca's cell phone was dead. O.K., come on, let's calm down, thought Marta Gaia. Luca was careless, he could have forgotten his phone somewhere. Or maybe the battery was dead. The charger didn't work well, right? That's what had happened. But night came and the phone was still disconnected.

The next day, Saturday, Marta Gaia talked to Signor Varani.

Sunday morning Marta Gaia was at work. The day's menu was fettucine all'amatriciana, pasta with mushrooms, scaloppini with citrus. As always on the weekend a lot of people came, the work was constant. At a certain point Marta Gaia looked up and found her mother there. How strange. "Hi, mamma, what's happened?" Her mother looked at her with a face that Marta Gaia had never seen. She found herself in her arms.

Now Marta Gaia was sobbing. *Dead*, they said. But every bone in her body maintained the opposite. It was as if they were assuring her that outside it was snowing while her eyes still saw the sun. Everyone was talking about Luca. The entire neighborhood was talking about him, soon afterward the entire city, in the evening all Italy was talking about him. You turned on the television and a picture of him appeared on the screen. Marta Gaia's phone began to be filled with messages, friends, teachers began to call, people of all types asked to come and see her.

A call also came from the police.

Marta Gaia presented herself at the headquarters in Piazza Dante after lunch.

She gave her personal information, shook hands with the marshal, and began to answer questions. She felt surprised by her own words. Bound to report the facts truthfully, she said things that seemed to prove the existence of some areas of shadow, ambiguities she'd never given the proper attention to. How much thought should we give to what we know we don't know about the people we love? And even if it were possible to know everything about them, would it be right?

After the talk with the police, Marta Gaia went home. She was dazed, grieved, she needed a place that would make her feel safe. She opened Facebook. Her profile was full of messages. A mountain of brief electronic missives, all for her. There were condolences, appeals to keep up her courage, short phrases of solidarity. Friends were writing to her, but above all a tide of strangers.

Sincerely struck by those manifestations of affection, Marta Gaia wrote a thank-you post.

Thank you all truly, for the thoughts, for the words . . . People I've never seen or met who've given me words of comfort. And then THANK YOU to my friends since forever, I got so many messages and calls. The pain is virtually immense and indescribable, in spite of everything one can't die like that. I'd like everyone to remember Luca as a sweet and sensitive young man and not as a "weak" and sometimes too arrogant one. I'm not interested in gossip, I'm not interested at all. I love him and I'll always love him, but not Luca how he was with everyone, Luca how he was with me . . . Rather, my MASCOTTINO.

Only later did she become aware of Valeria Proietti.

She found her on Messenger, asking for a private chat. How strange. Valeria Proietti was part of the Battistini group, she was a blonde with curves like a pin-up, and was everything Marta Gaia didn't like. She was ostentatious, exuberant (in photos she'd accentuate her lips in closeup, with freshly applied bright red lipstick, or stick out her tongue to show the piercing), and she enjoyed being provocative, with aggressive quotes. "I've always said that when you get to the point of being hated, then you know you're doing a good job." She was seventeen.

Marta Gaia and Valeria weren't friends: neither had the other's number; they were distantly acquainted. Valeria was the girlfriend of Alessandro Mancini. There were two other Mancini brothers, there was Valeria's sister, Daniele Spada, Gabriele Rivetti, then a guy named Adriano, a girl named Alessia, and various others. That was the Battistini group. It was said that some of them did coke. True or false, they had the reputation of being slackers incapable of making the smallest plan and uninterested in improving their situation. Marta Gaia hadn't wanted to have anything to do with them. She thought that for someone like Luca those guys were the perfect temptation, the ideal company to distract him from all his good intentions. The fact that he had continued to hang out with them was the only reason that Marta agreed to chat with Valeria. She clicked on the icon. Then she read.

Oh Marta they said they knew him for a short time but in fact when luca went out with us . . . he already was talking to that faggot and told us he lent him money and he disappeared for half an hour and came back . . . I don't know what he went to do there . . . but I swear to you I wouldn't have expected in that way, he was so good . . . and you can be sure he'll always be with you.

Because he always told me that he loved you madly he'll protect you from everything I know he will . . .

Despite the fact that Valeria showed a more than uncertain mastery of written Italian, it was all too clear what she meant. Marta Gaia was stunned.

I have no words. Why did he go to get money? What did he do? I can't believe it. I don't know if you know something, but if you do please tell me.

Valeria Proietti answered.

Yes
. . . so in my opinion he went there and had sex with the guy . . . . because he'd said so to me alessandro filippo my sister . . . . But in the end it was his business . . . he was my friend I loved him just as he was he was always good with us . . . . when filippo found out he went nuts . . . they really loved him . . . .but what happened to his phone??? From that you can trace something even if he always deleted everything . . .
He did take drugs . . . .
I always told him to bring you with him every so often or tell you when he was with us and went out . . . . He always said you didn't like him to be with alessandro and filippo . . . Who in the end always loved him . . . And anyway in the end he did that business on his own just the same . . . .

Was it only an impression, or was the fact that Marta Gaia didn't want Luca to hang out with the group from Battistini now backfiring on her? Was there a sense of reckoning?

Disturbed by what she seemed to read between the lines, Marta Gaia avoided answering. That didn't discourage Valeria Proietti, who returned to the charge.

Marta look if I wrote you it's only to help you also because besides the pain of having lost a friend I'm not getting anything out of it . . .

Then who knows what's the whole truth . . . who knows at their house how much drugs he took . . . how much they must have conditioned him . . . . Or maybe just because he didn't want to have sex they turned mean and did it by force.

But I advise you just to remember him as you said . . . . as he was because in the end he was always good with everyone, people loved him . . . and trust that he's near you and will always protect you because you were the woman of his life . . . he always talked to me about you!!!

Hugs

Sorry if I continue to write

But I swear that Filippo was home all day crying.

A concentrate of gossip and supposed philanthropic spirit. So in the end Marta Gaia gave in.

I don't know . . . I can't believe that Luca really prostituted himself . . .

Valeria's response wasn't long in coming.

But in my view he did it only when he needed money because he didn't always go. It could be that he told us as a joke. But that he went to him and came back with money . . . I'm totally suuuuuure. At first he told us that he gave it to him. But nobody just gives you money . . . .

After other exchanges of this type, Marta Gaia got upset.

You're telling me a load of bullshit.

Valeria Proietti changed her tone.

No way. Hahahahahaha. It wouldn't make sense. hahahaha
O.K. then Martaaaa
Think what you waaaant
For suuuuure you've been stupid For nine years hahahahahaha
I'm not writing you anymooore
Byyyye

Marta Gaia was taken aback; she certainly didn't expect such a reaction and had her only breakdown of the whole conversation.

Anyway, it wasn't 9 years, we broke up and especially what he did when we weren't together is his business.

It was true. In late 2010 she and Luca had taken a break. The fact that Marta had used the subject for defensive purposes should have inspired compassion. But Valeria Proietti wasn't the type to soften.

Oh in fact I knew you had broken up for a while but ooooooook, it also happened when you were together because he texted you that he was at school but he was with us
Now byyyyye
I don't care
You're right I'm full of shit
I don't think it would make sense to bullshit you I'm not saying anything bad about him. But since I knew him and saw him almost every day I could help you.

Marta gathered all her strength to end the conversation.

O.K., listen, don't write me anymore, I really have no desire to listen to more crap about him.

What the fuck got into people? What made them so cruel? Marta Gaia was too upset to go further into that reasoning. Also because, checking the screen, she realized something else. Her last post, the one where she thanked those who had offered condolences, had gotten more than two thousand likes. A post of a few days before the murder didn't get even ten. And since after the exchange with Valeria, Marta Gaia was starting to feel really angry, she decided to try out her new powers by placing her fingers again on the keyboard.

I'm not speaking because everything you're inventing makes you the equal of Luca's killers. Dishonoring the memory of a person essential to me in order to get ratings or money is really indescribable. For you it passes because fortunately it doesn't touch you, I will carry this pain for my whole life . . . . How disgusting are the Italian laws? How disgusting is what happened? Or simply how disgusting are the people who continue to make up trash about Luca?

She had barely published the post when the first reactions arrived. Dozens, then hundreds of likes and hearts. A swarm of new followers wanted to interact with her.

We have to unite so that justice is done!!!!

We all want justice because what happened to your boyfriend could happen to all of us.

Don't worry about people who talk nonsense, go straight on your path, warrior.

Many of us, in fact a huge number of us, are with you, demanding justice for Luca.

They all said she was right, they were all allies. In a short time the post got three thousand likes. In the space of a few hours phone calls from the newspapers and TV would arrive. She was no longer the girl of a few days earlier, but maybe she wasn't even the girl of a few hours earlier. Marta Gaia Sebastiani had become a public figure.

The next day it was Marco Prato's turn to offer his version of the facts.

The accused appeared before the judge for the preliminary investigation in the judges' chamber of the Regina Coeli prison. With him were Francesco Scavo and the defense lawyer Pasquale Bartolo.

Despite his recent hospitalization, Marco appeared in good health. He was calm and self-possessed. The absence of the toupee took something away from his charm, yet gave him an appearance in keeping with the game he had to play there, starting with a charge—premeditated murder—that could cost him life in prison.

"So let's begin with the personal information. Your name is Marco Proto, is that right?" asked the judge.

"Prato," the youth corrected him.

"Born in?"

"Rome, June 14, 1986."

"Do you live by yourself or with other people?"

"At the moment with my parents."

"Your family consists of?"

"I have an older sister, who's married."

"So your sister doesn't live with you."

"She lives in the same building, not in the same apartment."

"Are you married? What is your marital status?"

And here, a few minutes after the interrogation began, Marco Prato took his first liberty.

"Single woman."

"You must mean *bachelor*," the judge corrected him.

"Bachelor, I'm sorry," said Marco.

The journalists pursued Ledo Prato and Maria Pacifico, Marco's parents, exactly as they had the Foffo family in the preceding days. All requests for interviews were rejected by Bartolo, the lawyer. The reporters began watching the neighborhood of Piazza Bologna, they stationed themselves at every street corner, outside every bar or café where sooner or later a relative or friend of Marco might possibly emerge. The less they found the more anxious they got. The more anxious they got the more tempted they were to write negatively about him.

It was Bartolo who acted as the shield. The day of the interrogation, in Via della Lungara, just in front of the Regina Coeli prison, the lawyer offered himself as a meal to the journalists.

"Mr. Bartolo, wait just a second!"

Bartolo slowed down. A small army of TV cameras instantly surrounded this slightly bald man, enveloped in a dark overcoat, his face thin and a little nervous.

"What I can tell you is that we've decided to answer all the questions that will be asked."

"So the accused will not make use of his right to remain silent?" asked one woman.

"He will explain his role in what happened."

The reporter changed her tone: "How is your client? Have you talked to him?"

"He's like a young man who has just attempted suicide."

"But did he appear remorseful?"

"Look," said Bartolo. "He appeared remorseful like a young man who, after doing something, attempts suicide. I don't think there's anything to add."

Yes, but what *something* was it?

Luca Varani's father was starting to speak. Valter Foffo, with his interview on *Porta a Porta*, had given the press material to chew on for weeks. The Prato family created a void around themselves. Neither Marco's father nor his mother nor his sister, nor any other relatives or close friends, had let slip the slightest statement.

"Useless, they're all staying quiet," said the reporters, disconsolate.

What's hard to avoid is the police when they display a formal search warrant.

The investigators were eager to get their hands on Marco Prato's computers. The suicide notes written in the room in the Hotel San Giusto were clear: Destroy them. "They conceal my ugly sides." The police rang the bell at the Prato house at 8:40 P.M. Signora Pacifico answered the door. The investigators searched the apartment. In Marco's room they found a laptop. The second computer was missing. Signora Pacifico said she had given it to the lawyer to allow him to better carry out the defense work. That answer didn't please the police. The computer could have been given to the lawyer to destroy evidence. An emergency request for confiscation was also issued for the second computer.

After analyzing the iPhone and the two computers, the operations squad signaled the presence of some files to include in the trial documents: "Two openly pedo-pornographic videos" ("Some acquaintances sent them, I couldn't do anything about it" was Marco's defense), along with three videos in which Marco performed oral sex on other young men, including Manuel Foffo. The police also noted the Internet pages that Marco had consulted on his phone before they confiscated it: an article on adoption for gay couples; some porn videos; various searches on Google for food delivery; various searches on Google to find out how to kill yourself with an overdose of lormetazepam.

The problem was the cloud, that is to say the documents that Marco habitually kept remotely, and which anyone who had the password could have modified or deleted at any time. When the police accessed the cloud they found nothing important, but there had been recent modifications that no one could reconstruct.

"It's so ridiculous that Apple won't help you when it's a question of murder," I said later to one of the policemen who had worked most intensely on the case.

He looked at me in surprise, as if I had just landed from another planet.

"Really," he said, "do you remember the slaughter in San Bernardino?"

If Apple had refused to provide the FBI with the password of the iPhone of a terrorist who had caused fourteen deaths in the name of ISIS, what could you expect when the request arrived from a police station on the Esquiline for the murder of a kid from the slums?

"What is your degree in?" asked the judge, continuing the interrogation.

"Political science," answered Marco Prato, "and then a graduate program in marketing and event management in Paris."

"What work do you do?"

"I organize events. I'm a freelancer. I own a brand with two partners that's called A(h)però. I do consulting and artistic direction for various clubs."

"How long have you been doing this?"

"Since I came back from Paris. In Paris I was ill, I attempted suicide at the end of a relationship in 2011. I came back to Italy to lick my wounds."

"You came back to Italy."

"Yes, I spent some time in a psychiatric clinic."

"Can you explain what sort of problems you had?"

"Look," said Marco without having to be asked twice. "The problems for a personality like mine are complex and have various sources. One of these has to do with the fact that my sister has muscular dystrophy. She got the diagnosis when she was fourteen and I was seven. From that moment on I had no mother's love, and for me there was a continuous search for loves to fill that void. In my family the female figures are dominant. My mother is a woman with a strong personality. My sister, even though she's disabled, has a strong personality. My grandmother also had a strong personality. The role model is female. That encouraged homosexuality in me . . . and also, at a certain point, the desire to change sex."

"So you are homosexual."

"Yes, but not just homosexual," Marco explained. "I'm attracted to heterosexuals. I've had many relations with homosexuals. But my true attraction is to straight men."

Just as Manuel claimed for himself the right to bewilderment, Marco flaunted his awareness; he drew out the words as if he were revealing an affliction, demanding that no one question it. I know myself, I know who I am, he seemed to say, and you don't. Take notes. Write it down. Now I'll tell you.

"I imagine you are aware of the facts on account of which this proceeding is taking place against you," said the judge. "The charge is very serious. Homicide with aggravating circumstances together with Manuel Foffo. First of all I ask you: do you accept this charge or deny it totally?"

"I don't deny it totally."

He didn't deny having been at Manuel's house. He didn't deny having been the connection with Luca Varani. He didn't deny having seen him die. Nevertheless, there were clarifications to make.

"So, look. I've seen Manuel Foffo twice in my life. Four days, from the first to the fourth of January. Then four days for the latest thing."

The latest thing was the death of Luca.

"And you had a friendly relationship? Or was there something else between you?"

"Let's say I was his dolly."

"His what?" asked the judge.

"His dolly. His sex object for these four days. And since Manuel considers himself heterosexual, he rejected that I . . . in other words, he didn't want me to be male. So he shaved me. He used his razor. Then he put on the nail polish. I still have his mother's nail polish on my fingers."

"In essence Manuel made you up as a woman."

"Yes."

"And that happened in January?"

"You surely must have seen old photos of me that have been going around lately. You must have noticed that in those photos I have a beard. I don't have a beard now. I shaved it off at Foffo's house. He wanted me like that. I shaved my beard, I took the hair off my hands. The nail polish, as I said, is Foffo's mother's. The perfume is his mother's. The lipstick and the mascara . . ."

"All right, all right, let's return to January," said the judge. "On that occasion did the two of you consume alcohol?"

"Alcohol and cocaine."

"In what quantities?"

"Being with Manuel for four days without feeling tired, especially because of the things he had me do, makes it unlikely that it was just a little."

"Did you buy the cocaine?"

"I bought it, but the dealer came to his house. And since Manuel is embarrassed by the opinion of others, he went down to get it directly. He didn't want the neighbors to see me dressed as a woman."

They talked about the video that Manuel had made with his phone.

"He wanted reassurance that the video wouldn't circulate."

Then Marco went back to talking about himself. He said that he hadn't spoken to his mother for a year, that in recent months he'd had another romance ("with a gay guy, someone who bored me incredibly"), and that in March, when he returned to Via

Igino Giordani, he and Manuel had bought more cocaine and had invited some people over. This Alex Tiburtina had showed up. Then another guy. "Someone who works in Manuel's father's restaurant. I don't remember his name," said Marco. "I call him Cicciabomba"—Fatty Girl.

"This person who came . . ."—the judge interrupted himself. "Excuse me a moment," he said, "has a name? Try to remember, please, otherwise I'll end up calling him Cicciabomba, too."

Marco said they had also called Damiano Parodi, a friend of his, a good guy who was fairly wealthy. It was he who had introduced Luca to him. "Luca Varani was a mechanic in Valle Aurelia or Primavalle, I don't remember."

"And if I understand correctly," said the judge, "Luca was some sort of prostitute."

"He wasn't *some sort of prostitute*," Marco corrected, "he *was* a prostitute."

"He was a prostitute . . ." the judge repeated.

"A rent boy," Marco piled it on, "but he was also a pusher. Every so often he called to sell me some coke."

The judge asked how he had managed to get Luca to Manuel's house.

"I said to him: *Come and we'll give you a hundred and fifty euros.*"

"So, there's actually . . . an explicit agreement on the phone?"

"Of course."

"In which you . . . then . . ." said the judge.

"*Come over, there's two of us, there's my straight friend, and I'm dressed up like a whore: we'll give you a hundred and fifty euros.* I think I told him something like that."

"He said yes?"

"He said yes."

The judge asked what happened next. Here, too, Marco gave his version of the facts. He had behind him two suicide attempts, he did a lot of alcohol and cocaine, he got no affection from his mother, he had been discharged from the hospital, he had just experienced prison, where presumably he would remain for a long time, for four days he had been in a frenzy that culminated in the killing of a young man, and yet he spoke as if he had every-thing under control, as if he were capable of reorganizing every detail, every instant, even the altered states of consciousness into a coherent whole in order to relate an indisputable story for the benefit of his accusers.

Marco ended by reconstructing the dynamic of the murder: he offered his own version of who, he or Manuel, had done what, he stated in particular that he had never struck Luca.

Scavo said, "There are enormous differences between the two interrogations."

"Yes," the judge confirmed, "there are some major differences between his version of the facts and the one provided by Manuel Foffo." He turned to Marco. "Have you watched any television in the past few days?"

He was referring to the possibility that Marco Prato and his lawyer had planned their line of defense based on what Manuel had reported to Scavo, information they wouldn't have had if not for Vespa's television interview.

"We were also invited to take part in that broadcast," said the defense lawyer, "but we refused. However, watching TV, I couldn't help seeing that the report of the interrogation was displayed."

"It shouldn't have been circulated," said the public prosecutor.

"I assure you that for Manuel it's easier to think he killed someone for the experience of it than to imagine that he's gay." Marco Prato changed the subject.

"All right, you can sign" said the judge, ending the interrogation.

People competed to see who had more friends in common with them on Facebook.

I had three in common with Marco Prato. Everyone in my circle had friends in common with Marco Prato. None with Luca Varani. Very few with Marta Gaia Sebastiani.

My circle was made up of writers, journalists, high-school teachers, people who worked in the world of radio or publishing. In Marco's circle there were interior designers, fashion designers, television actors, club managers. The two worlds communicated with one another. A couple of phone calls and I was in a café in Trastevere with Stefano.

"One of those guys who snort cocaine, start sweating in the clubs, and think everyone's mad at them. That's who Marco Prato was."

Stefano was forty-seven. He managed various clothing stores in the neighborhood of Cola di Rienzo, and he moved between Prati, Rione Monti, Ponte Milvio, and Gay Street in San Giovanni. Those were the meeting places. Rarely did Marco's acquaintances go to the periphery.

"And this business of Dalida? Doesn't it seem like the *height* of ridiculousness?" he said.

Stefano took a swallow of his blueberry juice. Our worlds had points of contact. But Stefano and Marco Prato's circle, unlike mine, so prudent and chaste, included people who tried to gamble at least a little. They opened boutiques, night clubs, art galleries. They took risks. They kept a little money moving.

"He wore a toupee because he had a complex about being

bald. He tried to be seen with famous people. He was reduced to pretending to be the boyfriend of Flavia Vento."

"Flavia Vento the TV personality?"

Stefano said that Marco Prato's events weren't much. Had I ever been to A(h)però? All you needed was a bit of an aesthetic sense, he said, not to be impressed.

"What are his parents like?" I asked.

"With his parents he must have had the usual misunderstandings. But that has nothing to do with it."

We all had a complicated family story, he said, we all fought not to be destroyed by it. "My father was terrible. When he found out I was a faggot he stopped talking to me. We haven't seen each other for years. Do you think I go around killing people? What the fuck!"

He's getting too angry, I thought. We lived in a city in which reacting to tragedies with bursts of bitterness was a system for not giving in. We swelled up with cynicism to survive the cynicism that in Rome was the first lesson of life.

"Someone like Marco won't hold up in prison," Stefano said, darkening, "but the Pratos know a lot of people, they can afford the best lawyers."

Stefano had come to Rome twenty years before from Calabria. He had worked like a madman. Waiter, salesclerk, swimming teacher. He had opened his first store with the money from a liquidation. He couldn't forgive Marco for ending up in a story so horrendous when he had started out from a position of privilege.

"I had to work my ass off to get by in a place like this—you have no idea. Rome is a city that no longer produces anything." He shook his head. "There's no industry, there's no culture of entrepreneurship, the economy is parasitical, tourism is third-rate. The ministers, the Vatican, RAI, the courts . . . that's what Rome is made of, a city that now produces only power, power that falls on other power, that crushes other power, that fertilizes other power, that never makes any progress—no wonder people go crazy."

He ordered another blueberry juice.

"Get someone to tell you what your Marco got up to the last time he was in Mykonos," he said, increasingly contemptuous.

We talked a little more. Then I headed to my next appointment.

"It was a nasty night, in fact later that terrible storm burst over the whole city," Elisa was saying.

We were in Piazza Vittorio, a few steps from the police head-quarters where Manuel had been interrogated. Elisa was a few years younger than me. We'd known each other for a while. Blond, slender, with long black eyebrows. She worked in a graphic design studio, and hung out in the circle of DJs, people in advertising, young fashion designers who dreamed of working for Gucci.

"There was panic in Gay Street that night," she said. "People were all looking at their phones, seeing themselves as potential victims. Marco had various profiles on Grindr."

We were heading to Colle Oppio. True or not, she said a rumor had spread about Russian roulette. Marco Prato and Manuel Foffo, it was said, had sent dozens of messages to people chosen by chance on the phone. An invitation to a party. Those who answered risked signing their death sentence. So now, in Via di San Giovanni in Laterano, one of the most popular meeting places for the gay community, those who'd received a message from Marco Prato in the preceding days were having fits of hysteria.

We entered the Colle Oppio park. On the left was the bar, surrounded by pines; the air was cool, the light dim, homeless people were sleeping on the benches.

"Manipulative tendency, superiority complex, total absence of empathy. Add to that drugs," said Elisa, trying to give her personal version of the facts.

"It seems that they took twenty-eight grams of cocaine in three days," I commented, "but how could they have done that?"

"Almost all my friends are gay," she said, changing the subject. "The homosexual culture in certain circles is different from when we were young—I have in mind people who think in product categories. Each one has a defined role, each plays a character. Everyone's competing with everyone else. That's why the climate is so tense."

"It's not as if the straight world functions differently," I said.

Elisa spoke again of the torrential rain there had been right after the murder. It was as if the city, burdened for weeks by its troubles, had found a way to vent. But the relief was temporary, the itch returned and grew as soon as it was washed away.

It was then that we noticed it. The old amphitheater appeared suddenly at the end of the path, so pale and gray, like the moon when it's low on the horizon and seems to be coming at you. The Colosseum in the cold March air, amid the wastepaper, the homeless, the putrid water in the fountains. A short distance away, barely hidden by a hedge, a middle-aged man was peeing in the open. The fact is that in Rome everyone does whatever the fuck he wants, I thought. The fans of Feyenoord climbed into the Trevi Fountain drunk and threw bottles at Bernini's Barcaccia; in Villa Borghese vandals decapitated the statues of poets; big bags of garbage flew from one building to the next; everyone peed everywhere, full indulgence was in the air, and I myself, who in another city would have burst my bladder, had found myself more than once wetting the Servian Walls.

"What an incredible place," I said, thinking aloud.

"When did you and your wife move here?"

"I eighteen years ago, she sixteen. She from Piacenza, I from Bari."

"And what do you think of you here now?"

"When we arrived it was all fantastic," I said. "Rome never ended. Even now it never ends, but in a different way."

"Do you feel suffocated?"

"Let's say that every so often we feel like we're sinking.

Sometimes I'm afraid that we, too, in a certain sense, are part of the *thing* without realizing it."

"There's a guy named Michele," Elisa said, "who knew Marco much better than I did. Go talk to him."

Half an hour later I was in Portico d'Ottavia. I took the bus to Piazza Venezia. At Torre Argentina I saw a taxi driver coming to blows with a customer. Near Piazza Gesù, between the church and the palazzo opposite, I seemed to hear a wind echoing on the streets, like a lament, the inconsolable wailing of an old man. I found the pub where this Michele was drinking with friends. I introduced myself. Now we were talking outside the bar.

"Fat kid. Clumsy. Bullied at school for being gay. His parents taken by surprise. He might have come out of it destroyed," he said, "but he lay low for a few years and came back on the scene a new man. A lot of time at the gym."

Michele was thirty-five. Tall, flowing hair, jeans jacket, black cap.

"It's not true that they were some kind of circus sideshow," he continued. "A(h)però had grown recently. Some VIPs appeared. Nadia Bengala, ex-Miss Italy. Every so often a movie actor came by. Those faggots who look down on gay parties started showing up, which is the most a gay party can aspire to. Marco was smart, quick, intuitive, he was also an eccentric, but who doesn't like having all eyes on him?"

"He was a fucking egomaniac and a stalker," interrupted a young man who had heard us talking. "Hello, I'm Alessandro."

"But why do you always talk about Marco in the past?"

"He found me on Grindr months ago," he said by way of response. "I went out with him a couple of times. Marco was a bottom, he called himself bipolar—all nonsense to give himself a tone. Anyway: I wasn't his type and he wasn't my type, but some friends say they were harassed by him."

"Harassed in what sense?"

"Straight friends. Hey, I have to meet some guys in Re di Roma, if you want come with me."

He took me to a bar near Via Faleria and introduced me to his friends. They were all younger than me. We sat down and had a drink.

"He repeated to death the old saw that a blow job done by a man can't be compared to what even the most willing girl can do," said a thirty-year-old named Roberto. "He hammered guys until someone gave in. He felt so much like a woman that he went after straight men."

"He was strange in everything. When he did coke he seemed dull."

"Speaking of which, is someone making a pit stop in the toilet?"

"Wherever he was there was trouble."

"Once he literally kidnapped a straight kid. The parents wanted to call the police."

"I don't think it was like that."

"In high school he hung out with a left-wing group. During the film club meetings he showed off. He talked and talked. He was clever. He argued with the fascists."

"Pure gold," said one of the youths returning from the bathroom.

"In school he gave his friends free private lessons."

"In the past year business wasn't going well for him. He turned mean."

"In Mykonos he got into the villa of some filthy rich Milanesi. In the end they realized he just wanted to cadge a vacation. They threw him out."

"He was one of the most intelligent and sensitive people I've known," said a kid in a cable-knit sweater. "I don't think you understand fuck-all."

"He was tormented by his premature baldness."

They continued to talk about him as if he were dead. Even those who defended him kept a distance. I had the sensation that their fear wasn't so much of being associated with a murder as with being associated with an exaggeratedly ridiculous episode, as if that—ridiculousness, not horror—represented the danger.

"Sunday, when people found out about the murder, A(h)pero was about to start at the Os Club."

"Marco's partners were upset. They didn't know what to do. The handbook for the perfect aperitif doesn't have instructions for how to behave in these cases. In the end they did the event just the same."

"The situation was surreal."

"Everyone drinking a spritz and talking about the murder."

"It seems they did a casting call to choose the victim."

"Twenty-three messages all the same. *The Ring* at Collatino, by 20th Century Fag. Whose turn for the bathroom?"

The movie reference had been made by someone who went by the nickname Vaniglia, a man in his thirties who, while he talked, kept taking his fat foot out of his leather slipper and pressing it on the floor as if he were putting out a cigarette. A person I knew entered the bar. "Paolo!" I waved. He smiled, also greeted the others. He must have been at home there. He worked at a printer's outside Rome, and we had met years earlier. He sat down with us.

"Do any of you know Manuel Foffo?" I asked when the conversation resumed.

"Never heard of him before Sunday," said Roberto.

"He's not in our circle."

"Never seen or heard of."

"Seems like a loser."

"And Luca Varani?"

"The rent boy? No info."

"Never heard of him."

"No clue," said someone else, waving his hand as if to free himself of an annoying thought.

"Cigarette?" said Paolo, who'd gotten irritated after some more exchanges like this.

Leaving the bar, we started talking again. I saw cars going along the street.

"You hear how they talk?" said Paolo, taking me aside. "They act cool in Gay Street, but then at Christmas they go and visit their parents in their home town and tell them they've got a girl in Rome. Here everyone hates everyone else, and first of all they hate themselves."

Paolo was my age. He came from a world different from the one we were in now. He had come out when he was scarcely more than a boy, with pride and determination. As an adolescent I had a great admiration for people like him, kids who plunged, eyes open, into the mystery of their own sexuality and reemerged challenging people's prejudices. Boys of fifteen, sixteen, boys who loved boys and weren't even afraid to love much older men. It was always a question of desire, at the time.

"I don't understand the contempt for Luca Varani," I said.

"Pure and simple classism," said Paolo. "Remember there's a part of homosexual culture now that leans to the right."

"But if they all vote center left . . . "

"They confuse the cult of money with the cult of beauty. Beauty for them is Rihanna's eighty million followers. Power. Yachts. Vacations in the tropics. Anyone who doesn't live that life doesn't deserve to exist. The problem is that they themselves don't live that life."

Although they knew nothing about Luca they took it for granted that he was a prostitute, I thought, and in spite of the fact that this was irrelevant on the moral plane with respect to what had happened, they tried to attribute to it a discriminating value: they used reproach to hide their own hunt for the weak. And added to this was the fact that blaming prostitution for the murder and not chance made them feel safe. It could never happen to me, they thought.

Meanwhile around us the cars formed a gigantic swarm, radiating out from Piazza Re di Roma and along the Appia, rushing toward Cinecittà. Headlights in the dark of night, stop lights. Suddenly the breakdown of Rome regained a logic. Cynicism tipped over into faith, boredom became hope, slothfulness vanished into activity. It was the route of coke, the white electrical grid that enveloped the city. As the streets emptied of meaning, coke filled them with its own, pushing out of the house office workers, professionals, students, workers, managers, dentists, garbage men, connecting all to all without distinction of race, sex, religion, class—a formidable social glue that brought people together who would never have met. It forced them to get acquainted, to talk, to form bonds of every sort.

"Living in a world that basically despises us," Paolo was saying, "we gays have had to work harder to construct an emotional grammar. But they"—he pointed to the other men—"they lack points of reference. It's stunning. Society offers hundreds of empty models, if you want to avoid the brutal job of understanding who you are."

The surface of the water, I thought, but you couldn't see what was beneath.

"Why does this case interest you?" Paolo asked.

"I find some things that concern me personally."

"In what sense?"

I didn't feel like lying to him, but I had no desire to tell him my business.

"Things that happened to me as a kid."

"Whatever it is," he said, "it seems to me unlikely that you can find analogies. We're creatures of the past. The new generations have problems, resources, paranoias, qualities that we struggle to imagine. The past scarcely exists anymore. And the future is all theirs, lucky for us."

It was after midnight. I was tired, I said goodbye to everyone,

I crossed the gardens of Via Carlo Felice, then Santa Croce in Gerusalemme. The sky was crowded with stars. The Egyptian pizzerias were closing, likewise the Bangladeshi shops with goods packed in everywhere. I crossed the dead zone between Via Micca and Via Balilla. Back to a metal shutter, a man was inhaling a cigarette, staring at the void.

When I got home, I put on my pajamas and turned on the computer. I checked my emails, answered some. As I'd been doing for some nights lately, I left for last what most interested me. Google Alert. Hundreds of new notifications on the Varani case. I read the first articles. I jumped. The last thing I would have expected. Ledo Prato had come out into the open. The composed, sober professional from the Catholic bourgeoisie had decided to break his silence. He hadn't done it in the manner of Valter Foffo; he hadn't been so imprudent as to trust himself to the eye of a camera. He had written a long reflection on his blog. I clicked the link. *I Am Still Me, in Spite of Everything.* That was the title of the piece. I began reading.

Dear Friends,

I wish to thank you publicly for the many messages you've sent me, expressing closeness, affection, sorrow, sympathy for this tragedy that has struck my family, my relatives. Life reserves many surprises, some happy, others not. Both characterize it, mark it, give it color, form, substance . . . . In these long years I have tried to convey to many people hope, courage, trust, to construct beauty, to preserve the fundamental values of life, to believe in the future. Sometimes I've succeeded, others not, as this tragedy demonstrates. Maybe we think we can have a decisive role in human and family relations, but it's not always so.

Sometimes we attribute to ourselves capacities that we don't have, and the example of a life lived according to the values of honesty, respect for one's own life and that of others, a life that has been given to us and of which we are not the absolute masters, clashes with difficult contexts, fractured human relations, choices we can't always condone, bad values that cancel good values and seem to nullify the mission of a life to which you have given everything, unsparingly.

In these days in which the press has shredded the lives of three families, each stricken in a dramatically different way, summary judgments, partial or comfortable truths have been read, expressions that belong to the darkest times in civil life have been used. A passage from the Gospel of some weeks ago comes to mind. The protagonist is the fig tree that produces no fruit and, for that reason, people propose to cut it down. But then a different decision is made, to dig around it, water it, and set a time: if in three years it doesn't produce fruit, it will be cut down. It's not only an act of mercy, it's an act of wisdom that suggests prudence and patience, because the search for truth is not brief and human justice has profound limits . . . .

Feel free to leave this page today, to withdraw your friendship if this tragedy of ours causes you suffering or impatience, if you are no longer interested in reading, sharing some reflections, because you've lost the faith you had in the author . . . . I want to share only a short passage, among the many, that a very dear friend wrote to me, a better man than me in every respect, whom I've known for more than twenty years. He wrote: "Your boundless capacity to put together, mediate, minimize, search for the opening where you can insert a solution, or a small crack where you can place a wedge, will allow you to stay firm in your faith, not to fall into the black hole, to reaffirm the value of the things you've done and also to help Marco. You are a person capable of turning evil into good and now it's up to you to show it in a way that will surprise the world."

I can do it, I owe it to my whole family, my relatives, my many friends . . . . With your help, with that of the Lord who never leaves us alone because he is ready to interfere even in our lives as sinners, we prepare with a light step to get through this storm. May God help those who need it.

Ledo Prato

In the preceding days I had listened attentively, if I can put it like that, to Ledo Prato's silence. I had watched him in his absence, unsure what to think. His discretion could be an admirable show of respect or, on the contrary, the expedient by which certain people prevent others from understanding what is really going through their mind. When I'd had the temptation to blame Ledo Prato I had had the suspicion that it was because of my own bad conscience, and when instead I had been on the point of considering him a rare example of virtue I had been afraid I was falling into a rhetorical trap. But now Ledo Prato had broken the silence, putting his good principles in the service of the most ungrateful of tasks. His writing left me with a feeling of uneasiness. I reread the piece. Formally there was nothing wrong in the essay, not a phrase that the grammarian could isolate to reproach or condemn. It was what I seemed to see between the lines that left me perplexed. Ledo Prato lauded himself as a good family man, he attacked the press, he celebrated the values of honesty and respect as if it were the journalists who had trampled on them rather than those who had killed Luca Varani, he was pleased with the messages of solidarity he was receiving, he displayed understanding toward those who blamed him. He cited the Gospel. Behind this profession of humility I felt emerging indignation at his own threatened reputation. That's what impelled him to write, I thought.

Do not judge and you will not be judged, I continued to warn myself at the same time. He's a man who's been tried, I said to myself, overwhelmed by something larger than himself, and no matter how great an effort he makes to remain calm he's not the master of his actions.

In spite of that, I was astonished. Was it the way he risked putting the three families involved on the same plane? Was it the effort to show himself so virtuous? Or was it the calm tones, the attempt to contain the tragedy within an enclosure of reasonableness, the conviction that he could subdue by means of common sense something one could only surrender to? Then, when I was on the third or fourth reading, I stumbled on something I hadn't seen before, a detail I hadn't focused on but whose presence I had felt the whole time. Or should I say absence. Ledo Prato never mentioned his son directly. The only time the name of Marco appeared was in the mouth of the family friend, who named the son with the sole purpose of exalting the human gifts of the father. Suddenly Marco Prato seemed to me the person most alone in the world. And, as evidence of what an inextricable thicket of contradictions the story was, Ledo Prato's post, which was so aggravating me, produced in me a feeling of an opposite type. I was surprised to feel compassion for a young man accused of an atrocious murder.

When Marta had a math test in class, she'd take a photo of the problem and send it to him. He was really good at math. He'd send her the answer on WhatsApp. One day he showed up at her house with a sheet of paper covered with equations based on the important dates of their relationship: he demonstrated that according to the law of numbers, too, they were destined to be together forever.

Marta Gaia thought about it now, when he was no longer there.

The police detective had asked: "What do you mean when you say that Thursday Luca wanted to scrounge some money for a charging cable for the iPhone?"

"When he had to buy cheap things he often said he was going to scrounge," Marta Gaia had answered, "even just to buy a slice of pizza. It was sort of his philosophy of life. He lived by the day."

Luca would say: "Kiss me?"

And Marta Gaia: "Kisses aren't asked for, they're given."

To celebrate their first month together, he gave her a present. The *trinket*. That was what they jokingly called it after she opened the package.

"I got you a charm in the shape of a heart, girls like those things."

"I'm not like other girls."

"I got it because it reminded me of you who are my heart, but I was ashamed to tell you."

"That's better."

The marshal had asked: "Luca used to disappear? He left home without saying anything?"

Marta Gaia had answered: "When we had a fight he'd stop answering my phone calls. When he had a fight with his parents he might leave home for a couple of days—then he'd sleep in the car, at least until he had to scrap it."

My love, she had written to him on WhatsApp one night a few weeks earlier. And a few minutes later *My sweetheart*. Then *My disaster*. "Hey!" Marta Gaia had written finally. "Why don't you answer?" "I don't feel well tonight," Luca had written. "Then I'll call you." "I'm not in a condition to talk." Yeah, sure, she had thought. "All right, you're hiding things from me." They had fought a million times, and a million times Luca had promised her it wouldn't happen again. But it continued to happen.

The marshal asked: "Did he ever suggest that you take narcotics?"

"He told me he was afraid of those substances," Marta Gaia had answered. "And I don't even smoke cigarettes."

Like all couples, they had invented a language of their own. They pretended to be children. They used expressions like "What yooou dooo?" (*What are you doing?*), or "Sweeetiiie, kiiiisssy eemersensy (*sweetie, I need a kiss*). This amused them tremendously. *Yiii* was yes, *tiss* was this, while *taass* meant that. They wrote their names everywhere. *Marta + Luca 4EVER*. Or *L+M 20.10.2007*. Once, at the beginning, during a rainstorm, Luca tried to protect her with a leaf plucked from a tree. Years later, to celebrate the memory, he had a picture of himself taken with a clover on his head.

The marshal had asked: "Do you know any of his close friends?"

Marta Gaia had answered: "I know a guy named Filippo Mancini and his brothers. Luca had a group in Battistini, but I never wanted to go there: some of them used drugs, I didn't like that. A friend in common, Edoardo Petroni, confided to me that

Luca used cocaine *heavily*. He also told me that Luca freebased, and that he was a dealer. I don't know if it was true."

It was New Year's, 2012, and they were looking for a place to eat. He adored McDonald's, but it was closed. They switched to Chinese takeout. They celebrated in the car, took a selfie. In the picture he was sticking out his tongue, she was giving a thumbs up, holding the food in the foil container. They seemed radiant.

The marshal had said: "Who else did Luca hang out with?"

Marta Gaia had answered: "He was the classic 'everybody's friend.'" She stopped for a moment. "Edoardo told me that with the Mancini brothers sometimes Luca 'stole': in the sense that they'd go around stealing necklaces."

The marshal had asked: "Did he have so-called vices?"

Another time it was Carnival. Luca was taking her home. Suddenly he stopped the car in a parking lot, turned up the volume on Jovanotti's *A te* on the car radio, and they got out of the car and started singing at the top of their lungs, filming themselves on the phone.

Marta Gaia had answered: "Vices? Well, there were the slot machines: that was his vice. He earned a hundred and fifty euros a week at the auto repair shop and spent it on gambling. So when we went out I paid. Not always, but often. He *always* had money problems, every so often I thought he'd do anything for money, and once I asked him if he would take money in exchange for sex with women."

Once they had both gotten a bad grade in school. Their parents had punished them. Marta managed to get five minutes of freedom, she called him. He asked: "What nickname did you call me this morning?" and Marta Gaia: "*Amoruccio ruccio. And Luca: "Oh, I thought *Mascottino tino.*" Silence. Then he burst out laughing. He laughed and repeated: "*Amoruccio ruccio. Mascottino tino.*" He laughed unexpectedly, noisily. She had never heard him laugh like that.

"He said he would never cheat on me with anyone," Marta

Gaia had said to the marshal. "The times when he was the one who paid for dinner or gave me a present, I asked him where he got the money. He said some guy named Giorgio gave it to him. This Giorgio, whom I never saw, I know he's a homosexual. He had grizzled hair and wore glasses. I saw his WhatsApp profile on Luca's phone. Sometimes Luca showed me the messages Giorgio sent him. *You're sweet. I dreamed we had sex.* I asked Luca what that man wanted in exchange for money, he said he wasn't attracted to homosexuals."

Two weeks earlier, they were at the end of one of their nighttime chats.

"Good night, my love," she had written.

"Till tomorrow loovey," Luca had answered.

"I miss you."

"Me, too."

And she: "O.K., kisses."

And he: "I can't resist, I want to sleep with you."

And she: "Aww, so sweet!"

Then, suddenly, maybe not even knowing why, Marta Gaia had written: "Luca, I need to ask you something."

"What is it," he had written.

"Swear to me that you've never sold your body for sex, to get money, or buy me something?"

"What disgusting type of person do you think I am?"

"It was a question."

"And mine was an answer. I would never do a thing like that."

"I wish you were here."

"My love," Luca had written, "I'm with you, in your heart."

How had such a question occurred to her? Was she right to suspect something? Were the pieces of the puzzle set in her head even before Marta realized it? Or was it all a gigantic mistake?

D uring those same days Manuel Foffo began to attack his own family. He did it from the prison of Regina Coeli, where the public prosecutor was again interrogating him.

"Over the years I accumulated a lot of anger," he said to Francesco Scavo. "I feel a lot of resentment toward my father."

"What type of resentment?" asked the prosecutor.

"You see, sir," said Manuel, "my father always preferred my brother to me. As soon as I was born he thought: *This isn't my son, this one takes after his mother.*"

Manuel began to enumerate a long list of Valter's failures, negligence, abuses toward him over the years.

"My father, for example, wanted me to study law. I wanted to do economics, because my brain is more economic than legal. But no, it ended up that I had to do law."

Scavo looked at him.

"He always thinks he's right," continued Manuel. "He was convinced that if I did law I'd be more useful to the family businesses. Too bad that then he threw me out of the company."

The prosecutor tried to bring him back to the circumstances of the murder.

"There, too," said Manuel, "I think I lost my head, especially when the subject of my father came up."

"What do you mean?"

"The subject of my father," the young man repeated, "when the subject of my father comes up all the poison rises in me."

"Listen," said Scavo, "you didn't make this whole mess to get revenge on him?"

"I wouldn't rule it out," Manuel answered.

"And you and Marco Prato didn't, coincidentally," ventured Scavo, "also talk about killing your father? Even if only in the abstract."

"Probably yes."

"What does *probably* mean?"

"It means I have this flash."

"You're having this flash now or you've had it before?"

"I had it tonight. I went crazy because . . . well, I feel this whole story . . . this story that's been going on for years."

S o Manuel Foffo killed Luca Varani to get revenge on his father?"

"Like, Valter Foffo goes on TV to praise his son the murderer and the son badmouths him like that in front of the prosecutors?"

The journalists were back on the rampage. Interviewing Valter Foffo again became a priority for all the papers.

Alessio Schiesari was a young reporter who worked for *Tagadà*, the afternoon broadcast on the TV channel LA7. The network had done a lot of reporting on the case, and the audience was anxious for developments. Meanwhile, the people who were working on the murder persistently were getting to know one another, so they began meeting, writing to one another, exchanging opinions and documents. I got in touch with Alessio through a friend in common. He said he was coming off two days of useless stakeouts. He had been with the crew at Bottarolo (which was deserted) and then in Via Igino Giordani (it hadn't gone any better).

The night of our first conversation, Alessio had decided to go back to Bottarolo. Good luck had to be prodded. This time he didn't have the crew with him, and went into the restaurant with a girlfriend. Camouflaged among the very few diners, the two sat down, ordered something to eat, and began talking about this and that, pretending they were normal customers. A few minutes passed. Then Alessio saw him.

Valter Foffo was talking to a waiter. He ended the discussion, crossed the hall, looked around, and left the restaurant. Alessio

got up immediately. Not having the cameraman with him, he
started the video on his phone. Valter meanwhile was heading
toward a parked car.

The easiest excuse in the world.

"Excuse me, do you have a light?"

"Sure," said Valter Foffo bringing the lighter to the young
man's face.

"May I ask a question while I'm at it?"

At that point the man understood.

"Here's another," he said. "We're up to thirty-seven just
today."

He was wearing a pale shirt and a cardigan over the shirt; his
voice was tired.

"I'm a reporter from LA7," the youth introduced himself. "I
wanted to know something about the statements that came out
in the papers."

"What statements?"

"The ones your son gave to the prosecutor. The ones where
Manuel"—he looked for the right term—"got *worked up* after
talking about you with Marco Prato. Have you been able to find
an explanation?"

Valter Foffo sighed: "And where do you suppose I would find
an explanation? I turn the question back to you. I'm waiting for
the end," he said. "I want to read all the proceedings, I want to
see the toxicology reports."

"As a father how do you explain it?"

"I have complete faith in Scavo." Foffo went on the defensive:
"I defer to him and the authorities."

"Your son seems to have said that you made a whole series of
demands on him in the course of his life," Alessio insisted. "For
example, the choice of university. Manuel wanted to do economics and you would have forced him to do law."

Were they really talking about that? About the fact that his
son had become a murderer because, ten years earlier, there had

been a discussion in the family about what university he should go to?

"All the product of imagination," the man cut him off. "I don't know how my son came to say something like that."

"Do you still believe in Manuel's innocence?"

"At this point I no longer believe anything. Let's wait for the reports. Forensics is working on it. There's the police. All experienced people, am I right? Listen," he said, "what's your name?"

"Alessio."

"Listen, Alessio, I understand that you're doing your job. But can you imagine how we are feeling?"

"Believe me," said the young man, "writing about the scandals of Italian politics amuses me. When I'm in a situation like this, on the other hand, I have a hard time."

"Here business has stopped," the man said, "the restaurant is empty, people yell at us: *you're murderers!* You understand how we are doing? People who yell. People who make things up."

"Because it's a shocking story."

"Murderers," Valter Foffo repeated, "me, who never hurt a fly."

"I don't like stealing images with the phone," said the young man, "so I'll ask you: would you be available to answer these questions in front of a TV camera? Ten minutes, the time for the cigarette we just smoked."

"Alessio," said the man, "I understand you're doing your job, but, let's be honest, you journalists live on the misfortunes of others."

"The media spotlight is back on you because of your son's statements," he tried to explain. "He says that all his rage came from his relationship with you."

"His relationship with me," the man repeated. "I don't know what to say. We'll ask him one day, if we get him free."

"A few days ago I went to see the Varanis."

"Really?" he asked, curious. "What sort of people are they?"

"They sell candy."

"Candy," the man repeated, as if he couldn't really understand.

"They sell candy at fairs."

"Peddlers."

"Peddlers, yes!" said Alessio and his friend in chorus.

"Luca Varani was not their biological child," the girl explained.

"Listen to something," said Valter Foffo, impulsively. "Who usually adopts a child? Either people like famous actors, who have enormous economic resources . . . but in that case rather than adopting them, they hand them off to a nanny. Or families who are unable to have children adopt them, they adopt a child, and that child . . . how to put it . . . becomes their little treasure. You understand that someone took that treasure away from the Varanis. And so: how can you go and talk to the parents of Luca Varani? Who has the courage to see them? I go and see them, and what do I say? That I'm sorry?"

"You spoke to Prato's parents?"

"I don't know Marco Prato's family, I know it's a good family. We're all good families here. The problem is the children. I still can't believe I'm talking to you about these things."

The following Tuesday, Valter Foffo went to see his son in jail. Two more days passed and although Valter had again promised himself to keep away from the reporters, he nevertheless did not. It wasn't clear if he fell into the trap every time or if he was waiting for a chance to say what he wanted to say to an increasingly vast audience. This time it happened outside a bar on the Tiburtina, not far from the restaurant.

Camilla Mozzetti, from *Il Messaggero*. She introduced herself.

"Look at me," said Valter, as he ran a hand over his face to demonstrate, "I'm all breaking out. The doctors say it's stress."

The reporter took off.

"During the interrogations Manuel said he wanted to kill you."

"He absolutely didn't say that," Foffo counterattacked. "He

wasn't referring to me. He told me when I went to see him. You can verify it, in prison they record everything."

"Did he confess to you that he was the one who killed Luca Varani?"

"He told me that Marco Prato stabbed him first and last."

"The two are starting to accuse each other."

"My son was blackmailed. He met Prato some months ago, on New Year's. On that occasion he had sex with him. Prato recorded it all on his phone, and threatened to circulate the video. My son felt pinned in a corner."

"You're saying your son is a victim?"

"I'm waiting for everything to come out," he returned to the old script. "I have faith in the prosecutor, we're waiting for the toxicology reports. I'm convinced that cocaine, and who knows what other substances, contributed to clouding my son's lucidity, and by the way, he's not gay."

"Better a drug addict than a homosexual?"

Valter Foffo remained silent. The reporter pressed him.

"From the proceedings it would seem that your son had a sexual encounter with Marco Prato shortly before committing the murder."

"That's not true, either. They had one sexual encounter, on December 31. We Foffos don't like gays," he said, "we like real women. And my son no less."

That same evening Alessio Schiesari called me back. He said that the next day, early in the morning, he was going back to Via Igino Giordani with the crew. Did I want to go with him?

P eople were digging in the trash bins.

It happens in all cities, but things had changed since he had last been in Rome. Before it was immigrants and the homeless. Now old people were doing it. Young people were doing it. White kids, well dressed, heads stuck in a trash can. In Piazza dei Quiriti a thirty-year-old in jeans and gray sweatshirt had propped open the cover of a trash bin with a piece of wood and was busy. The Dutch tourist passed by him, reached Via Cola di Rienzo, and took a taxi. "Viale Trastevere," he said.

The driver drove like a madman, yelling and cursing. The Dutch tourist got out of the taxi clutching his stomach. He made his way into the neighborhood. Narrow streets and red roofs. The gold background of the mosaic of Santa Maria in Trastevere dazzled him.

Common mother of every people. Enormous garage of the Italian middle class. What happens when the monuments of a city last too long.

Reaching the restaurant, he asked for Signor Franco. The waiters began welcoming him. Sir, how are you. What a pleasure to see you again. "You're not tired of being in Holland?" "Of course he's tired of it," said another. "Otherwise he wouldn't be here." Signor Franco hadn't yet arrived. But why not sit down in the meantime? Today there was pasta and chickpeas, there were *puntarelle*. The Dutch tourist felt upset, it was wrong for them to recognize him. At the same time he knew it wasn't a well-grounded fear. As soon as he had left the restaurant, for them he would never have existed; in Rome you flow over the memory of those who treat you familiarly like water over stones.

The tourist gave in to the compliments, listening to the conversations of the customers as he waited to be served.

"At Villa Torlonia, where the war archive is," a man was saying to two friends sitting across from him, "I read the letters that Pope Pacelli had written to the British and American Air Force generals during the war. One went like this: *'Dear General Henry Arnold, we hope this finds you well. We're writing on behalf of the Holy Father. If it is your intention to continue to bomb Rome, we would like to request that you abstain from doing so between 2:00 and 3:30 P.M.: here at the Vatican during those hours His Holiness is resting. Peace and good will.'* His Holiness is resting. You see what sort of man he was, the Pope?"

"Golden coins on the retina" that last "through the whole blackout." A market where all confess publicly in order to tighten the knots of the secret.

The waiter brought coffee. The Dutch tourist asked for the check. The waiter looked at him almost with pity: of course they wouldn't let him pay. He said that Signor Franco wasn't coming, he saw the disappointment on the tourist's face. "No, what did you think," the waiter hurried to say, Signor Franco was having his coffee at Bar Caruso, he was expecting him there.

Someone at a nearby table sneezed. The Dutch tourist pulled back, annoyed, wiped his hand with a paper napkin, got up from the table, left, and headed toward the Caruso. Once he got to the bar, they told him that Signor Franco had gone to take care of some business nearby. The Dutch tourist didn't want a second coffee, but he drank it in order not to seem rude. *Il Messaggero* open on the bar. Headline: "If I had a gay son I would throw him in a furnace and set him on fire." A regional council member of the League had said it. At another table two men were talking about funerals.

"At a certain point a rain of rose petals fell from the sky. The music started. People wept. We were all moved."

The dead man was the boss of the second most important criminal organization in the city. The most important, people joked, was the real-estate developers. The funeral had been worthy of a head of state. Flowers thrown from a helicopter, a giant photo of the head of the family dressed in white like the Pope, and the band had accompanied the coffin to the notes of Nino Rota's *Godfather*.

"A day when half is enough. Sorry if I made you wait," said a voice behind him.

The Dutch tourist turned.

Signor Franco smiled, his purple face, his thick-framed glasses, just as he had left him the year before. He was wearing a nice blue jacket over a striped shirt. The Dutch tourist started to get up, Signor Franco said they could sit there quietly, no one would pay attention to them. He stuck a hand in his jacket pocket, took out the envelope; inside was the key to the apartment and a piece of paper with the address. The Dutch tourist, in turn, took out his wallet, counted the bills, seven of fifty each. The money passed from one man to the other. They stayed to chat about this and that out of good manners.

Every taxi driver in Rome was crazy in his own way. This one, for instance, at yet another traffic jam, did something the Dutch tourist had never seen. The taxi driver picked up some change from the dashboard, lowered the window, and started throwing the coins at the vehicles that were illegally occupying the reserved lane. "Hey shithead! Get out of there."

Rude manners were a distinctive mark of the city. But people were more nervous than the year before. Now they were mean. They'd gotten poorer, the black wave of the crisis was overwhelming them, they had good reason to be nervous. But underneath, he thought, they remained as spineless as ever.

When they got to Ponte Sublicio he saw a man who seemed to be throwing a bicycle down into the river. He was astonished. It must be one of the city's mysteries from which he was still excluded.

The taxi stopped at Santa Maria Maggiore. Not far was San

Pietro in Vincoli. He had been there a few days earlier, had climbed the shadowy stairway that leads to the basilica, had entered, and stood gazing at the object of so many tourists' supreme misunderstanding. To the eyes of the stupid, Michelangelo's *Moses* was the quintessence of inner strength, the glorification of the faith that makes possible the most grandiose undertakings. Nothing more false: it was the documentation of a failure. If those who came had taken the trouble to inform themselves, reading at least two pages of an art-history text, they would have known that Moses' passionate gaze expresses not faith but offense. Michelangelo had paralyzed the prophet in the act preceding the unleashing of his anger, when, descending from Mt. Sinai with the Tablets of the Law, he surprises the chosen people dancing around the Golden Calf. In the next instant—what the statue did not document—Moses breaks the Tablets, dashing them to the ground.

"Twenty euros, sir."

The Dutch tourist entered the hotel and went up to the room, where he washed his face, brushed his teeth, changed his clothes. He stood gazing at the magnificent sight of roofs and churches. Humanity had always been lost. He retrieved the keys that the restaurant owner had given him and left the hotel again.

You turned the corner and the scene was reversed. Now he was walking on Via Cattaneo. A minute earlier the gold and marble of the churches, now the drunks and the homeless. Piazza Manfredo Fanti was a garbage pit. He read the address on the piece of paper. Intersection with Via Turati. The Chinese shops. Here's the entrance. He took out the keys. The hallway was dark and damp, he got on the elevator, went up to the fifth floor. Through the stairwell rose shouts in unknown languages. He put the key in the lock.

The apartment was small and bleak. A double bed with a blanket, a night table, an ugly wardrobe. The sensation was intoxicating. There he was no longer anyone. No register existed with his name in it. The capital of vice. The most beautiful basket for those rotten apples.

I arrived in Via Igino Giordani by way of Casal Bruciato. I saw them from a distance. Alessio Schiesari and the crew were talking near the church of Jesus of Nazareth, so grand and graceless. Opposite was the building from which Manuel Foffo had left to go to his uncle's funeral. Besides Alessio there was a soundman, a cameraman, and two guys from the crew. We didn't have time to greet one another. "Shitheads," said a voice behind us.

Outside a bar, a small group of men were eyeing us with hostile expressions. Spit on the ground, disdain for the vultures who were coming to peck in their house. "Assholes," said another dripping contempt. "Let's move," Alessio advised.

We crossed the street, then went through the gate in front of the building. The entrance door was closed. Alessio pressed the buttons on the intercom randomly until someone opened it.

We started to climb the stairs, immersed in a leaden stillness illuminated by artificial lights. The structure seemed like a gigantic concrete intestine thrown upward. Gradually, as we ascended, the silence became so profound that it was possible to hear the sounds of dishes. Plates, glasses, pots tossed into sinks. People were locked in their apartments. They must feel hunted. And distressed, angry, frightened. A few meters from the rooms they lived in the murder that everyone was talking about had been committed, the building had been filmed and shown hundreds of times on TV and Internet sites, it had been renamed "the building of the nightmare," or "the cursed apartment block." On the fourth floor, an old man in a tracksuit vanished through the door of his apartment as soon as he saw us. On the next landing two doors opened and closed again, but no one came out. It was then that one of the boys on the crew added to the mood: he turned to Alessio and me, looked at us with an expressionless face, and said that, however absurd, to him it seemed that the entire place was submerged in a pool of blood. He smelled it, he added. It wasn't a real odor, he felt the need to specify; rather, it was the *idea* of a nauseating emanation that could drive anyone exposed to it for a long time out of his mind.

"Here we are, start rolling."

When we got to the ninth floor, Alessio nodded to the cameraman to follow him. He went to the door to read the name on the nameplate. "Here we are," he said. The apartment of Manuel's mother. Alessio rang the bell. The woman would open the door and find the camera on her, I thought, and a few hours later her bewilderment would become entertainment for hundreds and thousands of TV viewers. Alessio pressed his finger on the bell again. A second time, a third. The door didn't open.

At that point, while Alessio tried to get his scoop, I looked at the stairs, empty and cold on the sunny morning. I started up.

When I reached the tenth floor, the first thing I noticed was bars. In place of the classic building windows there was a half moon open to the outside and surrounded by heavy metal bars to prevent anyone, leaning out, from falling. I felt the wind in my face. From that height the eastern periphery dominated. You could see the highway for L'Aquila, the high-tension pylons. On the other side were the sheds, the bingo halls, the illegally constructed houses repainted white in the urban blankness. The wind continued to move between the bars, disappeared swirling down the stairs. Then I turned. A few meters away, in a cone of shadow made permanent by the arrangement of the walls, was the apartment. The door was crisscrossed by the police seals. The bands, with red and white stripes, were arranged like an asterisk on the door front, where three identical notices of seizure were placed. Everything had happened in there. I kept going, I had been brought up not to believe in the supernatural nature of marked houses, and yet the sensation I was feeling in front of that door was real. It was as if a sudden increase in mass around me led time to slow down until it nearly reached a stasis where there was no stillness but only idiocy, solitude, desperation.

Like having dipped your hand in the Styx and feeling it still swollen with shadow, I thought after I got home. Does an evil of places exist? I wondered, can one speak of the physical persistence of evil after it has been done? Or is it only the power of suggestion?

That afternoon I went for a walk on the Esquiline. I was nervous. After wandering among the Chinese shops I found myself at Porta Maggiore, then I took the Casilina. I was walking toward Tor Pignattara: on the right were the regional train tracks, ahead the view opened up. On the other side of the ring road, beyond the last buildings, past the countryside, with its ditches and ruins, the Castelli rose gently. Looking from a distance at the hills immersed in the blue light, I felt the answer to the sensation I had felt in front of Manuel Foffo's apartment surfacing. Going away from all that. Getting out of Rome.

I had never even formulated such a thought, and suddenly it seemed the only thing to do.

When I arrived, twenty years earlier, I didn't know anyone. I had a ridiculous job and not much money, and yet within a few weeks the city had overwhelmed me with its tumultuous generosity—it was chaotic, vital, and tremendously cynical, and thus unable to take seriously even its own meanness. If you had the least ambition then Rome demolished it, if you ventured to confess that you wanted to make your way in life, or in fact succeed, it gave you a pat on the back and began to mock you. Where did you think you were? Rome had existed for 2700 years, it had seen everything, it contained Italian politics' unique concentrate of paralysis and rhetorical artifice, and besides it was home to the epicenter of world theocratic disillusionment. In these parts people were not so ingenuous as to think that self-assertiveness or, even worse, glory was worth something in itself. In Rome you knew people of all types, you mixed with other bodies, if it went well you put some money in your pocket, you died, and the western wind swept away even the ashes of your memory.

Everything was suspended between harmony and chaos, beauty and indifference, sociality and dissolution. Then, however, everything had begun to slide rapidly toward the night. There had been the scandal of the Mondo di Mezzo. The investigation included private individuals and institutional authorities and involved crimes of every type. Rigged contracts, corruption, speculation on the housing crisis, immigration, garbage collection, buying and selling of public officials, extortion, money laundering—a gigantic thing. The name of the investigation had been derived from an interception by the police: "It's the theory of the Mondo di Mezzo, my friend," one of those intercepted had said. The world in between. "There are the living above and the dead below. We're in between because there's a world, a world in between, where they meet. You say: *Shit, how is it possible, say, that tomorrow I will find myself at dinner with Berlusconi?* But it is possible. In the world in between everyone encounters everyone else. You find there some people of the *upper world* because maybe they have an interest that someone in the *lower world* will do them favors that no one else can do."

The world in between wasn't something new. Everyone in Rome had always found ways of meeting everyone else. At night in 40 AD Messalina, the sixteen-year-old wife of the emperor Claudius, took off her royal garments and ("her dark hair under a blond wig, her nipples gilded," Juvenal wrote) went to prostitute herself in the city's lower depths.

I passed through Pigneto. I continued walking, following the railroad tracks. Rome had died and been resurrected many times, and I wasn't so arrogant as to believe that the present collapse was the ultimate. But it was at risk of being definitive, if I measured it against my life expectancy, and that of the people I loved. The city of below was eating the one above, the dead were devouring the living, the formless was gaining ground. Fostering a hope was no longer experienced as naïveté but considered a mortal insult, what was left of vitality attracted aggression, the bite of contagion; and that small wood-paneled barrier, the door of Manuel Foffo's apartment, I thought, looking again at the distant hills, symbolized the end of the line of a long degenerative process. At the same time it was a premonition, a promise. *You will all pass through here, if you haven't already.*

L uca Varani didn't work as a prostitute. I could swear on my life. I know him. I know who he is. I was his teacher." Davide Toffoli, forty-three, taught literature at the Einstein-Bachelet Institute, where Luca had gone to evening classes.

"He was a transparent kid," he continued. "He had trouble hiding his real feelings, he could hardly have had a double life."

I had met Toffoli in a café in Primavalle. We were drinking iced tea. It was five in the afternoon, a golden light struck the buildings, infusing everything with an idea of peace and vastness. He was a man with a gentle expression, dark-complexioned, with the lean physique of someone who plays sports. As a professor he was attentive and thoughtful, he took part in many extra-study projects that occupied him far beyond the class schedule. He immediately made a good impression on me.

"How was he in school?" I asked.

"Direct, lively, he always had a point of view, which he defended without overdoing it. On a good day he wouldn't stop asking questions, he became a chatterbox. You couldn't ask him to do much homework, but he was the classic kid who does half the work by paying attention in class. And then his emotional bonds. He had an uncommon maturity for his age: he always talked about Marta Gaia, their relationship was wonderful."

"So in your view what the papers are writing is false."

Toffoli looked at me, arching his eyebrows, but without irritation. He was only unhappy, tremendously unhappy that human beings could reach certain levels of malice.

"People who knew Luca know that he wouldn't have done certain things. These days the strangest rumors are circulating, people even talk as if what happened were his fault. I find it a disconcerting accusation. Do we need to find a fault in Luca? Innocence. It's become dangerous to trust the people around us. That's tough to admit for someone who does my job."

What Toffoli had said calmly I found in an increasingly excited form as I approached La Storta.

"He was only a kid," said the owner of a bar-tobacco store, "he came here to buy cigarettes. Ten-packs of cigarettes so he'd spend less."

"Every so often he ran out of gas," said a man of around fifty who worked nearby. "I remember last summer. There was a long line of cars on Via della Storta, I passed them all on my motorcycle and I realized that he was at the front. He was pushing the car. So I stopped, took out ten euros, we put gas in it."

"It annoys me to read the papers," said a tall, thin youth of around twenty, with wavy hair, leather jacket. "The news that's coming out is despicable. The gang of reporters. They throw garbage on anyone who can't defend himself."

"I found out he was dead on Facebook," said another twenty-year-old, with very short hair, white shirt, bomber jacket, and chain. "The rumors going around are ridiculous. They're even saying he was a fag. What are they talking about, fag. They're the fags."

"Luca wasn't a prostitute and he didn't deal drugs," said the girl with him, hair pulled back, plucked eyebrows. "We always saw him in Casalotti. If there had been something strange we would have noticed."

"Revolting. Pieces of shit. Slandering a poor dead kid." This was Stefano. White T-shirt, surly expression, we were talking outside a gambling arcade. "What they're writing in the papers makes you throw up," he continued. "People have no dignity.

They live on lies. Parasites." Behind him you could hear the sound of the slot machines.

"What are they talking about, dealer! What are they talking about, faggot!" a girl outside the Andromeda multiplex sneered. "He liked all my girlfriends."

Although generalizations always suffer from too many limitations, after I spent a few days asking questions it seemed to me that Luca's friends were more or less divided between adolescents of the lower middle class and those who were once called street kids. But the new century had changed, if not upended, the meaning of these categories.

If Marco came from progressive circles, many of Luca's friends couldn't tolerate those circles. It wouldn't be correct to say that they were right-wing, or that some of them had fascist sympathies (in a time of confusion, calling many of Marco Prato's friends left-wing would have been equally misleading), but without a doubt they hated the professionals of good causes, the politically correct, the rainbow culture, and a certain ostentation of virtuousness that they associated with the dominant classes. To say that certain of Luca's friends were homophobic, as some wrote, was equally wrong. The majority didn't hate homosexuals, or marginalize them, but that didn't prevent them from regarding gay culture with suspicion; in their view it used sexual orientation as a tool of class discrimination. Naturally, they considered Marco Prato and Manuel Foffo not only members of the gay lobby but two privileged papa's boys who should be left to rot in jail for the rest of their days.

The kids of the Battistini group were very young, untethered, and manifested no political ideas in their conversations, but precisely for that reason they were the most political avant-garde of all. If Pasolini's street kids were confined to an enchanted prehistory, half a century later the kids of the Battistini group—despite their shaky education, their nonexistent reading, their absolute lack of ideological protection—were more modern than their contemporaries of the city center. The youths of Parioli listened to De Gregori shut in their rooms. The youths of Battistini went to techno concerts and danced all night with people sweaty and high on ecstasy. The youths of the center showed off their nice clothes, the youths of Battistini often had beautiful bodies. Among their parents there were no legal professionals, journalists, or heads of foundations but, rather, plumbers, shopkeepers, hairdressers, night clerks. They didn't live in nice houses, they couldn't afford expensive cars, they focused on their bodies: smooth, hard, muscular, aggressive, enhanced in some cases by cosmetic surgery, displayed in every aspect on the street and on social media. Bodies were their patrimony and their revenge. Otherwise they were impudent, exuberant, and they went through adolescence with the suspicion that neither adulthood nor a normal dose of good luck would free them from their condition.

But whatever the Battistini kids were, or the savvier ones from Primavalle or La Storta, they all angrily rejected the hypothesis that Luca was a prostitute.

They rejected it because they considered it dishonorable, because victim and executioners would be on the same plane, and also because to accept it would mean supporting the enemy's story. Not only the truth of the facts counted but the way in which they were narrated, the rhetoric that sustained them, and rejecting the idea that Luca was a prostitute meant refuting a narrative that was false even if it was true, rotten even if it was paved with good intentions.

This business of Luca's double life was polluting the heart of the story, I thought. It was the perfect rhetorical trick: it might be important for the personal relationship between Marta Gaia and him, just as Giuseppe and Silvana might have wondered about how Luca spent the time when he wasn't with them. But outside of personal relationships, on the ethical plane, not to mention that of simple responsibility, it had nothing to do with his death.

Why then did this type of story spread with such success, pushing people to believe that Luca had asked for it, or—worse—that he shared a fate with his murderers? Was it the fault of the reporters? Was it its dramaturgical effectiveness? (We were living in a time of storytelling, a period in which unscrupulous professionals wielded the tools of fiction-making to create consensus and feed hatred.) Or was it the hunger of a public always prey to low instincts?

I made an effort to understand, but it was like looking into a well after the sun sets, and it was perhaps because in the darkness we imagine the most absurd things, or guess the most interesting, that I reached the point of thinking it was the event, in its intrinsic viciousness, which distorted things. I thought this entity had a will of its own, its own interests, evil calls up evil and certain rhetorical forms are its instruments of contagion, and so evil snares us, I thought, it plays at confounding us, uses splinters of reality to convince us of things that aren't true.

I continued to wander around La Storta, I sought information, asked questions, solicited memories, looked for elements that would help me to understand. Luca dismantled an axle shaft at the shop. He laughed with friends. He talked to Marta Gaia on the phone, they planned to buy a Nissan Micra together. Marta reproached Luca for never managing to hold onto a cent. Luca went with her to volleyball, she was annoyed because the coach wouldn't let her play in competitive games. Luca said, "I'll call you later," then disappeared. So Marta Gaia called him a liar, she claimed it was impossible to stay together if he acted like that, worse than his disappearances were the silences, she wrote in messages, the way he shut down, wouldn't speak. But Luca, wherever he was, always talked about her. "When will you stop smoking?" Marta asked, freeing herself from his embrace. "In February," Luca laughed. "Did you change Stoppino's water?"

Stoppino was their hamster. Luca every so often went to Battistini. Marta didn't want him to see those guys, but he wanted to go out. Sometimes he got home late. His parents were sleeping, so Luca, after messaging with Marta, went into the kitchen and took out a pot, heated up the soup in the silence of La Storta. The trees danced in the darkness, beyond were the fields illuminated by the moon: he looked out, or thought only of eating, head bent over the plate . . . And suddenly a flame was kindled in my head and I seemed to see him, released from the coils that reduced the immeasurable to a narrative scheme: there's Luca, I thought with assurance.

In a few seconds the flame went out, and I no longer saw him. Outside of certain intuitions we are as if without faith. I went back to being a slave of the story. How did it come to murder? I wondered. Was there something in particular—a gesture, a dialogue, an exchange—that was destined to reveal itself as crucial for understanding?

In the following weeks, the events brought me back to the city center. To Prati, where I had an appointment with Savino Guglielmi.

Guglielmi was Marta Gaia Sebastiani's lawyer: she had decided to take legal action. The lawyer's office was on Via Valadier. He was a man in his forties, thin, in jacket and tie, an excellent conversationalist. He told me that, unsurprisingly, the impact on Marta of what had happened had been tremendous: "Their relationship was for years a sort of free zone, when she and Luca were together it was as if the rest of the world disappeared." Which obviously did not prevent the world, outside, from continuing to exist. Marta Gaia would begin a journey of understanding, she would have the support of a psychologist. She hadn't read all the pre-trial documents, some parts were very harsh, she would confront them when she was ready.

The life we believe we've lived. Life as it presents itself one day.

"Are you married?" Guglielmi asked unexpectedly.

"Yes." I was afraid to guess what he was getting at.

"Do you think you know your wife?"

"I know her very well."

"Well," he repeated, "would you hold your hand to the fire and swear that your wife doesn't have a double life?"

I almost seemed to see it, a big red flame, to the lawyer's right, between the ashtray and the civil code. I had only to stretch out my hand, and that modern ordeal would certify the absolute transparency of my married life.

"No, I wouldn't hold my hand to the flame," I said, "partly out of respect for the free will of my wife." Smiling, I added, "I wouldn't do it especially because we never know everything about the people we love."

"We don't know," the lawyer smiled in turn, "but maybe Facebook does."

We talked about that terrible exchange of messages between Marta Gaia and Valeria Proietti. We talked about the WhatsApp messages from Luca Varani found on Marco Prato's cell phone, about the thousands of bits of information—SMS, WhatsApp, conversations, browsing histories, geolocations—that at any moment could destabilize the private life of anyone, information that we luckily did not have access to where it concerned our loved ones, and that the big tech companies guarded in their servers like unexploded bombs.

C olonel Giuseppe Donnarumma was the head of the police operational division the case had been assigned to. I met him on March 11, a week before the remains of Luca Varani were restored to his family. The examination of the autopsy samples had required more time than expected, and for days the funeral was announced in the papers and then unannounced.

I arrived at Piazza San Lorenzo in Lucina at nine in the morning. A transparent light illuminated the palazzos and churches all around. The temperature had gone above 60 degrees for the first time since the start of the year. The parliamentarians came over here from Montecitorio to enjoy the sun and a coffee at Ciampini.

I was announced by a young policeman with pale eyes. I went up the stairway that led to the first floor.

"May I?" I asked in front of the door he had pointed out to me.

"Nicola, come in!" said a vigorous voice.

Colonel Donnarumma greeted me in his large, extremely neat office. He was an imposing man of around fifty. He shook my hand, and immediately afterward asked how old I was, where I was born, what I had studied, what type of work I did. It wasn't an interrogation. It was the State placing its ear to one of its children to learn his story more thoroughly. Behind Donnarumma was the flag and a photograph of the President.

"Please, sit down."

In Italy the distance between men of power and men of institutions is often huge. The men of power I'd known always had an air of being busy and, ultimately, untidy; they occupied cluttered rooms, full of papers and useless objects, or they sat in rooms that were too neutral, where the only real work had been done by an interior designer. In them greed was indistinguishable from a strong sense of impermanence: they were about to bite into a slice of the public good, but suddenly they vanished for other posts. They were gamblers. On the contrary, men like Donnarumma—and along with him old school principals, outstanding linguists, and other upright types for whom the spirit of service was more important than career—worked in uncluttered settings. The rooms were dignified, even comfortable, never luxurious, sometimes oversized.

"So," said Donnarumma, "how can I help you?"

I had prepared a list of questions, but first I tried to explain why the case interested me. I spoke generically about Luca Varani, Marco Prato, Manuel Foffo, I said that the life of each threw a different light on the city, I talked about how the press and public opinion were reacting to what had happened, I emphasized the absurdity that surrounds certain apparently unmotivated crimes, I talked about unrestrained violence, about how people considered normal could carry out actions indecipherable to themselves.

"Poor kids," Donnarumma said at a certain point.

The colonel started from the assumption that man is a frail creature, and only bombproof ethics and an unshakable force of will keep him from sinking at times into disaster.

"Besides, what's around them doesn't help," he added.

He was alluding to the city.

I asked what he thought of Mondo di Mezzo. Every day the papers were filled with the investigation, along with the Varani case. The extent of the corrupt system was objectively impressive. But it wasn't clear—and this was where opinions clashed in the public debate—whether it would amount to the crime of Mafia association.

"I have enormous respect for the judges," said the colonel.

"Whatever the judges decide I'll consider just. If you think about it, though, it's hard to know what's worse."

If the absence of a true Mafia organization—with its rites of affiliation, rigid hierarchies, paramilitary arsenal—would allow us to draw a sigh of relief, it could mean, on the other hand, that corruption in Rome had assumed an undefined form. Its edges were vague, it was a gigantic gassy presence that, mixed with the bit of pure air that remained, we all breathed. In environments where corruption is widespread, he said, people reach the point of committing crimes without realizing it.

"Let's return to the case."

"You were with Scavo in the apartment," I said.

"I've served for many years," the colonel answered. "I've seen it all. But when we were in that apartment . . . well, we left disturbed."

There was murder, and then there was this other type of murder. The cruelty, the savage violence, the complete gratuitousness of what had happened. Everything shifted the thing into the darkest of the cones of shadow.

"Nicola, do you believe in God?"

No one had asked me that question for a very long time. I would have liked to answer that I tended to believe in the Son but not the Father. Instead I said that like many I practiced a banal form of worship; I was agnostic. Colonel Donnarumma asked me what I meant. I explained.

"Well, there's always something to learn. You see, Nicola," he said, "I would say that we policemen, in order to do our job well, have to have special protection instead."

"Protection?" I wasn't sure I'd understood.

"An aura, a screen that protects us from what we have to deal with."

Evil. They had to deal with evil every day. The colonel said that evil wasn't an abstract concept, but you didn't have to imagine it as a definite entity, either. Evil was mobile, multiform, and above all infectious. The longer you were close to it, the more you risked starting to act according to its plans. There was nothing sadder, he said, than a cop who fouled his uniform. Every so often it happened. Thus those who were surrounded by a protective aura—those who behaved so as to deserve it, he seemed to mean—had hopes of doing their job without falling.

I asked what he thought about Marco Prato and Manuel Foffo. "They met," said Donnarumma, "and that's the problem."

Crimes of this type, in which the accomplices hadn't known each other for long, almost all followed the same outline. Not three, not five, not eight. Two was the recurring number. A dominator and a dominated. A manipulated and a manipulator, even if the roles were often interchangeable. It was a matter of individuals who, on their own, were unlikely to have committed the crime for which they ended up in jail almost without realizing it. We weren't dealing with serial killers. In theory, they were normal people.

"But in the end what is the truth about Luca Varani's private life? And Foffo's and Prato's?"

I, too, tried to ask my questions pointblank.

"You see, Nicola," Colonel Donnarumma smiled, "that, unfortunately, I can't tell you. We have some ideas, and as we proceed with the investigations those ideas are reinforced, let's say you have to be prepared for every type of scenario."

"Is it true that Foffo and Prato sent twenty-three identical texts in order to choose the victim? A kind of lottery of death?"

"They sent messages. I wouldn't swear it was twenty-three, as the papers write, and I wouldn't necessarily call it a *lottery of death*. They spent three days shut in the house snorting cocaine and talking non-stop, and at a certain point they also sent text messages."

"Is it true that Manuel wanted to kill his father?"

"Manuel accumulated resentment toward his family. I saw it during the interrogation, it was dramatic."

"Did you notice that in this affair it's mainly the men who've talked, while the women have been silent?"

"Listen, Nicola," the colonel changed his tone, "the investigations will go forward, and at some point they will be made public. You will go forward with your research, I imagine you'll meet a lot of people, do interviews, put the pieces together, and, piece by piece, you'll manage to reconstruct the whole story. We'll do as much as we can so that the law is applied as well as possible. But I imagine that you want to go deeper. I see it. And so, if I may," he said, "I'd like to give you some advice about this."

Colonel Donnarumma opened a drawer. He took out what at first sight seemed a file of newspaper stories. In fact it was clippings. He began to rummage among them, and took out one. "Here," he said, "you should focus on this." The piece of paper passed from his hands to mine. I began to read. At first I thought he had mistaken the article, I looked up at the colonel, and he nodded. I diligently returned my eyes to the page.

It was an article from *Il Giornale*. The article, which had come out some days earlier, reported the words of Father Amorth, one of the most famous exorcists in the world. Old and now ill, Gabriel Amorth had been struck by the murder of Luca Varani. "The hand of Satan must be concealed behind this crime," the priest had said to his followers. "In this sense I borrow the saying of a famous atheist psychiatrist, Professor Emilio Servadio, who said: *When we see wickedness reach heights that are not humanly explicable, there I see the action of the devil.*"

If at that moment I had risen and turned my back to Donnarumma, I would have noted a certificate of merit hanging on the wall. It was a medal for bravery in peacetime bestowed by President Giorgio Napolitano in 2007. Years earlier, in Cagliari, the then Captain Donnarumma had played a decisive role in saving people who were trapped in a burning building, although he wasn't on duty. After having evacuated the building he had rushed inside again. He had gone up to the fifth floor and entered an apartment that no one had come out of. Inside he had found an old woman immobilized in a hospital bed. Donnarumma had picked her up and saved her, too; he'd gotten carbon monoxide poisoning, and had been hospitalized for a week.

That is to say that before me was a man courageous to the limits of heroism, whose rectitude was indisputable, and whose intelligence—he had a degree in industrial engineering—rested on rational bases. In spite of that he was comparing the murder of Luca Varani to a case of possession. And seeing me with an only slightly astonished expression—I didn't want to seem disrespectful, plus I felt that there was something interesting in his point of view—he continued to speak.

He said that once, many years earlier, when he was working in northern Italy, he had investigated a shocking case. A very poor family, a mother with three daughters. A house deep in the countryside, not far from the river Adda. The father dead or left. The mother supported herself with menial jobs. The youngest daughter, a girl of eighteen, was a waitress. At a certain point this girl became engaged to a game warden. In an environment like that it meant the possibility of social ascent. The game warden was, besides, a handsome man, which didn't hurt. But human emotions follow the most tortuous pathways. Although she had a hard time admitting it—at least you had to assume that at first that was the case—the mother found that she had a burning feeling of jealousy toward her daughter. As the days passed the more worked up she became. One evening, while she was in bed, the mother heard her daughter and the game warden in the next room. A few hours later the game warden left to go on his rounds. The mother got out of bed, looked into the bathroom, where her daughter was washing. The woman picked up a scrub brush and began beating the girl savagely with this improvised weapon, until she killed her.

"We had a lot of proof, but we lacked a confession," said Donnarumma, "so we called the mother to the police station and the interrogation began. I will never forget it. I made it clear to the woman that she had no escape, that it would be better if she confessed. She looked at me without saying a word. So I changed my tone. *Unnatural mother! We have plenty of evidence against you! We'll also pin on you concealment of the body. It means life in prison! Confess, evil mother, confess!* At that point the woman took my arm and I felt an indescribable warmth spread through my whole body. She made the confession and fainted. I was still shaken. Look, you see, in that unnatural heat was something similar to what we felt entering Manuel Foffo's apartment."

We talked a little more about this and that. I listened and tried to reflect. It was too easy to relegate to superstition the last part of the colonel's reasoning. Donnarumma was a Catholic, but even if you disconnected religion from his words the frame of an interesting argument remained. If you imagined evil as possession, then you could fight it without completely losing faith in human beings. We were not irremediably bad. We were weak. And someone, out there, was much stronger than us. That was one possible explanation. Depending on the etymology, *he* was "the adversary," "the calumniator," "the bearer of light"; he was also "he who divides." What was dividing us so sharply from one another in those unquiet years? And what slanderer, to succeed in his intention, doesn't also need to be a good narrator?

A lex Quaranta was on the phone with his girlfriend when he saw the TV news report. He had already heard about the murder. At that time, he had no money, and often slept in hostels and friends' houses. He had strange encounters. In Rome strange things happened constantly.

"Excuse me a second."

Alex moved the phone away from his ear. The report was showing the apartment where the murder had taken place.

"What the fuck . . ."

Television frequently tells stories about people to whom the most incredible things happen. But what about when the person they're talking about is you?

"I'll call you back later," Alex said to the girl. He felt his heart pounding.

He had nearly been murdered and discovered it only now. And he had a kind of stage name that everyone seemed to know but him. Alex Tiburtina.

A few days earlier it had been Damiano Parodi's turn.

Sunday afternoon Damiano was driving to Milan. He was going to the San Raffaele hospital to be treated for the obsessive-compulsive disorder he'd suffered from for years. On the car radio he heard about the murder of a twenty-three-year-old. He didn't pay too much attention to what the announcer was saying, he changed the station.

A few hours later, though, he got a phone call from his friend Angelo Vecchio. Just then he was in the hotel gym.

Angelo's voice sounded very worried. "I thought you were dead, or were involved in that business in Rome," he said.

"Why, what happened?" Damiano didn't understand what he was talking about.

Angelo Vecchio told him that the murdered guy was Luca Varani, and that Marco Prato had been arrested.

Tiziano De Rossi found out from his mother. She told him that the TV news had broadcast a story about finding a body at Manuel's house. "I can't believe it," said Tiziano, trying to keep his emotions at bay, and his memory went back to what had happened a few nights earlier.

They would be questioned by the police, then pursued by journalists. The three didn't know each other, nor did they ever meet. Nonetheless, they were bound forever by the story. They had been the only ones to see, to set foot in the apartment in Collatino before Luca Varani arrived. If things had played out differently, would it have been one of them? Did they have to imagine themselves as survivors, escapees from disaster? Certain questions are inevitable, and at the same time pointless.

Luca Varani's funeral was held on March 19, two weeks after his death. The forensics department of Sapienza University gave Scavo the results of the autopsy exam. The prosecutor arranged for the return of the body to the family.

It was a Saturday, the sun shone over the entire city. The church of Santa Gemma, a structure from the nineteen-fifties, began to fill with the curious in the early morning. Boxlike and imposing, the building dominated a small group of houses in the suburb of Porcareccia, not far from La Storta. The square outside was full of TV crews and cops, bouquets of flowers and wreaths lay on the steps. Flowers from the Einstein Institute. Flowers from Luca's relatives. Flowers from friends. Then a lot of white balloons held together by a string. On the door of the church was a sign: "By express desire of the Varani family, reporters, photographers, and video cameramen are forbidden to enter."

As soon as I was inside, I realized that the space was hopelessly packed. Impossible to move toward the altar. There was a small balcony, so I tried to get up there. The balcony, too, was full of people. Adults with bent heads. Kids with clenched fists. I found a place at the back. The priest, hidden by the crowd, was reciting the Beatitudes. His voice rang out clearly. He said that the men and the peoples of whom the Beatitudes spoke were "the missing," they were men who had endured violence, who had endured injustice, but God said to them: *Do not despair, this is not the final word on your life, I am your guarantor.* The crowd listened with emotion. The priest said that the final word on Luca couldn't be what had happened. God hadn't wanted him to die like that; one might think that the span of his life defined him, but the mystery that every man represents could not be exhausted even if that individual man lived a hundred years. There is always a missing part, he continued, the part we don't see, and it's that which gives meaning to the whole. God sees it. God was the guarantor for Luca. "And us with him," said the priest, asking us to open our hands with the palms turned upward. The organ began to sound and a girl started singing, followed soon afterward by a male voice. Isaiah 62. The hair on my arms stood on end. The girl sang marvelously, her voice was melodious, powerful, and the boy's voice, so steady and serious, was the ideal support. The passage of the Bible that had been set to music spoke of the vindication of the chosen people after the destruction of Jerusalem. "For Jerusalem's sake I will not remain quiet, till her vindication shines out like the dawn, her salvation like a blazing torch."

Then the organ stopped playing and, in the most absolute silence, the girl sang the original motif.

No longer will they call you Deserted,
or name your land Desolate.

The woman next to me burst out crying. Two rows away a woman began sobbing. Next to her a man, arms wide and palms spread, gnashed his teeth, his cheeks lined with tears. I felt a lump rising in my throat. As has happened for millenniums in collective rites, hundreds of people vibrated in unison. We were so unused to feeling such an emotion that we were overcome even by the surprise. Suddenly we knew we weren't alone, we were living in a city that included everyone, the living and the dead. The priest asked God to welcome the weeping of Luca's parents, of his girlfriend Marta Gaia, of his friends. He said that having faith did not rule out the expectation that human justice would take its course. He called to the pulpit Davide Toffoli, the literature teacher I had talked to a few days earlier. I stood on tiptoe to see him.

"Those who sow death are sordid and unacceptable," Toffoli

was saying, "those who confuse the victim with the executioner are sordid and unacceptable. *Weep less bitterly for the dead, for he is at rest*, says Ecclesiasticus, *but the life of the fool is worse than death.*"

When the Mass was over, people poured out of the church. Faces red. Gazes feverish. And, kept at bay until that moment, rage.

"Bastards!" a murmur could be heard in the crowd. Men and women, boys and girls, charged with the energy that had held them together during the mass, began to scatter through the square as if they knew perfectly what to do, what words to say, what sort of profile to maintain. The reporters were on them.

"He worked with me at the shop," said a twenty-year-old as soon as the mike was stuck under his nose. "The last time I saw him was the day before the murder. An exceptional person. He came to work with a smile and left with a smile. Now the important thing is justice for those beasts, the fear is that they won't do the time they deserve." "I remember him from school," said another in a black jacket. "He was a kid like us. He was innocent, they lured him into a trap." Luca's mother and father received one hug after another. Marta Gaia, sunglasses and dark dress, wept in the crush.

Speaking with the reporters were Luca's former schoolmates. Some of them had made a collage in which Luca was portrayed at different moments of his life: two girls held it, one on each side, carrying it in view like a piece of evidence, a witness. Then there were the kids from Battistini. They kept their distance from cameras and cops. With proud, sharp gazes, they controlled the surrounding space as if they were the true guarantors of order. A roar was heard, clapping began. The coffin had come from the church. Carried on the shoulders of eight men it was laid amid flowers in the empty back of a black station wagon. The priest advanced through the crowd, approached the coffin, said the benediction. People began to converge on the station wagon. Those who could stuck their head in and kissed the coffin. First Luca's relatives. Then the kids from Einstein. Now it was Marta Gaia's turn. Finally the kids form Battistini. The leader was a tall, very thin youth, with a fleshy mouth, head shaved on the sides and a tattoo even with his right eyebrow. He put both hands on the coffin. Someone behind him hissed: "Life in prison for those fuckers." The youth continued to stare at the coffin with his arms crossed, his serious gaze became a bitter smile, as if he were talking to Luca's ghost and he alone were authorized to do so. Finally he slapped the wood, like a farewell, let the ghost go. It was hot. The crowd was increasingly agitated. Someone cut the cord, the balloons began to rise into the sky. A rustle of clapping, then voices. People raised their fists to the sky.

"Justice!"

"Justice!"

"Justice!"

PART III

The Chorus

My own business always bores me to death; I prefer other people's.
—OSCAR WILDE

All that you say speaks of yourself: in particular
when you speak of another.
—PAUL VALÉRY

W hen I was a child," Marco Prato said to the prosecutor, "there were times when I went to bed and prayed. I prayed that in the morning, magically, I would wake up in the body of a girl. I wanted that so much."

FEDERICA VITALE

I've known Marco Prato for around fifteen years. We were in the same class until we graduated. Our relationship became closer over time, maybe because we're both homosexuals. I always thought Marco was a sensitive person. In school his classmates massacred him, they made fun of him because he was gay and also because he was fat. After we graduated he enrolled in university and we saw less of each other.

In 2011 he attempted suicide. He was doing a master's in Paris. I never really understood what happened, I think he'd broken up with his boyfriend at the time.

Around the end of last year we began seeing each other again. I was glad. We got together for a pizza once a week. He'd talk to me about his new business as an event organizer. During one of these conversations he confided that he wanted to change sex. I had the impression that he was telling me only so that I would support his decision. Right afterward he asked if I had any intention of doing the same thing. I said no. I've never thought of changing my sex.

The last time we were supposed to get together was March 2.

Unexpectedly he cancelled the date, he wrote that a work meeting had been moved.

Three nights later I was at a restaurant with some friends. Suddenly Ornella Martinelli calls me. She was really agitated. It seems that the police had telephoned Lorenza, had told her that Marco had been admitted to the hospital and that his family had to be told. There was a round of phone calls among us to find out what was happening. We couldn't figure it out.

The next morning I was sent a link with the news of two guys arrested for a murder committed in Collatino. Then I understood.

SERENA PALLADINO

As kids we played in the same volleyball court. I consider Marco my best friend. Over time we developed an almost symbiotic relationship. I've always believed that, whatever happened to me in life, he would be there.

We almost always met at my club. I leave at one in the morning, he'd show up for the last glass.

In recent times he didn't have a real partner, he had casual encounters with both gays and straight men. I want to be specific that these were encounters between consenting adults. I say that because I've read some strange things in the papers.

Very rarely, around once a month, he used cocaine. I wanted to make him stop. He also wanted to get away from it, so in November we made a pact: Marco would hand over to me what he earned from his events, I would keep the money for him. For maybe a month we organized ourselves like that.

Unfortunately business didn't go well for him. He wasn't working the way he had before, which meant he had a lot of free time, and that was a problem.

Extremely intelligent. Cultured. Brilliant. A steel-trap memory. Skillful with words. That's Marco Prato. I don't consider him capable of physical assault, he's not violent. He's very empathic and compassionate. And generous.

Around a month ago, we were having dinner, and he said he intended to talk to his mother. The situation wasn't easy. Marco said he couldn't have a conversation with her, and he suffered because of it; he thought his mother's love was conditioned by his homosexuality. He had told her he was gay when he was just a boy. I recall that at the time his mother called me. She said her son was ill, she had to take him to a psychologist. *A psychologist?* I said there's absolutely nothing wrong with being gay—we're not talking about an illness. From that day on Marco's mother wanted nothing more to do with me.

Last Sunday I read the article on the *Repubblica* website. I rushed to the Pertini hospital, but they wouldn't let me in.

LORENZA MANFREDI

We were undergraduates at the LUISS, he was a friend of my boyfriend.

During high school he'd had some problems with how he looked. He was fat. He'd told us about it himself, and even showed us photos. I should say that when we met him he was still a little heavy—he didn't have the physique he has now. He talked about it ironically, but I think he never completely got over that type of discomfort.

After the LUISS he went to France, he did his master's in Paris. That's where he tried to kill himself. Pills mixed with alcohol. He sent a message to us girlfriends. In the message there were lines taken from Dalida songs.

When we got that text, I remember, we immediately sprang into action. We managed, I don't know how, to unearth a girl who lived in Paris, an acquaintance. She was the one who saved him. The reason for the suicide attempt was a guy named Nicolas, French, it seems they'd broken up.

Given what had happened, Marco didn't finish his master's. When he got back to Rome, he tried again to kill himself. The reason was still Nicolas. The odd thing is that, as far as I recall, it was Marco who'd left Nicolas, not the opposite. Marco must have been upset when he found out that Nicolas was going out with other guys.

After that we lost sight of each other. I went to Chile.

We got in touch again almost by chance in September. He told me that he was now making money, but added that, like an idiot, he was spending all the money on cocaine. I was stunned. As far as I could remember he'd never even had a joint in his life.

Also during that phone call he told me about an incident that upset me.

He said that one night, coming back from a party he'd organized, he was passing through the Tiburtina station, which is near where he lives, and had noticed two guys sitting in a parked car. He realized they were a little drunk, and were foreigners. Marco knocked on the window, asked these two kids if they needed anything. It turned out that they were Australians, and that they did in fact need help. They were lost. They were looking for their B&B. So Marco, on the pretext of helping them, took them to his house.

MAURIZIO VALLI

The first time I talked to him was September 6 of 2015. I remember because it was my friend Paolo Lepore's birthday. Paolo and I arrived on the Tiber Island at twelve-thirty. Claudio Bosco, another friend of ours, worked there. We were a little drunk, and although I'm not the type who usually takes drugs I accepted Marco Prato's offer when he stepped in to fire up the evening.

But let's go in order.

When we arrived, the situation was calm. Claudio was at the

bar. Nearby Marco Prato was looking at us. He, too, was, so to speak, working: with some partners he'd taken over management of the place. First cocktail, second cocktail, the evening began in earnest when Claudio came out with that idiot remark of his, saying I looked like Kim Rossi Stuart, the actor. At which Prato looks up and goes: *O.K., come on, you're a handsome guy but let's not exaggerate.* I agreed, there's not much of a resemblance. Marco came over, he asked us what we did. I told him that I worked in movies, in the sense that after the Academy I started working on film crews, or with videos, things like that. Paolo said he was a *trader*, even though in reality he sits at a computer all day checking the situation, and in essence the one who actually does things is this algorithm that enables you to invest in stocks through betting on a series of factors.

We talked, I have to say pleasantly. At a certain point Marco goes: *So, this coke?*

Maybe it was that we'd been drinking, maybe it was the party atmosphere, the fact is that Paolo and I said yes. Claudio went home, he had to get up early the next day.

Marco started preparing the lines, not too thick and not too long. After the first snort he suggested we continue at his house. He was nice. When we asked if we could pay for the cocktails he said: *You really think I'd make you pay?* Before leaving I confessed to him that I don't snort frequently. He said: *No worries, what do you think, I'm not a big user, either.*

Marco's apartment was in a basement. A small place being renovated. Pipes were sticking out from the walls, it didn't even have a kitchen. In the living room there were couches, a low table with a computer, there wasn't even a phone line, so he used the cell phone as a hotspot.

Marco was wearing shorts and a patterned shirt buttoned up to the neck. It was hot, so at a certain point he suggested we take off our pants and be in our underpants. We went along with that. Marco meanwhile was making drinks. Vodka, gin and tonic. We drank. We started snorting again. At first Paolo and I sat next to each other, then Marco got between us.

Then he began talking in a rather allusive way, which I would call "testing." *I know you're not gay*, he said, *I know you're afraid, but don't worry, now we're going to watch a porn film*. There was also music. We snorted again. At that point, feeling comfortable, intoxicated by everything we were doing, I wanted to show Marco some videos I was making. The videos are loaded onto my site, it's my work, I wanted to show them to someone who could give me advice. Marco watched them. Then he said: *O.K., now let's watch the porn films*. He also offered to give us a foot massage. We agreed. The sensation was pleasant.

At first it was Marco who chose the films, he went on XTube, on TubeGalore, on YouPorn. To tell the truth TubeGalore was my idea. We watched a few. Marco said he liked them because he identified with the women.

At that point we entered a dimension that I would call "confessional." Marco started with something like: *So Maurizio, you go in the other room and Paolo will tell me a secret*. All of a sudden I found myself out of the room. I tried to eavesdrop, but I couldn't understand a word of what they were saying. So I sat on the floor and started smoking. After twenty minutes, Paolo came back. *Paolo, what happened?* He let me understand that they'd had oral sex. Then he said: *Come on, Mauri', once in your life . . . what do you care, you try, too!* I said I had no intention of doing what he'd done.

I went back in the room where Marco Prato was. As soon as he saw me he offered to give me a second foot massage. He said: *Come on, relax*. I let him do it, and it felt good. After a while as he went on I said that the only other thing I would be willing for him to do was to masturbate me provided he did it with an object and not with his hands. Marco was astonished. *What's the difference?* he said. *That object, if you think about it, would only be a surrogate for the hand*. At that point Paolo returned. Marco moved closer and told me that, if I really wanted to know, Claudio, who notoriously likes women, had been in that house. Maybe that was the decisive revelation.

Marco began using both hands. Sitting in the middle of the couch, with his right hand he masturbated me, with the left he masturbated Paolo. Paolo didn't have an erection. I did. I don't remember if Marco did. I tried not to look at him. I was struck by his hairy legs, he had broad thighs, a large, rather shapeless rear. The porn films were still playing.

While he went on masturbating me, I stopped him a little before I came. *Stop*, I said. I grabbed his hand and pulled it away.

Marco reproached me: *It's stupid not to give in to desire*, he said, *I don't like people who do themselves such an injustice.*

I tried to respond calmly, I considered my words carefully, I was his guest and I noticed that my refusal put him out. We went back to snorting coke.

After an hour we decided to leave. Marco offered to take us in the car since Paolo was in no condition to drive the scooter.

Once I got home I was really sick.

I began to feel sick both physically and mentally. I felt so sick that I asked my father to take me to a psychologist. I told my father only the part about the coke. I felt a lump in my throat, I was disgusted by myself, I couldn't even masturbate anymore, which is something I used to do every day. I needed to talk, I had to tell my girlfriend *everything*. She's Danish, at the time she wasn't even in Italy, I texted her, then we talked on Skype. I told her everything. I said that if I hadn't talked to her about it I would have had a panic attack. It was also a form of respect toward her. After I finished talking, my girlfriend reassured me. She stayed close to me. Slowly things returned to normal.

The problem is that three days later I had to find Marco Prato. I had left my license and health insurance card in his car. I was upset at the mere thought of seeing him. We agreed to meet near my house. When he appeared my heart was racing. He asked how I was, I told the truth, that I felt like shit. He had a reaction like: *Hey, mamma mia, really . . .*

Around November I got in touch with him again. I sent him a WhatsApp. To tell the truth I wrote him something a little perverse. I wanted him to arrange for me to have sex with two girls. He had said that he had friends he could introduce me to. I wrote: "If you set me up with two of your friends, I'll let you finish what you didn't finish."

He didn't answer.

ORNELLA MARTINELLI

He's capable of psychological cruelty, he's certainly a manipulator, but he was never aggressive. I mean in a physical sense.

My name is Ornella, I'm twenty-nine, I manage a bed & breakfast with my father. I've known Marco Prato since high school.

He was openly homosexual even then, and had very close friendships with us girls. He tried to surround himself with women who had strong personalities, from us girl friends he wanted total, unconditional acceptance, the acceptance that perhaps he hadn't had from his mother. He imposed on us his excesses, a certain emotional intrusiveness, and he was always quick to deliver judgments on our lives. I saw him use his astuteness to hurt people. He could do it in a very sophisticated way: he had a mental archive of everything we'd done in the past, and he used it at the right moment.

When he attempted suicide in Paris I began to understand that behind all that exhibitionism, that narcissism, was a person who was suffering.

After the hospital he joined a gym. He changed his life. He devoted himself to the cult of beauty, so to speak. He got thin. He wore a toupee. As soon as he recovered on the physical level, he felt more confident, he began to neglect his old friendships, he moved away from all of us to plunge into the life of the Roman gay community.

The last time I saw him must have been three weeks ago. He came to my house with Monica and Serena. He practically emptied my fridge, he even drank the limoncello he'd brought. He was annoying as I hadn't seen him for a long time. He made strange speeches about certain sleeping pills. I know he was seeing a psychologist, Dr. Crinò. Considering how capable Marco is of imposing his version of reality on others, I wasn't totally sure how far this Crinò had really succeeded in understanding him, whether she realized, I mean, that Marco was in a truly messed-up period.

A file from the Sant'Alessandro clinic going back to 2011 turned up. Sant'Alessandro was the clinic where Marco Prato had been admitted after his first suicide attempts.

I commented on it with Chiara Ingrosso, a reporter who worked for *Il Fatto Quotidiano*.

We met in Piazza di Pietra. I was coming from Ostiense, where, half hidden between the Tiber and the station, there was an Italian school for asylum seekers. Some of the most incredible stories to be heard in Rome at the start of the twenty-first century came there every day: the Hamids who had crossed the sea in a boat full of dead children, the Shorshes tortured for months in Libya with a bottleneck, the Alis, the Syoums, the Gabriels . . . Despite the exceptional nature of the lives of these men, the majority of us preferred to ignore them; we pretended that they didn't exist, as if there were a spell, an evil spell that prevented us from opening our ears, opening our eyes before what was so near.

"I've reached the point where at night I dream about Marco Prato and Manuel Foffo."

In the city center coffee and juice. Lawyers. RAI executives. A whole other world.

I had got in touch with Chiara Ingrosso after listening to a radio report she did. From the way she spoke about the murder it was clear that she was deeply into it. She was fifteen years younger than me; she had worked for a while in a dance club, and at the same time had been doing short reports for the paper's website. Since she'd been following the case, though, she'd been unable to think of anything else. ("Saturday, March 5, I'm working the door at the club. I go to bed at dawn. A few hours later, I'm still groggy, the person in charge of the paper's website calls me. He assigns me the murder, assuming that the world where it happened is the same as mine. I struggle out of bed, leave the house, start interviewing the kids I know. It started like that. I didn't turn back, everything else has vanished from my life.") Chiara had quit her job in the club, she was on the case day and night, interviewing people, collecting documents—it was as if the murder had given her "a center" on the emotional level as well. At the same time it had opened her eyes to her true professional vocation: crime reporting. Marco Prato and Manuel Foffo, she said, were the people she thought about most in the course of a day.

"Let's see those papers."

From the Sant'Alessandro clinical file came the information that Marco had tried to kill himself in Paris on May 28, 2011 (antihistamines mixed with alcohol), and then in Rome on June 15 of the same year (a bottle of Valium, alcohol, superficial cuts on his wrists). The psychiatric case history spoke of a "premorbid" personality characterized by a feeling of emptiness, mood instability, continuous attention-seeking. The psychological evaluation revealed that he was a young man with a good intellectual level, used to observing the world around him attentively. He always needed to be in control of the situation, and he collected information about the people he dealt with. The so-called "rational method," which he also handled very well, began to deteriorate, however, when he got too close to others, especially if the relationship became a sentimental one. His "intellectualizing" approach to emotions (talking about them rather than experiencing them) could have a protective purpose. But protecting himself from what? He was discharged with a diagnosis of narcissistic personality disorder.

"Maybe he never recovered from his childhood traumas," I said tritely. "His mother's silence. Or the bullies at school."

"He reminds me of one of those radical philosophers of the

late nineteenth century," said Chiara. Meanwhile I was staring at a bike that had been incinerated next to a trash bin, garbage spilling out onto the pavement as usual.

"In what sense?"

"In the sense that by exaggerating, by straining limits, by violating boundaries, he found himself facing a sort of definitive void, a black hole that could strip meaning from everything else. You remember what he wrote in one of his farewell letters? *I discovered horrible things in myself and in the world.*"

"What makes you so passionate about this case?" I asked.

"I want to understand. I've seen a lot of guys like Marco. Maybe they don't end up in such horrendous situations, but the journey is similar. I recognize them immediately, I look at Marco and I see others. It's my generation, right? Dance clubs, afterparties, chemsex. I worked in a club, I've seen it all: once you start that life it's easy to tip over to the other side. If this case hadn't arrived to keep me focused, maybe at a certain point I would have gone over, too. Who can say?"

A t home my parents were always estranged," Manuel said to the public prosecutor. "Ever since I was born I've witnessed their arguments. When I was a child I went to bed with my ears straining to find out if they were arguing. My brother and I . . . always ready to jump up if there was a fight."

"Look . . ." said the public prosecutor.

"You see, sir," said Manuel, in his turn, "when I was younger I had a scooter. In those days life was wonderful—I had a girlfriend, I played soccer, everything was going well at school. And then what happens? High school's over, my father suddenly gave my scooter to a guy who worked in a bar. I was very upset."

"Why did he do that?"

"That's what I've always wondered. I had a profound emotional bond with that scooter. And then the Yaris. I had asked my father: *Will you buy me a Toyota Yaris?*"

"A Yaris?"

"I'd already made a plan for how I should live. For example, I needed an easy car. The Yaris was perfect. Comfortable, small, suitable for someone who just got his license. But my father said I needed a solid car, in case of an accident. He bought me a Maggiolone. That Maggiolone caused me a ton of problems. Right after I got it I started drinking, I starting doing drugs, I had to quit soccer, I broke up with the girl. Everything happened at once . . . a series of situations that, banal as it may seem, led to failure. I had this beautiful girl . . . I had the scooter that my father . . ."

"Sold," Scavo came to his aid.

"No," Manuel specified, "he actually gave it away. Without saying anything to me. I had a lot of accidents with the Maggiolone. Once I hit a wall, the airbag burst, the car caught fire, and I had to jump out to save myself . . . But I had told my father: *Get me a modest car.* Because you see, sir, many kids, especially kids from wealthy families, it's better if they don't have a big car right away, because women . . . girls, at that age, they don't go for money . . . they think about money *later* . . . when you're young you succeed with girls another way . . . like that, with a big car, you look like a guy with a lot of money but he didn't get the money himself. You see? That's why the Maggiolone was a mistake. In that car, which made me sick, I had to change my personality. Because, how do you behave? I mean, in the end I didn't know how to be . . ."

"Excuse me," said Scavo, "did you just say that the Maggiolone forced you to change personality?"

"Maybe I . . ."

"It seems a little disturbing as a statement."

"Maybe I exaggerated," said Manuel. "The fact is I feel very tense."

GIORDANO PEROTTI

I work at a service cooperative. I must have known Manuel since I was fifteen. We were friends, we spent a lot of time together. I'd seen him less lately. Manuel began to have problems after a long trip to Ibiza. When he came back he wasn't the same. At the time we used cocaine occasionally, at most a gram on Saturday night, not even every Saturday. Then I stopped with coke. But, after that trip, he snorted much more frequently, and he also drank a lot.

It started happening whenever we went out. Manuel would get drunk. He was a very strange drunk. When he drank he became cut off, he didn't talk to anyone, he got quiet, staring at nothing.

At first, cynically, we, his friends, laughed about it. After a while the situation became embarrassing. We intended to confront the problem, we said we ought to talk to him, but we didn't. Instead we stayed away.

On March 2 Manuel created out of nowhere a WhatsApp group called Cristian. Luciano Invernizzi and I were in it. We'd used that name years ago to allude to coke. We'd say: *Let's go out with Cristian tonight.* Manuel created this group and started sending us bizarre messages. In fact he was inviting us to snort coke at his house. "*Yo guys, blow, chill . . .* He used words that weren't in his vocabulary. Luciano and I commented on the weirdness of what was happening, but we didn't respond.

"I had to quit soccer because of my mother," Manuel said to the prosecutor, "because practically, if you're too good, what happens? The other guys started to get jealous. My mother, who's kind of a psychopath, got to the point where she thought they could hurt me, and she cried every day . . . so in the end I gave in."

"What sort of relationship do you have with your mother?"

"My mother is a housewife," said Manuel, "of a simple type . . . There's almost nothing I can talk to her about . . . In other words she's not a cultured woman . . . But she's a woman who can cook well, she'd never let me go without a dish of pasta . . . and that I like, it fills my heart, I love her . . . but, let's be clear, we can limit ourselves to that. If I have a problem, I can certainly not go to my mother."

"Then who is your reference point in life?"

"No one."

"No one?"

"My father," said Manuel, "after making me study law because then I'd be useful to the business, set my brother up in the business and threw me out. Basically they kicked me out, so I was completely disoriented, without the university course I wanted, without a job, I was really lost . . . So then I said to myself: *Manuel, the only thing left for you to do is to become self-taught.* I started reading all these books. I really liked to read . . . I read all the time . . . business magazines, economics, everything . . . until, after three years, I came up with this great plan, the soccer app . . . My Player. I went to the soccer federation, I had some conversations, I took my brother with me, I chose the best software engineers . . . It was almost done . . . We talked to the secretary general . . . the secretary was enthusiastic: *Now it's up to the president* . . . if we got the signature of the president I'd be a millionaire now . . . It's not only the money . . . it's the satisfaction . . . I was a hairsbreadth from the goal . . . I didn't make it . . . Every time I used coke I'd think of how I'm suffering inside . . . The fact is I've always been misunderstood. Even Anna, my maid, always told me: *Manuel, you're a misunderstood genius* . . . So maybe it means that stress, cocaine, alcohol, and all that lack of understanding—one day they caused me to flip out, and I did what I did."

The prosecutor looked at him.

"Marco Prato, on the other hand," said Manuel shortly afterward, "told me his relations with his parents were splendid."

MAURO BERGAMASCHI

I've been hanging out with Manuel since we were in school. He got his first tattoo on his left arm. It might have been 2007 or 2008. He had an M and an F tattooed, his initials, but the way they were drawn they could also be his parents' initials. The second tattoo is a carp. I was there that time, too. He stayed in touch with the people who did the carp tattoo, since later he also had them do a geisha. The next tattoo was an archer. Finally he had a barrel tattooed on his ankle. The barrel was supposed to allude to the name of the family restaurant, Dar Bottarolo, the cooper.

In recent months he'd stay shut up in the restaurant all

afternoon. Maybe he was working on the computer. Or he was reflecting. Maybe he was on the Internet. Once I opened a Facebook
profile for him so he could participate in a Fantasy soccer tourna-
ment. He never used that profile, he was afraid someone might
ask to friend him and he'd be forced to accept. He didn't want
other people to know about his life. Anyway, recently he seemed
distraught. I didn't understand why. Then, looking through the
papers, I read about that video that supposedly showed him and
Marco Prato having oral sex. I thought the change in mood had
to do with the existence of that document.

The last time I heard from him must have been March 2. We
talked about pointless things. Then, on March 5, at 6:56 P.M.,
out of the blue I got a very strange message on my phone. I'll
reproduce it word for word: "I have been a sincere friend to all
but I don't believe I deserve your friendship. Even if you can't
understand, I would like to be forgotten."

LOREDANA CASELLA

Everything was fine until 2015. Last summer the problems began.

I'm forty-nine, I work in the food business. I met Marco Prato in the summer of 2013, when I started managing a restaurant in Testaccio. Marco came there as an ordinary customer. He was polite, likable, and he was a savvy guy. I saw it, that he was savvy. Two years later, with my son and daughter-in-law, I took over management of a fish restaurant on the Tiber Island for the summer. Mediterraneo. Marco was also a partner in Mediterraneo.

CLAUDIO BOSCO

La falopa, la falopa, la falopa... La falopa, la falopa . . . Coke, coke, coke . . .

Good lord, I can't get it out of my head.

I'm twenty-six, I'm a real-estate consultant, I play electric bass in a band, but in the summer of 2015 you could find me on the Tiber Island. I was one of the kids who worked at Mediterraneo. The owners were Loredana and her son and daughter-in-law. Then he entered the partnership.

I think Loredana had brought in Marco Prato because she hoped he would attract new customers from the gay world. At the same time she relied on the fact that he would help manage the restaurant. Nothing more mistaken. Marco was involved with his A(h)però events and almost never came to the restaurant. Plus cocaine.

There were many things Marco should have done at the restaurant and didn't, many things he did he shouldn't have done. For example, Loredana had assigned him to restock alcoholic beverages, you can bet he didn't. In the end Loredana had to take care of it, she loaded all those bottles in her car, and I mean, she's not a kid. Another problem, the so-called VIP friends Marco invited to the restaurant, he never let them pay. Same thing with the drag queens who did the A(h)però events and then came to us. He was photographed with Flavia Vento on various occasions, once they were even kissing. They pretended to be having a fling. Those photos ended up in the papers.

Damiano Parodi I remember. Gay, a wonderful person, they say it was he who introduced Luca Varani to Marco Prato. Damiano was a low-key guy, a different character. Once I heard him joke: *To go to bed with a man, I don't need to drug him.*

The truth is no one ever forces anyone in this sort of thing. After I'd been working in the restaurant for about a week Marco asked me:

By the way, do you take drugs?

At first I thought he was asking because he was ready to throw out those of us who did coke. Nothing farther from the truth.

He started asking me if I wanted to snort with him. *You want la falopa, you want la falopa, you want la falopa . . .* That's what he called it, *falopa.* He was a hammer. After I'd been working at the restaurant for several weeks, I agreed to snort coke with him. I got to the Island around 5. Loredana arrived at 7:30. Marco arrived later. Every so often we snorted after the place closed. Marco began complimenting my physical appearance, then came the comments: *Will you dunk your biscotto in the cappuccino?* Stuff like that.

I'm heterosexual. The first time I went to his house, we did cocaine, we drank, then he made me choose porn on the Internet.

He made me take off my clothes with the excuse that it was hot in the apartment. He started touching me. To be truthful: he didn't have to be that persuasive. I made a bit of a scene, but in the end I let him do it. It was pleasurable, even if in fact I didn't manage to get an erection. That night we also talked about music, about the VIPs he said he'd seduced, about the girls I liked.

The next day I was overcome by sensations like: Oh God, what did I do? It's well known, the down from coke makes you a little paranoid. So I called Diego, a trusted friend. He said: *Did you enjoy it? Yes? Then calm down, there's no problem.*

But there was the business of Loris. As I said, I play bass in a band. Loris the drums. To make a long story short, Loris also ended up at Marco Prato's house. Too bad it wasn't just a day like the others. We had an important concert, Loris disappeared for the whole afternoon, he called me at eight that night, he was stoned, he told me he was ready to come and play. I would never have appeared at a concert with a member of the band in that condition, and also because my father was coming to hear us for the first time. In the end the concert was canceled. I was furious.

But let's get to the second time I went to Marco's. He had invited me. O.K., he's gay, I said to myself, but the other time I had fun in the end. Maybe we'd started taking some drugs at the restaurant. At his house we snorted some more. He said *another hit, another hit, come on* . . . . I let go. He began to suck me, even though as usual I didn't get an erection. At a certain point I told him I was sorry. I was sorry I couldn't reciprocate with anal sex. He reassured me: *Come on, don't worry, you're my guest . . .* I was his guest. He continued to offer me endless coke. In short, at a certain point I had a panic attack. To be precise I had *the* panic attack. Unlike the attacks I'd had as a boy, just a little anxiety and some trouble breathing, this time I was really sick. My heart racing, sweating, trouble speaking. I was shaking all over. I felt *detached* from my body, I thought I was about to die.

Marco, I have to admit, immediately came to my aid. He held

me, gave me water, made me lie on the couch, tried to put on the right music, tell me the right things, until I fell asleep. I woke up after two or three hours. At that point we went to have a kebab.

After that episode he began to say stuff like: *Hey, remember I saved your life.* Otherwise he seemed to have calmed down. But it lasted only a few days. He started again. *You want la falopa, you want la falopa, you want la falopa . . .* Like the Chinese water torture. He started saying things like: If you don't agree I'll have you fired. I said to him: *O.K., good, fire me, and then what are we going to tell Loredana?* Then he changed his argument: *Come on, stop it, I'll have you playing in some clubs belonging to people I know . . .*

Apart from what happened the night of the panic attack, I have to admit that Marco Prato is an intelligent guy, charismatic, even likable when he wants to be. The way he acted could make you laugh. At other times I hated him.

After the panic attack I began to hate cocaine. I started also hating the job of barman. It's a job that leads you to see coke everywhere, I really became disgusted with it.

When I found out about the murder I immediately talked about it with Loris. He told me he felt like throwing up, he was shocked, he said something like that could have happened to him. I also felt sick. I couldn't read the papers. My family didn't notice anything. Of course, my mother asked me some questions, she knew that Marco had been my employer. I also talked to Marco's father. After talking to him, I felt better.

Anyway, I try not to think about the murder of Luca Varani. As I said, I'm a real-estate consultant. It's a job where the client can immediately perceive your state of mind.

D id you suffer from the fact that your father preferred your brother?"

"Look," Manuel answered, "I always knew he was the chosen son, but there was never a feeling of envy. I love Roberto. When what happened happened, right after the arrest, I thought that *I* could get through even fifty years of prison, while *he* . . . Roberto has the same surname, he's thirty-two, has two children, works like crazy, he's a respectable person, and he loves me . . . Well, I thought I'd ruined his life. Then of course he and I weren't treated equally."

"That inequality had existed since you were children?"

"The first time my mother was pregnant my parents didn't want a child, and yet Roberto was born and was very much loved. Paradoxically, it would have been better if the second child, who was a child they wanted, hadn't been born. When I grew up, I tried to understand. I asked: *Mamma, tell me what papa said to you about me?* So once my mother told me something I've never forgotten. The anecdote goes back to a time when I was drinking a lot. It seems that during that period my father one day supposedly said to my mother: *You'll kiss your son when he's cold.* How can you forget a remark like that? When I fought with my father, he addressed me in the plural: you did this, you're responsible for that . . . I wondered for a long time why he used the plural. Then I understood. He lumped my mother and me together, as if to say that she and I were made of the same clay."

"But you're sure that your mother was completely sincere when she talked about your father?"

"Could you repeat the question?"

"Your mother," said Scavo, "is perhaps a person who harbors some resentment toward your father."

"Certainly. But my mother also told me that she had some great times with him."

"You said you can't consider your father a point of reference."

"I'll try to give you another example. Some of my friends know how to act around girls . . . like, they must have slept with more than four hundred, five hundred girls . . . These friends know that girls today like beards. But if I grow a beard at my house . . . well, then I'm a disgrace . . ."

The prosecutor was puzzled.

"My father doesn't like beards," Manuel continued, "they make him suspicious. He says: *If a guy has a beard I don't trust him, men who have beards are revolting* . . . In fact friends asked me: *Manuel, why don't you ever grow a beard?* As a result, when I started letting my beard grow, partly to defy my father, then my friends thought I'd had a personality change . . . So for one reason or another, Mr. Scavo, everyone thought I was a little crazy."

"How would you define your relationship with women?"

"Fundamentally based on sex. Let me be clear, I'm not a playboy. But the relations I've had with girls are . . . well . . . as I was saying it's never really been about love . . . and besides, women don't like me the way I am. I can't guarantee a woman real financial stability . . . and I can't guarantee, as you've seen, good humor . . . because that, too, good humor, along with financial stability, is important for a couple's relationship."

"So," said Scavo, "can you tell about any girls who have been a little more important for you lately?"

"Sincerely no . . ."

"Girls, let's say, you've gone to bed with at least three or four times."

"Well," said Manuel, "one's called Marcella."

"Marcella what?"

"Santoro. Marcella Santoro. This Marcella . . . in real-ity . . . she's kind of an ugly girl . . . she's ugly but she's useful, because when I'm at home, doing nothing, I call Marcella, she comes over, she gives me a blow job and then I send her away. She complains, because among other things I never have sex with her. The fact is that I don't like her enough. Otherwise it's fine. Anyway, I don't just have her give me a blow job. I also spend a couple of hours chatting with her, because she . . . well, I also value her brain . . . She has a degree in economics, she says inter-esting things . . . I always talk to her about my business, she gives me a lot of advice."

"Your father came to see you in jail."

"When my father came to see me in jail, he started off saying how much he loves me. For me, sir, that's . . . it's like the Jubilee, it happens once every twenty-five years. It's emotional. I cried for half an hour. But then the moment when you're moved is over and so . . . in the end everything comes back. I mean rage. Rage came back."

MARCELLA SANTORO

I'm twenty-seven, with a degree in economics, I'm an intern at a consulting company. I met Manuel ten years ago through friends in common.

A calm guy, self-possessed, intelligent, also very polite. He was never violent, he never raised his voice. I knew that on the weekends he used cocaine with his friends.

What I'm about to tell happened a few times. When he and I met at his house, after talking, exchanging opinions, and so on, we'd now be lying on the bed. Then, right at the last minute, he pulled back. I mean, he pulled back from the possibility of hav-ing intercourse. Because then, instead, he asked me to satisfy him in another way.

In the past five months I must have been with him just two or three times. We talked a lot. Manuel's favorite subject was his app project. He talked about it constantly. He said he liked debating with me, he considered me intelligent. I gave him quite a bit of advice. Don't forget that I know about economics.

Anyway, in the end if I hadn't had to insist when it came to sex, then maybe we would have seen each other a little more. Or maybe he should have just said plainly that he only wanted to talk. There would have been nothing wrong. But he didn't do it. So at a certain point I blew him off, especially recently.

"Manuel," said Scavo, "didn't your father, at certain moments of your life, function as an alibi for you?"

"My father always went against me," said Manuel. "Once he tried to beat me just to relieve his nerves. I remember, there was also his new woman friend . . . who then, this woman . . . he's the type who likes to be seen by people, he grooms his eyebrows, he goes to tanning salons . . . he's all charm, my father . . ."

"When did he try to attack you?

"It was 2014, we had just opened Bottarolo. When my father starts a new business he always says he's doing it for the family. If you go and talk to him, Mr. Scavo, he'll tell you that he works for the benefit of his children. It's not true, I can tell you, he does it completely for his own pleasure . . . But I want to tell you another story . . . In 2010 we opened another restaurant, a restaurant conceived and planned by my father and my uncle Pietro, a great person. What did they think up? Practically they opened a fancy restaurant in Pietralata . . . I mean, an area that, however much you like it, isn't exactly exclusive . . . It's not Tor Bella Monaca, but we're not exactly talking about Parioli. So they open this restaurant and call it Les Chic. You could see already from the outside . . . it seemed to be . . . it was very ostentatious . . . The customers felt constrained to speak softly . . . It was all embarrassing. At first my father and my uncle wanted to make it a fish restaurant. After a month the proceeds were small and they changed it: just meat. After another month and a half the restaurant still wasn't doing well . . . because, let's be clear, in the end that restaurant was neither this nor that . . . In the meantime they didn't do any advertising . . . I mean, they thought they could make an expensive restaurant work without attracting people of a certain level. In Pietralata. The problem is, I tried to tell them, the restaurant couldn't work, people today get information on the Internet, things function differently from how they did in the past . . . Pointless, they didn't even consider my advice. In the end the restaurant failed."

"And that's what created in you . . ."

"Stress," said Manuel, "it created stress. It's not over. Take Bottarolo. I'm the one who invented the formula. Did you know that? I started doing the so-called 'food cost percentage,' I studied a whole series of commercial situations . . . the media campaign . . . *everything*, I studied . . . at that point I go to my brother, because my father would never have listened to me . . . I go to Roberto and suggest this restaurant to him . . . a restaurant with a certain décor, a certain profile, people who could get up from the table and pour the wine directly from the barrels, Roman cooking . . . my sister-in-law designs the logo, my brother finds this appealing name, Dar Bottarolo."

"And so the restaurant starts up."

"In reality, I invented it. At first the three of us worked there. My brother and sister-in-law and I, each with different responsibilities."

"And then?"

"The first five months I worked as a waiter. Then, reading *Millionaire* and other financial magazines I subscribe to, I got the idea of the startup . . . I started going to the restaurant less . . . and so it happens that my father . . ."

"Your father cuts you out?" the prosecutor guessed.

"Ostensibly what my father said was: *We Foffos decide.*

While in fact he was always the one who decided, or he and my brother."

"And you argued about that?"

"No, I just let it go. I devoted myself to the startup. I worked on it like a madman. I was so angry inside that then at night . . . well, I drank."

"Why didn't you have the strength to react?"

"I tried!" said Manuel. "For example, once, some time ago, given that our family relations were always stormy . . . I signed up on the Internet with an employment agency . . . And I went to London to work. I lived in Whitechapel with some other guys . . . I liked it, in the morning I was busy in a café, I made cappuccinos, I carried plates . . . in a few months I was fluent in the language, I even started to dream in English . . . *incredible* . . . dreaming in English . . . I felt good, I was finally independent . . . but at a certain point what happens? My brother calls me and says: *Listen, Manuel, you have to come home, Mamma's sick.*"

"What was wrong with your mother?"

"My mother has problems with stability. Paranoid schizophrenia. Some doctors said so. My brother, in turn, is someone who in these situations . . . he can't suffer by himself . . . If Mamma's sick, he pretends not to see, until he's forced to . . . That's why he asked me to come home . . . And so I came back to Italy."

"You came back for your mother, then."

"After the separation, my mother had to fight with my father for alimony . . . That woman has suffered so much . . ."

"You were bothered by the way your father treated your mother?"

"Of course I was bothered. Imagine, once . . . we were in a restaurant in Belpoggio . . . I remember like it was yesterday . . . my father was talking to my brother . . . My father that day was really spiteful, he said I'd better respect him, because if he let my mother *fall,* psychologically, then I would *fall*, too . . . if one falls the other falls . . . as if there were this bond . . . between her and me, not

between him and me . . . You get the thinking? . . . There's always
been a lot of tension, a lack of sympathy in my family life . . . In
fact some nights when I was a child I'd go to bed and before
falling asleep I'd think: *Either I become a soccer player or there's
going to be trouble.*

AURORA VALENTI

I was on the beach at Ostia with some friends. It was early
August. Manuel and another guy, who's a cop, joined us on the
shore. The cop knew one of my friends. We introduced ourselves.
It started like that.

In Rome we started going out together. He was very quiet.
Some evenings he didn't say anything. If I asked him what was on
his mind, he'd say: *I'm thinking.* Or: *I'm thinking about startups.*
I understood that he had some problems with his father, the fact
that many of his friends were rich wasn't easy for him. His family was well-off, too. Except that Manuel found it hard to ask for
money.

Our sexual relations were absolutely normal.

On the other hand the way they let me into their family life
seemed to me a little ridiculous. Almost immediately I was invited to the baptism of his brother's son. We'd only been together
a very short time. I recall that during the baptism dinner his aunt
came over, looked at me, then looked at Manuel, incredulous and
amazed: *Did you see, Manuel? You've found a fine girl!* She said
it as if it were something extraordinary. Everything seemed to be
happening to Manuel for the first time.

We started going out almost every night. Now and then he'd
stop in a bar and order gin and cola. At first it didn't seem like a
big deal. Another detail did strike me, though. Manuel never had
a car. Never, ever, had a car. When I asked him why, he said he
had loaned it to his mother. Well, what a coincidence, I thought.

I wondered how it was possible that his mother had to take the car whenever I went out with him. I started to ask him questions on questions. Finally, cornered, he confessed that he'd lost his license. Drunk driving. He'd been drinking and crashed into some garbage bins.

Every so often the subject of his father and brother came up. He went as far as telling me that his father had threatened him with death. I didn't think it was true, sometimes Manuel exaggerated. The day of the baptism, for example, I noticed that it was his father who approached him. But Manuel avoided him.

About his mother he told me that she was schizophrenic, and that it was his father's fault if she was ill now.

The business of the alcohol became a problem. Manuel could drink half a carafe of wine in practically a single gulp. He'd empty one glass after another, as if he were always missing something. And he didn't limit himself to wine. Once we had an ugly fight. We'd had dinner at his father's restaurant, and already he'd had half a carafe there. From the restaurant we went to a bar. We sat outside, and he drank gin and cola. I started to get nervous. Among other things, since I don't drink, it seemed disrespectful toward me. Plus I was bored. I threw that in his face, too. He got really angry, raised his voice. So did I. It was a terrible fight. We were causing a spectacle, everyone was looking at us. At a certain point he said if we were going to fight like that, it was better for me to go home. He took the phone and called a taxi. Too bad he couldn't tell the dispatcher even where we were. He was so drunk he couldn't read the address.

Then came the last straw.

One night, after we had dinner together, and then had gone as usual to a bar, we went to sleep at his house. Manuel couldn't sleep. At one point in the middle of the night, he got out of bed and went to the kitchen. He came back in a state of delirium, disoriented. He was muttering incomprehensibly. I asked: *Manuel, what did you do there? Did you take a sleeping pill? Why are you*

226 · NICOLA LAGIOIA

mumbling? And he: *I can't hide anything from you . . . yes, I took a sleeping pill.* He said it in a tone that was still acceptable. Strange but acceptable. I assume it was Valium or something. He came back to bed. But a little later he suddenly jumped out again onto the floor, went to the drawers in the wardrobe, and started opening them furiously, one after the other. He opened the drawers and rummaged through the clothes, he was looking for a bathing suit. *I have to find a bathing suit to put on, otherwise they'll see me!* And I: *Manuel, who will see you?* I was starting to get scared. I had the feeling that something terrible could happen at any moment.

Manuel kept rummaging through the drawers, meanwhile saying to me: *You're a pain in the ass! You're always criticizing me! Like my father and mother! I can't take it anymore!* Then he went into the kitchen again, came back to bed, got under the covers, closed his eyes and finally fell asleep.

The drug, I thought, the drug had this effect.

Now he was sleeping. But I couldn't close my eyes. I was terrified. I wanted to leave. At the same time I felt petrified with fear. So I decided to wait until morning, then I could get out of bed in the normal way, leave the house and not see him anymore.

I just remembered another episode. One night when we had first started seeing one another, I joined him at the family restaurant. I brought a gay friend with me. This friend took a selfie and put it on Facebook. He also tagged the restaurant. The next day Manuel called me. He was angry. He shouted into the phone that I had to tell my friend to absolutely take that photo down, he didn't want people to see *that he hung out with faggots.*

That time, too, we had an ugly fight.

Our relationship must have lasted a year and a half altogether.

ORNELLA MARTINELLI

That night we all went to eat at the Indian restaurant. Then I went back to the B&B. There were guests arriving and I had to take care of them. The others came later. We went into one of the rooms of the B&B and started drinking and talking. I want to make it clear that we didn't take any drugs.

The next morning I found out that Samuele hadn't come home. At that point all hell broke loose.

FULVIO ROSINI

I'm sixty-two, I work at the tax agency. On January 20, 2016, less than two months ago, I reported my son missing at the Vescovio Police Headquarters in Rome. I'm Samuele's father.

SAMUELE ROSINI

I confirm, that night we went to the Indian restaurant. Then we moved on to Ornella Martinelli's B&B. Besides Ornella, Enrico Bevilaqua, Serena Paladino, and Marco Prato were there. We were talking. At some point someone said we needed a bottle of vodka. I offered to go get one. Marco came with me. As soon as we got to the street I noticed a dark silhouette. It was a man, he was looking at us, he was short and had short wavy hair, a foreigner, certainly from Eastern Europe. In fact the man was expecting him.

Marco joined him, they talked a while, then went together to an ATM. The man was evidently a dealer. Marco came back to where I was. Before going to get the vodka we went back into the building. Right there, on the landing, Marco laid down a line on the screen of his phone. He snorted. He also did one for me. I accepted. I shouldn't have, but I was tired, I'd been shut in the house for two months working on my thesis.

We went to get the vodka.

Back at the B&B, we started drinking and talking. I felt on the edge of euphoria, the others were having fun. Marco poured me some vodka, said in a low voice that another line was ready in the bathroom. When I came back from the bathroom, my vodka glass was full again.

Around three in the morning the party started breaking up. I'd told Enrico I'd give him a ride on my scooter. While we were going down the stairs, Marco came up to me, whispered: *Tell me where you live, see you outside for a last snort.* I gave him the address. Not satisfied, I also gave him my phone number.

We went out into the Roman night. I took Enrico home and went back to my house. As I was locking the scooter I realized that Marco Prato's car was already sitting in front of my entrance. Considering what he'd said before, I got in the car. Once inside, however, rather than laying down the coke as I thought he would, he started the car and left. I didn't understand what was happening. I asked him where we were going, I had to work on my thesis the next day and I didn't want to be even later.

Don't worry, he said, *I just don't feel like sitting in the car. I live close by. We'll just be a moment and I'll take you home.*

That's how we ended up at his house.

The apartment was still being renovated, he hadn't finished furnishing it. I sat on a sack of cement near a small table. But there was a fridge, in fact he pulled out another bottle of vodka, poured two glasses, laid out the coke, we started talking again. At a certain point he confided that he wanted to change sex, he wanted to have the surgery, he talked and talked, and in the meantime he kept pouring. Then he started to come on to me. He became more and more insistent. He undid my pants, pulled them down, gave me a blow job. Everything happened right there, on the sack of cement.

At that point I told him I had to go home. *My thesis*, I said. And then I fell asleep.

Or at least I think so. My memory isn't really clear.

What I do remember clearly, though, is that as soon as I woke up Marco asked me for the password of my Facebook account. It seemed that my family was looking for me. I gave him the password, he wrote to my brothers on Messenger. They understood it wasn't me writing, the style was different. I think it was eleven in the morning. The blinds were lowered, you couldn't really tell. I must have fallen asleep again. At a certain point there was Marco with a strange expression, he was staring at the phone screen, he looked worried. Soon afterward, the phone started ringing, Marco answered, handed it to me. It was Enrico Bevilacqua, he told me that my parents had made a report to the police. They thought I'd been kidnapped. I started to get agitated, all hell was breaking loose. I have to recover, I thought. Marco's phone rang again. It was my mother. Marco handed me the phone. I talked to her. I ended the call. I quickly washed my face, put on my jacket, told Marco I had to go.

The next day Marco showed up again. He started sending me messages on WhatsApp. He was angry. He demanded an apology from my parents, he considered it absurd that they had gone to the police, he wasn't a criminal: if that apology didn't arrive, he would "instruct" his lawyers to intervene. I was gripped by anxiety. I called Marco and immediately handed him my mother. They started talking. After a few minutes I heard my mother apologizing to him, I suppose it was a way to end the matter.

Final clarification. I hadn't used drugs for ten years.

The newspapers associated Marco Prato and Manuel Foffo with the cutthroats of Isis. You had to imagine them as urban foreign fighters, they wrote. Some columnists maintained that the killing of Luca Varani recalled the ancient practice of ritual sacrifice, with the difference that in the past the victim died as a result of a social pact intended to placate the anger of the gods, while here, now, there was only disgust and obscene desire, disorder and self-denigration, and a tragic inability of the killers to see anything beyond themselves.

I was in a café on Via Flaminia. I was waiting to find out where to meet the reporter who had promised to let me read the criminal evidence from the prosecutor's office. I was listening to the conversations of the customers at the nearby tables. A few meters away a rather seedy-looking, long-haired man in his sixties, his beard unkempt, was entwining his fingers with those of a much younger, better-looking, and, one would have said, wealthier woman. Not far from them, as if wishing to offer instant compensation, a young man was passionately kissing a woman who seemed to be twice as old as he was. I got the text from the reporter. He would meet me at Termini. I paid. There were moments, I thought, looking at the tables in the café, when the city offered some nice surprises. In Rome social and biographical barriers, aesthetic contrasts could collapse in an instant.

I walked along the Lungotevere. I got to Prati. Having passed the neighborhood of Piazza Mazzini, I realized I was early. So I decided to go down the stairway that leads to the bike path, where the noise of the traffic diminishes, the river runs slowly beside you, the vegetation grows untidily along the banks. Walking, I noticed the carcass of a bicycle stuck on a patch of ground emerging from the gray waters of the Tiber. The shadow of Ponte Umberto I over my head. Again the sky. Some kids were listening to music a few steps from the mud, amid the trees sticking up out of the water. A little farther on there was another bicycle. It was beached on a tiny island. Something kindled in my mind; at first I couldn't bring it into focus, but I knew it was about to upend the sensation I'd had in the café. When, five minutes later, I saw something that might once have been a bicycle but was now a mass of metal, probably burned, or repeatedly kicked and hammered, the situation suddenly became clear. All week, wandering around, I had *continuously* seen abandoned bicycles. Bicycles with the frame bent or broken in two, with the tires destroyed, with the seat bashed in, with the handlebars torn off, bicycles stuck in the ground, thrown under bridges, shoved brutally into trash cans. Bicycles, among other things, perfectly identical. They were so tightly woven into the urban fabric that I hadn't even realized it. They were the models from the new bike-sharing system. For several years, Rome had been trying out bike sharing. First the city had tried it, and failed. Then it was the turn of some foreign companies, American or Chinese multinationals. They announced their project with great pomp, and a few weeks later hundreds of brand-new bikes arrived. After a month, nothing remained of those bikes. The Romans threw them off bridges, burned them, vandalized them in every possible way, destroyed them with a blind, primordial fury.

In a word, they rejected charity. Bringing those bicycles to Rome meant having the arrogance to cure a dying man with some aspirin, it was an insult, a humiliation. Even worse, it was an insistence on attaching to the latest technological novelties a city that had shaken off the concept of progress and was floating in stagnant waters, in a chronological void, like the dust on the

pyramids after the end of Egyptian civilization, with the paradoxical difference that Rome, instead, continued to be bursting
with life.

I met my contact at Termini station. The reporter worked for
a big national paper. He was a man of fifty. We'd known each
other for some years. "So, shall we find a place?" he said. We
settled ourselves in an ugly bar on Via Marsala and ordered a
drink. He took out of his backpack a document of some seventy
pages, which contained the criminal profiles of Marco Prato and
Manuel Foffo, and the so-called victimological analysis of Luca
Varani; obviously, unlike the profiles of those charged, it was the
result of work carried out in absentia, an investigation of someone who was no longer there.

GIUSEPPE VARANI

Let's get to the point, otherwise we'll never understand. Luca went to Collatino in good faith. Understand? Without for a moment imagining what might happen.

How many things have been said, taking advantage of the fact that the victim can't speak. That my son went to prostitute . . . that he went to the apartment for a hundred and twenty euros . . . they've said that. *But who said it*? Luca didn't need money. He worked! That story of prostitution was invented to cover up a party gone bad . . . But I repeat, Prato and Foffo had the party . . . and I repeat, those are the motives . . . The motive was to see a person suffer. It was to *enjoy* that suffering. They enjoyed it, until the end. It has to be said. There has to be an end to it. They said that *he* was a prostitute. But they haven't said who *they* are.

I won't stop until justice is done. Life in prison. There's nothing else to say.

MARIO ACETO

I'm the owner of the car-repair shop in Valle Aurelia where Luca Varani came to learn the job. Besides working for his father, obviously. He was a willing kid, a good kid. I think he had some debts with the government for something about unpaid taxes.

On March 4 he sent me some WhatsApp messages saying he

wasn't coming to work. The next day his father called me. They couldn't find him.

Luca never asked to borrow money. At most I advanced him some small sums that came out of his salary, we're talking ten or fifteen euros. I never thought he used drugs. It's something I always get straight with people who work for me: I don't want people who take drugs.

ANTONELLA ZANETTI

That morning I ran into Luca Varani. I've known him for years, we were at school together. I ran into him on the way to work, because as it happens we take the same train. That morning we met at the bar at the La Storta-Formello station. I got coffee, he bought cigarettes. We had a chat, I asked how he was. Good, he said. We got on the same train. I sat where I usually sit, while he went to the upper section, where there are outlets, because he had to charge his phone. Between Appiano and Valle Aurelia, a quarter of an hour later, he nodded to me from the stairs. I went over. He asked me for information about getting to Tiburtina. I didn't know if he had to go to the station or just the neighborhood. Then we said goodbye and have a good weekend, and didn't see each other again.

EDOARDO PETRONI

Luchetto, that was his nickname. I met him in a rather odd way. I was on a bus, at some point it was just the two of us. I mean he and I were alone on the bus. We started talking. We talked about our girlfriends and other things. He was nice, chill, friendly, it was a pleasant conversation. After that I didn't see him for a while. I saw him again when I started hanging out with a group in the Battistini neighborhood, near the metro stop.

As far as I knew him, Luca was a guy with a weak character. He spent the little money he had on the slot machines because the people around him told him to. They told him to play. Or simply he saw them playing, and that was enough.

After that summer I stopped hanging out with the group, partly because it's far from my house, I'm at Casal del Marmo, partly because Luca and I had a fight. Actually, I hit on Marta Gaia. I haven't seen him since.

I read the news of his death on Facebook, then I saw the papers and I can say with absolute certainty that the two guys suspected of the murder weren't part of our group.

MARTA GAIA SEBASTIANI

Everyone asked me *How can you say you'll love him forever?* I answered simply *I know and that's all.* That answer wasn't enough, so I patiently started listing all the reasons I knew absolutely that Luca would be the one, but it still wasn't enough, people made fun of me, I saw mocking faces that said: *For sure you'll break up, you know how many guys you'll meet over time?*

It's true, I've met a lot of guys, I've talked to a lot, I've laughed with almost all of them, but he was the only one who left me speechless, simply because he understood everything about me just by looking at me, and it's not easy to communicate without saying anything, if you do then it means there's something great between you and that person.

Look, I'd like to tell you that if you've never loved a person so much, then don't insult the feelings of someone who's put mind, time, heart, and soul into it. I'm a dreamer, I think all people have some good deep down, I live with the hope that one day things will change for the better. No one can root out of my mind the belief that Luca would have been the one.

(From a post published on Facebook April 10, 2016)

ALICE PEPE

I met Luca in early November. I remember because during that period, November 17 to be exact, I became Filippo Mancini's girlfriend. I live in Muratella, I'm seventeen, I'd see Luca Varani in Battistini, in a café near a school, or we'd meet at the McDonald's in Cornelia. He worked at the shop in Valle Aurelia, he got off around six, we'd meet afterward. He didn't talk much about his job, but he complained about money, he would have liked to take his girlfriend out to dinner, give her presents, but he didn't make much money and he couldn't manage to save anything.

At the time he was sick about Marta Gaia. They had temporarily split up just the day we met. I don't really know what happened.

He was cheerful, likable, when we met he said he felt better because I made his smile come back. He never dressed ostentatiously. In fact, since he wasn't with Marta Gaia, he was even a bit untidy. Then, when they got together again, I think in January, he was a lot better. Of course at that point he stopped hanging out with the group so much. She was jealous.

He was comfortable with us from Battistini. He especially got along with Filippo Mancini. They'd known each other a long time. I met Filippo when he was working in a pizzeria in Casalotti; later he was fired and didn't look for another job.

The last time I saw Luca was after my birthday. I'd already broken up with Filippo. Luca was in Cornelia. He was alone. Maybe he was waiting for Marta Gaia.

MARTA GAIA SEBASTIANI

Hi everyone!!!!!
Tonight my interview is being broadcast on RAI 3, on *Chi l'ha visto?* I don't know at exactly what time (very likely the episode

will begin with it), but from what I've understood they will be talking at several points about Luca in a way that gives him voice and lets him be seen and live through my eyes and my words. My profound thanks to the staff and to those who will watch the broadcast tonight.

(Post published on Facebook April 13, 2016)

"Luca is the person I would have shared my life with," said Marta Gaia to the camera, "I've never been in love with anyone else. I said to him: *Only your eyes are more beautiful than the stars*. I just had to look at him to be happy. I know he was a guy like many others, but for me he was everything."

"What were your plans?" asked the interviewer.

"He wanted to marry me. He said every day: *Come on, let's get married, even in secret from everybody*."

"How long were you together?"

"Nine years. Luca didn't like studying much," a smile touched the girl's lips, "but eventually he'd decided to go to night school. His parents are peddlers who sell candy. Luca said as an adult he'd like to continue that work. He liked being with people."

"Was Luca what Manuel Foffo and Marco Prato say about him?" the reporter asked at one point.

When the interviews got to that moment, the atmosphere usually changed. "No, that isn't Luca," the girl said, darkening. "They're talking about someone else. It's not my Luca."

"But we know that Marco Prato had his phone number."

"I didn't know that." Her gaze conveyed intense suffering.

"What was Luca's relationship with money?"

"He loved to earn it in order to spend it, like everyone else, otherwise what are we going to work for . . ." sad Marta, a little bewildered.

"I asked you that question," the interviewer explained, "for a precise reason. On the morning of March 4 Marco Prato sent Luca a text in which he referred to possible earnings. He talks about a hundred and twenty euros. Would Luca sell himself for a hundred and twenty euros?"

"No. Never," said the girl. "He wouldn't sell himself for any figure in the world. Absolutely not."

"So, in your view, and it's a question that many are asking, what really happened that morning? Why did he go to those two people?"

"Honestly, I don't know. I ask myself that question every day, and I find no answer."

VALERIA PROIETTI

I'm nineteen, I live near Torresina, I've known Luca Varani for about a year. I know he worked. I also know he had a girlfriend. I don't know her. But I saw Luca when he called Marta Gaia. When he talked on the phone with her he often lied, he'd say he was at school when in fact he was with us in Battistini. Every so often he disappeared for say an hour, he went to see a gay friend of his. We thought he went to have sex, maybe in exchange for money. I think that because once I read some messages where Luca said he had to go and get like thirty euros. I saw those messages just in a flash, I saw the number of the person he was writing to, on the phone it was saved as "fag." And anyway he didn't always go there, to that guy.

"It was Damiano Parodi who introduced me to Luca Varani," Marco Prato said to the prosecutor. "Damiano went to my events. He's a well-to-do person, very well-to-do. Homosexual. Sometimes he resorts to paid sex, in certain circumstances with cocaine added. I took part. Not in paid sex but I was at some of those parties. It must have been October or November. I saw Luca for the first time there. We met at Damiano's, in Piazza Ungheria. Luca went to see him more or less every week. Damiano gave him

money even without having sexual relations. You see," he continued, "Damiano suffers from an obsessive-compulsive disorder, I
think he gave Luca money out of fear."

DAMIANO PARODI

I'm a student who hasn't finished at the LUISS, in law.
Although I'm enrolled in the university I haven't finished my
studies because of the illness I'm being treated for in both Milan
and Rome. I live in Rome, my parents live in Lugano, I'm thirty
years old, I suffer from an obsessive-compulsive disorder.

I met Marco Prato one night last October through my friend
Angelo Vecchio.

That night Angelo and I had gone dancing at the Lanificio.
Afterward we went to my house, in Piazza Ungheria. Since breaking up with my boyfriend I've lived there alone. Marco Prato
arrived late, invited by Angelo. Later Luca Varani also arrived, invited in turn by Andrea. This Andrea is a guy of twenty-five who I
had a paid sexual encounter with, around the end of September.
In other words, a prostitute. Andrea picked me up near Piazza
dei Cinquecento. So in fact Varani was brought by Andrea, while
Angelo invited Prato. That's how Prato and Varani met.

Marco had some cocaine, we drank and snorted, for me it was
the second or third time. Soon the house began to fill with people.
Two drag queens also showed up. The situation was starting to
get a little out of hand. Marco was sulking on the balcony. An old
friend of mine, Ivan Beretta, also arrived, and was, to say the least,
rather disconcerted. At a certain point Andrea said in front of everyone that Luca was a prostitute, too, he added that Luca's was
bigger than his, and so Luca, to give a practical demonstration,
pulled down his pants. We were all drunk. People began to leave.

Marco I saw a month later, he came to see me again in Piazza
Ungheria. For the occasion we bought three hundred euros' worth

of cocaine. A guy named Armando provided the cocaine, the trusted dealer, so to speak. Armando was around forty, brown hair cut short, five-six at most. Because of a sort of handicap that I didn't understand, he couldn't drive a car, so he insisted we pay the cost of the taxi, a request that we always satisfied. Armando isn't Italian, he told me he's an Albanian reporter persecuted in his country. Marco had him in his contacts as Trovajoli. Armando Trovajoli.

But let's get to our last encounters. In late February Marco and I went dancing at the Qube. At the end of the evening we went to my house, Marco called the dealer, Armando arrived with the coke. We ordered some alcohol, then we used Grindr to try to get in touch with some guys. We couldn't find anyone who would come to the house. A little later, however, someone rang the doorbell, I went to open it and found two guys I'd never seen before. They introduced themselves as friends of Marco, they were both named Alessandro, one was called Alexander because he was of German origin, and the other "Alessandro the Japanese," because he had some clearly Asian features. After asking Marco to confirm that he knew them—he did—I let them in. We used cocaine, drank alcohol. I had oral sex with Alexander, performed by me on him. Then Marco and Alexander locked themselves in my study, while I stayed to talk with the Japanese. We talked about a lot of things. Alessandro the Japanese is straight.

When I returned to my study, I noticed that Marco and Alexander had broken a blind. Alessandro the Japanese, before leaving, asked to borrow some sunglasses. I was very fond of those glasses, they were maybe the only ones I could bear, I don't know why I ended up giving them to him. The next day I tried to get them back, I asked Marco to get in touch with Alessandro the Japanese, I asked for his number. But no, Marco wouldn't give it to me.

A couple of days ago I realized that two rings were missing. The rings were kept in the study where Marco and Alexander had locked themselves in. The first is a gold ring from my mother, inherited from my grandmother, worth ten thousand euros. The

THE CITY OF THE LIVING · 241

second ring has great sentimental value for me, it was a ring going back to ancient Rome, also gold, with a stone set in it, I have a picture of my grandfather wearing it. These two rings were shut in a metal drawer under the desk. I'm sure those two stole them, I'm thinking of lodging a formal complaint of theft, obviously in addition to the mess that happened with the ATM.

IVAN BERETTA

When Damiano told me that Marco Prato had let him take some drugs I was worried. Damiano is a very dear friend, he was my partner until the summer of 2015. He suffers from an obsessive-compulsive disorder, he takes medicine, and I think mixing it with cocaine is dangerous.

I know that Marco and Damiano had started hanging out, I knew about the coke, but I wanted to understand the situation better, so that Saturday night I went directly to Piazza Ungheria. I found the remains of a party, there were bottles scattered everywhere. Besides Damiano and Marco, there were also two guys I didn't know, two very young guys, one I think was foreign. I asked Damiano to send them away: they appeared to be gigolos. Then I took Marco Prato aside and told him to leave Damiano alone, also because I had never seen people like that there.

I'm afraid that Damiano was in a situation of psychological subjugation. I also thought that, since I left him, he'd been lonely. And so Marco took advantage of that.

FILIPPO MANCINI

I'm the only one who knows where things stood.

My name is Filippo, I'm nineteen, I live in La Storta, I've known Luca a long time. My friendship with Luchetto was reinforced one day when—I was at the bus stop as usual—he offered me a ride in his car. He had a white Micra. I was coming back from Montespaccato to meet my friends. From that day on, Luca was one of our group of friends.

In the group Luca talked to everyone, but he became friends with me in particular. I think because we have a similar character. We're both very simple, and in particular we don't hang out with people out of self-interest.

Over time Luca did some things that cemented our bond. I reciprocated because it was a true friendship. For example he drove me to my girlfriend's, and waited until I came back. In turn, I left the auto-repair shop where I worked, and he started there thanks to my suggestion. In fact I quit to leave the place for him.

In the period when I met him he was sleeping in the car because he he'd had a fight with his father, but I don't know about what.

When I was interviewed for the broadcast *Chi l'ha visto?* I said Luca didn't work as a prostitute, I did it out of respect for him. He had started for the money. He said: *Oh, please, bro . . . don't say anything to anyone.* Luca was the type who even if you left ten thousand euros on a table and went away he wouldn't steal it, he would never do it, he didn't do those things, but this other thing, unfortunately he'd started to do, maybe it seemed more "honest," given that he needed money.

I realized it about a year ago. It was the spring of 2015. Luca went to the house of someone in Selva Nera, in the new buildings. I don't know who this guy is. Someone older than us, I think he was thirty-five. Luca would go there, and I went with him. When we got to the building, I'd stay and wait for him, and he came back every time after an hour with a hundred euros. The first times he said vaguely that this guy owed him money, but in the long run that didn't hold up. So the third time I asked him to tell me what he was really doing in Selva Nera. It wasn't hard to understand what was happening, but he should have told me. So he did. I'm sure that Marta Gaia knew nothing about this business.

At a certain point Luca had a fight with the man in Selva Nera, I think it was a question of money.

Then came Marco Prato and Damiano Parodi, and another period, so to speak, began.

"May I ask you a question?" Flaminia Bolzan asked Marco Prato.

Flaminia Bolzan, age twenty-nine, was the criminologist whom Scavo had named as the consultant for the prosecutor's office.

"Of course," said Marco.

"What did you think of Luca Varani?"

"In what sense?"

"On a human level," said Bolzan.

"I didn't know him well enough," said Marco. "But at Damiano's house, as we were talking while taking drugs, he started telling us too flippantly about his double life. That bothered me, it wounded me because I thought of his girlfriend."

"Do you remember ever having called him *a whore with a second-grade education*?"

The phrase ("I'm not a whore with a second-grade education") had been used by Marco in a WhatsApp exchange with Damiano Parodi. According to Parodi, Marco was referring to Luca.

"*A whore with a second-grade education.* Jeez . . . I don't know," said Marco. "It seems a little too caustic for my . . . ."

"We're just saying," Scavo interrupted, "that you didn't have a high regard for Luca Varani."

"From what point of view, Mr. Scavo?" said Marco. "On an intellectual level obviously no, I didn't have a high regard for him. But Luca was a cheerful person, he was someone who was always laughing, that I will never forget. Once I went to a costume party, at a friend of mine's, a very special party, there were various important people, that friend of mine is a big lawyer. I was disguised as a TV showgirl, I had been made up professionally, I even had fake boobs . . . When the party was over I got in touch with Luca, and we met. As soon as he saw me, Luca started showering me with compliments, he said I was *fascinating*. That really pleased me, so it seems strange that later I would have put him down. Of course, intellectually it's likely that I didn't have respect for him, but I would separate the human level from the intellectual."

"You didn't consider him a person who would satisfy all your desires as soon as you asked him?" Scavo asked. "In short, he wasn't, for you, a weak individual who would acquiesce in . . ."

"Not really," Marco interrupted him. "On the contrary. A kid who grows up on the outskirts, who deals, who's a prostitute, well . . . that's an individual a person like me should *fear*, not consider weak. Someone like me could think that someone like him could be armed, or anyway violent. But I thought that for money Luca would do anything. I knew his financial situation. I knew he had family problems. Luca confided in me."

FILIPPO MANCINI

One night, a Thursday or Friday, I went with him to Piazza Ungheria, but first we went to pick up a guy named Andrea. That guy was waiting for us on the benches in the metro. I don't know how Luca had met him. I think he's Tunisian.

That night I'd gone out with a girl named Giorgia, a girl from Milan who'd come to Rome on vacation. I never saw her again and didn't even have time to ask for her phone number. I was driving, she was sitting next to me, Andrea and Luca were in the back. Andrea asked if I could take him to Piazza Ungheria, he had to get some money, then he asked to borrow my phone. I gave it to him. I heard him say: *Can you give me Damiano?*

When we got to Piazza Ungheria, Luca unexpectedly got out with Andrea, he asked me to come back and get him around midnight.

Unexpectedly—not entirely. During the trip, Luca and Andrea were whispering. But I heard them. I heard the phrase "blow jobs" clearly.

After midnight Luca started calling me. Three, four, five calls. At first I didn't hear because I'd ended up at a party on the other side of town, I'd gone with the girl from Milan. Then I saw the calls.

I went back to Piazza Ungheria, it might have been one-thirty. I got out of the car, I looked around, I went to the intercom and pressed the same bell I'd seen Andrea press. I expected an unknown voice would answer. Instead Luca answered. I said: *Come on man, come down, it's late.* In a kind of strange voice, he said: *Hey man . . . listen, I'm staying here, but anyway I'm coming down a sec and I'll bring you the money.* He meant money for gas. I said: *Hey man, why are staying there? If your father catches you he'll give you a beating.* It was late and his father was very strict. Among other things it was important for Luca to come with me because I didn't have a license. I told him that through the intercom, the thing about the license, he answered that I could let the girl from Milan drive. Yeah, sure. The fact was that the girl from Milan had left. I asked Luca to let me come up, at that point I wanted to see what was going on. He said: *No no, I'm coming down a second, you can't come up.*

Except that instead of Luca coming down, Marco Prato appeared. He looked me up and down. And I looked him up and down. He handed me twenty euros and said: *This is from Luca.* I asked why Luca hadn't come down. *Because Luca's busy and doesn't want to come down,* he said. I was starting to understand the situation, so I let him know that I, too, was "open," I'm referring to drugs. More than anything I wanted to see what was happening upstairs. Marco Prato said: *Wait.* He disappeared into the building and returned with a bag of cocaine. It must have been five grams. He suggested doing a line, I said O.K., he laid out a little on his phone, we had this snort, and only at that point he invited me up. *Come on,* he said, *I talked to Luca before, I know we can trust you.*

So we went up. A guy around thirty-five opened the door. It was his place. Damiano. It was clear from his voice that he was gay. Then I heard the voices of Andrea and Luca. You couldn't not hear them, because they were arguing. They were yelling violently. They went by me, they left the house shouting. I ran down the stairs after them, Andrea was really furious, he was saying that Luca had taken more than him, they'd given Luca a hundred and him only forty, and to say that he had introduced those clients. Luca tried to hand him twenty euros, Andrea grabbed the bill and tore it in his face, he told Luca he shouldn't behave like that, then he turned on his heels and left.

At that point, we should have left, too. Instead we went back up to get Luca's stuff, jacket and backpack.

But as soon as we got there Marco led us to a room with a lot of books, a couch, and a small table. Basically, it was a study. Marco got out the coke and started preparing four lines. Someone poured vodka in glasses. I barely tasted it because vodka makes me sick. We started to snort. This went on for a while, each time Marco prepared three big lines for us and a small one for Damiano, I don't think Damiano understood a thing about this stuff. Marco took advantage of the situation. More than once, that night, he went to get money with Damiano's bank card.

Damiano didn't try hitting on me. He asked if I was bisexual, I said I had a girlfriend, and that was sufficient. But Marco, after the second line, began to bother me. He said: *What do you think, you came to get free coke? At least you have to have a blow job, we gays do it better than girls* . . . But I pretty quickly shook him off. Those games don't appeal to me. I let Marco understand that if he just tried to get close to me there'd be trouble. He didn't even graze me.

But then Marco approached Luca, and Luca pulled down his pants, also his underpants, and stayed like that, with his dick out. I lost it, the scene shocked me, I yelled at them to do those things somewhere else, even though I was then the one who left the room. I stayed in the hall doing nothing. After a while I tried knocking, they didn't respond. I opened the door, I found them in the same situation as before.

At that point I went into the living room, turned on the TV, and lay down on the couch. Damiano went into the bedroom. Marco and Luca were still shut in the study.

We took off when Damiano's ex arrived. Luca and I said good-bye, went downstairs, got in the car, and left.

Of the hundred euros that Luca had earned that night, Andrea had ripped up twenty, we used ten to buy cigarettes, the twenty he had given me for gas we played on the slots, so all he had left was a fifty-euro bill.

We never talked about that night again, because that stuff makes me sick.

M y journalist friend ordered a second coffee. Sitting across from him, I continued to page through the report from Flaminia Bolzan, the prosecutor's criminologist. The document revealed how the murder had no functional purpose; it had been carried out in a disorderly way—apart from the location of the crime, a carefully chosen place, intimate, familiar, inaccessible to outsiders—with an impressive amount of brutality and cruelty.

Referring to Marco Prato, the evaluation mentioned "psychic withdrawal." It was a mental state that led to alienation from a reality considered intolerable. (In Marco's case, that intolerability, the report maintained, could be associated with the weak or failed perception of a male self owing to childhood problems, perhaps stemming from his relationship with his parents.) So it was a "withdrawal" into an ecstatic dimension that found in perversion a possible way in.

For Manuel Foffo the evaluation hypothesized the presence of narcissistic and paranoid features due to a long-held frustration: the wounds tied to family rejections, whether actual or perceived, could have generated in him grandiose fantasies destined to shatter continuously against the reality principle.

I went on to read about Luca Varani.

"Varani did not have a high-school diploma or the skills necessary to find a better-paying job than the one he had in the car-repair shop," the criminologist wrote. "Probably he didn't have even the relational skills necessary to deal with a context different from the one he came from, or the possibility of entering one except as a *rent boy*." Leaving aside the assumption that no victim deserves to be

one ("he asked for it" is always nonsense), Luca Varani, the criminologist explained, risked being a sort of ideal victim for Prato and
Foffo. His social class, financial weakness, way of life, character,
physical constitution, lack of skills and diplomas, and, in addition,
the way he related to Marco when he tried to ask for money—an
approach "from inferior to superior," the report noted—made it
more likely that Luca would fall into the trap, compared with those
who had been in the apartment before him.

The WhatsApp conversations, taken from Marco Prato's cell
phone, seemed to confirm this type of dynamic.

"Can you come to Piazza Ungheria tonight with Andrea?"
Marco asked Luca in one of the exchanges. "I don't think so,"
Luca answered. And Marco: "Why not? I'll pay you!" And Luca:
"What time?"

In another conversation it was again Marco looking for Luca:
"How are you? What are you doing?" Luca answered: "I'm up,
tell me." And Marco: "I'm at Damiano's, snorting a lot of coke and
drinking. If you have nothing to do, come by." Luca answered:
"No thanks, I'm not interested in that life anymore. I just need
money. So thanks anyway Marco and thanks the same anyway to
Damiano." But then, a few minutes later, it was Luca who wrote:
"I need 50 euros: if there's that I'll come by. In fact, you know what
there is, I'll come by anyway."

Another time it was Luca who got in touch with Marco: "Evening,
friend, can you help me? I have a gram of snow to give away. You
need it now?" Marco answered: "No, Luke, I don't need it." And
Luca: "Shit, I need 50 euros for a doctor's appointment." Marco cut
off the matter concisely: "Luche', I don't hand out money."

When I got to the WhatsApp message that Luca had felt the
need to write to Marco the night of Christmas Eve ("Very best
wishes to you and your family"), I realized my vision was blurred.

"Hello? Anyone there?" my journalist friend asked impatiently.

The fact is that I felt angry, I had the impression that in Luca
a conflict was playing out from which he periodically emerged

defeated. He would have avoided seeing Marco, but he ended up by giving in. Marco had in turn developed an uncommon capacity to recognize in others hesitation, weakness, he knew whether to go on the attack or lie in wait. But the point wasn't even that—I thought while my journalist friend looked at me with a bewildered expression—the true reason for my frustration had to do with the mechanism in which we were all in danger of ending up. Murder casts its light on victim and killer, and it's always a partial light, a perverse light, murder is evil and evil is the narrator of the story. Murder casts light on itself to leave the rest in shadow, so that victim and killer are confused in the exceptionality of the event. Seeing the murderers as monsters keeps us from approaching them at the emotional level; reducing the victim to the extraordinary nature of his fate distances him from our empathy. Drug dealing and prostitution were activities alien to the habits of ordinary people; it was hard to recognize oneself in Luca through them. But outside that deceptive cone of light, there was the rest: Luca who worked in the car-repair shop, Luca who warmed a plate of pasta at home, Luca who talked with Marta Gaia, Luca up against his old teachers. And yet even that, I thought—extracting the right cards from the deck, going in search of Luca's moments of ordinary life to provoke a recognition—was offensive, since it put the victim into the aberrant situation of having to provide evidence. The innocent victim doesn't require proof, his body is sacred. If the narrator, that is to say the plot of the murder, seeks to distort our gaze (leading us, on the one hand, not to feel love for the victim, on the other to delude ourselves that what we despise in the murderer is alien to us) we should redouble our efforts to free ourselves from that trap. We should love the victim without needing to know anything about him. We should know a lot about the murderer to understand that the distance separating us from him is less than we think. This second motive we learn, it's the result of an education. The first is much more mysterious.

"Will you explain what the hell you find so interesting about this case?" asked the journalist again, after finishing his coffee.

More than once Luca confided to me that he didn't like Marco. He was polite, smart, very nice and humble. I think he worked as a prostitute because he needed money, not, certainly, for pleasure. More than once he asked me for a loan. More than once I satisfied his request, I'd give him twenty or thirty euros. Sometimes he'd ask directly for a hundred and fifty euros, and then he'd lower the amount. He let it be understood that he would pay me back on the sexual level. Often he said he needed the money to take his girlfriend out to dinner. He inspired tenderness in me, and I was fond of him, even though I'd seen him only a few times. He said he was very attached to this girl, I think they'd been together since they were children.

If Marco said I loaned him the money out of fear he's wrong. I was never afraid of Luca Varani.

Yes, it's true, I think he sold drugs. As early as the first times I saw him he told me that if I wanted to find cocaine better than what Trovajoli brought, I could ask him. He would provide it from a mysterious guy who worked in that world. I have no idea if it's true. I never went to him to buy coke.

Every so often Luca came with that Filippo. Filippo also offered to sell me drugs, but I always said no.

I gave Luca a Rolex. A fake Rolex, belonging to my father. He looked at it, so I gave it to him. *Go on, take it*, I said. Naturally I told him it was a fake. He didn't bat an eye. *I think I can make some money*, he said.

"*Guys, I do everything, but I'm a top*. About that he was always clear," Marco Prato said to Scavo. "He could penetrate me, I could perform fellatio on him, I could lick him from head to toe, he could pee on me, he could do a ton of things to me—sex has infinite nuances—but he would never suck me, and he would never be sodomized. He was really categorical. I think that's how he drew the line that separated his normal life from his secret life, and in his own eyes he preserved his heterosexuality. Provided the line between *topping* and *bottoming* wasn't crossed, in other words, Luca could continue to be with his girl as a heterosexual."

FILIPPO MANCINI

The next time was a few days later. Luca and I were together in the shop when the call came. He asked me to take him to Prati. He had to go to someone's house. We left the auto shop, got in the car. We arrived at the meeting place. Luca got out and asked me to wait for him. I waited for more than half an hour. Then I called him. He didn't answer. I got nervous. We had to get back to the shop. After other attempts, finally he answered, he said: *Go on, go, they'll take me back.*

In the next months we didn't see each other much. Luca had gone back with Marta Gaia, and she was very jealous, so he showed up less often in the group. But I think Damiano continued to give him money. Luca told me that sometimes, when Damiano wasn't home, he left the money right under the doormat.

A lot of that money Luca then played on the slot machines.

I'm pretty sure I saw him for the last time at the Joker, which is a gambling arcade. I remember because that day I must have lost almost seven hundred euros. Luca was there playing by himself. Before leaving he gave me thirty euros for a taxi. I played that on the slots as well.

The next Saturday his father called me. He said that Luca

hadn't come home, they'd been unable to find him for two days. Then I wrote him: *Hey man, where the fuck are you? Your father called me, he says you haven't been home, let me know and call me.*

I no longer have the messages I exchanged with Luca. I got rid of my SIM card because I decided to cut off my old group. I changed my life. I also changed cities. I've been working in a shopping mall in Verona for two weeks.

And so December 31 arrived. Marco and Manuel met. That night, Lorenza, my girlfriend, and I had dinner at the house of a friend of my brother. Other friends had decided to go with Manuel to eat at Bottarolo. When our respective dinners were over, we all went on to the New Year's Eve event Marco Prato had organized at the Quirinetta. It was there, so to speak, that the two story lines converged.

"So look," said Manuel Foffo, "I met Marco the morning of January 1. I spent the evening with friends, then decided to go to my house with some of them. Marco Prato introduced himself there, I'd never seen him, he was a friend of Lorenza's. We started talking, we talked about this and that, sniffed a little coke. At a certain point, since I didn't have any liquor at home, Prato said: *Who's coming to buy some vodka?* Since I knew the area, I offered to go with him. We went out, bought the vodka. On the way back, Marco Prato goes: *Hey, what would you think if I take another little hit?* He was referring to the cocaine. *I'll take another little hit, but then can I stay at your house?* I still didn't get it."

"You had no idea . . ." said Scavo.

"That he was hitting on me? I didn't get it."

"And how did Marco do it? Did he touch you? Or did he hit on you just with words?"

"No, no, what do you mean words . . . Marco got close,

and started touching. And I . . . you see . . . even though I had never had a homosexual fantasy in my life, even though basically the thing also made me a little sick in spite of all that I got hard."

Trains entered Termini continuously. The few taxis in Piazza dei Cinquecento were stormed by travelers who had just arrived in the city. The noise rose slowly from the street. The Dutch tourist observed the sunset from the window. The television antennas. Two magnificent clouds above the old water tower. The tramps along the marble railings. The Chinese in their shops. From the stairwell cries continued to rise. Cries of indignation. Cries of pleasure. The television antennas turned red, sparkled, then fell back into their usual color. The sun had disappeared.

The Dutch tourist opened the window, the evening breeze caressed his face. A city where everything has already happened. After a week here in Rome, the president of the United States would become just another schmuck. Those who need illusions should avoid long stays in the city. In Rome the powerful look in the mirror and see a skull, the knowledge that we are all destined for shadow. That after Augustus is Tiberius. That every man has a price. That the flesh is weak, that a one-armed window-washer works at the intersection of Via di Porta Maggiore and Viale Manzoni.

The woman on the floor below continued to moan. She stopped pretending, she burst into a long laugh.

A triumph of offal and wine stretched with water. Eternal void of memory.

The Dutch tourist heard footsteps on the stairs coming closer and closer. He heard a knock at the door. The door opened and the boy appeared.

He was dark, thin, curly-haired. Wearing jeans and a pale cotton sweater. Libyan, maybe Egyptian or Tunisian. He wasn't more than fifteen. The Dutch tourist took his hand out of his pocket, showed him the 50-euro bill. The boy started to undress. No frills. He couldn't do without the boy's body, the boy couldn't do without his money.

"Shower first," he said in English.

The boy nodded without smiling.

W ill you explain to me what the hell you find so interesting about this case?"

When I was seventeen, I didn't say to the journalist, I almost murdered a girl I didn't know. The next summer I ran a similar risk. The fact is that I was very angry. My parents had divorced when I was five and they struggled to deal with the situation. At the time I lived in Bari. I won't list the silences, the lies, the low blows, the attempts of my father and mother to hurt each other. I will say only that they were not prepared to confront the situation, and obviously I wasn't. At the time, in certain parts of Italy, divorced families carried a social stigma. We came from a small town, where censure could be fierce. My parents found themselves up against the hostility of friends, even of relatives. My distress was so great that in school, in first grade, I lied totally. I said that my parents were still together. I sustained this fiction until middle school. It was painful, embarrassing, the end of middle school was like a liberation: a few months, I thought, and a new school would allow me to start over. The first day of high school, however, I found three of my middle-school classmates in my class. Luck was no help. I thought it over, but I didn't have the strength to do anything, I let the others speak for me, condemning myself to keep the fiction going, with the aggravating circumstance that constructing his social life on a lie was an adolescent who at the end of high school would be an adult. I felt trapped.

If I reflect on it now it all seems so implausible, but at the time there was nothing truer in my life. I spent days of anguish, I didn't know what my classmates or teachers had intuited, and I wondered, among other things, if my parents were aware of the situation. If they weren't, they were blind. If, on the other hand, they knew, why didn't they help me get out of it? Later, to my surprise, I realized that my parents not only were aware of the situation—although they continually tried to forget about it—but encouraged it. Rather than help me get free of the lie, they backed me up, so to speak, with their silence. They were even more ashamed than I was. I started drinking. Also in that period, I started going out at night. Bari was an open-minded city, cosmopolitan in its way, at least compared to the small town we came from. On the one hand I hung out with my contemporaries in the city. On the other, the situation I'd got myself into made me feel inferior. At night I got drunk. I drank and shouted at the top of my lungs. Or I drank and blacked out on the street. At first my friends found these exhibitions interesting. Very soon things got complicated.

One evening in June, one of those magnificent Adriatic summer evenings, there was a party on the top floor of a building in Via Camillo Rosalba. I was there with some friends. After drinking everything I could find in the owner's fridge, I started raving, I took some people who were dancing aside and said some very strange things. I don't know what I could have been talking about. But I remember very well when I began throwing bottles off the terrace. Five or six vodka bottles, which I grabbed one after another and hurled into the void, eight floors down. I started dancing again. The intercom was ringing madly. Ten minutes later I was cornered by a furious girl calling me a dickhead. Other people began yelling at me. I was surprised, I didn't understand what was happening. What happened, they explained to me, was that that that girl was walking on Via Camillo Rosalba when, suddenly, a few meters away a vodka bottle had crashed on the pavement. The girl had yelled. Ten seconds later a second bottle had smashed on the ground, then a third, terrifying her but luckily leaving her unharmed. The girl had burst into the party just to see the imbecile who had nearly killed her. She was wearing a white T-shirt and overalls. She railed at me with such rage that, in my drunken fog, the fact that someone was giving me all that attention charmed me. I muttered a declaration of love. It all sounded ridiculous. I was so insecure, and at the same time so exhilarated, that I wanted to sweep away the already nonexistent possibility of success. "Fuck you!" she shouted before leaving.

There were other episodes. The next week, in the middle of the night, after drinking too many bottles of beer, I climbed on a scooter, forcing four friends to get on with me. We crashed into a garbage truck. Two months later, more bottle throwing. This time I was on a train going to Calabria, I was going camping in Sibari for the summer vacation. During the trip I got drunk (Cointreau) and threw the empty bottle out the window. A little later a man started hitting me. The bottle had struck a pylon a few meters from the tracks, a rain of glass had hit the travelers, coming in through the window of the next compartment. "What have you got in your head, shit?" the man shouted. And I, completely drunk: "Yes! Shit! Shit!" Arriving in Sibari, I was expelled from the campsite in a few days for destroying some garden lights by throwing rocks. I remember the night spent in the station.

We come to 1991. I was in twelfth grade, I barely did any studying, I had a girlfriend. I stubbornly continued to maintain the fiction. My girlfriend was in the dark about everything. My mother had had a new relationship for years. My father had remarried and had two other children. It's easy to imagine the complications of having to hide all this from a girl I saw two or three times a week, with whom I talked and exchanged confidences and tried to take to bed whenever my parents (yes, but in what sense?) weren't home. On a Sunday in late May one of the friends who were reckless enough to hang out with me, Cristiano, invited me to lunch at his house. His parents were gone, and so, when we got to the house, we immediately were able to take advantage of the situation. We emptied into a large salad bowl three bottles of rum and five cans of Coca-Cola. We drank it all with stupefying speed. Drunk, we decided to seal our friendship with a blood pact. Cristiano got a pocket knife and tried to cut his wrist. The attempts were timid, there wasn't a drop of blood. Impatient, I said, "Let me do it." "O.K.," he said. Encouraged by his answer, I grabbed a big kitchen knife, of the type used for cutting bread. For demonstration purposes I began making some cuts in my left forearm. I kept going with determination until the blood began dripping. "Give me your arm," I said to Cristiano. I struck him two or three times, until the blood flowed. The sight of blood exhilarated us. He said: "Now we need a human sacrifice." I saw him disappear into his room. A few minutes later, he returned brandishing *The Name of the Rose*, by Umberto Eco. His literature teacher had forced him to read it during Christmas vacation, he had hated it, now he wanted to get revenge. "Let's kill Umberto Eco!" We took the kitchen knife we'd used for the blood pact and started stabbing the book, reducing it to shreds. At that point, maybe three in the afternoon, I remembered I had a date with my girlfriend. "We have to go get her," I whined. "We can't," said Cristiano, "we're drunk." "I'll drive, I feel like it." "You don't have a license," he reminded me. "I have a permit," I corrected him. Certain stories about young men are inevitably also stories about cars. Cristiano was persuaded to give me the car keys. We left the house. We got in his mother's Clio, I was driving. We were now speeding toward the Poggiofranco neighborhood, I was driving with élan. In fact my head was spinning. Proving that chance is the best orchestrator of human events, or that some places conserve the memory of what has been, transforming the memory into a magnet, on Via Camillo Rosalba, the same street where I had earlier tossed the bottles off the terrace, I lost control of the wheel. We crashed into a parked car. Luckily there was no one inside, but the impact was violent. Windshield shattered, big boom. A few seconds of darkness. Then I was conscious again. "O.K.?" I asked. "I think so," said Cristiano, in a very strange voice. "Hey, what have you done?" "What a mess!" "What the fuck!" Those voices came from outside. Our car, I realized, was surrounded by people. A little before the street had been deserted, now a small group had gathered around us. They were all men and were looking at us with hostility. Suddenly I felt perfectly lucid, maybe it was the shock. I cautiously lowered the window, tried to calm the crowd, which continued to grow. I recall that I said: "We're insured." I said: "Clearly it's our fault." I said: "We'll pay the damages, no one was hurt." At that point I heard a window open and close violently. A voice, Cristiano's voice, shouted: "We killed Umberto Eco!" Still obviously drunk, my friend had gotten out of the car. His shirt was bloody, the kitchen knife clutched in his fist, his arm covered with clotted blood. "We killed Umberto Eco!" he repeated. "What the fuck!" The crowd surrounding us wasn't made up of literary experts. It should be added that in Bari, in that period, murders were not rare, because rival clans were constantly settling scores. Some started to think that we really had stabbed a guy named Umberto Eco and, not satisfied, had the impudence to claim it. How to explain all that blood? And the knife? "Murderers!" "Call the police!" I heard the door open, two powerful arms lifted me bodily and threw me out of the car. I felt the pavement on my lips, a taste I was used to. The crowd closed in around us. We were in danger of being lynched. A man we knew saved us, the father of a girlfriend of ours who happened to be passing by, recognized us, and shouted: "Let them go!" This man, evidently a saint, talked to the bystanders at length, vouched for us, reassured them that we weren't murderers, managed to calm the crowd and then to disperse it.

After that episode something snapped in my head. I changed my life. I confessed to my girlfriend the true story of my family. I told everyone everything. I stopped drinking and started studying with total commitment. I got my degree in law with the highest grades and in a short time. In bed before eleven, up before dawn. I subjected every gesture to an iron discipline, but I was young and still very inexperienced. After I graduated, I left Bari, destination Milan. After less than a year, I moved to Rome. I had very little money, the promise of a job, and a granite conviction: not to return to Bari for any reason in the world. In Rome I didn't know anyone. I felt the generosity of the city, but I had just arrived, I didn't know how to take advantage of it. I was unemployed a few days after I moved. I'd taken too seriously the words of a small entrepreneur who had promised to give me work. I had been ingenuous, and now I was broke. If I didn't find a solution in two weeks, I would have to leave the place where I was sleeping. It was the dawn of the Internet. Among the various solutions I came up with to avoid defeat was to put up an ad on a site for meetings between men. On another site I offered to be an escort for ladies. My heterosexuality didn't prevent me from understanding that one market was more flourishing than the other. As I imagined, I got responses only from the site for men. Mainly it was old men who wrote to me. I waited to answer. When the deadline I had set for myself before starting on my career as a prostitute—a solution I imagined as temporary—passed, I waited a little longer. I played for time. I didn't want to degrade myself like that. Yet I wanted *also* to degrade myself. A few days later I found a real job and never thought about it again.

In ascribing my youthful problems to my parents' divorce I gave only a partial version of things. Suffering, at times, is merely a pretext for giving an outlet to one's personal stupidity, or to the most unrestrained narcissism. As for me, I can't say if it was an excess of stupidity or of fragility that got me in trouble. I'm sure, however, that, once in trouble, if I hadn't reacted foolishly I would have come off worse. That is the most complicated consideration to bring into focus: my resources of the time, I mean, were so scant that they wouldn't have allowed me to emerge without excesses—and rather dangerous excesses—from the dead end I was stuck in. It had taken more than a violent jerk to pull me out of it.

I was fortunate.

But what would have happened if a bottle had struck the girl?

And if, rather than a parked car, I had hit a pedestrian?

If in exchange for a hundred thousand lire I had had sex with an old guy I didn't know, what would have happened to my self-respect? Would I have held up? Would I have collapsed?

That's why, when I first heard about the Varani murder, I instantly felt something familiar. An electric shock. Naturally, the familiarity was less than partial. Throwing a bottle from a balcony was certainly not stabbing another man. I knew what it meant to take half a step into the cone of shadow, I knew it was necessary to pull back as soon as possible. But then? What happened to those who didn't stop, or couldn't? There, that I didn't know at all. What happened to those who, sunk in the shadow, continued to go down the steps? Beyond a certain threshold an unknown world opened up.

PART IV

At the Bottom of the Well

> The descent to Avernus is easy.
> —VIRGIL

> I believe I am in Hell, therefore I am.
> —ARTHUR RIMBAUD

Locked in his cell, Manuel tried to reconstruct certain events. At night, when he was lying on the bed, memories rose suddenly in his mind. *Bam!* The image was cut out inside a flash of light, then swallowed up by darkness. Manuel had asked the prison guard for a pen to make a note of these flashes before losing them forever, and the guard had answered: "You see about going to sleep, I'll bring you the pen tomorrow." But the next day there was no sign of the pen. They were afraid he'd use it to kill himself.

As far as he could remember it had been Marco. To listen to Marco it had, rather, been Manuel who asked him to dress as a woman. It was January 1, that Manuel recalled, and after the unexpected—the incredible circumstance that a guy he'd just met had given him a blow job, along with the even more surprising circumstance that he had felt the need to film the whole thing using Marco's phone—they had stayed in the apartment together until the sun lighted up everything in the desolate silence.

"What shall we do?"

When the cocaine was gone, Marco had got in touch again with Trovajoli. "Armandino, sweetheart," he had written, "you must bring me three strong coffees. Via Igino Giordani 2. Hurry! I'll pay for the taxi." The dealer had arrived, Marco and Manuel had started snorting again, very soon slipping into a dimension of great intimacy. Manuel had told Marco all about himself, about his parents' separation, about his enormous unhappiness at how he had been thrown out of the family business, about his brother, his mother, his lost license, he had also talked about the "digital project" with which he intended to redeem himself.

Marco, too, had, in turn, been very talkative, he had even expounded to Manuel his theories of sexuality. Every heterosexual, he'd said, possessed a discrete homosexual element that it was a mistake to deny: "What happened between us two is the proof, don't you think?" That position had inspired in Manuel an argument that was no less odd. Gays like Prato, he had thought, used to being marginalized, dreamed of an exclusively homosexual society: if on the one hand this would mark the end of discrimination, on the other it would make possible the inadmissible desire of many of them, that is, to live in a world where the only recognized unit of measure was one's own image in the mirror.

Marco had talked about his plans to become a woman. "The process of transition is long and complicated. You have to do a year of hormonal treatment, after that the operations start: permanent hair removal, breast augmentation, and so on." Down in the street, in the glove compartment of the Mini, he had said, there was a tourist guide to Thailand, he always carried it with him, it was where he planned to go one day, where you could have the operation in peace, far from judgments and hostile gazes.

It was then that the business of cross dressing had come up.

Who had had the idea first?

Manuel remembered only that they had got in the car and headed to San Giovanni. Here was the apartment of some friends of Marco, makeup artists, people who worked in the theater world. Marco had taken out fifty euros. The makeup people had dressed him as a woman, they'd put on a wig, plasticine, greasepaint; with Manuel's help they'd chosen the right skirt and bra. Returning to Via Igino Giordani, Marco asked: "Is your mother home?" Manuel had shaken his head, and given him the keys. Marco had gone down to the ninth floor and had come back with nail polish and perfumes belonging to his mother to complete the job. They had started drinking again, snorting coke. According to

Marco they had also started having sex again. Manuel didn't remember. It wasn't so much what they had done. It was what they had *said*. High on cocaine, but also on a strange sort of energy that was released every time their gazes met, Marco and Manuel had started to make plans. Rather weird plans.

It's not unusual for young people to fantasize about actions that will allow them to free themselves from the yoke of adults. Flee far away. Get possession of an inheritance. Find a revolutionary system for making a lot of money. That's how they would get rich: Marco's boldness combined with Manuel's entrepreneurial abilities. Marco would be a prostitute, Manuel would be his pimp, he would put at his disposal a house where he could receive clients, wealthy clients, people willing to pay a lot of money to pass the time with a sophisticated and fascinating person like him. Fantastic. Marvelous. But why be content with a pimp when there are managers? Marco would have the operation, he'd burst on the scene as a porn star. "A porn star?" one had said. "Fuck yes, a porn star!" the other had responded. The exploits of porn stars, on the Internet, got millions of views. Marco would become a porn star and Manuel would be his manager, he would get a percentage of the take, and with that money he would finally develop his soccer app. *Hit the big time.* Just like that. So in a few moves they had resolved Marco's problems with the sex change and Manuel's need to free himself from family ties. But why limit themselves to words? Why put off to an uncertain future what could be done immediately? "Come on! *Come on!*" After all Marco was *already* dressed as a woman. Wildly excited, they left the house and got in Marco's Mini.

And so, in the cold of the half-deserted city, Manuel Foffo had driven Marco Prato to walk the streets. Manuel said they'd gone first to the Lungotevere. Then they headed toward EUR. They'd turned onto Viale Cristoforo Colombo, crossed the big highway that connects the center with the southern part of the city, turned a little before the artificial lake. At that point the Fungo had appeared, the monumental water tower, more than fifty meters high, that dominates this part of the urban complex. They had parked. Marco had got out of the car and gone on his mission.

You could scarcely imagine a more alienating and melancholy scene: Marco Prato dressed as a woman, stationed under the gigantic industrial structure to wait for a client, enveloped in the silence of EUR.

Marco was waiting for a client. Manuel was in the car observing. From time to time he blew warm breath into his hands. Marco remained bravely under the Fungo expecting something to happen. After forty minutes, no one had stopped to pick him up. So he got back in the car, chilled, with no more money than he'd had before, but it didn't upset him. They had demonstrated that they knew how to put a plan into action. It was a start. Still full of optimism, they'd started the car and returned to Manuel's.

Once in the apartment, they had ordered more cocaine. "Armando, how's it going? Can you bring a couple of strong coffees?" They called King of Delivery, ordered pizzas. Manuel went down to get the coke, he didn't want the neighbors to see Marco dressed as a woman. The partying began again. They barely touched the pizza. At some point they were in the car again. How much time had passed? Was it the night of the 2nd or 3rd of January? Now they wanted to go dancing. They'd been at the Alibi. Then they'd gone elsewhere.

According to Manuel, the club in San Giovanni where Marco took him after the Alibi "was gross." Dark and rather seedy. Manuel felt uneasy as soon as he saw it, so he'd stayed in the doorway for a few minutes, unsure whether to go in. When he finally entered, the bouncer had looked him up and down with a sarcastic expression. "Evening eh." "No, sorry, I didn't really know how . . ." Manuel mumbled. Meanwhile he looked around for Marco Prato. Where had he gone? Manuel started wandering through the place, moving warily from room to room. What the hell sort of place are we in? he continued to wonder. It wasn't a gay bar, since there were also women, but it was clearly not a normal dance club. That it was a "special" place he understood when, after entering a room that was darker than the others, he had seen a totally naked woman sitting between two men who were drinking and smoking as if it were nothing. Manuel had deduced from that that it was a club for swingers. He started sweating. He felt inadequate, unprepared, he felt that everyone was looking at him, he started asking where Marco was. He looked for a safe place. Finally, after wandering around a little longer, he found him. Marco was talking with some guys at the back of one of the rooms. Every so often one of his interlocutors burst out laughing. Manuel approached the group cautiously. Before he could introduce himself, Marco pointed to him.

"See him? That's Manuel, he's my new boyfriend. Cute, right?"

Manuel blushed. He would have liked to disappear.

A few hours later they were back at his house, in Via Igino Giordani. Or was it *many hours* later? Probably it was the evening of January 4. Now they were having a rather heated argument. Marco wanted Manuel to go with him to another bar, and Manuel was afraid that he wanted to introduce him again as a sort of boyfriend. Among other things Marco wanted to go out dressed as a woman. "No way!" Manuel burst out. "You can't always do what you want." "What do you mean what I want?" Marco had asked, curious. "You can't say what you said about me before!" Manuel *was not* anyone's boyfriend. He *was* heterosexual. Clear? Marco had shrugged, as if to let him understand that it wasn't his job to soothe the paranoias of people with whom he'd had a little sex. Manuel had then asked him to leave him alone. In reality, he was throwing him out. Then Marco turned mean, called him mediocre, it was the only really tense moment since they'd met. After a few more minutes, however, the tone of the discussion softened. Everything returned magically to the tracks of normality. Marco and Manuel had said goodbye warmly, promising to see each other soon.

The next day, after a deep sleep that had erased the effects of alcohol and coke, Manuel looked out the window to contemplate the urban panorama. He had, so to speak, returned to the Manuel of every day, but, from that perspective, he had realized something very clearly: he'd gotten himself in a mess.

As far as he understood himself, he liked women. The confirmation was his fantasies. What is more reliable in the matter of sex? Since adolescence, he'd seen girls as soon as he lay down and closed his eyes. Smiles, legs, lips, asses, all was undeniably female.

And so why had he let Marco Prato put his mouth on him? He couldn't accept it. There's nothing more moronic than to behave in a way different from what you are. It means others will misunderstand you, and others are always ready to judge. In this unfortunate case, others were potentially *all*. Marco had given him a blow job and he had filmed the scene, filmed it with *Marco's* phone. How could he have been so imprudent? A simple click and Marco, just by wanting to, would share the video with friends. Another click, and he would put it on the Internet.

Exposing him to the world. Was Marco capable of doing such a thing? Manuel had no idea, he didn't know what sort of person he was, he barely knew him. He reflected some more, he wondered if he should call him and start controlling the situation from a distance, "monitor him" to find out if he had bad intentions. Manuel examined all the elements at his disposal, thought and thought, evaluated the various hypotheses for action, but in the end didn't act. He did nothing. He felt stuck. A few days later, it was Marco who acted.

I see you were so interested in friendship!"
The message sounded subtly accusatory.
Manuel observed the phone screen. He hurried to explain.

"It's not that I'm not," he answered. "I'm just stressed, because I have the test, and I'm not going out because of the gym!"

Marco wrote another message right away. "We need to hang out at your house." He was alluding to another night of alcohol and cocaine. Manuel said that until he'd had the test to get his license back he couldn't do anything of the sort. "Even if I wanted to I can't!"

Marco insisted, reminded him that traces of cocaine disappear from the bloodstream in a few days, then gave the final thrust. "Of course it would be hard to make money with that plan, given how strict you are."

Manuel continued to justify himself, playing down the importance of what they'd said after New Year's. "Consider that we were stoned," he wrote. Then he repeated: "I have to keep quiet for a while, just exercise and study rather than have a crazy life. But anyway there will be occasions, I promise!"

Ingratiating and stubborn. On the one hand Manuel defended his position, on the other he was worried about opposing Marco. "I felt I had to flatter him," he said later. "He had *the video*."

In the following days they continued writing to each other. The pattern was unvarying. One pressed, the other took time. Then, slowly, they came to an agreement. They would meet under Manuel's conditions. No drugs, no craziness. Two good friends who meet to talk.

They made a date in a bar on Via dei Monti Tiburtini. Neutral
territory.

Manuel saw him emerge at the end of the street. He took a
breath to release the tension and walked toward him. Marco wore
a nice dark jacket, brand-name jeans, his face was relaxed. "So,
how are we?" he asked in a friendly way. They sat down at a table.
They ordered something to drink, began talking. Pleasantries.
Small talk. Marco talked, Manuel listened and in the meantime
reflected, looked for the right moment to bring up the subject.
A few minutes later, he confessed. "Listen, Marco, there's something I've been thinking about for days," he said. He talked to
him about the video. "I'm afraid it'll circulate, if that happens
I'm ruined."

Marco seemed surprised: "Manuel, what are you talking
about? Videos don't get around by themselves. Unless you're in-
sinuating that I could circulate it."

"It would be a real mess . . ."

"Well, let me reassure you. I don't have the slightest intention."

But Manuel didn't seem convinced. He reminded him that
they had friends in common, Lorenza Manfredi, for example, the
one who had introduced them: what would happen if, maybe by
mistake, the video ended up in her hands?

"How could a thing like that happen *by mistake*? Don't worry,
Lorenza will never get it."

"Listen, Marco, I really . . ."

"Come on, sweetheart, enough," said Marco with an expression of boredom.

They changed the subject. Manuel was still scowling. So, at
the first chance, he brought the conversation back to the business
of the video. Marco got impatient.

"Again, with this video? You're like a broken record. I already
told you not to worry," then, more gently, "Manuel, do you believe me or not?"

Manuel answered yes, of course he believed him, how could

he not, and yet the only way to be truly relieved would be to know that that video no longer existed.

"Please, delete it."

"Delete it? But I like watching it!" Marco laughed. "It's a nice video, it would be a pity not to have it anymore." So on the one hand he wouldn't delete it, he repeated, while on the other he gave his word that no one else, apart from the two of them, would ever set eyes on it.

Manuel looked down.

"Come on, don't make that face."

Manuel returned home bewildered. The meeting had resolved nothing. Rather, it had made the situation even more complicated. Marco had been clever, handing him the lighted match: it was up to Manuel to decide whether to trust him or not.

But what means did he have available that might help him *understand*? And what tools did he have to *defend himself* if things went badly? Manuel headed to his father's office. There were computers there. He turned one on and started browsing. He looked into the legal aspect of the thing on Google. "Revenge porn." A whole universe emerged. As usual the material was confused, endless, and hard to interpret, thousands of articles on privacy in the time of global exposure. After a few hours of painful consultation, he seemed to understand that if Marco circulated the video online he would be committing a crime, but if he confined himself to watching it with friends it would be almost impossible to prosecute him. The number of acquaintances they had in common was enough to ruin his reputation.

But why would Marco Prato do a thing like that? Manuel asked himself again. And was he, Manuel, sure all he wanted was for him to delete the video? Or was there something else? Something that not even he could explain? What was *really* hiding behind his unshakable compulsion to please Marco, behind the politeness, the availability, the ambiguity he displayed every time Marco got in touch?

In the following days Marco and Manuel continued to write. And this time it was Manuel, not Marco, who sent, so to speak, the decisive WhatsApp message.

"Next Thurs if you can don't make plans! I'll call you in the next few days. I haven't forgotten!"

The message oozed enthusiasm and politeness. Manuel sent it on February 24, after he had the tests for getting his license back.

Marco's answer was immediate: "O.K. Perfect. How do you want me to dress?"

Manuel headed him off: "Normal. Just friendship, O.K.?" No cross-dressing. And the implicit message was no sex.

"What do you want to do?" Marco asked.

Answer: "Talk, then the stuff."

So no sex, but cocaine would be good. What a strange guy. When Marco, with a message that wasn't even too suggestive, pointed out that, once they were stoned out of their minds, the situation could get out of hand, Manuel gave no weight to those words. He answered simply: "O.K."

They made a date for Tuesday, March 1.

That day they messaged to decide what time to meet and how to get money for the coke. Marco arrived at Via Igino Giordani around ten at night. He parked the Mini. Despite the warnings of his friend, he had a bag with him. In it he had put an electric-blue wig, a leopard-skin dress, a pair of tights, high-heeled shoes, and a padded bra. He grabbed the bag, got out of the Mini, headed to the building that loomed over the church across the street.

Marco and Manuel on the tenth floor at Via Igino Giordani: here they are again in the same situation as New Year's. Even though it's never the same situation.

After letting him in, Manuel closed the door behind him. Marco put his bag down on the floor. Although Manuel had been explicit (no cross-dressing), Marco was convinced that the words didn't correspond to his real desires.

"I brought what was needed because I knew it would end up like that," he reported to the police.

"This time you pay," Marco said as soon as he was settled.

Manuel pulled out two hundred euros from his wallet without a blink. They ordered alcohol and pizza, Marco messaged with Trovajoli. Half an hour later they started drinking and snorting. The atmosphere was pleasant. After midnight, however, although everything was going smoothly, Marco and Manuel were afflicted by the subtle tension that grips consumers of cocaine when, with two good lines still on the table, they realize that the stuff will soon be gone.

"Do you have more money?" asked Marco.

"No. For today it's used up."

The two looked around impatiently, as if the solution would fall from the sky. Which, if on the one hand it testified to their nerves, on the other was evidence of an unprovable truth, and that is that on evenings devoted to cocaine the most unexpected things always happen. Strange coincidences. Small strokes of luck. People who show up and turn out to be critical.

What are you up to?

A message from Damiano Parodi appeared on Marco Prato's phone. "What are you up to?"

Marco looked at the screen, smiled, typed the answer on the keyboard.

"I'm at a friend's house drinking and doing drugs. You want to join us?"

Damiano was rich, problematic, absolutely naïve in situations that involved the use of drugs. And he wanted his sunglasses back.

"Maybe I'll come by," he answered.

"So what are you doing?"

Among Marco's techniques was that of showing himself especially interested in the situation of anyone who could help him get what he wanted. How are you? What's your mood? Feeling lonely?

"I'm bored," answered Damiano.

As Damiano saw it, Marco Prato was something of a mystery. He was struck by his changeability. Marco could go from empathetic to malicious in the space of a sentence. Damiano had experienced this directly already on a couple of occasions. That annoyed him. But it also made him feel for brief moments at Marco's mercy, and it was complicated to decide if the situation was only unpleasant.

In the preceding months Marco had asked to borrow money.

"Damiano, I wanted to ask you something in confidence," he had written on October 10, "but *truly* it has to remain between us. Since A(h)però hasn't reopened yet, I don't have a cent. Would you lend me something? Sunday we reopen and I'll pay it all back."

"I'd be happy to give you the money," Damiano had responded, "but I have an automatic withdrawal coming up and I can't take anything out."

Marco changed his tone: "Damiano, I'm not a bum or a whore. I'm a serious person from the same background as you."

"But of course," Damiano had responded, careful not to offend him, although the possibility of offense—the reference to whores—had been opened up by Prato himself like a trap.

"You could use your father's card," Marco had written, "he'd realize it in a month and in the meantime I would have paid back the money."

"Please," Marco added after a few minutes, "you're already not answering me?"

"Sorry, my battery's dead," Damiano had responded. "Can you wait twenty minutes till my parents leave? Even fifteen."

"In fifteen minutes I'm there," Marco had answered, and added some emoticons.

So Damiano had given him the money. He had been moved not by a simple spirit of generosity but by the blanket of threat with which Marco had subtly managed to surround the request, playing not so much on the sense of guilt as on the need not to disappoint expectations that obscurely evoked social approval. How would we be judged if we denied the money that we have in abundance to a good friend who needs it?

But then Sunday had come and Marco hadn't showed up to pay back the loan. When a few more days had passed, Damiano thought it was legitimate to remind him of the debt. But it was in these tight spots that Marco Prato was at his best.

D: Hi Marco, how are you?

M: Well. Pretty bad. You?

D: I'm writing because you said you'd give back the money I lent you on Sunday.

M: I never hear from you.

The phrase was textbook.

D: You're right, I haven't gotten in touch, and I'm sorry even to ask you like this. But I need the money.

M: Damiano, unfortunately I'm still not able to pay you back. I feel terrible. I hate having debts. A(h)però is still getting going . . .

D: You shouldn't feel bad. I tried you because I needed some cash.

On November 17, Damiano had tried again.

D: Hi Marco, how's it going? I'm leaving for Brazil on Saturday. Do you think you could pay me back at least part of the money?

M: I'm sick, at home. I'm in a bad patch.

D: I'm so sorry. Want to go out tonight? Want to come by my house? Or if you want I'll pick you up.

They didn't get together that night, and Damiano left for Brazil. Returning to Italy on December 2, he had written to him.

D: Marco, sorry if I'm asking you. It embarrasses me, too, a bit. I need the money I lent you. Can't you pay it back? Even part?

M: Unfortunately no. Believe me, it's much more embarrassing to me! I'm mortified. For New Year's (keep your fingers crossed) I'm organizing an event and it should bring in a good amount.

There were other exchanges in the following weeks. Then, on January 5, Damiano got back to the point, if in an allusive way.

D: Happy New Year Marco! How were the proceeds?

Marco didn't respond. After a week, on January 12, Damiano had written again. The tone this time was resentful.

"Marco, you could at least answer . . ."

"I'm in bed with a fever," Marco answered the next day. Then he had landed the punch: "When I read the message from New Year's I was upset. I don't hear even a Happy New Year from you and then you ask me how the proceeds were. The evening went well, but on the level of proceeds not much. Anyway, as soon as I get what I'm owed, and the fever subsides, I'll start giving you something."

Transforming his own failure into someone else's was an old trick, but it worked.

"Marco, sorry, I didn't mean to be rude. You were angry with me, then?"

"I wasn't angry, I was unhappy. As soon as I recover I'll write."

"Yes, I'd like to get a coffee with you. Feel better soon."

"So, are you coming by or no?" Marco typed on the phone, looking at Manuel, who was leaning over one of the last lines of coke.

"O.K., I'll come by."

"Good. We're in Collatino, Via Igino Giordani."

Marco took his eyes and fingers off the phone. He looked at Manuel and told him what was happening.

"You're sure?"

Manuel now had an expression of disappointment. In fact he seemed put out.

"Isn't it better if it's just you and me alone talking? What do we need to have your friend come for? We're fine just the two of us."

"Coke," Marco cut him off.

"Listen, Marco, let's be clear. I don't want to seem like a faggot again."

"Come on, don't worry," said Marco, smiling. "Damiano is useful for money. He's our ATM. Then he's also nice, you'll see, he's really a good guy."

I t wasn't clear even to Damiano what had driven him to accept the invitation. He didn't know how to spend the evening? Was he really bored?

The fact is that he was upset about the sunglasses.

He continued to curse himself for lending them to that guy,
the friend of Marco Prato's who had appeared at his house one
night some time earlier. Alessandro the Japanese. He didn't even
know his real name.

Obviously Damiano had tried to get to the bottom of it, he had
written various messages to Marco, but Marco had answered in
an increasingly evasive manner. So at twelve-forty in the morning
Damiano left his apartment and called a taxi. He arrived in Via
Igino Giordani, paid, got out of the car, and looked around. He
couldn't find the number. Collatino, at night, seemed a gigantic
beehive of concrete abandoned on a distant planet. He wrote to
Marco.

"Where are you?"

"This guy can't even find the building," said Marco when he
got the message. They went down to the ground floor.

Damiano saw them emerge from the darkness.

"Hi Marco," he said hesitantly.

"Damiano sweetheart, here we are. Let me introduce
Matteo."

Matteo? Manuel was disconcerted. He held out his hand to
Damiano, trying to appear normal. Why had Marco introduced
him by that name? Was he protecting him? Or was he getting
him into yet another mess?

The three went up to the tenth floor, entered the apartment. On the table in the living room three lines of coke were ready.

"This Manuel, whom I called Matteo," Damiano said to the police, "at first was very reserved. I was afraid he was annoyed by my presence. But then he began to open up. The atmosphere over all was pleasant. The problems began later."

The three snorted, put together money to buy more coke, or rather it was Damiano who got out what was needed. Two hundred and fifty euros. He wasn't a regular consumer and had no idea if it was an adequate sum. Marco called the dealer, it was two in the morning. After another couple of glasses, Manuel loosened up, he started talking to Damiano about the university. Marco looked at them with satisfaction.

"An e-campus? What does that mean?" asked Damiano.

"It's an online university. The lessons are on the web . . . like . . . you go only to take exams and discuss your thesis."

"Don't be offended," said Damiano, "but to me it seems a little ridiculous for a university to operate like that."

Manuel tried to explain better. Marco laid out three lines on the table. At this point something rather funny happened. Damiano had trouble snorting. He hadn't had any difficulty with the first lines, but he started to now.

"I suffer from nasal turbinate hypertrophy," he explained, "excuse me a moment."

So in the middle of the night Damiano called another taxi, was driven to an all-night pharmacy, bought some nasal spray, and returned to Via Igino Giordani.

The three went back to snorting. Now it was Marco who took the lead. While he entertained Damiano with chitchat, he observed Manuel out of the corner of his eye. And Manuel looked at him, looked at Marco, recognized *the thing*. Thanks to cocaine everything had started up again as before, two months ago, in January. The *magnetism*. A luminous white wave. Now they understood each other again. They drank another glass, snorted, and as soon as the wave exploded in their brains—a soft, bloodless explosion, like a waterfall of fireworks seen in slow motion—Manuel and Marco looked even more deeply into each other's eyes.

When two people under the influence of drugs look at each other like that, there are many things they can see. They can have the sensation that they're reading the other's mind. Or, on the contrary, they can be convinced that it's the other who is reading their mind. Which can lead them to open up in such a way that the other *truly* intuits what they're thinking. Or again, their interpretation of the other's thoughts may be outrageously wrong. Those who look at each other like this might emerge terrorized. Or intoxicated. They might feel pervaded by a sensation of happiness. Or of terrifying anxiety.

Marco stood up suddenly. "The meeting!" he exclaimed.

The next day, he explained, he had an important work meeting. He would have to get up early. Just that. He was talking to both but he continued to stare at Damiano. Damiano understood all too easily that the speech was addressed to him. He understood that he was superfluous. The altered state of consciousness, or the implicit threat that hovered behind each of Marco's words—the possibility that something would offend him—warned him not to ask too many questions. "Oh, of course, I'm so sorry," he was quick to say. He said goodbye to Marco, said goodbye also to Manuel ("Bye, Matteo, it was nice to meet you"), called a taxi, and left.

As soon as Damiano closed the door behind him, Marco and Manuel fell on the coke. Marco grabbed the canvas bag he'd brought with him. He rushed to the bathroom, shaved, removed the hair from his hands and arms, put on makeup, perfume, nail polish. He took the leggings, the leopard-skin dress, the bra, and the high-heel shoes out of his bag.

It was five in the morning and the atmosphere had changed. What had been in the shadows appeared in full light. The charade that had hovered in the air revealed its solution. Marco and Manuel felt strong, energetic, each able to understand the other, look even more profoundly into the other's depths.

D amiano woke up before lunch. He heard the sound of keys in the lock, footsteps in the living room. His mother had come to see him. He had lunch with her. A little afterward he went back to bed, feeling tired from the night before, and fell asleep instantly.

When he woke up again, the apartment was silent. It was afternoon and his mother had left. He watched some TV. After half an hour he thought it was time to go to the gym. He got his bag, put his stuff in it, prepared to go out. Then his cell phone vibrated. Marco Prato. He was proposing another evening together. This time they could sleep at Damiano's, he wrote. Basically he was inviting himself to his house. Damiano answered right away.

"Hi Marco, thanks for the offer to come to me ♥, but tonight I'm going to dinner at my grandmother's and I'll stay and sleep at her house."

Marco wasn't the type to yield to an emoticon.

"I'm going back to Matteo's house," he informed him. "Join us and then go to your grandmother's."

"I'd like to come, but I'm on the way to the gym."

Damiano put the phone back in his pocket, left the house, started walking to the gym. When he was almost there, Marco appeared with another message.

"You could go to your grandmother's for dinner tomorrow, too."

"Thanks, but today it's a bit of a problem."

He didn't have a great desire to see Marco so soon. Too bad that Marco, in some strange way, had sensed an opening between the lines of the conversation, and now he pushed to enter. He played an unforeseen card.

"Damiano, listen, the fact is I'm not well."

"How not well?"

Marco wrote that his mood was really low. He was "stuck," paranoid, felt he was close to a panic attack. Who could understand him better than a person who suffered from an obsessive-compulsive disorder?

"Don't leave me alone," he wrote. "I love you, seriously."

"Tomorrow if you want we can spend the whole day together," Damiano tried to calm him.

"Listen, Damiano," the tone changed again, "when you're in a rough spot, that's the exact moment you need help. And that exact moment for me is *now*."

"Yes, but I've organized a dinner with my cousins in Rome whom I almost never see."

Excuses on excuses. He was grasping at straws.

"Your cousins are in Rome," wrote Marco, "they're not coming from Australia. You can see them whenever you want."

"True," Damiano admitted, "but believe me, I can't."

"Damiano, I'm asking you *please*," Marco insisted, "I think it's mean of you to leave a friend in this condition for a dinner based on bourgeois civilities."

"I'd rather be with you, too, but honestly you're making things hard for me."

"So *come*," Marco wrote. "I don't want money, I don't want drugs, I only need YOU to be here. When *you* needed *me*, I was always there for you."

"But if I come I'm not drinking."

He had given in.

"Here's the address again. Via Igino Giordani 2. I ask you just one favor. Bring me all the tranquilizers, anxiety drugs, benzos you have. I'm sick."

Damiano turned his back on the gym. He called a taxi. He gave the driver the address and closed his eyes, exasperated. He sighed, then wrote to Marco: "On the way."

T his time he knew where the intercom was.

Damiano went up to the tenth floor. He found the door already open, but what he saw wasn't what he expected to see.

"Hi, Damiano."

Marco didn't seem in the least like someone on the verge of a panic attack. He was smiling, solid on his legs, and as if that weren't enough he was shaved, had removed the hair on his arms and hands, and put polish on his nails.

"But . . . why are you wearing nail polish?" Damiano managed to ask.

"I was bored" was the answer.

Marco Prato's appearance was surprising. But the appearance of the apartment was also surprising. It appeared to be the same place as the night before, and yet everything in it seemed to float in a new atmosphere, as if something were boiling up within those walls, and, even more, as if, once you entered, you were hurled thousands of kilometers away. Above or below or into some other dimension, Damiano wouldn't have been able to say.

"Where's Matteo?"

"Oh, he's in his room sleeping."

Marco handed him a glass of chilled wine.

Although he had promised himself not to drink ("I was also on a diet") Damiano couldn't refuse, he brought the glass to his lips. "The anti-anxiety meds?" said Marco. Damiano took out the package of benzos he'd brought. Marco grabbed it, started examining it carefully.

"How did the work meeting go?" asked Damiano.

"Oh fine, fine," Marco answered quickly. "Now I'm making you another cocktail." He went back to the kitchen.

Damiano sat in the living room, took everything out of his pockets, put his wallet and phone on the table. He looked around, increasingly disoriented. Some minutes passed, and since Marco didn't come back he decided to join him. "What's taking so long?" he asked, going into the kitchen. "I like to chill the glasses with ice" was Marco's answer. He had his back to him, and angled it more when he heard Damiano approaching. Damiano had the sensation that Marco was concealing the part of the counter where he was preparing the drinks. He took a few more steps. Marco turned with a faintly annoyed smile: "Why don't you go in there?"

"To do what?"

"Go and watch Matteo sleeping," he said.

"Watch Matteo *sleeping*?"

"It's interesting," Marco said, without changing expression.

Damiano thus found himself in the hall. He would never have dared to disturb the host in his bed, especially since he barely knew him. At the same time, though, he didn't want to irritate Marco. Reaching the end of the hall, he stopped, stood still so that Marco would think he was following his suggestion, but didn't venture even to graze the bedroom door. He counted to ten, returned to the living room.

"Oh, here you are," said Marco, and passed him a glass filled with a dark liquid. It looked like an amaro with herbs. Damiano took a swallow. The taste was strange. He tried to figure out where he could put the glass down without Marco getting offended. At that moment they heard sounds from the bedroom, then footsteps in the hall. A few seconds later, Manuel entered the living room, greeted them, walked, stumbling, to the table, sat down, and took his head in his hands. "I have a headache," he declared. Although he had just awakened, he seemed tired.

The three began talking. After a few minutes they reached the conclusion that it was time to buy more cocaine. Damiano pulled out his bank card and a piece of paper with the pin scribbled on it. Marco talked. Manuel talked. The voices expanded as they entered Damiano's head. The space around him began to move, the walls oscillated like curtains in the wind.

"Who can understand a person like that?" Manuel said to the prosecutor. "Who can understand a person who pours benzos in the glass of a friend who has also given him money to buy cocaine?"

Manuel reported that Marco told him he'd poured the benzos into Damiano's glass. Damiano said he wasn't sure that anything like that had happened (besides, how could he verify it?), but his memory in fact became imprecise starting at that moment. He recalled having awakened on the sofa. He was confused, lethargic, he didn't even know what time it was. "Let's go get a breath of air. Come on, let's go downstairs," Marco said suddenly. "What, go downstairs?" Damiano asked, surprised. It seemed to him that the apartment had taken on yet another appearance. "Come on, hurry up." He felt that he had to do what Marco said. Manuel also headed for the door. Damiano got up from the couch. A few seconds later he was on the landing.

"We're walking, you take the elevator."

He obeyed this time, too. He got on the elevator, looked at his feet as he descended from floor to floor. Then the doors opened and Damiano found himself in another world. "Hey guys, where are you?" He heard his own steps echoing in the emptiness, the place was completely dark. His eyes began to adjust to the obscurity and in the shadowy light he recognized a gray stain. He looked more closely. The shutter of a garage. He had accidentally gone to the basement. On the right was a stairway, he headed in that direction, climbed the stairs, found himself on the ground floor. His head was still spinning. He went to the door, opened it, and was again outside, on Via Igino Giordani.

Now he was breathing the cold night air. Across the street, past the church, he heard distant footsteps. He seemed to recognize two silhouettes in the dark. "Marco? Is that you?" "Over here," said a voice. Damiano tried to follow it. Arriving at a traffic circle he turned right, continued along a street bordered by hedges, turned to the left, and realized he was lost.

Now he was walking aimlessly, surrounded by apartment buildings and parked cars. He struggled not to be overcome by anxiety. After some more minutes of wandering he saw a moving figure in the distance. He hurried toward it. It was a girl. Damiano raised a hand cautiously; he wanted to attract her attention without scaring her. The girl came out of the shadows; she didn't seem alarmed. Damiano told her he was lost. She was nice, she explained what he had to do to get back to Via Igino Giordani.

After a few minutes Damiano found the street. As soon as he saw Manuel's building, he had an unpleasant realization. He dug in his pockets. *Shit*. The bank card. He hurried. He pressed the intercom.

"Damiano, where were you?"

It was Marco's voice.

"I got lost, will you please open the door?"

"Go home, I'll be down shortly."

Damiano sighed. It was like a nightmare.

"Marco, I left my bank card with you. If you let me up, I'll get it and leave."

"Go home, I said. I'll bring you everything in half an hour."

"I must have been in a very strange condition," he told the police, "because, really, if I realize I don't have my bank card and I say *can I come up a moment*? And they say no, well, in a normal state I would have insisted, right? I would have managed to assert myself. Instead I did what Prato told me to."

He returned to Parioli in a taxi. Once he was home, Damiano

waited. After an hour Marco still hadn't arrived. A few minutes later he heard a beep from his phone. He rushed to the phone, looked at the screen. It wasn't Marco. It was his bank. Damiano reread the message to make sure he'd understood. Beep. Another message from the bank. Although it was absurd and outrageous, although Damiano refused to think that something like that was even conceivable, he was forced to accept the idea that it was really happening. He immediately called Marco. No one answered. Then he started writing message after message.

"You can't do this to me."

"Answer, please."

"You don't behave like that, Marco."

"Please answer."

"Someone took another 250 euros with my bank card."

"Do I have to report the card stolen?"

"Marco, please, I'm going mad."

"Marco, I don't care about the money but answer."

"You're ruining my life."

Hours passed. Marco didn't respond to a single one of these messages. By the time Damiano decided to block his card, more than a thousand euros had been taken from his account.

Alone in the apartment again, Marco and Manuel found themselves with two grams of unused coke, several bottles of vodka, a bank card still available. It was two in the morning on Thursday, March 3. They wasted no time getting back to the coke. It was like picking up the thread of the incredible conversation that had been interrupted a little while ago. There was the surface reality, and then there was the subterranean world, which the cocaine rekindled instantly in their brains.

"We plunged back into delirium immediately," Marco recalled.

They resumed their conversation about how to make a lot of money. Marco again brought up the idea of transitioning. He would take the hormones, would become a transsexual soldier under Manuel's command. A body ready for everything, managed by an entrepreneurial mind with a passion for computers. What happens when Sasha Grey meets Steve Jobs? The young men's minds dialogued at a high voltage, they clung to one another for a few seconds, then each slid into his own thoughts.

"Manuel talked to me about an inheritance he'd get on the death of his father," Marco told the prosecutor, "but why wait for his death? Thanks to my sex change we'd be able to hatch a seductive plot."

"A seductive plot? And to what purpose?" asked the prosecutor.

"Manuel had described his father to me as a man very sensitive to female charm. If I introduced myself to him dressed as a woman, well, it wouldn't work. But if I were *really* a woman . . . I would seduce Signor Foffo, and persuade him to do things to

Manuel's advantage. I would even manage to seduce the heads of the soccer federation, and that way Manuel's app would be approved. In other words: madness."

As long as it was a matter of words, everything was settled at a dizzying speed.

"While we were talking, Manuel's eyes were unrecognizable," Marco said.

According to Manuel it was Marco who, at certain moments, had "the criminal gaze."

"It was then that he talked to me about rape," said Marco.

"It was then that I told him the pretend story about rape," Manuel clarified.

In Manuel's version, Marco put a hand on his shoulder: "Come on, you can tell me everything. What's your most unacceptable fantasy?" So Manuel, who had never wanted to rape anyone in his life, came out with the most extreme idea he could conceive.

"I like rape."

He saw it as a contest, he wanted to see his friend's reaction, Marco was a guy as strange as he was interesting, his answers were always disorienting.

Marco took out his phone and showed him some videos.

"They were horrendous," said Manuel. "They immediately made me sick." Adults having sex with children. A video of a girl raped by a group of men. Manuel looked at the video close up. He couldn't tell if it was a real rape or simulated. They drank more vodka. They snorted more coke. Manuel resumed talking about his fantasies. Now he was going non-stop, the sentences became a little disjointed, his gaze was further distorted. Marco tried to stay with him, but Manuel's eyes became so strange they frightened him.

"We need a third mind," he said.

With the psychic contagion a few degrees from boiling over, he had to try to lower the temperature. "He started saying some really *weird* things," Marco recounted. "I was distressed, but I liked him a lot. So I thought that if another person joined us, the situation would be toned down. I said: *Get some friend of yours to come over, so we can talk a little.*"

Manuel's version was slightly different: "Marco began to harass me with this business that I ought to call some friend of mine. He wanted him to come to my house. He was insistent. Very insistent. So at some point I got the phone and we started going through the contacts together."

As Manuel showed Marco his contacts, Marco commented on them.

He looked at the photos on the list and gave an opinion: "*This is a good guy; this one looks like a criminal; this is someone who snorts; we can't trust that guy . . .* He went so far as to tell me that many of these friends were using me, taking advantage of my kindness, my availability. The whole thing, just by looking at the photos."

Was it a way of weakening him? Keeping a hold over him? By saying that he couldn't trust certain friends, whereas he could obviously trust him, did Marco intend to increase his power over Manuel? For Manuel, among other things, the version in which the arrival of his friends was necessary for the theory of the "third mind" didn't completely add up. Or at least it seemed to him that it wasn't the only reason.

"Marco didn't say it, but I was afraid he also had some sexual aims."

Manuel started calling the contacts on his list who wouldn't be able to accept the invitation.

"I called a friend who had to go to work early the next day. Another who wasn't in Rome, and would have taken hours to get here. Another who hadn't snorted for years, and so would never come. I did it on purpose. I didn't want to get anyone in trouble."

After the first fruitless attempts, Marco, impatient, took the phone out of his hands. He scanned the list of contacts again and started sending some WhatsApp messages himself.

"I don't even know how many he sent. He wrote to people pretending it was me. But it was pointless, given how he did it."

Manuel spent long days reading the restaurant reviews on Tripadvisor in an attempt to distinguish the real ones from the fakes. He was convinced that that practice had given him a considerable sensitivity to linguistic analysis.

"It could never have worked. If you take my phone's history and read all the WhatsApp and text messages I've sent, you notice that I always express myself in correct Italian, while in the messages that he sent, he had me speaking in a different way. He used words like: *dudes, we got a stash of blow*, even *chill*. All nonsense."

Marco even sent a message to Manuel's brother. Manuel was resentful. Exasperated, he grabbed the phone, resumed patiently going through the contacts.

"I would never put my closest friends at risk."

It was 4:13 in the morning when Manuel called Alex Tiburtina.

W hile I was watching the TV news, I had a shock," Alex Quaranta said to the police. "It's incredible to discover that you've barely escaped a massacre."

Manuel Foffo and Alex Quaranta had met almost a year earlier, and hadn't seen each other again. On a summer night whose exact date neither of the two could pinpoint, Manuel, after spending some hours in the family restaurant, had decided to go home. From Dar Bottarolo to Via Igino Giordani was a twenty-minute walk. Although he had just come from a restaurant, he realized he was hungry. In Rome, when you're out on the street and hungry, sooner or later something will, inevitably, appear. Manuel hadn't gone far on Via Tiburtina when he noticed a pizza-by-the-slice place. He went in, sat down, started eating. He heard voices behind him. The voices became shouts. They were fighting.

"A guy had come in with some friends, they had ordered pizza and beer. When the moment came to pay, the guy realized he was short two euros. The pizza owner got mad. They started arguing. They wouldn't stop. Just so as not to hear them, I took out the money."

Alex Quaranta, with a certain punctiliousness, insisted on specifying that the situation had been a little different.

"I was short fifty cents, not two euros. And I hadn't gotten any pizza, only a Nastro Azzurro."

Manuel paid the little debt, Alex Quaranta went over to him smiling.

"Damn, you're the best! Thank you very much. No one has ever done me a kindness like that."

"O.K., but let's not overdo it," Manuel was disparaging.

"It's not that I can't even pay for a beer," said Alex. "It's that I came out with no money, I live around here."

"Around here where?"

"Right over there, around the corner!"

He was a big guy of thirty-five, dark-complexioned, very frank. He had a likable gaze.

He introduced his friends. One of the two was named Samir, he was Tunisian. "I have a restaurant right here, in Monti di Pietralata," said Manuel. "Really? I'm a pizzamaker!" said Samir. "Do you need help?" They went out to the street. Manuel liked meeting new people. Alex loosened up easily with strangers ("With a person you don't know you can speak freely, you don't have to constantly watch what you say"), and so he told Manuel his troubles. He came from a complicated family, he'd been in rehab ("problems with cocaine"), now, however, he was clean, he was training as an amateur boxer and looking for a regular job. He also had a new girlfriend. "Hey, why don't we meet for an aperitif?" "I'd really like that!" Manuel answered. They exchanged phone numbers. So as not to confuse him with a friend who had the same name, Manuel recorded him as Alex Tiburtina.

A few weeks later, Manuel tried to call him, suggesting they go get a drink. Alex at that moment was on the other side of the city ("Sorry, Manuel, I'm on the Tuscolana") and so nothing came of it. They hadn't had any contact since then.

Alex Quaranta did in fact have a complicated story. His father was a successful engineer, "a kind of scientist with a lot of degrees, but cold, very rational." His parents had met in Somalia. "My mother is from there, she's a political refugee, the daughter of a general in the armed forces." The two had moved to Rome, where they had lived together until 1991. Then they separated. "My father was a womanizer. My mother began to have problems with alcohol. When I was eleven she left home and, with the help of her parents, moved to Switzerland, then England. My father stayed with my brother and me. He was present for our material needs, but in the feeling department zero. Even now, when we see each other, he merely shakes my hand. Anyway, a few years later he left, too, moved in with his new partner. My brother and I stayed home, papa left us the house and a sum of money. I was eighteen, and even though financially nothing was lacking, I felt the absence of affection. That's why, I think, I've had a difficult life."

For Alex a period of excess began. "I wasted a fortune on cars, travel, drugs, every kind of dissipation. At a certain point my brother and I sold the house. When the money was gone, I realized I had to work. I started as a stocker in supermarkets. I went to Pomezia. In the meantime my father had moved to Spain, so I decided to join him. I was twenty-three, it was a chance to start over."

For a while, in Spain, Alex had gone straight. He had a beautiful girlfriend. But then he ended up in Ibiza ("I went there on vacation. I saw some old friends from Rome, and started again with Ecstasy and that whole business"). He returned to Italy for a while, and was convicted for dealing ("later reduced to *slight quantity for personal use*, it's important to be precise"). His Spanish girlfriend was pregnant, Alex couldn't wait to see her, only he had to get back his ID, which had been taken away because of the legal problems. He almost had it, but an ugly surprise awaited him.

"I'd already got the tickets to go back to Spain, my girlfriend had just had a baby girl, I couldn't wait. But right at that moment she had second thoughts. In the end she didn't want it. I refer to the fact of being with me. She left on her own with the baby. In agreement with her family, she decided to exclude me from everything. Another blow. I stayed in Italy."

In Rome a very harsh period began. "I was living now from house to house. I worked as a hotel receptionist, then a waiter in a restaurant, a barista, everything. I got a place in Centocelle, and was evicted. On some days, as they say in Rome, I made it up as I went along. Luckily I met Sonia."

This Sonia was his current girlfriend. Alex had met her after a stay at a rehab center. "In the center I finally was able to rest, when I left I felt well, I was strong again, ready for a normal life."

Sonia had two children from an earlier relationship. She and Alex didn't live together. ("When the daughter slept at her boyfriend's and we sent the other child to stay with a friend, then I could go to her house"). But they had serious intentions. "We had this idea of having a shop. A restaurant. I had come up with a unique concept. We wanted to open a gnoccheria, where you have fifteen different sauces, all homemade. We combined our savings, six hundred euros of mine, another six hundred from Sonia, another four hundred Mamma sent me. We were on this path, and were waiting for the insurance check that Sonia was supposed to get from a little accident: that check would allow us to finish the renovations on the restaurant, and so, at least for me, I'd finally join a sane working world." Waiting for the gnoccheria to get going, however, Alex gritted his teeth. "At this time I don't have a fixed address," he said to the police. "I sleep where I can. One night in a hostel, one night at Sonia's, one night the guest of friends. I'm a good guy, people help me, maybe one day I call a friend and say, *David, will you lend me twenty euros*? But it's rough, it's frustrating to be on the street when you come from a good family, stare at the pavement for hours, listening to the silence of the night—it's a destructive thing. That's why I found myself in that mess."

The police asked him to describe in detail where he was the night of March 3, when Manuel Foffo, pressed by Marco Prato, decided to call him.

I was in Piazzale della Radio with a beer," Alex Tiburtina said. "That night I was in a bad way, I didn't have enough money for the hostel. I could have slept in the shop that was being renovated, but it was full of plaster dust. So I was wasting time, in the hope that something would happen."

And, unexpectedly, something did happen.

At 4:13 in the morning, his phone lighted up. Calling: *Manuel rest*. Alex had trouble figuring out who it was.

"Hello?"

"Hey man!"

"Who is it?"

"Hey, it's Manuel, you remember?"

Alex's face lighted up.

"Manuel! How are you? I'm here having a beer."

"So come over. It's a party. We're having fun."

Alex couldn't believe he was having such good luck. "When you ask to sleep at someone else's house your self-esteem is always at risk, and you have to be careful, you can't say a word out of place because they can kick you out." But now it was Manuel—the guy who had already got him out of trouble once—appearing, and he hadn't had to ask him for anything. "I thought of the classic party situation, people drinking, picking up girls, maybe taking some drugs. But all I wanted was a couch where I could lie down and sleep. A warm place to spend the night."

"I'll give you the address, Via Igino Giordani 2," said Manuel.

Alex had his last fifteen euros in his pocket. Suddenly calling a taxi seemed to be a good investment.

Manuel Foffo gave a slightly different version of the phone call.

"While I was talking to Alex, Marco tore the phone out of my hand and started talking to him. *Come on*, he said, *but listen, I have a surprise.* When the call was over, I was angry. *Hey, what the fuck are you talking about?* Marco reassured me: *He didn't mind*, he said, *he said he's happy there's a surprise.*"

Prato recalled: "On the phone I anticipated the situation, I said I had a surprise. For a kid from the slums it's an unmistakable expression. There's also the song by Califano"—*Fling with a Transvestite.*

Alex confirmed that he'd talked to Prato as well. He denied that there had been any allusion of a sexual nature. Or maybe he was only very tired and couldn't really remember every word.

Alex took a taxi. Once he was in the cab, Manuel called him again.

"Hey, you coming or not?"

"If you don't hurry we won't let you come." That was Prato's voice.

When Alex reached his destination, the taxi meter showed twenty-one euros. He sighed. "I'm sorry," he said, "I only have fifteen." The taxi-driver was mad. "Hey, you don't do that, what the fuck." But Alex knew his business. "When I find myself in a situation like that," he told the police, "I'm always true, direct. Usually it works."

It worked. The taxi-driver took the money, grumbled, and let him go.

Alex found himself in front of the big building on Via Igino Giordani. He rang the intercom. Arriving on the tenth floor, he pressed the bell. He expected to find a lot of people dancing, loud music, girls laughing. But what he saw was something else.

"The door opened and there was Manuel. I almost didn't recognize him. He looked terrible. Behind him I saw a guy dressed like a woman. That's all. No music, no party, no girls. The situation was absurd."

It wasn't only absurd. In his life Alex had seen houses that were ugly, shabby, bleak, abandoned to themselves, but that apartment had a characteristic that no neglect or bad taste could instill: it leaked evil.

Manuel invited him in. His eyes were puffy, his gaze lost.

"Hey, man, what've you done?" Alex made an effort to keep his tone light. "You look *really* wiped out."

Manuel responded coldly: "We've been in here for two days taking drugs."

Alex drew on experience: normally it would take a week to be reduced to that state—if it had taken just a couple of days for the two of them it meant they'd *really* overdone it.

He was unable to reflect further, because the real attraction of the evening came toward him.

"Hello, sweetie, shall we make the introductions?"

Marco Prato was wearing an electric-blue wig, high heels, lipstick, and a woman's dress over jeans. "It was one of those dresses that girls wear in summer, when they rush out to go shopping," Alex recalled. "He spoke in a female voice, very pronounced. Under the makeup you could see the line of his beard."

Manuel claimed something happened at that point which Alex denied decisively.

"Before sitting down, Alex said: *What happens on the Mile stays on the Mile.*"

According to Manuel it was a warning: Alex didn't want anyone to say a word about what happened within those four walls. It meant that he wouldn't spurn the diversion that the transvestite seemed ready to offer. The allusion might make one smile, but in light of what happened later, it was chilling. What is the likelihood that Stephen King is evoked in the place of an imminent massacre?

Alex told the police that as far as he knew it was a movie quote but that he, anyway, had never uttered those words.

Marco said: "Sit down, honey. So good you came."

Manuel stayed between them in a catatonic state.

"He was like a zombie, completely wasted. I tried to talk to him," said Alex. "I showed him some boxing videos on the phone. *I practice every day. Look how good I am.* I told him about my daughter, about the plan of opening the gnoccheria. I tried to communicate. From him nothing, zero empathy. So I changed the subject. *Manuel, Jesus, you're really in a bad way, is the restaurant going well at least?* He said: *No, I don't go to the restaurant anymore, they threw me out.* He always had that tone of a dead person. I get shivers thinking about it."

It seemed like a bad dream. Meanwhile Marco had sat down opposite him. Alex looked at him more closely. "Tell me," he said, "where do you live? What do you do?"

"I'm a friend of Manuel's," Marco answered in a fluty voice, "I work upstairs. I'm supposedly a student, but you know . . . at the same time I work as a prostitute."

It wasn't true, but Alex couldn't know that. And in any case he wasn't thrown off balance. "On the one hand I thought: *What the fuck is happening in here?* On the other I said to myself: *O.K., stay cool, it's all very weird, but basically these two are harmless.* I mean, if you go dancing at Qube, Gay Village, Muccassassina, you see all types of people all the time. Gays, trans, transvestites. Sometimes families come. So I thought: *One's dressed like a woman, the other must be a bit of a fag, they probably have something going on, what's the big deal?*"

At that point Marco pulled out the first surprise of the evening. A bag of coke. He opened it and began to lay out on the table a nice big line. "Help yourself," he said.

Alex was suspicious.

"At my house, when they offer you too much cocaine it means something's wrong. And then if I snorted that much I'd be in danger of not sleeping. Marco saw that I was hesitant, so he took out the credit card and divided the big line into three. Now it had become a normal bump. We all three sniffed."

Right after sniffing the coke, Marco said: "Now I'll make you a cocktail." He disappeared into the kitchen. Remaining alone with Manuel, Alex tried again to start a conversation. "Listen," he said, "really, why did you call me? There's no party here."

Manuel said he'd tried to get some other people to come, but no one had accepted the invitation.

"I know it seems crazy," Alex told the police, "but at that moment I felt even more fortunate. I couldn't wait to lie down on the couch and close my eyes."

But there was no talk of sleep. Marco returned with a glass of a yellowish liquid. "What's that?" asked Alex. "Vodka tonic," said Marco. Alex got more upset.

"I had Marco opposite me," he recounted, "while Manuel went and positioned himself behind me. Now, ever since I was a kid people who get behind me have made me nervous—when I take the metro I always try to have my back against the side of the car. Now I had Manuel behind me, and I was trying to keep an eye on him. Every so often I'd turn around: *So Manuel? How's it going?* He answered *fine*, but he stayed like that, staring at me steadily with that lifeless gaze. And added to that was Marco going on about the vodka tonic."

Marco held the glass in his hand, stirred the contents using a pink straw. He handed him the cocktail. "Go on, sweetie, taste it." Experience again came to Alex's aid.

"I've worked in bars. I know how to make cocktails, and I know, unequivocally, that there's no need to stir a vodka tonic like that. The tonic water is carbonated, it mixes naturally with the vodka. So I thought: *Either this guy is an asshole who doesn't know how to make a vodka tonic or there's the risk he put something strange in the vodka.* I have strong instincts . . . sometimes I don't follow them and I end up in trouble. I had that voice inside that was telling me not to drink it. No, thanks, I said. But Marco insisted. So I got up and tried to talk to Manuel, but he was still trapped in his high. He was, as they say, in the groove. Meanwhile Marco was facing me again. *Come on, humor me.* He went on stirring it with the straw. I tried again to avoid him, but no matter where I moved he stayed right there with me. *Drink, this stuff is terrific.* He kept talking in a woman's voice. Finally I took a drop to please him. That wasn't enough for him. As soon as I put the glass down, he picked it up and put it in front of me. At that point I thought: *Listen, you're really pissing me off.* So I grabbed the glass and took a long swallow. I must have drunk more than half. It tasted like shit. Either they had put something strange in it, I thought, or they had used the worst kind of vodka. I bet on the bad vodka so I wouldn't get too paranoid."

After the drink, Alex sat down again. Manuel left his spot and went in search of his phone.

"It was as if they were waiting to do something to me," Alex recalled, "not necessarily what happened later, but I felt there was the *concrete* possibility that at any moment a kind of trap could spring. So I changed my attitude. I stopped talking, I started to move away with the chair. Manuel went into his room. Marco got up, came toward me."

"Listen, you . . ." Marco approached Alex, bent over toward him, grabbed the edge of his jacket, made as if to open it. "Let's see what you're hiding under there." Alex jumped up. "Hey, what are you doing? Hold it." He smiled to defuse the situation. Manuel came back to the living room, he was looking for the headphones for the phone. Marco approached again, Alex backed up, embarrassed. Marco showed his cards: "Come on, come here, I'll suck you off. I'm really good, you know." Alex looked at Manuel. But Manuel said: "If my opinion counts then I'll tell you it's worth it. I've tried it, trust me."

"He also gestured with his hand, closed fist and thumb up,

as if to say it was OK. Marco came toward me. He tried to open my coat, my jacket, my sweater, whatever the fuck I was wearing . . . He said: *Come on, let me see where you come from, what your origins are* . . . I smiled . . . I don't know how to explain it . . . as if to say, *Come on, stop it, what the fuck are you doing* . . . but in a way that was still polite, a foolish smile . . . part of me was thinking that maybe it was all a joke, they were making fun of me . . . but Manuel repeated *Listen to me, she's the best of all.* After which he disappeared into his room for good. It was just Marco and me. I retreated. Marco stretched out a hand. He touched my balls. I said: *Stop, hey, come on* . . . He came even closer to me . . . and suddenly we fell onto the couch . . . he knelt down, stuck his head between my legs, tried to open my fly . . . I tried to resist . . . I attempted to come up with excuses, *Listen,* I improvised, *you should know that after I've snorted it's hard for me to get it up* . . . he didn't bat an eye: *You let me suck you and see if you don't get it up* . . . He put his hands between my legs . . . I told him to stop . . . I have the impression that I should have freed myself more forcefully . . . but I was stuck . . . maybe exhaustion . . . or the fact that I'd been sleeping in hostels for days . . . I felt *dirty*, because it was as if I were selling myself for a roof over my head . . . even though nothing had happened, let's be clear . . . I was selling myself because I was hesitating . . . so finally I said enough."

Alex jumped off the couch with a decisive move. He stood up. He looked down at Marco.

"What the fuck are you doing, huh?" he shouted. Then he called Manuel: "Manuel, come out of that room, come here and explain to me what the fuck is going on!" Manuel reappeared in the living room. Marco got up off the couch.

"Suddenly he no longer had a woman's voice," Alex recalled. "He said: *Manuel, send this guy away, he's no use to us.* He said it just like that. I couldn't believe it. *What the fuck*, I said, *it was you who called me, you made me spend fifteen euros on a taxi, goddammit!* Manuel looked at me, he went: *Yes, Alex, but listen to me, it's better if you leave."*

At that point yet another bizarre episode occurred. It was now eight in the morning. The shops down in the street were reopening, and despite the fact that the situation was very tense, they asked him please to go get them something to drink.

"The vodka's finished," said Marco, "come on, do us a favor, go get us some bottles."

Manuel opened his wallet. Alex was stunned by the cash he counted out. Manuel took a fifty-euro bill from the pile, and handed it to him: "Get some vodka," he said.

Alex could have left the house and not returned: it would have been his revenge. He thought about it. He got in the elevator, went down to the ground floor, and out to the street. He started walking with the fifty euros clutched in his fist, he assessed the situation, finally he thought that certain shitty things he no longer did. He saw the sign for a Tuodì supermarket, headed there. As soon as he was inside, it was all suddenly clear to him. Pouf! He felt the wave spreading in his head.

"I took a few steps into the supermarket *and it happened,*" he told the police. "I still get the shivers when I relive the scene . . . at a certain point . . . suddenly . . . I felt a peace . . . but like true peace . . . like when I went to Ibiza and took a couple of uppers . . . like when I went dancing and swallowed two tabs of LSD . . . a *sensation* . . . and that sensation, let's be clear, wasn't the effect of the coke. At that precise instant I understood, incontrovertibly, a hundred percent, that they had put *something* in that cocktail—that shitty vodka tonic. I was still in the aisles, I felt that typical buzzing . . . I felt the cool air I'd felt in Ibiza again . . . then I really tripped out . . . and I decided that instead of the vodka I'd get beer . . . just that. On the shelves I saw those nice half-liter Barleys I like . . . I thought *What the fuck do I care about vodka, I'll get the beer, I'll get all the beers I want, like when I used to go and have fun* . . . I got seven or eight beers . . . I felt good, so good I thought *In the end the two of them will be glad, too, that I got beer.*

But when Alex returned, he got a reaction different from what he had imagined. As soon as he set foot in the apartment, Marco Prato looked at him with contempt: "What the fuck did you do?" he said. "You weren't supposed to buy that stuff, you were supposed to get vodka."

Alex looked into Marco's eyes. Something crossed his gaze. He put the beers down on the floor. He approached Marco without for an instant looking away. He arrived a few centimeters from his nose. "Listen," he said harshly, "now you've really pissed me off. Give me back the money for the taxi and I'll leave."

It was over. Manuel immediately opened his wallet, Marco objected: "Manuel, what the fuck are you doing, you're giving him more money?" Manuel had taken out a twenty, Alex tore it out of his hand, put it in his pocket, took their measure with one hand raised: "You really make me sick," he said.

Manuel and Marco looked at him. A few hours earlier Alex had showed them what he could do in the ring. They didn't even think of stopping him.

When Alex heard about the murder he freaked out. On the one hand, he felt he had escaped a massacre. On the other, the fact that he had become a sort of public figure bothered him. The newspapers wrote about him, people he didn't even know called him "the boxer with no fixed abode." It wasn't at all pleasant. In the following days he avoided reading the papers, and couldn't even watch TV—he felt hunted. Was I the chosen one? he wondered, was I the one who was supposed to die? When he went out he avoided the newsstands, the shop windows where a TV might be turned on. He was afraid of seeing his name appear at any moment.

But if he sought refuge from the media, the media came to him. One night, after the statement to the police, his lawyer called him and said that Mediaset was looking for him, offering him fifteen hundred euros: he just had to go on TV and describe what had happened. Alex refused. More phone calls came. "My lawyer said that all the shows were looking for me now. The offers had increased." But he was afraid of making a bad impression on Sonia, the girl who had changed his life, the girl with whom he was trying to build something sane. He should have told her what happened, but then he would also have been forced to explain to her why he hadn't fled as soon as he saw the guy with the blue wig. His lawyer reported that one show was now offering a figure with four zeroes.

"My answer was, yet again, no. I can't sell myself and then be on YouTube for the next hundred years. Sonia is worth more than fifty or a hundred thousand euros. Every man has a price, mine is my loved ones."

A few weeks later, however, the police returned. They asked more questions. At a certain point—by now they knew him, the atmosphere was almost friendly—they asked about Sonia. Alex darkened.

"She left me," he said.

"What?" one cop let escape.

"For the first time in my life I'd done things really in a serious way," Alex told them, disconsolate, "because, look, you see, I asked Sonia to marry me when this ugly story was over. I did it. I asked her officially. All the answer I got was she gave me back the engagement ring. Stop, the end. Maybe it's me who can't get to the bottom of what is in a woman's mind, but this time I'd done everything right."

As soon as Alex left the house, Marco and Manuel had sex. They talked for a few minutes, then collapsed into sleep. They were exhausted. They woke in the early afternoon, the cold and cloudy afternoon of Thursday, March 3.

"What should we do?"

They still had Damiano's money. Marco sent yet another message to Trovajoli.

In two days they had bought more than ten grams, they would come close to twenty by that night, a quantity sufficient to intimidate a small group of hardened cokeheads.

In the meantime Manuel's apartment was utterly neglected. Empty bottles. Paper garbage. Clothes scattered everywhere. Marco bent over the table. Bill, nostril. Except for the makeup and the nail polish, he was again in male clothing. "For you I'm willing to do anything!" he said, satisfied.

They began plotting again. Every time they slid deeper into delirium. The effect was like a record where the needle keeps going over the same track, but at an always higher volume and greater speed. They talked again about how Marco would use his powers ("He said he would seduce even my brother," Manuel said, "he would blackmail him, and that way we'd also resolve the question of my father"). They talked about Manuel's fantasies ("Manuel would have liked what in Roman slang is called *batteria*," Marco said, "that is to say a woman who services several men. I would have to take the role of the woman. We returned to the rape fantasy, we looked for ways to put it into practice, I wanted to satisfy his desires, it was my way of feeling like a woman"). They talked about Valter Foffo, and Manuel got nervous ("Whenever that subject came up all the poison flooded me"). Marco in his turn was upset ("When Manuel talked to me about his father he became unrecognizable"). But also to Manuel it seemed that Marco was strange ("I don't know if it was the effect of the cocaine, but he gave me a look . . . in that look, between him and me, there was a *sincere* communication").

In a look between the two a sincere communication. What did Manuel mean?

According to some of the professionals who worked on the case—criminologists, psychologists, psychiatrists—it was at that moment that a crucial step was taken. So-called psychic contagion, like a racing engine, brought the two young men close to the point of fusion.

"We need a third mind, a third mind!"

Marco again suggested luring someone else to the apartment. "We had to let in some oxygen, the air in there was mentally foul."

The choice fell on Tiziano De Rossi.

Tiziano was an employee of Valter's. Manuel was worried: Alex Tiburtina was one thing, another was a waiter from Bottarolo, a person his father and brother knew very well. He asked Marco if he intended to hit on Tiziano, too. Marco answered: "So what? will you get it into your head that everybody likes the surprise?"

O.K., but if Tiziano doesn't like it? Manuel respected him, he considered him smart. Also, he was a formidable observer. "Like all experienced waiters, Tiziano is perceptive. Because of his job he's used to assessing customers in a few instants, he understands immediately who he has to deal with." At night when Tiziano finished his shift, Manuel would go drinking with him in a bar near the restaurant. At a glance Tiziano could make predictions: "Let's bet that in the end she'll give in?" he'd say, pointing to a couple of kids who were flirting. He always guessed right.

So on the one hand Manuel was afraid that Tiziano would immediately understand, for example, that there was something between him and Marco. On the other, given Marco's persuasive powers, he was terrified by the possibility that Tiziano, despite his acuity, might fall into the trap, as he had. At the same time, he hoped between one snort and the next, wasn't it perhaps possible that Tiziano's great experience was precisely what might help him get out of this mess? Maybe, since he could no longer manage, Tiziano could figure out what sort of situation he'd gotten himself into.

Giving in to the illusion, so much more seductive than the reality principle, Manuel sent a WhatsApp to Tiziano De Rossi. It was 9:57 P.M.

"Lucky situation. A guy who lives in the building is offering everything. Let me know, and if you come bring a bottle of vodka."

At that hour Tiziano was very busy. He was moving among the restaurant tables, taking orders, discussing with customers, running to the kitchen. He didn't even realize he'd gotten the WhatsApp. A little over an hour later, his phone started ringing.

"It was the son of the owner," he told the police, "asking me to come by, to bring a bottle of vodka. I seemed to understand that he was partying. He had never invited me to his house. While he was talking, I heard some rather strange voices in the background. It disturbed me, I said I wouldn't come."

But a few minutes later Tiziano noticed the message. He read it with attention. He took some time to think about it. He called Manuel back. This time there was no voice in the background, Tiziano calmed down, said O.K., he'd come by. "Can you also bring some cigarettes?" Manuel asked.

Tiziano waited for the end of his shift, left the restaurant, got a bottle of vodka, bought the cigarettes. He headed for Via Igino Giordani.

Manuel had done yet another line when he heard the intercom squawking. He hurried to open the door. He went back to the living room before Tiziano came up. He looked around and was stunned.

"What the fuck are you doing?"

With astonishing velocity, Marco had again put on women's clothes. Manuel panicked: what would Tiziano think as soon as he entered the apartment?

"Don't worry," said Marco, "you'll see, nothing will happen. I'll take care of it."

Tiziano De Rossi found the door open, entered the apartment, immediately noticed the chaos. Manuel met him. He was in a pitiful state. Then Tiziano saw the man dressed as a woman. "Manuel, what the hell is going on?" he asked under his breath.

"Oh, hello sweetheart, a pleasure," said Marco, looking up. He was preparing three lines of coke with the credit card.

Tiziano remained standing for ten minutes ("The situation was extremely strange, I couldn't explain the presence of such a person in Manuel's house"), but since getting used to the strange things in life isn't so difficult, after a bit he also sat down.

Tiziano asked if it was the first time the two had met, Manuel answered that Marco lived upstairs. "He let me know that it was all under control, the building was full of weird people, he added. I think we had already introduced ourselves, but I no longer remembered the name of the transvestite. I asked him. He said: *Sorry, sweetie, I speak only once.* I didn't like the way he said it. So I provoked him: *O.K., but you have a dick, no?* and he: *I don't have to answer you.* He referred to himself in the feminine."

Marco began to hold forth on sexual orientation: even the fanatical fans of Curva Sud, he assured them, every so often welcomed the company of a trans. It hadn't escaped him that Tiziano was wearing a Rome team jersey. Tiziano looked around as if to assess the situation better, reflected for a moment, then got up from the chair, approached the table, leaned over, had a sniff of coke ("Not even one, it must have been half a line"), straightened up, and said he didn't want to take further advantage of the generosity of his hosts. "Thank you very much," he said, "but my partner is waiting at home. She doesn't know I'm here. She'll be wondering what became of me."

He waved goodbye, went to the door, and gave Manuel a dirty look. And then he took off.

They were still present to themselves with Damiano Parodi. They were half stoned during Alex Tiburtina's long sojourn. But by the time Tiziano De Rossi also left, their perception of reality was close to hallucination. Eye to eye, they started talking again, they snorted, they drank more vodka. The theme of what they would accomplish together was entwined with their friendship. What was the deeper meaning of what they were doing? They had met in January and become intimate, they had confided things that had brought them closer than they were to people they'd known forever, but now they could do something more, something that would make their bond more lasting, that would join them forever.

It was Marco who uttered that phrase.

"My intuition is that you want to recruit me to kill your father."

Manuel was startled. The sentence, uttered unexpectedly, wasn't connected to what they were saying, and yet it sounded mysteriously plausible. Pay him to kill his father? He didn't recall that he'd ever made such a request, and yet, on a purely theoretical level, the idea didn't displease him. If he'd had his father standing in front of him and a gun in hand, he would never have been able to pull the trigger. But to imagine the destruction of the man because of whom his life had been a chain of failures, well, that was satisfying. Marco, although he had uttered the phrase, considered that they were in the grip of an unrealizable fantasy. Pure speculation, abstract thought. And yet playing with that fantasy, well, it was pleasant.

They returned to the subject of rape. Manuel said that in a

drawer in the living room there must still be a package of Alcover. "There it is, that's it." A psychiatrist had prescribed it to keep him from drinking. If you mixed the Alcover with alcohol, he said, you'd be in danger of collapsing, you'd get the effect of GHB, the rape drug. Drink. Rape. Maybe kill. The mental associations leaped out one after another, the topics got mixed up. They snorted. They drank another glass. They said things they would have trouble reconstructing in the days following. At four-thirty in the morning they left the house.

"My inference is that we were supposed to kill a person," said Manuel.

"Not at all," Marco recounted. "We left the house to try to fulfill Manuel's fantasy. We left in search of someone to rape."

"I don't think we left to rape someone," said Manuel. "I don't even know if we left to kill someone. To beat someone up, probably yes. We had bad intentions, I'm sure of that."

"We weren't going to *actually* rape someone," said Marco. "It was supposed to be a fake rape. Everything was supposed to remain in the realm of fiction."

"I was poisoned by the matter of my father," said Manuel, "maybe Marco Prato was poisoned by something else. I don't think we were looking for a whore. What's it take to pick up a prostitute?"

"I wanted to make Manuel happy," said Marco. "At first he suggested a girl, a prostitute we'd pay to stage the rape. I was opposed: no women, I wanted to be the *only one*. We had to get a boy. For once I could be the top. It would cost me, but for Manuel I would do it. He would be limited to watching."

"When Prato told me he had intuited that I wanted to hire him to kill my father he had the eyes of a madman again," said Manuel. "His statement was also a way to reinforce our friendship. If he really had killed my father, we would have shared a huge secret. Even though, sincerely, I can't explain how Marco could stir up in *himself* the rage for something that *I* felt on my skin."

Psychiatrists and criminologists wondered if in that last statement, however disjointed, there was a clue for reconstructing the mental pathway that put them on the road a little before dawn. Human nature is sensitive to self-deception. How many times, to fulfill a desire of our own, do we need to misunderstand the desires of another? And in how many cases do we use words uttered by a friend, a parent, a lover to feel authorized to do what those words did not in fact contemplate? Words are ambiguous, fleeting, they resonate in different ways according to the material they collide with. And since words—cousins of witchcraft—often produce deeds, it's important to understand what expectations or misunderstandings they carry at the moment of crossing that fatal border.

They left the house, got in the Mini. Manuel drove. Marco, in the passenger seat, besides the makeup and the woman's dress, was wrapped in an ostentatious dark fur.

They decided that the first stop would be Villa Borghese.

"We headed for the usual places for male prostitution," said Marco. "If there was someone we could pick up it would have to be there."

They skirted Porta Pinciana. Via Veneto stretched lifeless and sleeping to the left. Villa Borghese was nearby: pines and fountains and statues rose in the cold of the night. They passed a police car.

"Marco wanted me to drive," Manuel recounted, "in case the police stopped us, he said, he would have his hands free to disarm the cops. He would perform fellatio and they would let us go."

They were in a pitiful state. But they still had some money. Marco knew that street prostitutes don't ask a lot, sometimes thirty or forty euros is enough, and his intention was to offer as much as a hundred and fifty. For that sum a whore would do anything, and they had in mind at the very least the simulation of a rape.

They entered Villa Borghese on the road reserved for taxis and buses. They drove on among trees and hedges and ponds and temples. The black of the vegetation was deeper than that of the sky. They passed some headless statues, then the vault of the Orangerie, housing works by De Chirico, Manzú, Warhol, Severini. They left it behind. When the vegetation stopped, there was asphalt again and artificial lights. They headed toward the National Gallery of Modern Art. It was here, at the start of Valle Giulia, that boys sold themselves every night. The clients arrived in cars of every type, stopped at the bottom of the stairs, waited with engines idling. After a while, the boys emerged from the bushes around the museum. Prostitutes of twenty, quick as guerrilla fighters, approached the clients' cars.

"Shit, there's no one," Marco stated.

Traditionally the traffic disappeared after three in the morning. That Marco knew, but he had hoped. He told Manuel to head for Piazza della Repubblica.

"We went first to the place where Pasolini picked up his murderer, the stalls behind the piazza," Marco Prato recalled, "but it was totally deserted."

Not far away, in Piazza dei Cinquecento, was another historic place for prostitutes. Among the branches of the pines and the showers of guano, Italians, North Africans, Romanians walked the street, boys of all colors and all ages. For the most part they were desperate. That fact had its relevance: if the two were to simulate a rape, they needed people ready for anything. But even in Piazza dei Cinquecento there was no longer anyone.

"Damn."

Meanwhile the first pink streaks were beginning to imprint themselves on the opaque texture of the sky. The light would filter gradually through many small fissures, then the sun would explode and a river of angry people and cars would sanction the start of a new day in Rome. As in a story about vampires, Marco and Manuel felt their minutes were numbered.

"Let's go to Termini."

Marco said that at that hour some drifter in search of a ride might be wandering around after getting off a night train. They pulled up on Via Giolitti. The street ran straight and dark. Marco got out of the car. Wrapped in his fur, he started walking back and forth on the sidewalk. It wasn't clear if his intention was to be picked up, as in January in EUR, or to pick up someone. In front of him a silhouette took shape in the darkness. A middle-aged man. To start a conversation Marco asked for a cigarette. The man examined him, handed him one, and quickly vanished.

All Marco could do was light the cigarette, he took a couple of puffs, threw it away, and got back in the car. Manuel started off again.

Here they were, then, empty-handed at six in the morning. How was it possible that it had ended like this? Was it the confirmation that something wasn't right in their lives? If in the past they had had the suspicion that they would never be able to fully realize what they proposed to do, how could they avoid it now, faced with the evidence of being unable even to pick up a prostitute, though they were ready to offer a price at which those who sell themselves for money usually fling themselves into the arms of the client? Were they total failures? Were they worth less than a whore?

As they returned to Collatino, Marco tore the phone out of Manuel's hand and started making calls. He called presumed friends of Manuel's. He sent messages. At a certain point he called Alex Tiburtina again. He had been favorably impressed by the ex-boxer's condition of indigence. "Alex was dead broke. My reasoning was: if I offer Alex Tiburtina a hundred and fifty euros and tell him, *For this amount I'm going to walk on you with high heels*, he immediately lies down on the ground and thanks me."

But neither Alex nor the others who got phone calls and messages responded. Manuel was now driving along Via dei Monti Tiburtini. The closer they got to Via Igino Giordani, the more indisputable their failure seemed.

It was then that Marco Prato had the idea of calling Luca Varani.

M arco remembered that kid, so handsome, and young, and always short of money. Basically, he thought, Luca was usually willing to go halfway across the city to scratch up a little change from Damiano Parodi. He'd go all the way to Piazza Ungheria for fifty euros. If Marco gave him the prospect of a sum triple or quadruple that, he would drop whatever he was doing and rush to them.

Meanwhile the first light of morning descended on the Tiburtina. Marco grabbed the phone, looked for the number in the contacts. The hook disappeared under the surface of the water.

"Hello, Marco, is that you?"

Marco and Luca spoke rapidly on the phone. The conversation continued on WhatsApp.

Marco Prato to Luca Varani: "Call when you're almost here."

Luca Varani to Marco Prato: "O.K. But I have to leave by 12."

MP: "Listen, don't say anything to Damiano, otherwise I can't pay you. If you keep it secret, I'll give it to you today."

LV: "But when will you give it to me? When I get there?"

MP: "Luca, do I seem like someone who would cheat you?"

LV: "No, no, but at least I'll have it in my pocket."

Manuel turned onto Via Igino Giordani. Again the church, the giant apartment buildings. They got out of the car. Manuel stretched his legs. Marco, in fur and spike heels, hugged himself, breathing in the cold morning air. At that moment they were still two young men of nearly thirty with their lives before them. Who hadn't done stupid things in his youth? The world was full of adults who, calm and contented in their houses, paged through the album of memories and stopped, incredulous, at the absurd episodes whose protagonist they'd been so long ago.

"Down there," Marco pointed. Near the traffic circle, a man's dark profile, straight and solitary in the morning.

"I'll take care of it."

Manuel headed toward the man. Trovajoli delivered the goods. Then he took his phone out of his pocket and called a taxi. His work was never done.

"And now for some vodka," said Marco.

"We went to a bar between Pietralata and Tiburtina," Manuel recalled. "A girl with brown hair sold it to me. It wasn't even seven in the morning. *Come on, really?* she said, and sold me the vodka."

Returning to the apartment, Manuel turned on all the lights. It was a little cold. They adjusted the thermostat, raising the temperature. Marco checked his phone.

Marco Prato to Luca Varani: "Hurry up."

Luca Varani to Marco Prato: "You think I'm driving?"

MP: "So where are you?"

LV: "Waiting for the bus. I'm coming, don't worry."

The heater was going full blast. Now the apartment was really warm. Manuel began to strip, he took off his sweatshirt, his pants, keeping on boxers and T-shirt. He took a Camel from the pack and lighted it. Marco had prepared some lines. Manuel stretched out on the couch, looking through the helix of smoke at the tip of the Camel, the shapes of the living room. Morning, night, evening, afternoon. How long had they been there? Down there, in the depths, perhaps nothing even existed that could correctly be called time. The doorbell rang. Manuel heard behind him the sound of footsteps. The door opened. Voices. The door closed. Then more footsteps. "Hello." Manuel Foffo turned.

"At a certain point this kid showed up at my house," Manuel recalled. "I was lying on the couch, and I didn't even get up. And I didn't even wonder why he'd come. Considering the absurd life we were living, knowing who he was didn't matter."

But then Manuel looked more carefully at the new arrival, focused on him beside Marco, and something happened.

"As soon as I looked at him *I knew*. I looked at him. Then I looked at Marco, and it was as if we'd mentally said to each other *it's him*. A kind of tacit agreement clicked between Marco and me. As if that thing that was there before were . . . still *alive*."

A tacit agreement to do what?

"When Luca arrived I was wearing a pair of purple sunglasses, with gradient lenses, like Mina in the sixties," Marco recalled. "I was wearing the wig, a kind of black coat, a leopard-skin dress with prostheses in the bosom, tights, shoes with heels, and red socks."

And Manuel: "I said hello to Luca, we introduced ourselves. At that point I remembered that Marco had told me about him. He had said Luca was a prostitute. He had said that he was adopted. We all three sat down at the table and started talking."

"We drank some vodka. It might have been nine-thirty in the morning," said Marco. "We talked in a friendly way. *So, how are things? How long have you been like this?* Luca asked. And we: *And you? where are you coming from?* I started to lay out the coke, the biggest line as always for Manuel, then Luca, finally the smallest for me. We snorted. Luca also snorted."

And Manuel: "We snorted. We talked. We drank vodka. At a certain point, on my left, I found Luca naked, he was lying on the floor, face down."

"I'd said I would pay him," said Marco. "I just asked him not to say anything to Damiano. There was still the business of the bank card. Luca took off his clothes and lay down on the floor."

And Manuel: "Prato told me, because I didn't see it, that Luca had licked his shoes. They encouraged me to climb on Luca's back. To me that seemed stupid. But I did it."

"Luca licked my shoes," said Marco. "I started walking on his body, I said to him: *Maybe, if you suffer a little, we'll even give you three hundred euros.* He had a hundred-watt smile because he'd never seen a figure like that. I supported myself on Manuel's shoulder and walked on Luca, and at a certain point I slipped and scratched his thigh. I was wearing heels, I hurt him by accident. Then Manuel walked on him."

And Manuel: "I tried to do it gently, I got up on his back, they asked me to. I didn't even know it was an erotic game. Afterward I sat down again. Anyway we didn't have sex with Luca."

"We didn't have sex," Marco confirmed, "we started talking again. After a few minutes, very casually, Manuel took the Alcover out of the drawer and said: *Come on, let's go make cocktails.* I followed him to the kitchen, he said: *Let's put this in it and start to rape him.* At least that's how I understood it."

And Manuel: "I'd gotten the Alcover in a pharmacy some time earlier, it was prescribed to make me stop drinking. But I'd never taken it."

"Alcover can cause a kind of alcohol coma," said Marco. "But it's an alcohol coma that's absolutely reversible. Manuel poured the Alcover in one of the glasses and we went back to the living room with the three cocktails."

And Manuel: "Marco put in the Alcover. I agreed."

"Manuel wanted to fulfill the rape fantasy," said Marco. "Luca Varani was a top, he would never let himself be sodomized. That's why the Alcover. We had to stun him. I would have to rape him, unfortunately. Unfortunately because I'm a bottom, it was a compromise I had to reach with Manuel so that we wouldn't bring a woman into the house, it was a sacrifice I was making for him."

And Manuel: "Luca drank from a bowl, all the glasses were dirty, in the sink."

"We drank, we talked," said Marco. "After a few minutes Luca began to feel sick."

And Manuel: "While he was drinking from the bowl I knew he would feel sick, even though at the same time I doubted it. Given the state we were in, everything seemed plausible, that we walked on his back, that he drank the Alcover. Completely absurd. And completely normal."

"First Luca took a sip, then he took a slightly bigger sip," said Marco.

And Manuel: "He went to the bathroom to throw up."

"He started to feel sick," said Marco. "At a certain point he stopped the conversation, he said: *Guys, just a moment, I'm sick.* He got up. He was swaying, he felt nauseated, he went to the bathroom and Manuel followed him. I followed Manuel. Luca began to vomit an orange liquid."

And Manuel: "Luca vomited in the sink, he was in a confusional state, he leaned on the bathtub."

"He went into this sort of alcohol coma," said Marco. "He started to spin around, lost his balance, and ended up in the tub. He fell asleep instantly. I remember he snored."

And Manuel: "He had fallen with his bottom on the edge of the tub, his back to the wall. Marco gave him a slight push, I don't remember if with his hand or his foot, a little push, but enough to make him fall into the tub. It was then that he uttered that sentence."

"I never said any such thing," said Marco. "Manuel must have said it in his head, and thought I was the one who'd said it."

And Manuel: "As soon as Luca fell in the tub, Marco said:

We've decided you have to die. I looked at him and thought: So it's really happening."

"I never said any such thing," said Marco.

And Manuel: "But he did say it. Luca was in a confusional state, I don't think he even understood the meaning of the words. Right afterward Marco attacked him. I remember that I stabbed him in the neck, I hit him in the head with the hammer."

"The violence didn't begin in the bathroom," said Marco.

And Manuel: "After what Marco said I have a gap in my memory. I remember that we were strangling him, we were both trying to strangle him, first his hands, then mine. I have the image of Marco who was trying to cut off his penis. If I make an effort I can visualize the most distressing images, not the chronology."

"Nothing happened in the bathroom," said Marco.

And Manuel: "Marco started to hit him. I followed, I kicked it up a notch. I must have taken the weapons from the kitchen. A hammer, a knife with a short blade, another, bigger knife. I immediately grabbed the hammer because I thought if I hit him with the hammer it'd be over right away."

"We took him out of the bathtub and dragged him to the bedroom," said Marco. "I was still in my heels, so it was difficult. Manuel picked him up under the arms, Luca's bottom slid along the floor, our biggest effort was when we had to lift him onto the bed."

And Manuel: "We started hitting him in the tub. In the next flash we had carried him to the bedroom. Prato had talked to me about the plumbing. In the bathroom, he said, the blood would run out through the bathtub drain into the pipes and we'd be found out. That's why we moved him."

"Once he was in the bed, I straddled him," said Marco. "I took advantage of the fact that he was stunned and began to play a little. I caressed him, I kissed him. Manuel said: *Strangle him, sweetheart.* And I put my hands around his neck, I started to squeeze, but it was only a sexual practice, and besides, Manuel had said: *Strangle him, sweetheart*, not *Kill him, sweetheart*."

And Manuel: "Marco told me to grab a weapon, and I took the knife."

"*Strangle him, sweetheart*, he said. But while I was strangling him Luca came to," said Marco. "He revived, he gave me a shove and knocked me to the floor. I fell with my butt on the floor. Luca got up, staggering. He fell down next to the bed, on the floor. Then I saw Manuel's silhouette, he had both hands in view. In one he held the knife, in the other the hammer. I looked at his eyes. They were the eyes of when he talked to me about his father. Luca was staggering toward the door. Manuel hit him with the hammer and he fell to the floor."

And Manuel: "I realized I had to kill him only when I actually started to attack him. I hit him in the face with the hammer. I used the knife. Marco also stabbed him."

"I said to him: *Manuel, calm down. Calm down! What the fuck are you doing?*" said Marco. "He replied: *No, no, no, I have to kill this jerk!* And I: *What do you mean kill, what are you talking about, stop!* He hit him with the hammer. I heard the dull sound, an indescribable sound. Then I ran out of the room. I feel guilty that I wasn't able to stop him, I was in a panic."

And Manuel: "We hit him. Luca had some red Kleenex in his mouth. Marco must have put it there so he wouldn't scream."

"I went back and forth, I tried to make him calm down," said Marco. "Going in and out of the room was a way of protecting myself from what was happening. After all that hammering, Manuel got up and started to look at him. He looked at Luca. He leaned over him again, took the knife, slashed him again and again, on one side, then the other, as if to draw asterisks on his skin. Then he started hitting him in a different way, he went straight in, stabbed him in the chest, I heard a noise . . . Something indescribable. I went back to the living room. I was upset. I took off my shoes, I lay down on the couch, I started thinking."

And Manuel: "Stabbing, hammering, but Luca wouldn't stop breathing. It seemed as if he'd never die. He suffered so much."

"He was unable to die," said Marco. "I wanted his suffering to end. Manuel also wanted him not to suffer. *That bastard won't die, he won't die!* he said. He attacked him with the hammer, with the knife, he hit him randomly. I went back and forth with my hands on my head. Manuel said: *He has to die now, sweetheart, he has to die, but how can I kill him?*"

And Manuel: "At one point I recall that I wanted to break a vodka bottle on his head to kill him, but Marco stopped me, because I would have left too much glass around. But really, sincerely . . . there was already so much blood the glass would have been the least of the problems."

"He grabbed a two-liter bottle of Sambuca," said Marco. "He wanted to break it on his head. I shouted: *Manuel, stop it!* He put the bottle down on the table, picked up the knife again."

And Manuel: "Marco also stabbed him."

"I had retreated to the living room again," said Marco. "I was on the couch with one arm around my legs, I wanted it to end as quickly as possible. Manuel was shouting from the other room: *Come here, come and help me!*"

And Manuel: "He was suffering so much, but he wouldn't die, he just wouldn't die! He wanted so much to live, we didn't know what to do."

"I was still on the couch," said Marco. "Opposite, near the television, there was a tangle of cables. Manuel kept shouting: *Help me kill him!* So I brought him one of these cables. I said: *Take it, he just has to stop suffering!*"

And Manuel: "We tried to strangle him with the cable. We tried to press the pillow over his face. Nothing doing. He was breathing."

"Manuel tried to strangle him," said Marco. "At some point he asked me to kiss him on the head, he wanted me to go on kissing him on the head so he would find the strength to strangle him, to take his life."

And Manuel: "While I was stabbing him, Marco was kissing

me on the head, he was saying: *Go on, kill him*. It was something we both wanted to do."

"I put a hand on his shoulder, and then, yes, I kissed him on the head," said Marco, "I started kissing him while he was strangling Luca."

And Manuel: "Marco said: *Give him the death blow*. Then, instead, he gave the final blow, he put his right knee against Luca's chest and stabbed him in the heart with the knife, he stuck the blade in."

"Manuel came into the living room and told me that Luca was dead," said Marco.

And Manuel: "I realized he was dead when we tried to lift him. He felt cold."

"He said he was dead," said Marco, "so I went immediately to the bedroom and covered him with a quilt. I couldn't look at him."

And Manuel: "While we were killing him I also made a video. I did it with the phone, the video must have lasted about fifteen seconds, I made this video but then I deleted it, because I thought: *What am I doing? First I kill him and then I film it?* Maybe I wanted to make up for Marco's video. I don't remember. Anyway the video doesn't exist anymore."

"After I covered him with the quilt I went back to the living room," said Marco. "Luca was dead. I was petrified. Manuel had had a fit and I had been unable to stop him. At that point I began to talk. What have you done? I said. I noticed that Manuel's expression changed. I was afraid and I used the plural. *What have we done? Do you realize?*"

And Manuel: "We were very tired. We went to bed. He and I got under the covers, with Luca's corpse nearby on the floor."

"Manuel went to the bathroom to wash," said Marco, "then he came back to the bedroom, and lay down next to me. I was about to go to sleep. but he was talking, he said that we would be bound for life, that what we had done would join us forever. *Yes, but we killed a person*, I said. I was still dressed as a woman."

And Manuel: "There I lay on the bed, with the corpse practically next to us. It was then that we had the first anal sex of our relationship."

"That is absolutely untrue," said Marco.

And Manuel: "I had just fallen asleep. He got on top of me, like a woman who gets on a man who's lying down. He held it, he wanted to put it inside him. That position disgusted me. But I had an erection. So I flipped him over and we had sex. Since he insisted, I did it more to keep things calm than out of real excitement."

"We had sex," Marco said, "but that happened in the days before. He sodomized me several times, without a condom. But after the murder we didn't do anything. How could we? The mere idea is sickening. We lay on the bed and fell asleep."

And Manuel: "I possessed him. But it was as if he possessed me. We had sex and then we fell asleep."

M arco opened his eyes again several hours later.
He had fallen into a deep sleep. Waking was like being tossed up from the bottom of an ocean, his breath
failed, he opened his mouth to take in oxygen, abruptly sat up
in the bed. Like water from a leak, a thought began to invade
his head. Next to him was Manuel, asleep. Marco observed him,
bewildered, then he turned the other way and saw, clearly, Luca's
body on the floor. *So it's true*, he thought.

In certain science-fiction stories the protagonist dreams of
killing someone, and then, on waking, finds the murder weapon
on the night table, the disturbing testimony of something that
happened elsewhere. In this case Marco and Manuel had shattered the glass that separates the plane of reality from the imagination by inverting the relationship between light and shadow:
starting today, and forever, they would awaken every morning in
a nightmare.

Marco got out of bed, left the room, wandered into the living
room, brought his hands to his face, and burst into tears.

His sobs woke Manuel. He, too, sat up in bed, but slowly. The
room was enveloped in shadow. Smell of stale air. He saw the
corpse on the floor, he got up and joined his friend in the living
room.

"I don't think I deserve to live!" Marco was shouting. "I
shouldn't be alive after what happened!"

Manuel looked at him. He couldn't tell if the grief was genuine
or if Marco was pretending.

"All right," he said, "but now sit down and let's think."

In the apartment waste paper, open drawers, empty bottles, scattered clothes. And blood everywhere.

"I don't deserve to live!" Marco wouldn't stop crying. "And I don't think you deserve to live, either."

"I understand," Manuel answered, "but at least let's try to clean up a little."

Marco looked at him, his cheeks lined with tears, then nodded.

Somewhere, in their fogged brains, there was still, perhaps, the idea that they might get away with it. When Manuel was interrogated by the prosecutor, he said he hadn't thought of the legal consequences as he was hitting Luca with the hammer, and had believed, on waking, with the body in the bedroom, that, in the end, there would be a way to get out of it. Naturally there was no way to get out of it. They had left behind an infinity of traces, some of them impossible to erase. The reckoning was a matter of hours, even if at that moment they were the only keepers of an abominable secret: a large group of people had been flung into the state of not knowing something that would change their lives forever. Luca's parents. Marta Gaia. Manuel's family and Marco's. They were going around Rome in ignorance. Outside it was an ordinary March day.

Manuel called his mother on the landline. The phone rang in vain. Assured that she wasn't home, Manuel took the keys and went down. He wanted to get buckets, rags, detergent.

"I was completely dazed. I went back to the tenth floor and realized I had forgotten the rags, for instance. So I went down a second time to my mother's. But when I got upstairs again, the detergent was missing."

Every time he went out, Manuel double-locked the door. Marco thus found himself alone for several minutes, locked in, surrounded by silence, staring at the walls with the body in the bedroom. At a certain point he went out on the balcony feeling nauseated. He clutched the railing and leaned forward. O.K., he said to himself, it's a drop of at least thirty meters. He thought of the actor who had played Superman, Christopher Reeve, paralyzed from the neck down after falling off a horse.

Manuel returned. Now he had everything they needed. He called Marco. He handed him a rag and detergent. They had to clean, he said, and then they had to think how to get rid of the body.

"He claimed we had to bury it at Circeo," Marco said, "we had to go and bury it there, but first we had to buy a shovel at Leroy Merlin. He insisted on Circeo because, he said, it was a protected area. Who would go digging in a nature reserve? That was his reasoning."

They were still under the influence of the drugs. And yet certain sides of one's personality don't change along with states of consciousness. Manuel had always hated housework. Straightening, washing floors, dusting—all jobs for which he relied on his mother. He asked Marco to take care of it.

"And maybe take off the wig," he added.

Marco looked at him strangely.

Manuel returned a glance that wasn't really reassuring.

For the first time, in their games of looking, something was misaligned to the point of heading for a collision.

"There, now you want to kill me, too!" Marco burst into tears again.

"When I told him to take off the wig he looked at me with a furious expression," Manuel said. "I didn't understand if he didn't want to take off the wig because he was bald underneath or because, without the wig, he would become a male again."

"When he told me to change I was very frightened," said Marco. "As long as I was dressed as a woman I felt more protected, because I was his accomplice, his lover."

"When he said: *You want to kill me, too?* I thought in fact that I could go to the other room and get the knife and make a bit of a scene," Manuel admitted. "I only thought it. I certainly wouldn't have done it. I was really falling apart."

"I was afraid he was about to do something to me," said Marco, "so I said: *If you've decided to kill me, at least try not to let me suffer. And anyway,* I added, *remember that if you kill me then you'd have the problem of having to get rid of two bodies.* At that point he calmed down."

"I never really thought of beating him up or killing him," said Manuel, "but I did think he was a scumbag. I thought of how he had lured Varani to my house and I was very angry, then I saw him crying and all my aggression was . . . was as if disarmed."

Marco saw the calm return to Manuel's eyes, Manuel saw the fear drain from Marco's features. The moment of conflict had passed. Then Marco tried to waste time ("It was night again, I was trying to drag things out, I was waiting until the stores closed because all we needed was for him to drag me to Leroy Merlin to buy a shovel"), and finally he accepted Manuel's invitation. "O.K., let's clean up."

They went back to the bedroom. They turned on the light. They lifted the body off the floor, put it on the bed, and again covered it with the quilt. They picked up the clothes and carried them into the other room. Now they were in the living room again. Marco collected the dirty glasses, put them in the kitchen, grabbed the knife and the hammer, folded up the pizza boxes, threw them in the garbage. Manuel followed him with his eyes, but at a certain point he froze.

Incredible as it may seem, the sensation was real: Manuel wondered if it was really happening or if the horror of which they had been protagonists had entered into him and now was enjoying pulling the strings of his mind. *Luca.* He looked at the bedroom door.

"I heard Luca breathing. I know it's ridiculous. He'd been dead for hours. We had slept with the body and nothing had happened. The body was indisputably cold when we lifted it off the floor. And yet I heard him breathing. He was gasping. I had it fixed in my ear. So I got up my courage and went into the bedroom. As soon as I entered the gasping disappeared. The body was still there, I stood looking at it, waiting for I don't even know what, obviously nothing happened. But then I went back to the living room and the gasping started in my ear again."

Meanwhile Marco had filled the bucket with water, poured in the detergent, and wet the rag, and was running it over the floor.

"I got down on my knees, I had begun to run the rag over the floor, I really seemed like Cinderella. I was trying to clean that floor properly, but then I saw the rag all bloody and I said that's enough."

Marco dropped the rag. He stood up. Again his cheeks were streaked with tears. He told Manuel that what he was doing made no sense, they had behaved atrociously, and at least as far as he was concerned the moment to die had come.

"Are you serious?" asked Manuel.

"Of course I'm serious."

"And how would you kill yourself? with the knives?"

Marco shook his head.

"He wanted to kill himself, but using the knives bothered him," said Manuel. "He wanted a less bloody death. I thought maybe I could still dissuade him, the situation was confused, we decided to leave the house again."

Manuel picked up Luca's things. Clothes, shoes, phone. He put everything in Luca's backpack. On the one hand he was beginning to understand the situation. On the other, every so often the illusion of an escape appeared, like a sudden clearing in a cloudy sky. But where could they go? It was eight-thirty at night, they had a body in the house, darkness had fallen again over the entire city.

"Come on, let's go get a drink," said Manuel.

Raffaele Braga was thirty-one and lived in Guidonia, and every day he traveled back and forth the thirty kilometers that separated him from Rome. He worked at the Café Oval, in San Giovanni. Minimal fixtures, outside tables, a bar quite well supplied with alcohol.

That Friday evening Raffaele was dividing his time between the tables and the bar. It was a little after 9 P.M. The bar was starting to fill up but wasn't yet crowded. Two girls had climbed up on barstools and were drinking. Two guys were sitting outside. They were pretty much keeping a low profile; they weren't regular customers. The one with his back to him was all hunched over, the other was wearing a kind of dark jacket that came to his knees. After a few minutes the guy in the jacket got up and went to the bar. He ordered two glasses of white, sat down again across from his friend.

After serving them, Raffaele went back inside. When, two weeks later, he was summoned by the police, he said that if there was a characteristic that those two guys shared, without a shadow of a doubt it was the fact of seeming "perfectly normal."

After leaving the house, Marco and Manuel had wandered around for a while in San Giovanni. On Via Magna Grecia, paying no attention to the police patrol cars, they had pulled up next to a garbage bin. Manuel had gotten out of the car, thrown Luca's backpack, containing his clothes and cell phone, into the bin. Then they had gone to the Oval.

Marco Prato finished drinking his Falanghina and said: "I want to die."

Now he was dressed like a man. The only visible traces of the preceding days was the polish on his nails and the now smudged makeup under his eyes.

Manuel tried to calm him. Marco kept whispering: "What have we done . . . what have we done . . . my God, we deserve to die."

"Wait a minute," said Manuel. "Now let's have another glass and get a better sense of what's the right thing to do."

"We took the life of a twenty-three-year-old kid," said Marco. "We played at being God. Now the moment has come to pay. I want to die, and you have to help me."

He said that he wanted to kill himself with sleeping pills. He knew that Manuel had a prescription for benzodiazepine at home. Two one-milligram tablets and you'd sleep all night. Four bottles mixed with alcohol and you were in danger of not waking again.

In the end Manuel seemed to be convinced: he would help him end it. They paid and went back to Manuel's house. Reaching the apartment, they began searching for the prescription, examining the floor, opening drawers, adding disorder to the disorder: careful not to look in the bedroom. In the end they found the piece of paper. The prescription had expired. Manuel looked for a pen and altered the date, trusting in the tolerance of Roman pharmacists after nine in the evening. Now the problem was money. They didn't have a euro left.

"The restaurant," said Manuel.

"Besides the money, try to get some vodka," said Marco when they were in the car.

Not even twenty-four hours after he had fled the apartment on Via Igino Giordani, Tiziano De Rossi again found himself face to face with Manuel Foffo. The son of the owner burst into the restaurant a little after eleven. Tiziano was waiting on some tables. The young man was obviously agitated. He must have snorted more coke, thought Tiziano. The other waiters also looked at him in bewilderment. Manuel went straight to the cash register, took out a hundred and fifty euros, then opened the fridge. No vodka. After dinner, the waiters at Bottarolo would offer the customers a liqueur or limoncello. Manuel grabbed a bottle of Amaro del Capo, said a confused goodbye to the onlookers, and rushed out.

It was illegal to buy more than three bottles of sleeping pills at a time. First they went to a pharmacy on Via Nazionale. Then to a second, near Porta Pia. In neither case did the pharmacist notice the altered date on the prescription. Marco got back in the car with five bottles of benzodiazepine. Now he had everything he needed.

Before they separated, Manuel proposed a last glass. Marco agreed ("Considering my goal, drinking would play into my hands"), so they turned onto Via Livorno. On the Tiburtina, long and straight and enveloped in shadows, the sign for Dallas appeared. "Let's stop here," said Marco.

It was a small bar across from the Verano cemetery. From the tables you could see the cypresses. Marco ordered a straight vodka, Manuel a rum and coke. Now they were very silent. They looked at one another without speaking.

"Manuel, listen, now let me go," Marco said finally. "I can't take it anymore."

"I'll drive you to the hotel," Manuel agreed.

Marco shook his head.

"The Mini Cooper was registered to my father," he told the police, "the person I love most in the world. I was afraid that, once I had gone to kill myself, Manuel would hide Luca's body in the car. So my father would be in the middle, he'd be in a lot of trouble. I told him I wouldn't leave him the car."

Manuel shrugged, said, "O.K.," and paid the bill. He and Marco left the bar. It was the moment to say goodbye. They embraced.

Marco said: "I hope never to see you again, but not because of you."

Manuel walked home. It was three in the morning. He patiently followed the Tiburtina, leaning forward with his hands in his pockets, one step after another. When he was back on Via Igino Giordani he looked for the house keys. He got on the elevator. Arriving at the tenth floor he opened the door of the apartment, turned on the lights, went into the living room, and sat down on the couch.

With his back to the bedroom, Manuel lighted a cigarette, and reflected. He smoked calmly. Then he lighted another. He got up and went to the kitchen. In the refrigerator there was still a bottle of rum. He opened a Coca-Cola, carried everything into the living room, tried to improvise a Cuba Libre. He took two sips, then gave it up. He smoked a third cigarette, stood up again with the idea of putting things in order. He had to make the time pass. He retrieved some garbage bags from the kitchen, started tossing in the empty bottles and the remains of dinner. Having filled two bags, he went to throw them out. Every chance to get away from the body was good.

When he got outside again dawn was breaking. Manuel looked at the deserted streets, and the cold began to enter into his bones. After throwing away the garbage, he returned to the apartment. What else could he do? Again in the elevator. He opened and closed the door, sat down once more in the living room. He felt the presence of the body in the bedroom. He took a cigarette out of the pack, played with it between his fingers. Light began to filter through the half-closed blinds. At seven-thirty his brother was coming by to pick him up and go to his uncle's funeral. Good, he thought, looking at the clock, it's almost time.

He wasn't the only one who'd found a den in that neighborhood. There were many places like his around the train station. The rumor had been circulating for years. The landlords had multiplied. The clients came from all over the world. Like Bucharest but better. A child emerged from the tunnels of Piazza Indipendenza, stretched, began his day.

The Dutch tourist paid for a coffee in a bar on Via Lanza, left to walk along the street. The Magic Gate. Derelict gardens in the sun. Then women with their shopping bags.

Now and then he encountered men like him on the street; he recognized them by the mask of desperation and benevolence. Every so often someone was caught. The hand of the law fell on the shoulder of a coat. The name of the guilty party appeared in the papers, but new news devoured the old, and so, within a few days, that name was as if unknown. The financier. The town councilor. The artisan. Recently even a judge.

The judge had defended himself by explaining to the assistant prosecutor that he had been "pushed by impulses toward boyish faces." He said he always inquired about the age of the boys. The money was a gift, not compensation.

The Dutch tourist observed the luminous dust that rose slowly from the market. At Santa Maria Maggiore, he seemed to hear behind him a small whirlwind, a wind that echoed like a laugh. He checked his watch. There wasn't time to stop by the hotel. He hurried toward his den. From the sidewalk now the fragrance of spices. Then shouts. Italy was an atrociously old country. A garden of angry, spiteful old people. But in that area the biological age dropped.

The Thrill on Via Giolitti. The revolting kebab shops on Via Manin. Eternity was revealed in anonymity. The stink of frying. Sweatshirts. Glitter on nails. Only an occasional leather jacket. The array of minors was dazzling. Maghrebis. Egyptians. Adolescents from the periphery came here to go out together. They took a broken-down bus from Labaro, from Primavalle, they crossed the city amid potholes and jostling and creaking and curses. In sneakers with colored laces they arrived at the station gardens.

But the Dutch tourist was there for the invisible ones.

They were mainly Romanians. There were also Egyptians, Tunisians, Libyans. They slept in the gardens, amid the rats and the garbage bags. Or in the tunnels, in the ditches, in the sewers. Huddled together in the cold. They slept for five, six hours at most. Dreamless sleep.

The Dutch tourist opened the outer door. He got on the elevator, went up to the fifth floor. He observed the antennas from the half-closed window, the water tower of Via Giolitti. He heard the cry of swallows in the sky. Someone knocked on the door. The Dutch tourist went to open it and found him there again. This time the boy was wearing a sweatshirt two sizes too big. It was the third time they'd seen each other. The Dutch tourist gathered his courage, ran a hand through his hair. The boy didn't smile. Then he moved aside, in such a way that he could feel the autonomy of that body before making it his own. Everything on loan and nothing given. "No," said the man. The boy stopped. He was about to go into the bathroom. He would take a shower like the other time. "No," he repeated in a lower voice. The boy didn't understand. The man pulled fifty euros out of his pocket, rubbed it blatantly between his fingers and the boy understood. He didn't want him to take a shower, he wanted to smell the street. The boy took off his sweatshirt, undid the belt from the belt loops, took off his shoes, then his pants, terrycloth socks, underpants. Naked as he was, he lay down on the mattress. He intertwined his hands openly behind his head, retracing, in the man's mind, a scene that had been repeated for millenniums. They were there, nameless, fleetingly. In a hundred years they would both be dead and that room would no longer exist.

After an hour, it was the boy who examined the afternoon sky through the half-open window. The man was sitting on the bed. He heard knocking at the door. Four decisive thuds. "Open the door, please!" The tone unmistakable. The Dutch tourist tried in vain the protection of language. "I don't speak Italian." The voice remained firm. "Open the door, please. Police!" They were on the fifth floor. He couldn't jump out the window. And in a few seconds they would kick the door in. So he opened it. A small squad of officers entered the room. They saw the boy. But they already knew he was there. "This is not your son," one officer declared. "Your passport, please?" said another. They asked him to hold out his wrists. They handcuffed him. They escorted him down the stairs.

S ome months later we left Rome.

It all happened very rapidly. One Tuesday morning I got a phone call from the head of an important Turinese cultural institution. The next night I was at dinner at his house. Between the antipasto and the first course, he made me a very interesting job offer. Of course, he said, you'd have to move to a different city, and the idea of moving elsewhere, he smiled in a friendly way, always risks sounding blasphemous to anyone who's lived in Rome for a while. I answered that I would think about it. That night I recounted everything to my wife. It was a little after midnight and, sprawled on the couch, we found ourselves assessing the idea of changing our lives with an unusual calm: we confronted the subject with fewer difficulties than when we discussed summer vacations. I had this opportunity, she could work from home, where was the problem? To infuse depth into our words we listed a series of good reasons that giving it all up might seem a mistake, and we did it as if it were not we who put forward the objections but a grim presence scrupulously hostile to our happiness.

At breakfast the next morning, fresh and rested, we knew we had decided.

We tore ourselves away from Rome with the dark satisfaction of someone freeing himself from a vice. Our friends were incredulous. "Are you really sure?" was the question I heard repeated most frequently in those days. We organized a small farewell party at which, amid canapés and glasses of wine, we defended our decision perhaps too insistently. Why continue to suffer, we said to the guests. We had the unhoped-for prospect of moving to a civilized, orderly, clean city, where the concepts of work, politeness, honesty, and social responsibility still had a recognized meaning. We had the chance to start again, it would be stupid to waste it.

A month later we were gone.

The first days in Turin I remember held small quotidian surprises that could leave Chiara and me in a numbed state of relief. We'd get in a taxi and not be insulted by anyone, nor did we witness savage fights between the taxi-driver and other drivers. We left a government office, and bureaucratic problems that in Rome would have consumed us for months were resolved by a text message from the local government office. At work, meetings began when they were scheduled to begin, rationality and common sense were tools to be used in an attempt to contain the natural chaos of the world. Everything proceeded in a normal way, and the impalpable sensation that nothing was happening was due, we said to ourselves, to an emotional prejudice that we would soon get over.

But weeks passed, and my wife and I began to feel ill. A veil of sadness descended over our faces which we didn't understand at first. The morning was dark when we awoke. At night the disorientation became dizzying. Each of us received confirmation in the face of the other and, so as not to reckon with it, turned our gaze elsewhere.

In the next weeks this silence became the undisputed protagonist of the time we spent together, and so at a certain point Chiara and I were forced to talk about it. The problem was, we admitted, that we felt an overwhelming homesickness. We missed Rome desperately. Maybe we were tied to the city like an addict to his drug, and maybe the excessive impudence with which we had announced our farewell was the rage toward the faithless lover we flee though our feelings haven't changed.

The occasion for leaving had been a job offer, but I knew that for me it had all begun the day I found myself in front of Manuel Foffo's apartment. It was there that the bad feeling latent in recent years had become evident. The knowledge of what had happened on the other side of those seals had made all the rest visible. What to think of ourself when, despite good will, and even the courage to act (we had confronted a move, we had subjected ourselves to a radical change of habits, friendships, occupations), we are surprised to find that we love what until a short time before was poisoning our blood? Maybe we were so used to disaster that we couldn't separate from it? Were we part of it? There are cities of the living, populated by the dead. And then there are cities of the dead, the only ones where life still has meaning. I continued to think about the murder. Although I had handed in my report months before, it still occupied me. There was no longer a commissioner or a newspaper to meet with, there was no one to get paid by, there existed no practical reason that I had to go to Rome whenever I could. And yet I did. The first chance I got, I was on the train and in less than five hours was in the city again. Arriving at Termini I was overcome by a wave of happiness and trepidation. I took the metro, I walked for hours, I wandered with a lump in my throat through Tor Pignattara, through Garbatella. *Will I still be worthy of these places?* I wondered on the dusty streets, *or will I be considered a stranger, a traitor?* Traitor of traitors. What I missed so much was the sensation of absolute freedom that in Rome was synonymous with breakdown, anarchy, and neglect, and I missed the sometimes staggering certainty of living simply as human, in the wild state, released from the ties of a State and even from the chains of a community that wants to be called a people. (If the eternal city were truly eternal a past couldn't exist, as a result a present to respect didn't exist nor a future to be taken care of.) Was I mistaking disaster for freedom? Impossible to cure. Unless—I thought, in search of absolution—I were like someone who flees a burning house, then returns and plunges into the fire armed with a glass of water.

Staying in a hotel during my sojourns in Rome would have made me feel even more of a stranger, so I slept at the house of a friend in Piazza Sanmicheli. I took long walks on the Casilina before going to bed; the smells of the city seemed to me different from what I remembered, similarly the colors, the shape of the buildings, the traffic on the streets. It was as if on a gigantic face, reduced to a puzzle by long contemplation, I had recognized a new wrinkle that might perhaps redraw everything. On the right the train tracks, on the other side the run-down buildings. It was incredible, I thought, how Marco Prato and Manuel Foffo had succeeded in destroying their own lives with the killing of Luca Varani. Not financial advantage, not career, not fame, not personal revenge: there was no classic motivation that could explain what had happened. Add to this the fact that Foffo and Prato had acted so as to reduce to zero the likelihood of getting away with it. It was as if by luring Luca to Collatino they had set off on their own tracks to celebrate a rite planned in the preceding months with a meticulous lack of awareness.

Foffo was in conflict with his father; he felt crushed, humiliated, badly treated, but he had never been able to confront him effectively. The only punch he had landed was to confess the murder to him. There he had really felt him waver, sensing, perhaps, along with revenge, the regret that grips us when we hurt those we think have betrayed our love. In the car heading to his uncle's funeral, Manuel, absorbed by the bond that binds sons to fathers, could have savored the eternal instant in which the young man has the best of the old and the roles of domination are reversed. But revenge was impossible, it was a dead end: all the more when that moment had passed, time had begun to flow again, and his father hadn't toppled.

Marco, too, grieved for a failed recognition. His mother, he said, couldn't see him, couldn't accept him for what he was, re-paid his devotion with silence. Even Ledo's love, the unquestion-able paternal love, might not have been enough, or not robust enough, to vacate the sentence that Marco felt he had been given, and that he had exorcised over time by becoming an actor, a cha-meleon, a conjuror who tries with his arts to fill the abyss. But what happens when, unable to go through the looking-glass, un-able to cross the threshold of pain, we construct our life accord-ing to a code that continuously erases and repeats the shame? (This was an aspect that would have inspired tenderness in my wife, with whom I'd talked about it, if it hadn't involved murder; she had a weakness for those who react to personal disasters by scattering glitter over the void they walk on.)

They hadn't defeated the father, they hadn't changed the mother's mind. They had destroyed themselves. There was some-thing else. One afternoon during a stay in Rome, sitting in a café in Ponte Milvio, I read in the paper a long article that appeared to pile disaster on disaster. It seemed that an international net-work of pedophiles had been active in Rome for a while in the area of Termini. I had lived nearby for a long time, and hadn't realized it. (The papers report horror, I said to myself, they don't recount normality, "people with their intelligent indifference and sad desperation," as Marco Pannella had written: Rome is also that, stores of healthy normality, tons of banal sadness countering the horror.) However, what I thought right afterward, as I contin-ued reading the paper, was something else. You have to make a reservation on a plane that takes you to Rome. You have to rent a room where no one will ask for documents. You have to contact a middleman if necessary. You are, in short, aware, from begin-ning to end, of what you're doing. The pedophile who had been arrested, in a bleak studio apartment on Via Cattaneo, knew he had committed a crime, knew he had broken a moral law, plac-ing his own desire ahead of it, if not a divine law at which he had hurled his challenge. But what remains of guilt when the criminal is no longer capable of recognizing it? Marco Prato and Manuel Foffo had no idea that they would be able to commit a murder when they met for the first time, they hadn't considered it when they met the second time, and even in March, when, shut in the apartment, they had descended into delirium, they hadn't understood what they were doing until they found themselves doing it. They even seemed not to be aware of it *while* they were doing it. "But then it is really happening," Manuel had thought when the massacre began. Although each had recounted the crime in a different way to the police, adding or leaving out significant details from the legal viewpoint, they had talked about it as if it had been not they who were acting but *something else*, an obscure director who had taken over. Manuel had given his father a nearly complete confession, and Marco had actually attempted suicide. In spite of that, both seemed to be driving at a mysterious cause-and-effect nexus rather than at a classic type of crime. It was here, I thought, that the narrator again had a hand in it. Recognition of one's own responsibilities in a base act was becoming, at the emotional level, an unsustainable trial. No one could see himself as culpable anymore, no one recognized in himself the possibility of evil. Was it mass narcissism? Was it the fear of social condemnation that found in the pillory its preferred spectacle? Conscious delinquents were thus replaced by murderers unbeknownst to themselves, sincere liars, loyal traitors, merciful thieves, responsible scoundrels. It was no longer the man who plunges the knife knowing what he's doing but the criminal who is surprised to be recognized as such—when he's not outraged by it—although he has done exactly what those like him have always done. What hope could Marco and Manuel have of recognizing themselves as guilty—and of understanding, of going through the looking glass beyond which they would finally recognize *Luca*, their victim? On the one hand it was hard to attribute to Marco and Manuel a true planning of the crime; on the other, the path that led to the murder had a shape that only they could fill in. "As soon as

I saw him *I understood*," Manuel had said, recalling the moment when Luca crossed the threshold of the apartment. But understood *what*? "I looked at him, then I looked at Marco, and it's as if mentally we had said to each other *it's him*."

Imagining Luca as a predestined victim was blasphemy. Rather, you had to try to find an act of will in what Manuel and Marco seemed to attribute to the joint between two interlocking pieces. Not the victim being predestined but *them* making themselves into probable killers. And when, I wondered, did that probability increase to the point of becoming a certainty? Here you were dragged down by the hair, into the nocturnal, ancestral part. Luca didn't have the experience or the strength of Alex Tiburtina, he wasn't quick-witted like Tiziano De Rossi: the criminological report had emphasized his weakness in every category compared with the aggressors. In addition, Luca was meek. Some commentators continued to blame the cocaine. Others insisted on sexuality. Luca's unproved homophobia had made him odious to Marco and Manuel or, on the contrary, they said, a failure to accept their own homosexuality had kindled in Marco and Manuel the spark of violence. We lived in a backward country, terribly behind on questions of gender and sexual orientation, but the perception of one's own sexuality and that of others, I thought, in this case was one of the filters through which—in order to emerge from its latent phase—something even more remote passed. A shadow had stagnated in us since the night of time. Destroy the weaker. Or weaken the stronger in order to destroy him. Aggression as guarantee of survival. Strike to avoid the fear of being struck. Feel impotent, reduce the other to impotence. Feel in danger, put the other in danger. Feel like nothing, reduce the other to nothing. To let oneself be conquered by that weakness, by that atavistic fear, meant to choose: it was here that individual responsibility should be found in an era when, rhetorical circle after rhetorical circle, that concept was hiding at an increasing distance. Otherwise it would have been barbarity;

otherwise, as soon as science (to which not a few jurists looked trustingly) reduced our every gesture to a predetermined set of chemical reactions and electrical impulses, the concept of guilt would dissolve along with choice, and, free of guilt, we would be imprisoned forever.

Were we as one, indistinguishable, with the instinct for abuse of power? Who could sever the tie? Was it the job of upbringing, of culture? But culture and upbringing, in themselves, were not the contrary of violence.

I couldn't understand. I folded up the paper and looked straight ahead. The light fell on the tennis courts of Ponte Milvio and the lovely colored houses, the birds were flying from one side of the river to the other.

PART V

The Seagulls

It's beautiful, said the devil behind Adam's back.
But . . . is it art?
—ORSON WELLES

They sleep in the same bed,
but they don't have the same dreams.
—ZHOU ENLAI

S ummer had returned. The shadows of passersby were lengthening on the Esquiline, in Casal Bertone, in Tor Pignattara. The heat stagnated, ravenous. Porters spent hours looking out on the street. Girls' bare arms. Old people moving slowly among the potholes. On weekends people fled to the sea, but those who could left work in the middle of the week. Deserted offices. Blue skies. Phones that rang unanswered. It was one of the most intense pleasures for the city's residents: finding themselves with their feet in the Mediterranean discussing futile things, as if, from the shore of the dead, one could already look with a sense of superiority at the sad troubles of the living.

It was in this atmosphere of eternal demobilization—identical every year, but every year hotter—that people in Rome voted again for the first citizen. In the space of two weeks the city emerged from provisional management and officially returned to normality. Out with the special commissioner, in with the new mayor. The first woman mayor of the city.

The situation, I observed from Turin, did not go back to normal. The city continued to sink into a chaos made more egregious by the presence of someone at the helm of the boat, armed with a popular mandate.

The mayor—elected on a wave of protest against the old political class—seemed even more powerless than her predecessors. Tourists drifted among infinite dysfunctions. Exhibitionists swam naked in the fountains. The garbage increased everywhere. Photos of the disaster went around the world. Articles arrived from foreign papers. "Rome in Ruins" (*New York Times*). "City's

Reputation Now Near Zero" (*Le Monde*). Some citizens began to protest against those who, in protesting, had favored the new political course. Some protested against those who were protesting against those who had protested.

Strange things began to happen. Like mechanical Buddhist monks, buses set themselves on fire. At Torre Rossa, on Via del Tritone, right in the middle of Piazza dei Cinquecento. It was discovered that the episodes of spontaneous combustion, worryingly frequent, were due to the poor quality of the parts installed in the buses by the city's mechanics for lack of funds. At the end of June, a group of children playing in the bushes on Colle Oppio found a giant pig's tongue. In Campo dei Fiori kids started throwing bottles on the weekends. In Tuscolano brief urban battles exploded, fought with garbage picked up off the street. The merchants of Centocelle were beaten by people who wanted to force them to leave the area: when, with their swollen faces, they turned to friendly cops, they might receive in confidence an unexpected response: "If you want we'll give you a guard," the cops said, "but at that point prepare for a life as the prey. You have a wife, you have children, you have a little money: why the fuck do you bother? If you want some advice, sell it all and get out." Public works, between delays and inefficiencies, as usual consumed a lot of money, but there was less and less of it. Private citizens, discouraged by the direction of the economy, put their own houses on Airbnb. A tide of the new poor, homeless, needy, pressed uneasily from the outskirts. Everything was corrupted, nothing ceased to exist.

To the rat emergency was added the scourge of seagulls. With their mean expression and their glassy eyes, they lorded it. They hopped amid the garbage, devoured small dead animals, dove fearlessly into every source of food.

"They'll eat us alive," commented the Romans, expressing impatience or hope.

Although months had passed since the murder of Luca Varani, interest had not diminished. At the police station in Piazza Dante the police continued to listen to experts and people informed about the facts, they filled out summonses and reports. Reporters thronged in pursuit of news.

Marco and Manuel were both locked up in Regina Coeli, but they hadn't seen or talked to one another. However, they had been forced to endure one another's company. Marco was continuously asked about Manuel, Manuel continuously asked about Marco. When, before the murder, the two had said that, accomplishing something big, they would be bound forever, they hadn't imagined *this*. They had had no way of reflecting, that is, on what it meant not to be able to sever the bond. Their minds, interlocking with one another during the days of delirium, had been thrown out of alignment, then frozen, and now they were consumed with resentment. Locked up in the darkness of their respective cells, far from their homes, affections, routines, they were forced to realize, with dismay, that, unreachable, and yet so close, separated only by a half dozen corridors, was *the other*, the person without whom they wouldn't have been there.

All they did was accuse one another.

Manuel Foffo told the interrogators that it was Marco who had stabbed Luca Varani in the heart, killing him. Marco Prato claimed he had never touched Luca with a weapon. Manuel said he had been manipulated by Marco. Marco stated that he had fallen for Manuel, and that it had been amorous folly that led him to make the mistake of going along with him.

Even though the verified elements already offered sufficient material for any type of narrative drift, the suggestiveness of the stab to the heart was irresistible on the symbolic level. Who had given the final blow?

There was speculation and hypothesis, experts were interviewed and editorials written, until the analysis requested by the prosecutor became official.

The tests detected the presence of GHB in Luca Varani's blood in a much larger than recreational amount. The quantity of cocaine, on the other hand, was compatible with normal recreational purposes, and did not rule out further consumption in the more recent past. The genetic-forensic report was important for understanding who had handled the weapons of the crime. The tests detected "the presence of genetic profiles" traceable to, besides the victim: a) both Foffo and Prato on the handle of the hammer; b) Prato alone on the handle of the kitchen knife; c) Varani alone on the knife with the short blade that had been stuck in his chest. Concerning this last, the expert said that the result was due to an excessive quantity of DNA traceable to the victim's blood, which might have covered other traces.

The forensic report finally made it clear that there had been no lethal stabbing. Despite the incredible number of blows, and the fury with which they had been delivered, there wasn't one that could be considered "decisive." Or, if you wanted to look at it in a different way, the decisive actions were *all of them*.

In reality Luca Varani had bled to death.

We're all afraid of being in the victim's shoes. We live in terror of being robbed, deceived, attacked, trampled. It's more difficult to fear the contrary. We pray God or fate not to find a murderer on the street. But what emotional obstacle do we have to overcome to imagine that it could be us, one day, in the murderer's shoes?

It's always: *Please, let it not happen to me.* Never: *Please, let it not be me who does it.*

"If Marco and Manuel had never met, that murder would never have been committed."

It was Francesco Scavo speaking. I had arrived in Rome from Turin the night before, now I was with him at one of the tables of a café just across from the court. To get there you go through Piazzale Clodio, where the urban fabric suddenly opens up, revealing Monte Mario. Up there, amid the hills, you can see the astronomy observatory.

"In the past fifteen years I've worked on cases that made me reflect. I'm an open-minded person. But the panorama that this murder spread out before me is breathtaking."

Scavo was sitting very close to me, in his light-framed eyeglasses, the tuft of black hair falling over his forehead, his gaze perpetually focused.

The first destabilizing aspect, he said, was the ease with which two absolutely normal young men had become guilty of a crime like that. The investigators were used to professionals. Organized crime. Terrorism. Family crimes, of course. Or small-time hoods.

All people whose motivation was clear. If Manuel Foffo and Marco Prato had been told at the end of February that a week later they would be in jail charged with murdering a twenty-three-year-old (a victim who, in the case of Manuel Foffo, didn't even have a name), it would have seemed to them the plot of a science-fiction film.

According to the prosecution, the accused had to be considered of sound mind. It was true that Manuel and Marco were stoned when Luca Varani entered the apartment, but they had freely decided to buy and consume all that cocaine. It was also true that, unlike in the classic premeditated murder, there was no concrete, confirmed plan (for example, the purchase of a murder weapon in advance), but, although it was more difficult to prove, the prosecution aimed at a sort of *psychological premeditation*; that is, at an interwoven volition that, step by step, had first believed that it wanted the murder, then had truly wanted it, then had carried it out.

The second important question had no penal relevance, but for Francesco Scavo it was no less a subject for thought.

"Adults criticize young people. It's normal," he said. "When I was young, the adults were horrified by our long hair, they despised the music we listened to, the way we dressed, they were skeptical of the values we said we believed in and many of us said we were willing to fight for. But these kids," he asked, "what values, precisely, are they fighting for? For many of them, no matter the social class, if you tell them that winning a civil-service competition will get them eighteen hundred euros a month, they say contemptuously: *What would I do with eighteen hundred euros?*"

As an intelligent person, Scavo wouldn't dream of despising them. He felt pity and sorrow, a profound sorrow. He could examine the depths of their hearts, but once he found what he was looking for, what else could he do?

"The thing that struck me is that many of them are from good families."

Speaking this time was one of the cops who had been most valuable in the investigation. He was referring to the friends of Marco Prato. He had managed to get crucial information without ever giving the young people the impression that he was judging them.

Even now, faithful to his role, he made an effort not to express a judgment. However, that the world had taken a rather strange turn, well, that he believed he could say without offending anyone.

"We were all young, we all did stupid things. If, however, I compare what we did with their life style, I realize that I spent my youth in a state of complete innocence."

He could understand how certain kids from the underclass reasoned. He knew the children of the unemployed, of thieves, of drug addicts. Those who grew up in devastated families, or in contexts where poverty and violence were one, were open in their defiance of the established order. In those cases the police knew how to behave, and even before that they knew what to think. It's easier to oppose an illegal act when it's clear what's driving the person who carries it out. But the reason that absolutely normal kids, lacking nothing on the material level, seemed to live like the truly desperate—the drugs they took, their inability to focus their identity, the convulsive preoccupation they had with the judgment of others, the disrespectful use they made of their own bodies, the relationship they had with money, their apparent indifference to wasting entire periods of their lives—left him in a state of absolute puzzlement.

"In the conversations on WhatsApp, some of them speak disdainfully about public transportation. If they don't have money for a taxi they feel inferior. They call the metro *trascinapoveri*: poor people mover. Twenty-year-old kids. I take public transportation even now. I had to make an effort not to feel offended."

At Regina Coeli the conversations with relatives continued. A couple of times a week, for months, Manuel had visits from his brother Roberto, his mother, and his father.

"That guy is dumping all the shit on you," said Roberto during one of the first conversations. "He says you decided everything, that he only obeyed your wishes."

When they talked about Marco they almost never called him by name. They said *that guy*, or *the other one*.

"But if *I* was the one being blackmailed," Manuel protested, "if *he* was the one who made all that repressed rage come to the surface."

"He incited you to violence, the scumbag," Roberto declared. "I'd just like to get my hands on him."

They tried to calm him by comforting themselves that way as well: circumscribing Manuel's responsibilities kept them from thinking that his guilt was absolute, kept them all from going mad.

"How are you spending the days?"

Manuel said he was treated well in prison. He was still in isolation. He had regular meals. He had periodic interviews with psychiatrists. Every day he got a mood-stabilizing pill and a tranquillizer. The correction officers got to know him. Some didn't like him, but the majority understood that he wasn't a problematic detainee. He thanked his mother for bringing him a change of underwear. He said there was some problem with the shower: "I don't have any body wash." If they'd sent it from home, the guards hadn't delivered anything.

"You can buy body wash in the prison commissary," his father said.

"Every week we put seventy-five euros on the prepaid card," said his brother.

"Right, thank you."

They went back to talking about the murder.

Roberto said the lawyer was at work, the experts were at work, the whole team was working for him.

"You'll see, things will turn out for the better." The other's situation, Roberto continued, was, on the contrary, much more compromised. There were precedents: the papers said that months earlier Marco Prato had kidnapped a boy, drugged him, and abused him. He was a recidivist. The judges couldn't ignore that.

"I saw the criminal eye in him," said Manuel.

"He incited you," said Roberto.

"He put psychological pressure on me," Manuel kept going.

"But is it true that the kid was tortured, as the papers say, or not?" his father asked.

"It's true," Manuel admitted yet again.

"Is it also true, though, that you were high on cocaine," said his father, "but wasn't the drug cut with some bad substance?"

"If that guy also erased the evidence, there are the experts," said Roberto. "The work of forensics will show that . . ."

"Listen, let me say this right away," Manuel interrupted him. "If you're getting funny ideas, get it out of your mind that I'm not guilty. Because I *am* guilty."

"Yes, of course," said Roberto, "but it all started from the initiative of that other guy."

"I don't understand anything," said Daniela. "This business is absurd."

The brothers were quick to silence their mother. Manuel thanked her for the help she was trying to offer. But, he said, it was pointless to ask questions about the legal aspect of the case, she didn't have the tools to understand what they were talking about. Roberto said that in the future it would be better if they met without her.

In the following weeks only his father and brother visited him, sometimes only his brother. They continued to talk about the defense strategy. They talked about life in prison. Manuel alternated moments of distress with moments when he could even imagine a future. It was then that he began talking again about startups.

"Lately I've been thinking about it."

"Your projects will go forward," Roberto comforted him. "I'll help you, I'll make it so you can follow even from here inside."

"All the materials for the project are in the backpack."

"I'll get you the contents of the backpack," Roberto said. "I'll put you back in touch with the software developer. I'll try to arrange for you to have a conversation with him in prison."

"First the backpack," said Manuel, "then pencil and paper. They still won't let me have pens or pencils here, they're afraid I could use them to harm myself."

"You'll be able to use pens," said Roberto. "You'll get back the contents of the backpack. We'll put you in touch with the software developer. You'll start on your projects again."

"But my name will be on those projects," Manuel turned gloomy, "and my name will be forever linked to this story. The truth is I'm finished."

He darkened. And when he darkened he touched on another problem. Prison, he said, he could endure, life in prison was a terrible thought, but he could deal with it. About one thing, though, he felt totally at the mercy of events.

"The fact is that everyone now thinks I'm a faggot."

"Who thinks you're a faggot?"

"My friends, acquaintances, strangers, *all of Italy*."

"They don't think you're a faggot, it's the other guy who's the faggot."

"Roberto, I had sex with that guy. He was dressed as a woman."

"So what does that mean? For a little anal sex it means you're a faggot? You were the one topping him. People know you're not a faggot."

"Even here in prison," Manuel said, "every so often someone goes by and calls me a faggot. They've read it in the papers, they've heard it on TV, every time I hear the TG5 credits from a nearby cell my legs shake."

"The papers also say you're heterosexual. The proceedings say it. It's written there. Now they've made us leave our phones at the entrance . . . otherwise I'd let you read it, what's being written."

"Everybody thinks so . . ."

"No, Manuel, it's not like all Italy is sitting around thinking about your sex life. Who the fuck do you think you are, Berlusconi?"

Some days Manuel alluded to the possibility of putting an end to it. Then Roberto got agitated.

"Don't talk nonsense, Manuel. That's not an honorable act, it's the act of an idiot."

"Depends on how you do it," said Manuel. "If you end it with alcohol and benzos the way Marco wanted to, then yes. But if you cut your throat that's another thing."

"You're a total jerk," Roberto responded, "and you want to ruin my life. I have two children."

"Precisely, you have two children. You have two children, you have a life, and I get myself out of the way and . . ."

"My life *is you*. Don't ruin me. I tell you as a brother. I don't deserve it. I really don't deserve it."

"I'm finished, I don't even feel like making it to tomorrow."

"I'll get you out of here, I promise. I'll do it for you. But you, if you love me, you have to be strong, you have to be stronger *for me*."

"Maybe you don't understand what it means to be in here, you don't understand what it means to be finished. I don't even have the courage to look people in the face."

"What the fuck are you talking about, Manuel, what the fuck are you talking about?"

"It was a brutal crime. A terrible, cowardly, fierce crime."

"But it was committed in a state of . . ."

"I'd like to have plastic surgery. Not be me anymore. I asked the lawyer if there's a way of changing my name, he said it's very complicated."

"Change your name?"

"When I get out of here what can I do, with my name? And my face? It would be better to change countries as well."

"Abroad," said Roberto, exasperated, "we'll all go abroad, all change our name, leave. The children, too. We'll send them abroad to study."

"They say I haven't expressed remorse," said Manuel. "In the proceedings it's written that from my behavior there's no evidence of remorse. But that's not true. I think of that poor guy every day, at night I dream of being him, I dream that someone does to me the things I did to him. I have these nightmares and then I wake up with my heart in my throat. If I get to the end of this story alive, not in two, not five, but ten, fifteen years . . . then, apart from his relatives, apart from his parents, I will be the one who loves Luca most. I'll love him more than his friends. Because here inside I have to think of him every day."

Marco also had visits in prison. It was mainly his father who came to see him.

After Ledo Prato's famous post—which the newspapers had predictably massacred, describing the professor as a narcissist with a lofty prose style—neither interviews nor statements had been released. No one in the family appeared in public to speak about what had happened. As for Marco's mother, Signora Mariella, not even a photo appeared in the papers. The silence gave credibility to all interpretations. It was the reason that I regarded Ledo Prato with mistrust.

But then I saw him in the interview room at Regina Coeli.

It happened when I was examining the recordings of Ledo Prato's visits to Marco. Although the surveillance cameras didn't enable closeups, what they showed was sufficient. In one of these recordings Ledo Prato entered the prison interview room. Marco hadn't yet arrived. Jacket and shirt under black coat, Ledo had looked around, observing the deserted space, the walls of reinforced concrete, the backless chairs, until his eyes happened to meet the camera. It was a very long instant. To me, looking at the video, he seemed a man entirely without defenses. No one bargains for coming to see his own son in jail. The impact with suffering takes the majority of us back to a sort of original innocence. At a certain point we no longer have defenses, or resources, there is absolutely nothing we can do to avoid the worst, and so—along with our defenses—privileges, strategies, class identity, rhetoric collapse, letting us glimpse the frail nakedness of the species that unites us all.

A few seconds later Marco entered the room and, as far as possible, everything returned to normal. Marco wore jeans and a black sweater, and was almost completely bald. Father and son embraced. They sat across from one another and began to talk.

"You're cold," said Ledo, squeezing his hands.

"It's because they search me before the visits," said Marco. "They put me naked in a freezing cold room."

"But now it's better, right?"

"Yes, here it's comfortable."

They began to discuss the trial. Ledo was as always very cautious. He spoke in a low voice. He told of his meetings with the lawyer. "Bartolo is someone who knows his business." They were trying to figure out how to move among expert reports and depositions. Marco said it would be a good idea to get in touch with Franca Leosini.

"Franca Leosini?" Ledo was surprised.

"The reporter for RAI 3," Marco confirmed. "She might

have advice about good experts. She's an authoritative person. Progressive. A woman of the left. We can try her."

Franca Leosini wasn't simply a reporter for RAI 3. Franca Leosini was the indisputable queen of crime stories on TV. For years she had had a show seen by millions of fans who harbored feelings close to idolatry for her. Marco continued to mix the arguments of the law with those of the theater; he said that when all the material was taken from his phone a bomb would go off. There were many VIPs among his contacts, there were messages that could be compromising for several of them. At that point, in order not to be dragged into scandal, they would shield him.

"But didn't you say there was nothing to worry about in your phone?" Ledo asked.

"Right. Nothing to worry about," Marco answered. "All that material merely confirms the hypotheses about the complexity of my life, my contradictions. It will be useful for making people see that I was really at the mercy of all this. Even if ugly things come out of the phone, even that will be useful, it will help outline the profile of an ambiguous personality but not say, or prove, that I did a given thing."

It wasn't important how closely Marco's reasoning adhered to the plane of reality. But it was odd that it was *he* who felt the need to reassure Ledo. On the one hand he seemed to feel tenderness for his father and, as far as possible, tried to protect him. On the other—even in jail—he insisted on keeping absolute control of the situation, on holding, so to speak, the true interpretation of what was happening. Which might lead one to feel a burning antipathy toward him but also deep pity: what type of wound does a young man want to hide when, locked up in prison and charged with murder, he feels constrained to display assurance like that?

They talked about the conditions of life in prison.

"There are four of us in the cell," said Marco. "Besides me there's a prisoner who knowingly infected a bunch of girls with HIV, a photographer who drugged his models in order to rape them, and a pedophile. Their trials are under way, and maybe they're innocent, but you can understand that with the four of us together in there we seem to be in Satan's cell."

Marco asked Ledo if they had managed to get in touch with his psychoanalyst, Dr. Crinò. That woman knew everything about him. She might be useful in the trial.

"You all should talk to her, meet her. Trust what I tell you."

Ledo said that the lawyer had tried to get in touch, but the psychoanalyst hadn't answered the calls.

Another day—it was just him and his father in the visitors' room—Marco plunged into politics. He continued to complain about the conditions of life in prison, he said the heaters didn't work well, the windows were "medieval," the cells were unfit, it was likely that the minimum threshold for livability prescribed by law was not respected. Maybe, he added, his father's acquaintances could help.

"Look," said Ledo, "the problem is that now they're in the middle of an electoral campaign. Which luckily will be over in a week."

"But there's a senator, in the Democratic Party," said Marco, "born in Sardinia, very sensitive to the subject of human rights in prison."

"You're talking about Manconi," said Ledo. "Yes, of course, there's Manconi. But there are a lot of others."

"But what about what's-his-name?" Marco asked. "What's his name . . . that friend of yours who's in the Senate."

"You mean Giorgio."

"Not Giorgio, the other one," said Marco, "his son was at Giulio Cesare with me."

"I know," said Ledo, "he's now the minister's chief of staff. He was under-secretary. But it was a long time ago, he's been out of Parliament for years."

"But he's the chief of staff, and *you* still have a relationship with *him*."

Yes," said Ledo, using the most sympathetic tone possible, "but when you start taking on certain duties . . . If he has to receive the members of Parliament who are going to talk to the minister you can understand that he has priorities of a type different from . . ."

"You were a consultant for the ministry."

"I wasn't a consultant. I worked with the minister, yes, but you have to consider that some of these people face the problem of appropriateness."

Ledo added that, except in certain situations—for example a prison brawl—they couldn't solicit intervention in individual cases.

Marco asked Ledo if he had checked his Facebook page. What was happening on the Internet? What were people saying about him? His father said that things had calmed down, every so often someone left offensive comments on the profile but you had to expect that. "Rather," said Ledo, "to close the account I'd need the password."

"But why should we close my Facebook profile? I'm not dead."

Then Marco asked about his mother.

She was trying to come to terms with what had happened, Ledo said, she was occupied with the house, for the moment she didn't feel like coming to the prison.

When his father returned, Marco insisted again on Dr. Crinò.

"Papa, imagine what it was for me to see that woman three times a week for *years*. She knows everything about me, there was never any filter, I never *fooled* her. She's the only person who never allowed me to use shortcuts, if I'm still standing I owe it to her. You remember how patronizing, rude, spoiled I was? If it hadn't been for therapy with Dr. Crinò I could never be in prison in these conditions, with dirty bathrooms, broken radiators . . . You have to find her. I need her. She must be feeling destroyed. I want to help her, I want to say to her: *Look, doctor, you were great.* I have to make her understand that. Otherwise she'll kill herself, professionally and humanly. She'll kill herself."

His father said they had tried, the lawyer had written to Dr. Crinò again, had phoned her. But she had refused, had avoided answering, had let him understand, very clearly, that she had no intention of helping with the case. She didn't want to talk to the lawyer. She didn't want to talk to the Pratos. And, one might presume, she didn't want to talk even to him.

Marco said he had managed to enroll in a music and literature course. "Yesterday during the class the other inmates started singing love songs to me, they sang *Ciao amore, ciao,* and I was moved, I started crying."

The situation also improved regarding the basics of life in the cell. "They gave me an upgrade," Marco continued. "Now I can buy gas cylinders for cooking, I can make myself coffee." In any case, he said, he was always full of good will, always available to socialize, to stay busy, everything, in order to endure in this situation.

"Do you need anything?" asked Ledo.

Marco asked if he could have a bathrobe, some shirts, his polo shirts, a pair of jeans. Then he came to the point. He did it with delicacy, but they couldn't go on avoiding the issue. His mother. She hadn't appeared on this occasion, either.

"She needs time," said Ledo.

"I sent her a letter several days ago," Marco said. "I wrote to her: *Take all the time you need.*"

He spoke with an unnatural calm and composure. But it was clear that he was skirting an abyss. He told his father that as a child he had felt a lack of affection, a void, and had tried to fill it in the worst way, with sex, with drugs, and if in the end what had happened had happened, the explanation was there. Despite the values that they had tried to instill, that emotional deficit had been with him all his life. He said he would never blame his mother, and yet, he repeated, she had opened that void.

"Months ago," Marco continued, "she told me she was tired of being a mother. So the other day I wrote to her: *I don't want you to be the mother now, but at least let me be the son, give you strength, make you understand that life goes on.* Then I wrote: *You don't have to come here to be the mother, but let me be your son.*"

They began talking about the trial again. They agreed on the fact that they would rely on the ordinary criminal process.

His father said that, after what had happened, years would pass before things found an equilibrium.

"Thank goodness you didn't register anything in my name," Marco responded.

He thought *he* could offer his mother strength. And at the same time—locked in a cell, destined to endure a trial that could end with a sentence of life in prison—he thought *he* had to protect his psychoanalyst from human and professional collapse, all to be demonstrated. The way in which Marco continued not to appear wounded, in need of help, or psychologically unstable was stunning. It was hard to understand where arrogance began and where suffering. One thing struck me above all. On the one hand Marco accused his mother of ruining his life, on the other he had decided resolutely not to blame her. In this he was sincere. I thought he was fighting with all his strength to keep from hating her, to keep from thinking that she didn't care enough about her son, hoping—like the child who, staying in the place where he has been left beyond any reasonable time, believes he's bringing about a happy ending—that these were the premises that would enable his mother sooner or later ("when she was ready") to show her love. Was a more intricate feeling—made up of a protective instinct, demand for love, narcissism, violence, and self-destruction—imaginable?

I had the impression that Marco and Manuel, close to touching their own private tragedies in the days following the murder—close to acknowledging themselves, seeing themselves, discovering inescapably what substance they were made of—had gradually begun to distance themselves from it. When the exceptionality of what had happened was replaced by their daily life as defendants awaiting trial, the opportunity for truly focusing had vanished. The meetings with relatives, the discussions with lawyers, the bureaucratic refinement of legal strategies, the confrontations with the media . . . Their new condition seemed to have the blunting and reassuring power of enabling them to assume—although different from the way they'd left them—the roles they had always played.

During the following weeks some of these sensations of mine received confirmation, others the most total denial.

Apart from the conversations with relatives, Marco Prato and Manuel Foffo were busy with many other things during that period. They talked at length with their lawyers—the start of the trial was approaching—and although the construction of their respective defense strategies was the most important matter, they were also involved in dealing with their correspondence. Every week hundreds of letters arrived at the prison.

Prisoners who are talked about on TV are an irresistible attraction. Obviously friends wrote to Marco and Manuel. There were requests for meetings from journalists. But mainly letters arrived from strangers, hundreds of strangers, ordinary people whose irrational part was incited by the facts. They were letters of few words and torrential ones, letters from people who hoped the worst for Marco Prato and Manuel Foffo and letters from people who wanted to save them, letters from people who, on the pretext of bringing comfort, wanted *to be saved*. There were plenty of letters with a macabre tone. The author of one of these signed himself Luca Varani, claimed to be observing Prato and Foffo from a dark, remote place, invited them to reflect on the evil they had done, and said he was waiting for them, impatiently, where he now was.

Manuel Foffo received a letter from Pietro Maso, the kid from San Bonifacio who had become famous twenty-five years earlier for killing his parents in an attempt to get his inheritance. Handsome, rich, arrogant, Maso had at the time become a kind of star. Now, somewhat diminished, he was free again and, his confidence undamaged, visited spiritual fathers and television studios.

"I can't blame you for what you did," Maso wrote to Foffo. "I was worse than you, but I can understand why you wanted to kill your father. A dark and rarefied instinct of rivalry to capture all the affection of the women of the house and prove you're not just the frail, defenseless puppy." After a long dissertation on what, according to Maso, would happen to Manuel in prison ("You'll get a lot of psychiatrists who will dismember your mind and soul, some in good faith, in order to understand, others merely to relegate you to a false normality. You'll be the monstrosity to exhibit as a target for every reproach, the shared reference for 'contemptible'"), the letter concluded with recommended reading: "You'll need a lot of books. I'll give you one, the one I wrote when I was freed."

The book had been published a few years earlier, and there was no need of a world-famous psychiatrist to understand that jail hadn't had much of an effect on certain aspects of Maso's character.

Manuel answered contemptuously, making the letter public. "Signor Maso, if you mean to get publicity by taking advantage of the tragic death of Varani, and in particular publicity for the book you wrote, which I don't intend to read, you have mistaken the address and the addressee. You have not wasted a word of remorse for those who gave you life. Unlike you I will never have peace for what I did. So leave me in my profound repentance, don't write to me and bring in my father, whose name you are not worthy of uttering. I hope not to have to write to you again, in that case my lawyers will take care of it."

Marco Prato preferred not to do interviews or make any type of public statements. That didn't mean he was shut up in himself. On the contrary, he was very active at Regina Coeli. He held classes in English and French for the other prisoners, helped them write letters to their families, participated in the prison's cultural activities. Although the place had nothing to do with the network of clubs he was used to, his name began to circulate. Marco Prato became, so to speak, known among the prison population. Which, perhaps, not everyone was happy about.

On August 6th, unexpectedly, against all his wishes, predictions, and expectations, Marco was transferred to the prison of Velletri. The reasons for the transfer weren't clear, but the consequences were all too obvious. Velletri had the reputation of being a much harsher prison than Regina Coeli: few cultural activities, socializing reduced to the minimum—a desolate place where the prisoners might spend entire weeks looking at the ceiling of their own cell.

Marco was plunged into despair. At Velletri he felt isolated, marginalized, without even the least occasions for comfort that make prison a place where one can try not to go mad. His lawyers protested immediately: if re-education and social rehabilitation were supposed to go along with punishment, it was Regina Coeli, certainly not Velletri, that offered greater assurances from that point of view. At Regina Coeli Marco had managed to find a sustainable human dimension; there, through the activities offered by the facility and good relations with the other prisoners, doing time was consistent with the purposes of rehabilitation. The transfer to Velletri seemed a pointless as well as an unjust punitive measure, and as such should be repealed.

After a further appeal to the national guarantor for the rights of prisoners, Marco Prato returned to Regina Coeli.

The summer passed and fall returned. The trial of Foffo and Prato approached, and rumors about the preparations for it varied greatly.

Rash commentators, passing off their own emotional state as a coherent vision of the world, began to maintain that Marco Prato and Manuel Foffo could be out of prison within a few years. Some went so far as to claim that they would even be acquitted: the accused came from good families, they said, they had the best lawyers, a lot of money, the right connections—reasons that penal justice would be bent to their desires.

Those who observed the events with a modicum of rationality confined themselves to pointing out that, because of the way things had turned out, it was likely that the defense strategies of the accused would diverge. Manuel had admitted his own material involvement in the crime, Marco never. Manuel had confessed from the start that he had raised his own hand against the victim, Marco had always denied it. One might therefore hypothesize that Manuel would rely on mental infirmity, on diminished mental capacity. Marco—whose lawyers, from the day of Valter Foffo's interview on *Porta a Porta*, after Manuel had shown his cards, had had the advantage of being able to play their own game—could go so far as to totally deny the charge of murder, asking for the case to be dismissed.

It wasn't impossible that the trial could offer surprises. If it did, however, the reasons would have to be traced not to some arbitrary decision or other but to the tools of defense normally offered to any accused under the normal rule of law.

I continued to go to Rome whenever I could. I also talked about the murder to people who had nothing to do with the facts. Usually my interlocutors knew enough about what had happened to have their interest piqued as soon as I opened my mouth. But, unlike me, they weren't obsessed by the case, and that greater freedom, I thought, allowed them to look at the story from points of view not available to me.

One evening, after going to a book presentation, I ended up at dinner in Ostiense, where the Tiber moves into the tangled darkness of undergrowth and trees with the skeleton of the Gazometer behind it. This was a part of Rome that had always fascinated me (the pallor of the moon over the steel structure, the unruly vegetation). I had arrived in the early afternoon on the usual train from the north. The presence of the river nearby in the darkness made me feel at home. At this dinner—at a small fish restaurant—were two writers, the publicist for a publishing house, a psychologist, the editor in chief of a newspaper, an architect. The conversation on the Varani case arose when, to the inevitable question ("What are you working on these days?"), I gave the inevitable answer. But first, as happened increasingly, the talk was focused on the grave problems afflicting the city. It became specific. The movie theaters were closing. The bookstores were closing. Cultural life, said the journalist, was now reduced to the more and more fantastic curses you heard on the street. "Rome is getting disgusting, trash for tourists," said the architect, "only junk-food restaurants are opening. Or desolate wastelands where even the ATMs don't work." "The economy is based on bars with slot machines, illegal taxi-drivers, social cooperatives that pay under the table," said the psychologist. "Then there are those who rent to tourists: self-cannibalism on a carcass that's already been gutted," said the journalist. "At this point it seems clear that the problem is us," said one of the writers, "I mean us Romans. The governing class is the mirror of our rot, everything is rotten, even the tourists. Imagine Rome free of our presence." "So boring," said the psychologist. "Imagine this city deserted," the writer continued, "made up only of fountains, porticoes, gardens, basilicas, made up of statues in the middle of squares, but also of lampposts, hospitals, pylons, portable radios left on balconies. With the people banished, things would at last be having dialogues with one another. Nowhere would this dialogue be more musical, more inspired, more fertile, more dense with meaning than in Rome."

"What the fuck are you talking about?" The architect laughed heartily.

We went on to talk about the murder.

"If it were a novel," said the first writer, "it would be Frankenstein in the time of the smart phone, with Marco Prato in the role of Victor Frankenstein and Manuel Foffo as the Creature. Marco Prato uses his rhetorical abilities to manipulate Manuel, plays with his weaknesses, incites him against his father, then, without Manuel realizing it, he transfers to him all his paranoias, his traumas, his nightmares, I mean Prato's nightmares and paranoias."

"Think of those horror films where a group of kids goes on a retreat for a weekend in a house at the edge of the forest, and at a certain point, at night, while they're all sleeping, monsters arrive?" said the other writer. "Except that in this case the monsters arrive not from the outside but from within, they come from the obscure depths of those kids."

"Walt Disney's *Fantasia*," said the journalist. "*Mickey Mouse the Sorcerer's Apprentice*. It's that sort of stuff. Marco and Manuel summon up a *force* that at a certain point they can't control. Besides, think of what's happening *in the world*. The economy, politics, the digital revolution, the mood of the masses . . . everything's going incredibly out of control."

"I have the impression that Manuel sees in Marco his father," said the psychologist. "I know Marco's gay and even wants to change sex, but on the psychic level he's the male of the relationship. On the sexual plane, Marco is the passive part. On the psychic plane, he is the active, manly, dominant one. Manuel feels Marco's authority over him."

"And then Marco, cross-dressing in wig, tights, high heels," said one of the two writers, "has his female part take on the maximum guilt, but at the same time he unloads it on the figure that is quintessentially iconic, his mother, the person who has marked his life more than anyone. Dalida, from that point of view, is the supreme disguise. He disguises his private nightmare as a dream."

"Cross-dressing as a form of evasion. And a refuge," said the architect.

"Marco and Manuel are not simply immature," the psychologist added. "They are the triumph of impotence. In that poor kid, reduced to a state of absolute prostration, they recognized themselves and were horrified. One body for another. Luca Varani's death is a ritual murder."

B
ut how could Giuseppe Varani consider even a single one of these theories? How could he accept that the childhoods of Marco Prato and Manuel Foffo and their family traumas and repressions, drugs could be used as explanations, not to mention attenuating circumstances, for what had happened? How could he think that a crime like that didn't deserve to be judged on the simple evidence?

"Why did they drug him?" he asked with an expression of challenge. "To rape him!" he answered. "To torture him, to see him suffer! What else is there to say? That they tried to cut his throat to keep him from crying? That in the funeral chapel my son had a head covering because they had even bashed in his head? We want proper justice, p-r-o-p-e-r!"

He shouted it at the lawyers, he shouted it in front of the TV cameras, and he shouted it also at me when, on a morning of sun and wind, we met for the first time. We were sitting in a café in Piazza Mazzini. Chiara Ingrosso, the reporter for *Fatto*, with whom I had shared Marco Prato's clinical file, had introduced us. Giuseppe Varani had parked the sweets van close enough to keep an eye on it. Jeans, gray sweatshirt, unkempt beard.

"How can they say it wasn't premeditated?" he asked. "It *was* premeditated. And there's deception, there are torments, torture, there's cruelty, and there are the vile reasons. How," he widened his eyes, "in a trial of any type, summary or not, shortened or whatever you like, how can you not talk about the victim? What he endured. What he suffered. They broke his hands to keep him from defending himself. They hammered his mouth to make his teeth fall out."

Criminal law—lawyers never tired of repeating—did not obey a criterion of retributive justice. The punishment was always less harsh than the crime. Otherwise we would have returned to the law of retaliation. But that wasn't what Luca Varani's father challenged. He accepted the limits of our system. He respected them. But he couldn't tolerate that in front of that boundary we took a step back. In Italy there was no death penalty? Fine. There was, however, harsh imprisonment, there was life in prison.

"They haven't repented. And it's not all right with me that they're going to do sixteen years. They *eviscerated* my son. I have photographs, and I'll show them in court. I'll talk to the judge. I'll make him understand just what happened."

It was like that every time. His voice began to vibrate, then it exploded. Then not only the voice but everything in him seemed to be climbing on a tongue of fire. When he was on television these explosions were usual; maybe he had understood that it was the way to be noticed, to keep attention on what was happening alive. But he also did it far from the video cameras. He did it with every person—he did it with me, that windy morning—in whom he recognized the power to carry his mission farther than he could.

To some his volleys seemed excessive. But he certainly wasn't a judge, Giuseppe Varani, he had no control over the fate of Manuel Foffo and Marco Prato, he wasn't even a reporter, and he undoubtedly wasn't one of those commentators who pontificate on social media about the lives of others, protected by their incorporeality and crazed by an abstract thirst for violence. Giuseppe Varani was a man in the flood tide of grief, and this, I thought looking at him, was a sacred image. Besides, although he had Roman dialect under his breath, theatrical gestures, and burning expressions, it seemed to me that Luca's father was appealing to a principle on which—with less force than he—I had recently been interrogating myself. Individual responsibility, free will: into what would we be transformed, or dissolved, if we were liberated from those two fundamental weights? We lived in a world perennially analyzed, measured, sifted by innumerable investigations and statistics, but at the same time an unknowable world, in which it was increasingly difficult to understand who was really responsible for what. The economy was collapsing. Whose fault was it? The Earth was threatened by climate change. Were there specific responsibilities for that? It was paradoxical that, in the era in which the principal changes on the planet could be attributed to our actions, tracing an effect to its cause, and above all doing it on a human, individual level, had become the most difficult exercise of all.

A kid was lured to an apartment by two other guys and came out of it dead. Was it possible to *classically* charge that crime to the two—with all the appurtenances of crime and punishment— or was it necessary to surrender to the thought of having entered into a *completely* new time and world, where these concepts no longer had any value?

It was in this guise—wild gaze, gaunt figure, black eyes, twisted lips—that Giuseppe Varani appeared to me as a Biblical figure. If Marco Prato and Manuel Foffo, I thought then, continuing to reflect on the questions that nagged at me, had let themselves be overcome by the atavistic fear that leads to tormenting the weaker—and it was here that one had to isolate their guilt, trace their responsibility, circumscribe their choice in such a way that it wouldn't evaporate (strike to avoid the fear of being struck; feeling oneself to be nothing, reduce the other to nothing)—how was it possible to lead them, at least abstractly, to that type of awareness? Since, I kept repeating to myself, a guilty person who no longer has the tools to recognize himself as such damages the very idea of guilt, of responsibility, and therefore of choice, what had to be done to prevent these concepts—which were disintegrating for an increasing number of people—from also becoming corrupted in those who considered them fundamental? What were we supposed to look at?

"You should have seen him at the fairs, it was a magnificent sight!"

Giuseppe Varani was talking about his son, and as I listened a thought surfaced for a moment—a precious intuition, perhaps decisive—that I lost immediately afterward.

"You should have seen him with people—what great pride!"

Giuseppe Varani was telling about when he and his wife went around to the fairs in the van and took Luca. His son was so handsome and bright he was magnetic, the customers saw him and came to the counter, bought sweets, bought dried fruit, Luca chatted with everyone, and the girls, hidden behind their mammas, were crazy about him. "They all loved him. Every time, it was a party." Giuseppe said his wife was at home, devastated by grief, but life had to continue. It wasn't easy. He now had to go alone to the fairs and festivals. It was very difficult, as well as dispiriting. He and his wife would sue for damages, they would ask for some compensation, but it wouldn't be easy, given that the sins of the sons, as far as assets were concerned, didn't revert to the fathers. Then Giuseppe said that they hadn't called him. "Who didn't call you, Signor Varani?" I asked. "Ledo Prato and Valter Foffo," he answered. No one had showed up, no one had said he was sorry, no one had managed to make even just a phone call. Of course, it took guts to pick up the telephone and ask for forgiveness, he knew that; given the enormity of what had happened, asking forgiveness might even seem offensive, would have exposed one who did so to insults, or, worse, to chilling silence. It might be wrong, agreed. But also *not* to ask was wrong. And they hadn't asked. There was no truly decisive option, but since they hadn't called, well, then they had made the worst of all choices.

Giuseppe said then that every so often, during the week, he happened to go into Luca's room. His wife had arranged it so that from the day of his death everything had remained untouched—the notebooks, the posters, the alarm clock, the stereo—as if Luca would return at any moment. Giuseppe entered the room, and stayed, looking around, for several minutes. But it was at night that the hard part came, he said, when he and his wife sat down at the table for dinner and neither of them could take their eyes off the empty place.

"Signor Varani," I tried to change the subject, "the trial will start soon."

Now he could hold on to that, I thought, to analyses, experts' reports, testimonies, the judicial process with all its traps and formalities.

"Yes, of course, the trial," he muttered to himself, his gaze still dark, as if he had read my thought and my question had forced him to cast a glance on the *aftermath*. The tongue of fire that enveloped him was extinguished, and for a second—it was the only time I saw it—I glimpsed on his face a naked expression, the same defenseless look with which, perhaps, shut in his son's room, he continued in secret to talk to him.

"Two trials for the Varani case?"

In early 2017 the papers reported news that those who followed the case with full knowledge of the legal facts considered almost predictable. The lawyers for Manuel Foffo had asked for a summary procedure. Prato's lawyers instead wanted a normal one. It meant that—if the judge for the preliminary hearing agreed to the requests—there would be two separate trials.

On January 26, the judge for the preliminary hearing, Nicola Di Grazia, agreed to Foffo's and Prato's requests. The prosecution charged both of them with premeditation and the aggravating circumstances of cruelty and depraved indifference. The judge also accepted the civil suit for damages brought by Luca Varani's parents and Marta Gaia Sebastiani.

Michele Andreano, Manuel's lawyer, delivered to the court a hefty medical report in an attempt to demonstrate the diminished mental capacity of his client, also taking into consideration the damage that, according to the defense, the prolonged use of drugs had done over time.

Unlike what many believe, the summary procedure is not an admission of guilt. It weakens the defense. The accused renounces argument, can neither call witnesses nor try to dismantle further the elements collected by the prosecution. Naturally these disadvantages have a counterpart: in the case of guilt, the punishment is reduced by a third.

Trying to interpret these diverse strategies, as the more

farsighted had already done, one would have said that Foffo was relying on a reduced sentence, while Prato on a dismissal. Both of the accused rejected premeditation. Prato was aiming at a more sensational result, but he had chosen the normal trial, so he risked even more.

Since the physical presence of both at the summary procedure was ruled out by law, Prato and Foffo would find themselves face to face when Marco's trial began.

Luca Varani's parents were forced to recognize that, for at least one of the two accused, there was a good probability that life in prison would be avoided. The summary procedure did not in reality exclude the worst punishment, but the judge would have to consider a whole series of aggravating circumstances, and it was precisely that which the legal experts considered unlikely. First of all, premeditation. From the prosecution's investigation no indisputable elements had emerged that attested to the pre-existence of a plan for murder. If there had been such a plan, it was made in the minds of the accused, and it was precisely that which was very difficult to demonstrate.

"But how can it be said they hadn't planned it?" Giuseppe Varani thundered. "They lured him to the apartment with a trick! They stunned him with Alcover! It was thought out. And the unlawful restraint? They kept him there by force. You don't call that unlawful restraint?"

On the Internet, many commentators saw in the news of the summary procedure the antechamber of acquittal.

What did I tell you? Now they'll get out of it!

In Italy that's how it works, you just have to have the right friends and you get out of jail even if you killed your mother.

It went on like that for weeks, on the Internet a tide of over-excited types mouthed off unchecked until the foam of theories broke yet again against the reality principle.

On February 21, 2017, after a very eloquent summation by the lawyer Michele Andreano, Judge Nicola Di Grazia sentenced Manuel Foffo to thirty years in prison.

Andreano tried to demonstrate a mental capacity that was at least diminished. He called on medical consultants and the results of examinations, and even resorted to neuroscience. The material gathered was abundant and extremely detailed. Andreano tried to prove not only that Manuel was affected by chronic alcohol and cocaine intoxication but that his habits—reinforced by his physiology—had over the years caused irreversible neurobiological changes.

Despite the medical documents, the judge declared Manuel to be of sound mind. The accused, he said, had consumed excessive quantities of alcohol and cocaine consciously, had asked consciously for the summary procedure in place of an ordinary trial, had taken university exams not too long before. All these elements, according to the judge, disproved the hypothesis of even partially diminished mental capacity.

The sentence ruled out premeditation.

The sentence recognized the aggravating circumstance of torture and cruelty: both Foffo and Prato had been fully aware of the suffering inflicted on Luca. The aggravating circumstance of trivial motives was acknowledged: Prato and Foffo had made the life of Luca Varani "an object" at the mercy of their compulsions. The wish to inflict suffering on the victim until his death, the judge wrote, had as its only purpose that of having an experience "beyond every limit" linked "to a very high degree of sexual perversion." The way Luca was killed indicated the formation of "a despicable feeling that might reveal a degree of perversity such as to arouse a deep sense of repugnance, and unjustifiable because of its abnormality with regard to human feeling."

The first hearing in the trial of Marco Prato was set for April 10th.

On February 13th, despite his wishes, and contrary to all his hopes, Marco Prato was again transferred to the prison in Velletri. The protests of his lawyers were to no avail this time. But it was only the beginning.

A few weeks later, his face was splashed unexpectedly across all the newspapers in the country. What lighted the fuse was *Giallo*, a muckraking weekly specializing in crime.

THE HORROR HAS NO END: PRATO IS HIV-POSITIVE!

ANYONE WHO PARTICIPATED IN HIS WILD SEX PARTIES IS AT RISK

The headline, in block letters, occupied most of the cover. The piece was signed Albina Perri. It seemed that the reporter had obtained possession of Prato's clinical files, kept in the archives of Regina Coeli. In one of these documents, going back to the days of his arrest, a doctor from the local health authority had written by hand: "Clinical record of prisoner Marco Prato. HIV: positivity verified in March. Last test, negative two years ago. Transmission: sexual. The prisoner reports he was informed of his HIV-positive status."

The text of the article did not skimp on adjectives ("We found the page with the *terrible* diagnosis," "The report is *unequivocal*") and seemed to want to justify the violation of privacy by safeguarding Prato's preceding partners: it was likely that the majority of them didn't know about his HIV-positivity. The article noted that Marco had seduced many heterosexuals; as a result their girlfriends could also be infected.

The papers repeated the news in a disorderly manner. Some pointed out that Prato's HIV-positive status could sow panic among the VIPs of the capital whom Marco claimed to have seduced. When show business trembles, the reader buys.

Accused of murder and possible plague-spreader. The situation was becoming increasingly complicated. Judges and prison administrators should rely only on documents, but few believe that the media atmosphere doesn't influence their decisions, and the atmosphere surrounding Marco Prato was now very heavy. He needed a move that would attempt to redress the situation, and lead at least some segment of public opinion to see the accused in a different light. A few days later, Marco broke his silence and granted an interview to *Panorama*.

The interviewer was Annalisa Chirico, a former university classmate of Marco's. The interview took place by correspondence, mediated by Prato's lawyers.

"It wasn't me who struck him with the hammer and the knives," Marco affirmed. "I can't be sentenced to life in prison. I know I didn't prevent Luca's death, but I didn't kill him and I didn't call him in order to kill him."

It was difficult to deny the hypothesis that Luca had been invited to spend a day of excesses, just as it was difficult to deny that Marco's life had been, in recent years, rather turbulent.

"Is transgression the sister of death?" asked the reporter.

"If observed under the microscope, or through the keyhole," said Marco, "we all have a dark side that's more or less moral, more or less acceptable. Mine simply came to the surface. Yes, I took drugs, but not that much. Yes, I had sex, but like an ordinary thirty-year-old. The extreme requests, the most bizarre, came from the men with whom I surrounded myself, they drew them out of me. I endured a lot of violence to please heterosexual males who attracted me and made me feel female. It's evident that when such prurient details come into the public domain they're useful for the collective consciousness to point the finger rather than look in the mirror. Public condemnation satisfies us because it keeps us far from our monsters, makes us feel more normal inside. Convinced as I am that normality is an abstract concept, I would eliminate the first three letters of the word 'perversion.' They are all different *versions* of humanity, distinct shadings of individuality, sometimes experienced with suffering."

The journalist asked him about living conditions in the prison at Velletri.

"When I was at Regina Coeli," said Marco, "I held language courses for the prisoners, I tried to help them with letters and written communications. Here at Velletri I do nothing of all that, there are no activities, there's nothing, which is outrageous, because, besides the inadequacy of the bathrooms and the food, prison reality like this is reduced to mere expiation, without re-education. I pass almost the entire time lying on my cot, I continue to think about what happened, I go back over every minute. I miss everything there is outside. I miss walking and listening to my adored Dalida. I really miss everyone."

"What would you say to Foffo?" asked the journalist

"I would say to him: *Manuel, give up hate. Just as you did the night you calmly left me to go and die, now let me live and restore the truth to that tragic night.*"

If the purpose of Marco Prato's discourse had been to chastise the worst instincts of the masses, he would have hit the bull's-eye. Outside there were a lot of people eager to crucify the guilty, to burn monsters at the stake, people engaged in setting up every type of pillory just to satisfy a devastating feeling of revenge. But revenge for what? We felt humiliated, we needed to humiliate. We felt wounded, we needed to wound. We felt basically mediocre, stupid, fearful, and inessential, in the twilight of an era that had promised to make us rich, intelligent, courageous. As a result we kept very busy so as not to look reality in the face, we flaunted our failure, passing it off as proof of our honesty, our kindness, our lucidity, when not of our purity, and we hunted for the guilty (or began to fabricate them) just to keep our castle of cards standing. If Marco Prato had wanted to recount this psychological collapse, this profound social illness, he would have been right. But the problem lay in the fact that—apart from what the trial would establish, and the punishment he would be sentenced to—he was indisputably responsible for what had happened. Marco Prato pointed at the fanatics of the pillory to avoid lingering on his own failures—uttering a truth about others in order to avoid one about himself; this, too, was, ultimately, a widespread social illness—not to mention avoid lingering on the most shocking aspect of all, that is to say that a boy of twenty-three was no longer there.

I saw the skein getting tangled, I wondered how, and when, all those tangles would be straightened out.

Thus, at a certain point in the interview, Annalisa Chirico, the former university classmate, the journalist to whom Marco had entrusted some hope of public rehabilitation, recalled Varani's family. Luca's parents, she said, didn't believe that the word "forgiveness" deserved to be uttered.

"I will write a letter to Luca's family," Marco answered. "I've been thinking about it for some time, but I don't think now is the moment to talk about it."

W hat letter? He never wrote anything!" said Giuseppe Varani.

Luca's father, furious about how things had gone with Manuel Foffo, feared they might go even worse with Marco Prato. He didn't understand the principle behind the summary procedure: how was it possible, in a murder like that, to trade the terrible nature of the facts for the reasonings of the bureaucracy? Giuseppe Varani was also frustrated because, during the trial, he said, he hadn't ever been allowed to speak to the judge. What sort of rule was that? If he had been given a chance to show the photos, to describe his own suffering, to recall, outside of documents and expert reports, who his son was and what end they had inflicted on him, if someone had simply allowed him to place on the pan of the scale—so conclusive, symbolically, for representing justice—the particular type of suffering to which he and his wife had been condemned ("We're the ones on whom they've inflicted *never-ending punishment!*" he said), maybe things would have gone differently. Now Signor Varani was nervous and worried. If Foffo had received thirty years by declaring that he was guilty, what would happen with Marco Prato, who was shouting his innocence from the rooftops?

Then there were the expectations of the public. The summary procedure had taken place behind closed doors. No one had seen Marco Prato and Manuel Foffo in the dock. Now, with the onset of the ordinary trial, there was the possibility that the two would find themselves in the same courtroom. The curious would be able to see them face to face with one another, at the height of a confrontation (one would speak his own truth, the other would deny it) that promised to be dramatic. People were impatient to enjoy the spectacle. Thus began the countdown to April 10.

When April 10 actually arrived, however, the trial did not take place, because of a sudden lawyers' strike. The hearing was put off until June 12.

On May 19, less than a month from the start of the trial, Luca Varani's parents took part in a torchlight procession organized by a recently formed group, We Are Luca. More than a hundred people—friends, family, ordinary residents of the neighborhood—paraded after sunset on the streets of Boccea. They had prepared the banners carefully. They had had T-shirts printed with an image of Luca along with the legend "We Are Luca." The small demonstration did not have only a commemorative purpose. When the procession began, and the participants started marching, holding up the banners with a proud and sorrowful gaze, the curious could observe, on the backs of the shirts, another saying: "Life in Prison and Exemplary Punishment for the Murderers."

So June 12 arrived, the day of the first hearing in the trial of Marco Prato. That morning Luca's parents, sustained by the committee that had promoted the torchlight procession, held up a banner right in front of the court. "We Are Luca. Justice for Luca Varani." A gesture of preventive protest.

But again, completely unexpectedly, the trial wasn't held. A new strike by criminal lawyers caused it to be put off a second time. Luca Varani's parents went home carrying their banner along with members of the committee. The hearing was set for June 21.

The wait was getting unnerving. All attention was on Marco. The stories that for a year had rained down on him had made him in imagination a character in a film—chameleon, contradictory, fearfully lucid, divided, hypersensitive, manipulator, capable of every sort of cunning, willing to do anything just to see his image sparkle—even though almost no one, since the day of the murder, had seen him in action. What would happen at the trial? How would Marco Prato present himself in public? What face would he offer photographers and video cameras? In what tone of voice would he address the jury? Would he speak of himself in the feminine? What might happen if he was faced with Manuel Foffo? Would he try to destroy him rhetorically, as he seemed capable of doing with everyone? Even if he did, people said, it would be far more complicated to get the better of the prosecutor. Scavo was tough. Did Marco have aces up his sleeve that he could still play? Which of his many personalities would he resort to, and with what subtle reasoning, what miraculous job of deconstruction, would he refute the chain of evidence thrown at him? What exceptional lie or annihilating truth would the accused disclose at the crucial point? In Rome the heat was again atrocious.

T he news began to circulate on the radio on June 20, the day before the hearing. It was on the Internet, then the news shows.

I got a WhatsApp at 9:08.

I was in Turin. The night before, to prepare for the trial, I had fallen asleep reading some documents in the gigantic folder I had put together over the months. I heard the sound of the notification while I was drinking my second coffee of the day. I picked up the phone.

"Nicola did you see? I'm shocked." Writing me was a friend I hadn't heard from for months.

It could be any news capable of rousing dismay, from an earthquake to a terrorist attack. And yet—even before answering "No, what happened?"—I felt I knew what it was about. I'd known for months, maybe from the start of the whole thing, I had reckoned with it but at the same time managed to ignore it. It had taken that message for me to assess seriously what I had perceived only unconsciously.

A few seconds later, again on my phone, I got a link to the home page of *Il Messaggero*.

MARCO PRATO SUICIDE IN PRISON

I collapsed on the couch as if someone had punched me in the face.

During the night, in the prison at Velletri, Marco Prato had been found lifeless in the bathroom of his cell. He had killed himself by inhaling the gas from the cylinder used for cooking. He had put a plastic bag over his head, tying it at the base of his

398 · NICOLA LAGIOIA

throat, and had put the gas canister in it. His cellmate hadn't noticed anything, or at least so he told the prison guards. The body was found at 12:45 A.M.

In the bathroom, next to the body, the papers wrote, was a piece of paper with a brief farewell written in block letters.

"Suicide isn't an act of courage or of cowardice," Marco Prato had written before dying. "Suicide is an illness from which you don't always recover. It doesn't have ethical connotations, it's not an escape or an egoistic gesture. The media pressure is unbearable, the lies about that night and about me are unbearable, this life is unbearable. Forgive me."

There followed a signature and a postscript.

"Make sure that when my father is told a doctor or my mother's sister (a retired head doctor) is with him, because he suffers from hypertension and heart trouble!"

T he next day, June 21, the judges of the First Court of Assizes of the Court of Rome opened and closed the case against Marco Prato. The crime was declared no longer punishable because of the unexpected death of the accused. The apartment on Via Igino Giordani was ordered released from seizure.

The court was besieged by reporters. Marta Gaia Sebastiani was present at the hearing. As soon as she left the building the reporters were on her.

"Marta Gaia! Marta Gaia!"

"I don't want to talk."

The girl, protected by a large pair of dark glasses, had a determined tone. The day before she had written a post on Facebook saying she was shocked by what had happened.

"You really don't have a comment?"

"No." Marta raised a hand at the microphone as if to protect herself. "A life is a life," she said, "the families' mourning has to be respected."

"A tragedy within the tragedy?"

"Yes," she said before hurrying off.

It was the turn of Savino Guglielmi, her lawyer.

"I believe that everyone comes out a loser here," he said, surrounded by TV cameras. "The state, the community, poor Varani. We all lose. The safety of a prisoner was not protected. We are unable to conduct the trial of Marco Prato. Unfortunately we'll never know the complete truth."

Valter Foffo, Manuel's father, was reached on the phone by reporters.

400 · NICOLA LAGIOIA

"You're harassing me with calls. What can I say in the face of this other sorrow? I found out on the radio that Prato had taken his own life. Now my son alone remains. The danger? That he remains the only scapegoat of this endless drama."

Giuseppe Varani was also reached by reporters.

"We're sorry for the family of Marco Prato," he said, "no one deserves to die like that, not even the worst criminal. We heard the news from a journalist friend. My wife burst into tears. We're sorry for what happened. But our suffering is clearly worse than theirs. My son was killed, he didn't decide to die."

The psychiatrist for the health service who was following Marco in the Velletri prison had written in his last note: "Seen regularly since February 14. Weekly visits and supporting talks. During the clinical evaluations suicidal intentions were not reported. Mood reported as not depressed."

But Mauro Palma, the national guarantor for the rights of prisoners, declared: "In many ways this suicide was predictable. We had already intervened last year to bring Marco Prato back to Regina Coeli, in light of the fact that the so-called psychiatric care unit at the institution of Velletri is nonexistent, and that there, in Velletri, a person who had already attempted suicide would have had less assistance than what is guaranteed in the prison in Rome."

At 11 in the morning, Ledo Prato was in the mortuary of the polyclinic at Tor Vergata. In front of him was Marco's body. "We had seen each other in jail, who could imagine it," he whispered in a very low voice. He had gone to see his son the previous afternoon. He had gone to see him as he had continued to do ever since Marco had been in prison. They had embraced. They had talked. Now they were there.

The suicide of Marco Prato was the saddest turn of events and, at the same time, threw over the case a heavy black mantle. Although the legal proceedings were not over—there would be Foffo's appeal, the Court of Appeals, the civil suits of the Varanis and Marta Gaia Sebastiani—from that moment the tension began to diminish. The peak had been reached, the contents had caused the container to explode. There was no shortage of after-effects, but a clear sensation like the end of a match hit those who, for more than a year, had followed the murder, unable to break away.

On the causes of the suicide there was speculation for months.

"Try to come up with some hypotheses," said Francesco Scavo, with whom I was now on fairly intimate terms.

We were in the usual café in Piazzale Clodio. I had again passed by Monte Mario, had seen the observatory in the distance. I felt the usual upset of returning to Rome knowing that I would have to leave it soon afterward, I heard the traffic on Viale Angelico, I knew that farther on was Piazza Mazzini, the stores of Cola di Rienzo, and then, past the Palazzaccio, the court building, right on the river, the museum of the Souls in Purgatory, whose small collection was focused on documenting the conduct of the souls of the dead. Divine imprints on priests' robes. A pillowcase stamped with fire by the spirit of a deceased nun. That day, before meeting Scavo, I had been stopped on the street by a little girl. "Hi, do you like animals?" The child was outside a store where her mother, I saw, was buying cat food. "Of course," I said, "like you I have a cat." The child might have been nine or ten, tall for her age; she was wearing a pair of green pants that left her ankles exposed, her hair had a bowl cut, and she had one of the liveliest, most intelligent gazes I'd ever seen in my life. "How do you know I have a cat?" she asked, after ironically rewarding my correct guess with the first four notes of a famous symphony. "Because I read your thoughts," I said. "Oh yes," she said, serious, but as if the attention she was granting me shouldn't remove her completely from the parallel dimension, the magnificent submerged land that anyone over twenty would give everything he has to return to. "So if you read my thoughts," she continued, "you must also tell me the name of my cat." "What sort of questions are these?" I answered. "His name is Beethoven." "How did you . . ." She smiled almost imperceptibly. Her mother called her from inside the shop: "Come on, stop bothering people!" The voice was full of loving exasperation. Life would be tolerable if I could stay talking forever with this child, I thought. She, who was truly able to read thoughts, had been so generous as to give me the illusion of being able to do so as well.

"Everything that's said about the suicide seems plausible," I was saying now to Scavo, "maybe there isn't a single explanation."

Some claimed that the criminal lawyers' strike was the last straw: the continual delay of the trial had undermined Marco's mood: he was already worn down by prison and the media onslaught. Many interpreted the suicide as the peak of its author's need for attention. Killing himself two days from the trial, they said, Marco had contrived an exit worthy of a diva, philologically retracing Dalida's tragic end. "Forgive me, life is unbearable to me," the singer had written in her farewell note. "This life is unbearable. Forgive me": Prato's note was almost identical. As if that weren't enough, through his suicide Marco had launched a dramatically effective attack on the machine of justice. Killing himself was the only way to prevent the trial from taking place. With an extreme gesture, Marco had regained control of the situation, preventing anyone else from writing the finale in his place.

"Then there's the business of Ettore Catanzaro," I added.

"There's also that," said Scavo.

Some weeks earlier, Ettore Catanzaro, age forty-one, formerly incarcerated in the prison at Velletri, then transferred to the district penitentiary of Latina, had asked to be heard by the judicial authority. He had told a marshal from the police that at the prison Marco Prato had commissioned him to beat up Manuel Foffo. "In the prison at Velletri I was in cell no. 7," he had said, "Marco was in no. 5. At first he was in isolation, they made him go out every so often to socialize a little, he'd talk to my cellmate, Medina, a Cuban he'd met in Regina Coeli. One day Medina comes to me and goes: *Listen, Ettore, there's Marco Prato who hates Manuel Foffo, wants to have him beaten up, he's convinced that it was he who spread the rumor of his being HIV-positive. He wants to know if you can help him.*" Catanzaro was inside for serious crimes, he had friends in other prisons. "I would never have had Manuel Foffo beaten up," he told the marshal, "but I played along." When his isolation was over, Marco visited Catanzaro in his cell during free time. Catanzaro cooked for him ("fettucine with ragú, cutlet"), every so often he rolled a joint ("I had some weed hidden in the salt tin"), and after lunch he talked and listened to music. In fact, Catanzaro continued, Marco had tried to commission him to beat up Manuel. "He offered me two thousand euros to get Foffo beaten up, he said he could get the money. I would have had to write to a friend from Tor Bella Monaca in the prison where Manuel is, asking him to do the job. Marco and I became intimate. He told me about his parents, he said his mother had never come to see him. Another day, also in my cell, since by now we'd told each other everything, I asked him: *Tell the truth, did you take part physically in the murder?* Marco answered: *Yes.* and I: *How many times did you stab him?* He said he'd stabbed him twice."

Catanzaro's account was put in a report. The report was given to the prosecutor. Presumably, a copy had also been sent to

Prato's lawyers, who, I thought, must have informed their client. Assuming this version was true—and that Catanzaro's story was—Marco had found out where his confidences ended up. It might have been the collapse of his defensive structure, and at that moment he might have seen lengthening over him the black shadow of a life sentence.

"Ledo Prato came to see me," Scavo said then.

When a trial is over, it happens more often than you'd think. The relatives of the condemned seek out the accusers. They feel the need to explain, to clarify, as if the person who had set in motion the heavy machinery of justice were the best one to confront the problem on other levels as well.

In this case, however, Ledo Prato only wanted an inquiry opened into the suicide of his son. Why had Marco been transferred to Velletri? How was it possible that the prison psychiatrists hadn't realized his state? They all knew that Marco had tried to kill himself before. And so why had *no one* done *anything* to prevent the situation from getting out of control?

I said goodbye to Scavo. I checked my watch. I walked aimlessly for half an hour, then I put in an envelope the letter I'd written to Manuel Foffo, the only survivor of the three men. I took the metro.

I had lunch in a terrible osteria near Via Cavour. Since I still had time before my next appointment, I went to San Pietro in Vincoli. I went up the stairs of the Borgias, perennially shady thanks to the overhanging arch and, at the same time, enlivened by a cascade of vines. At the top, I saw the smooth, regular façade of the church. I went to the side nave, walked along it until I was facing the statue. It had been there for almost five hundred years, and would remain long after our death. Michelangelo's *Moses* was the rare case of a puzzle in grandeur, which people had been debating forever. When Sigmund Freud was in Rome, he went to San Pietro in Vincoli every day and stood before the statue for hours, trying to understand, alight with hope when he seemed to have grasped something important, disheartened when the intuition vanished. He looked at the statue's muscular arms, the tablets of the law under his right arm, the left hand resting on his lap, the fingers of his right hand entwined in the curls of his beard, the left leg raised so that only the tips of his toes touched the ground, the head turned to the left and, in the gaze, a mixture of anger, contempt, and sorrow. Scholars believed that Michelangelo was documenting the moment immediately before Moses, outraged at the behavior of his people, breaks the tablets, hurling them to the ground. Then he grabs the golden calf, burns it in the fire, grinds it to a powder, scatters the powder over the water, and makes the Israelites drink it. Well, after yet another visit, Sigmund Freud, observing the statue without pause, suddenly thought he had had a revelation. It seemed to him, that is, that Michelangelo, carving his *Moses*, had made a powerful gesture of free will, venturing to change the Biblical narrative, and documenting not anger about to explode but, what is not in the Book, anger subdued. According to Freud, Michelangelo's Moses, after moments of inner torment, a mysterious battle with himself, changes his purpose. Indignation is curbed, violence dissolves, suffering begins to be healed. The prophet no longer smashes the tablets on the ground, and for that very reason the tablets, that is, the law, assume new meaning.

Replace one narrator with another. What had happened in Moses' mind, in Freud's interpretation? And what should we do? I wondered, looking at the statue and thinking of Marco Prato. What was the task of the living, if the dead had failed in theirs?

I left the church. I walked aimlessly for a few minutes. Then I headed to my next appointment. After having been in Piazzale Clodio, where justice is administered, and in San Pietro in Vincoli, where souls are cared for, the palazzo where democracy is saved and threatened on alternate days awaited me.

I knew that Ledo Prato had turned not only to Scavo but to Senator Luigi Manconi.

At that time Manconi was the president of the Senate's special committee for the safeguarding and promotion of human rights. I went to see him at three in the afternoon. We had already met; Manconi was then nearly seventy, he was in his third term, and he conducted his battles with enough independence to seriously jeopardize the possibility of a fourth. He worked on the rights of migrants, the conditions of the Roma communities, prisoners, refugees, the disabled, abuses of power by the police against ordinary citizens. For several years he had been almost completely blind, because of glaucoma. He didn't carry a stick or wear dark glasses, and every so often he nearly got killed crossing the street. Otherwise he worked tirelessly, surrounded by his assistants, in a tiny office in Palazzo Madama.

I arrived at the Senate. I handed over my documents and was led into the gigantic forge of Italian democracy. Into one of its lungs, to be precise. The clerk led the way. Looking around, I thought that the places of power in Italy resemble one another. Crossing the monumental thresholds you find yourself in a cramped labyrinth of rooms and corridors. Every so often a museum-like view. Then another spider web of corridors, small offices, and elevators as narrow as coffins. Power lives in the interstices. "This way," said the clerk, and pointed to yet another elevator.

Senator Manconi's office was a small, long room, full of papers, files, and just published books. They were sent by the publishers.

"He came to me after trying other politicians," he confirmed.

Manconi said that Ledo Prato was trying to act at the institutional level. It wasn't so easy. He went from one interlocutor to the next, was put on hold, sat in anterooms in vain, waited for phone calls that were slow in coming.

"He wanted to talk to men closer to his area first. It's natural, I think. But they wasted his time, or got mired in some bureaucratic problem or other."

Manconi said that very soon he would be submitting an inquiry to the Minister of Justice, Andrea Orlando.

"You know how many people kill themselves in Italian prisons?"

One a week, he informed me before I could come up with a hypothesis.

"You know how they kill themselves?"

Senator Manconi said that often they hanged themselves. The second cause of death was gas. They used the canisters, as Marco had. There was a way to avoid this last type of death, or at least in part reduce that horror, a way so simple that he couldn't understand why it wasn't adopted. "They'd merely have to replace the gas canisters with electric hotplates." For years, Manconi said, they'd been sending requests to the Ministry of Justice.

It was then that I recalled what Marco had said to his father during one of the last conversations in prison. "They've given me an upgrade" were his words regarding the fact that he had been authorized to use the gas canister to make himself coffee.

Before I left, Senator Manconi wanted to give me a small gift.

"I don't know what conclusions you've come to in your research," he said. "We can't ever know everything about the human beings we're interested in."

"We can't ever know everything about ourselves, either," I said, "otherwise no one would write a damn thing anymore."

"Yes, but one has to reach a certain degree of understanding. These things follow complicated paths, at times it takes years, other times we never get there."

"Understanding doesn't last, we're transitory even in that."

"Whatever happens," he said, "I want to give you something that might be useful."

He asked an assistant to dig in the small mountain of books that occupied one of the desks. After a brief search, the assistant found the volume. He weighed it in his hands, held it out to me.

"No offense to those present," he said smiling. "I consider it the finest Italian book of the past ten years."

The inquiry (signed by Manconi, Corsini, Stefano) was submitted to Minister Orlando on July 6th. The response arrived after five months, on December 7th.

The minister wrote that, although aware of the tragedy of every act of self-harm, he couldn't ignore the fact that in recent years the number of suicides in Italian prisons had decreased. As far as Marco Prato in particular was concerned, one could not conclude, based on the reports from the prison administration, that his condition had been "underestimated or neglected."

The report, five pages long, continued in that tone. It seemed rather like a game of role playing. Stuffed in among the usual reassurances, however, there was a piece of information that couldn't go unnoticed. The petitioners had asked how in the world Marco Prato had been transferred to the prison in Velletri. The minister's answer was typical.

The proposal for transfer from Rome to another institution was justified by the tendency of the prisoner to exploit the weaknesses of his prison mates in order to assume a dominant role.

From that response—obtained presumably after asking the prison authorities for information—one could imagine that at Regina Coeli Marco had managed to reproduce some of the dynamics he'd practiced when he was free. Manipulating others. Bending their will. Making them do what he wanted. Among those who followed the case were some who recalled what Marco had said about a music and literature course he'd done in prison.

The other prisoners had sung to him Dalida's *Ciao amore, ciao*. "You don't persuade a group of prisoners to sing your favorite song to you if you don't have them in the palm of your hand." Someone hypothesized that Marco hadn't confined himself to exercising his seductive gifts on the intellectual plane. If he had had sex with other prisoners, then the news that he was HIV-positive could have had consequences. From seducer to spreader. He might have been transferred to escape the revenge of other prisoners.

M ore weeks passed. On October 16, 2017, I received a WhatsApp from Chiara Ingrosso. Something unexpected had happened, she wanted to talk to me. We met a few days later near Ponte Milvio.

It was the period in which the appeal was taking shape. Manuel had been transferred to the prison in Rebibbia. We had also learned that he had decided to change lawyers. Out with Michele Andreano, in with Fabio Menichetti. It was said he had done it for family reasons: after all Andreano was his father's lawyer, and although Manuel allowed Valter to take care of many financial tasks, he continued to harbor toward him a feeling of distrust. In the moments of greatest confusion he had gone so far as to think that Valter might conspire against him.

Otherwise, contradictory news arrived concerning the Foffos. Some said they had started business activities abroad, others that they were in Rome, occupied in trying to get out of the financial problems brought on by the murder.

From the Pratos, as always, no news.

"That's precisely what I want to talk to you about," said Chiara Ingrosso.

She was now working as a correspondent for some Mediaset TV channels. She traveled around Italy, tracking the protagonists of the bloodiest crimes and trying to get decisive statements out of them. There was no lack of material; human beings continued to kill one another. Chiara said that the cases disturbed her, but she managed to erect a protective screen of professionalism. The Varani murder was different: every crime reporter had her case of a lifetime, against which her defenses were fragile. Chiara was surprised by how far from her old life the murder had cast her without her realizing it. Anyone who got too close when it came to certain brutal stories, she said, received *the mark*, and strange things began to happen to the marked.

"It happened a few weeks ago," she said. "I was at the airport in Brindisi. I was supposed to go to Rome. I'd checked in, I was waiting for boarding to start." Suddenly ("until that moment it had been a clear day, in fact sunny") the sky darkened and practically out of nowhere an exceptionally violent storm hit the city. The wind was so strong that the airport was closed, the flights were rerouted to Bari-Palese, an emergency shuttle was made available for the passengers to get to the airport. "Once we got there, we prepared for the boarding process again." Before going through the metal detector, right on the escalator that led to the upper floor, Chiara seemed to see a known profile. In front of her was a tall, distinguished man, enveloped in a dark suit. "It seemed to me that it was him, and at the same time a coincidence so incredible I couldn't believe it." Once on the upper floor, Chiara Ingrosso walked quickly, passed the man, and turned to look at him. "I think I've seen you before," she said. "It's possible," he said without changing expression. "You're Marco's father," she said. Ledo Prato's eyes grew misty. "I started crying, too," Chiara recounted. It was a genuine moment of recognition ("I think he felt, clearly, my involvement in the event"). "Were you a friend of my son?" Ledo Prato asked, regaining his composure. Chiara said no, she was a journalist. The man's expression changed again. "Out of candor I listed the reports I'd done on the case. He grew cold, he remembered every one; after all, Marco had attributed the decision to kill himself in part to media pressure, and I might have added to it." The two re-established their distances, made an appointment to talk in tranquility some days later. "We met at Villa Torlonia," Chiara said. "But the atmosphere of that day at the airport couldn't be recreated. I brought him as a present a record by Dalida, he said that it seemed a choice in bad taste. I tried to explain that it was my way of honoring Marco's memory." Ledo had remained rather cold, he had been wary for the rest of the meeting, letting no confidences escape, and without agreeing to be interviewed.

"Anyway, it isn't a coincidence that I met him," said Chiara.

"What do you mean?" I asked.

"I deserved it," she said. How likely was it that she would find herself on the same flight as Ledo Prato, and how likely was it that out of nowhere a crazy storm would burst over Brindisi without which she wouldn't have noticed his presence? In the past year and a half she had thought so intensely about the murder, had interviewed so many of the people, read so many documents, listened to so many voices that chance, or fate, she said, had put her in Ledo Prato's path.

"I don't know," I said, but everything in me believed she was right.

It was then I thought that I had to separate from the case. I had to release my grip, it was time, my need to understand had become a dependency and now I was in danger of succumbing. There's the moment when you dig into the murder, and then there's the next moment when it's the murder that's digging into you, mercilessly. You begin to interpret everything as a function of the case, you see signs everywhere, coincidences, premonitions, you are transformed without realizing it into your own object of investigation. A point is reached beyond which you can't dig anymore, cast light, so it's the darkness, a blind spiritual void, that forces its way into you. Then you have to turn your head in the other direction, you have to separate yourself from the case to have even just a hope that the last piece, the most important, the one you still haven't managed to find, will appear without your realizing it.

When I got home I found Manuel Foffo's answer to my letter. I read it. It contained no overwhelming revelation. I also found an email responding to the request for an appointment I'd asked for. I printed the train tickets, got ready to leave.

F irst I worked in an architecture studio. Then I started in a photo agency. I quit today."

We met in Porta Venezia. The traffic was quiet, the streets tidy, the sidewalks full of busy people. Nice shops, great exhibitions, brand-new skyscrapers. A feverish energy rose from the city. Milan. Coming out of the metro, I sent him a message. His name was Andrea, he was twenty-six years old, he was Marco Prato's last boyfriend. When I tried to get in touch with him on the phone, days earlier, he had been very polite. I was a total stranger and I was asking him to talk about a terrible experience. His apparent calm struck me.

We shook hands. We went to a café. He was a young man with delicate features, well dressed, an intense, alert gaze. We sat down, ordered two glasses of juice.

"Marco and I met on Facebook," he began the story. "In a certain sense it was thanks to the algorithm." The social network, as it did every day, suggested profiles of users you might ask to be friends with. "I saw the photos of Marco, he immediately looked like a handsome guy. I started liking and hearting his posts. We started chatting. Only then I realized that he had already tried to get in touch with me on Tinder. In that case I had ignored him, but now I was interested. We decided to meet."

They began seeing each other in October of 2015. They were together for several months. If Andrea had had to describe Marco as he had known him up to the day of the murder, his judgment would have been totally positive. "He was always kind, protective, he took care of me. An angel. I never saw him angry, he was never violent, in fact he was very gentle."

Andrea lived alone in a big house in Rome. ("My family was rather scattered all over Italy.") So Marco often came to see him. "I never saw him sniff cocaine, he never talked about prostitutes, he never even said he wanted to change sex. I found him to be an intelligent, very sensitive person."

I wondered if he was the man with whom Marco, interrogated by the prosecutor, had said he was "incredibly bored."

Andrea meanwhile continued to tell the story. On December 31 of 2015, he said, he was invited to lunch at the Prato house. He knew that Marco's homosexuality had created some uneasiness in the family. Marco had talked about problems with his mother. "In fact it was better than I expected." The lunch went relatively well. At the table were Marco's parents, his sister, and aunts. The aunts, according to Andrea, had been "fantastic." The sister ("a very smart girl") also welcomed him kindly. The mother was polite but detached, maybe some tension was noticeable but nothing that wasn't manageable. Ledo had behaved strangely.

"Soon after my arrival, he got up from the table and left. I was afraid that he was annoyed at finding his son's boyfriend in his house. Or maybe he was only tired."

That same evening, at the New Year's Eve party, Marco would meet Manuel Foffo.

After the holidays, Andrea and Marco began to separate. "He made the break, because I didn't seem enthusiastic. He was right. A few months after our relationship started, I wasn't interested anymore."

They broke up in February, but their relations remained good. They continued to see each other, and went out together. On March 1 they met at a club.

The next day, Andrea tried to send him a message. He got no response. On March 5 he sent him another ("You're slipping to the bottom of my chats, and I don't like it. I'm writing even if you ignore me"). Then, on the 7th, he read about the murder on Facebook.

"I couldn't believe it. I was shocked. There was a photo of Marco in a black sweater and underneath the news that he had been arrested. I knew that photo because I had taken it, which made it all even more distressing. I thought it was fake, Marco was known in Rome, someone could have played a nasty trick on him. In a few hours I realized it was all true. I was plunged into a state of chaos, total confusion, I recall the next days as a kind of hallucination."

During this period Andrea was preparing his thesis for graduation.

"The next day I went to the university. I had decided to tell my supervisor that I was giving up the thesis. I found her in the corridor, she was talking to a group of lecturers, I approached, I realized they were discussing the crime. I felt my blood freeze. She didn't know that Marco and I had been together. It all seemed madness."

Andrea talked to his supervisor, told her everything.

"The professor took me under her wing, encouraged me, tried to support me in every way. If I got my degree it was because of her, I will never stop being grateful to her."

At first Andrea wrote Marco letters. Marco responded from Regina Coeli. In the beginning he didn't talk about prison, and he never talked about the murder. Then he started to open up. He seemed to be becoming part of the prison population, interacting with other prisoners, socializing. It went like that for several months. Then another bomb burst. The news arrived that Marco was HIV positive.

"Then I stopped writing to him. I broke off all communication. I felt betrayed, and I was obviously in a panic. I hurried to get the HIV test. You can imagine the tension. Luckily it was negative."

But the nights were difficult. As soon as he fell asleep, Andrea was assaulted by nightmares, literally crushed by bad dreams.

"What did you dream?" I asked.

"I dreamed that Marco killed me. Or, worse, I dreamed that *I* killed someone. Those were terrible nights. Finally the nightmares disappeared."

"When did that happen?"

He sighed, gave me a long look.

"I know it's sad to say, but the nightmares ended when Marco killed himself."

After Marco's suicide, Andrea decided to leave Rome. It was too much, it had been an unimaginable year, he had to leave that story behind.

"After a few days in Milan, I got together with a guy. Maybe not the best idea, but I was shattered."

Several months passed. Andrea started working, and didn't return to Rome for a long time. He didn't feel ready to face the city. But sooner or later he would have to.

"I let more months go by, finally I made up my mind and came back. I thought that as long as I couldn't set foot in Rome, I couldn't say that I had really got over it. I remember the train journey. When I got to Termini it was wonderful, the confusion, the heat, the giddiness. But then someone shouted at me on the street: *faggot!* It happened twice in one day. I decided to stay in Milan."

Suddenly, as he was talking, I felt guilty. Guilty because I was forty-five and he was not yet thirty. A chronological, objective guilt. Adults are always guilty when young people live in a terrible world. Who else's responsibility could it be?

"I'm trying to return to Rome."

I hadn't yet said it to anyone. My wife and I had started talking about it a few days before, we felt our plans were too fragile to share, but at the same time, if they weren't shared sooner or later, those plans might not become acts.

"Once, on the street, I ran into one of the people connected to the *crime*," Andrea said meanwhile. "We looked at each other, and kept going without saying anything. We were survivors, and it's as if the survivors were all suspects."

He and the other shipwrecked men of the Pequod, I thought. Shortly afterward Andrea got up, we shook hands, I paid the bill.

"Why did you quit?" I asked finally. "Did you find a better job?"

"No," he said, "it's that after a while I didn't feel comfortable at that agency."

"What will you do now?"

"Who knows."

"Do you have particular plans?" I insisted.

"I don't think so," he said smiling.

Thus he seemed freer than I was, younger than ever. He seemed shining, victorious. I felt again, but only for a moment, the thrill of the days when you're sure you have nothing to lose, and you're strong even though you're weak. I made an effort not to envy him, but it was only fear. In fact I felt liberated, vicariously freed. I don't know how he'd done it, but he had, so to speak, shaken off the curse of the story, broken the evil, defeated the adversary. It had cost him suffering, he had said so himself, but now he was on the *other side*, temporarily outside the zone of shadow, on the other bank of the river, on the path that leads to the future. I thought he didn't belong to a lost generation. How could we think such a thing? We would have been the lost ones if we had left them alone. I saw him disappear beyond Porta Venezia. I felt something rise to the top, I saw it sparkle on the surface of the water.

PART VI

The Book of Encounters

> The sense of guilt can be fought only
> with the practice of virtue.
> —SIMONE WEIL

> If from the love of discipline originated the step of the soldier
> who doesn't win but retreats without striking a blow . . . .
> —AMELIA ROSSELLI

I got off the bus at Piazzale Flaminio. The sun was shining over the entire city. The month before, the driver of the 46, on the way to Piazza Venezia, had been beaten by a group of drunk kids. In May something similar had happened to the ticket inspector on the 545. In neither case had the passengers intervened. The bus resumed its route, I saw it get lost in the traffic. I crossed the street. I was walking without a purpose. My wife and I had returned to Rome. We had settled in with friends as we waited to regain possession of our old house. I could observe the city with new eyes for a little while longer, I thought. Santa Maria dei Miracoli, bell tower in the morning light. Months earlier the Appeals Court had confirmed Manuel Foffo's thirty-year prison sentence. His new lawyer, Fabio Menichetti, a man of impeccable eloquence, had brought clinical files and medical studies to the hearing. The Court experts, although observing in Manuel a moderate personality disorder, had not considered it decisive. Manuel was lucid when he killed Luca. I looked at the water clock on the Pincio, enclosed in its glass cage and surrounded by plants. I had also been in court that day. Manuel had arrived in jeans and white shirt, hair nicely cut, a well-tended appearance. He sat between prison guards. During the entire hearing he had looked at the judge with a serious and respectful expression. He had turned toward us only once. There were journalists, some of the curious, Luca Varani's parents. Neither Manuel's parents nor his brother was present. Cars sped along the Muro Torto, I saw them disappear into the mouth of the tunnel. The Court of Appeals had confirmed the thirty years, putting an end to the legal proceedings. For the final appeal Manuel had turned to two new lawyers. That restlessness might be explained by a search for a specific defense strategy. Or it testified to the bewilderment of the prisoner. I had talked to one of the new lawyers, Giammarco Conca. He was a calm, cordial man of forty, who lived outside the city, and had at heart the fate of his client. He told me that Manuel was in a difficult situation: no matter how he tried to get to the bottom of what had happened, he was often overwhelmed by confusion, by solitude, by guilt, by bitterness.

I had been exchanging letters with him for months. Manuel responded to my questions politely and punctually. He wrote in block letters, and his prose was so elementary that some passages weren't easy to interpret. I felt that he was making a huge effort to isolate the concepts he cared about from the force of chaos. From what he wrote I understood that he hadn't gotten over his problems with his father; there were reporters with whom he'd cut off relations as soon as he found out they had interviewed him. What most worried him was that Valter or other people would speak for him, saying inaccurate things. There was a correct version of the facts and then there was another story—an artificial, sophisticated, diabolically false story—that could betray the correct version brutally. His father, the reporters, all of us had to be careful not to end up in the trap. But who was the creator of these distortions? Who set the traps? I had the impression that, as Manuel saw it, the hand that continued to write the apocryphal story so feared by him was, yet again, Marco Prato's. He couldn't get rid of Marco's ghost. Through the lawyer Conca, Manuel let me have a brief "memorial" (as he called it), which was his version of the facts. He asked me to read it carefully. I did, but in those pages I could find nothing that altered in a meaningful way the reconstruction of the facts. In every word written by his hand, rather, line after line, breathed an inexhaustible, powerless, endless struggle with Marco Prato, a fight for the last word. It was Marco who had manipulated him, Manuel wrote, it was he who had confused and blackmailed him, pushed him to leave home that cursed night, it was his fault if he had reached the point of killing, and it was he, Marco Prato, who had slandered him, spreading the rumor even in prison—Manuel received continuous confirmations from other prisoners—that Manuel was "his boyfriend." It was as if Manuel still felt the force that had subjugated him in the early months of 2016. That force confused him, tired him, *survived*.

I passed Via Rasella. I entered the small park next to the Quirinale, the so-called Villa Carlo Alberto, where an equestrian statue is surrounded by roses. I continued to receive contradictory evidence about Marco Prato. There were some who described him the way Manuel had. But there were others who continued to speak of him as a gentle, empathetic, generous person. I reached Via Lanza, climbed the stairway of the Borgias, and shortly afterward was in the courtyard of the Mechanical Engineering Department. I thought of Prato's family. I could scarcely imagine how they would hold up under such a violent blow. The murder charge, then Marco's suicide. Every so often I received news of Ledo Prato. He helped organize shows, was present at literary events, always appeared in public with great discretion, polite and impeccable in every gesture. A way of carrying the tragedy on his shoulders without letting himself be destroyed by it, I thought. A beating of wings. I saw a flock of doves through the windows of the department. Of Signora Prato there was no news. Did she represent the black hole in her son's emotional universe or was she a woman overcome by grief who asked to be able to weep far from the spotlight? Guarding San Pietro in Vincoli were two bags of garbage. I could have speculated infinitely on whether Marco or Manuel was the greater manipulator, on how the frustrations of one and the affective deficits of the other had rendered them capable of unimaginable things. If, however, I had to point to the evil that, immediately after the instinct for aggression, seemed to me to precede any others, I would have traced it to a particular type of solitude. The solitude that, all the more if crowded, causes us to rot inside our ego, and is one with the fear of not being understood, of being wounded, robbed, damaged, the fear that forms our invisible spheres, that leads us to calculate in anguish, the fear through which even the good we try to do passes, and is perverted.

In Piazza Vittorio the sun shone on the palm trees and the buildings. A tram crossed the square. In the past weeks I had read the book Senator Manconi had given me. It had sat for a long time on the night table, then in the boxes during the move. I had recently found it again. It was called *Il libro dell'incontro* (*The Book of Encounters*) and offered testimony of a long-term experiment in restorative justice involving victims and perpetrators of the armed struggle in Italy. For years, between 2009 and 2015, relatives of the victims of terrorism had met some of those responsible for the deaths of their loved ones. The project was inspired by famous experiments in restorative justice, and started from the assumption that ordinary justice, whose course no one doubted, rarely gave full satisfaction to the victims and at the same time didn't offer the guilty the tools that might facilitate full comprehension of what they had done. The encounters between the parties, far from the clamor of the media, had been mediated by the authors of the book, with the addition of a small group of external "guarantors." They started from few assumptions: on one side the perpetrators of the armed struggle were aware of having destroyed the lives of entire families; on the other the relatives of the victims were ready to recognize the full humanity of their counterparts. "Our purpose," one of the authors wrote in the book's preface, "was, and still is, to complete a journey together, we mediators *in the middle*, between people who have suffered a terrible injury and those who caused that injury, all joined by something as mysterious—and in many ways inexplicable—as it is strong, inescapable, and decisive: the demand, or search, for justice. During this journey," the preface continued, "we encountered problems, questions, knots that only the *difficult other* could untie, and doubts that only trust in the *difficult other* could dissipate." More than once Luca Varani's father, I thought, had complained that he had never received a phone call from the parents of Manuel or Marco. Breaking a terrifying silence. Taking the first step. It was unlikely that a thing like that could happen, considering the level of incomprehension the two sides had reached, the distrust—even greater in the absence of mediators or guarantors. In play were feelings and states of mind difficult to master, such as anger, shame, despair. But maybe only something like that—a counterintuitive move, an impossible gesture—could break the spell, stopping the cycle of evil and solitude. A shout. Then a child, released from his mother's grasp, ran for a few seconds under the porticoes of the square.

The cars sped along Via Flaminia, but we were on Via della Villa di Livia, alongside it. We were choosing flowers. I had never been to Prima Porta. The immense city of the dead spread eastward, with its kilometers of internal streets along which even buses travel. I was with Chiara Ingrosso, and we were waiting for Luca's parents.

"We'll take these," she said pointing to the chrysanthemums.

Stalls, numbered from 1 to 40, wound all around the cemetery. Mostly they were selling flowers, but there were also marble workers who displayed pure white statues and plaques in the early afternoon air.

We saw the Varanis arrive in an Alfa 167. Chiara waved. The car began to slow down. We got in, and all together entered the biggest cemetery in Italy.

In the city tourists were suffocating at the doors of the Pantheon. Here summer was less violent. A honey-colored light, a moderate heat descended indifferent amid stones and chapels, in the enormous Catholic section and in the areas devoted to other religions. Next to the crematoriums was the Garden of Memories, three hectares on the hillside where the ashes of the dead were scattered amid trees and bushes.

We passed some other intersections, and Giuseppe Varani parked. We got out of the car. "Wait to go in," he ordered.

The chapel was a small parallelepiped repainted orange. As soon as I crossed the threshold I understood why Luca's father had told us not to. "Come out, come out, Nico'!" In an instant I'd been attacked by a swarm of mosquitoes. I retreated.

So I watched this operation, which the Varanis had to perform every time they came here, at least in summer. Signor Varani
went around the car. He opened the trunk. Then he headed to
the chapel with a spray can. He sprayed the insecticide. In the
meantime his wife had taken a plastic bottle and poured water in
front of the threshold of the chapel to keep the dust from getting
encrusted. It seemed to me that together they gave life to a sort
of sacred gesture.

In the chapel were some fifty niches, arranged vertically one
above the other. I looked at the dates of birth on the plaques.
Luca was the youngest. The old populated the cemeteries, and
populated the squares. Luca's tomb was overflowing with flowers. It was hard to add new ones every week, Signor and Signora
Varani didn't even know who came and put them there. There
were notes, poems, a letter from a teacher, a Navajo proverb. All
together they formed the equivalent of a small altar. We recited
the prayers together. Then Luca's mother made a gesture that, we
understood, was habitual. She knocked with her knuckles on the
marble of the niche.

I left the chapel. In front of me the tombs and the green of
the trees. Somewhere around there lay Sandro Penna. It was the
middle of the afternoon. Insects hovered in the air and the light
was perfect.

Then Luca's parents invited us to their house.

Chiara and I followed them in the car. We stopped along the
highway. Signor Varani got gas. He offered us something to eat
from the service station café. Chiara and I accepted without much
argument. Sandwiches and Coke. Giuseppe Varani brought them
on a small tray. I had always seen him angry. Now both Varanis
had a disarming politeness. They had had LUCA tattooed on their
wrists. We got back in the car and followed them to Via della
Storta; the city center was definitively behind us. Here was the
house where Luca lived. The building was constructed on three

428 · NICOLA LAGIOIA

levels. To get in you had to climb a scaffold: the ground floor was being renovated. In the Varanis' plans, it could have been Luca's apartment. But now? We went up to the first floor, sat in the living room. On one side the dining table. On the other the television and the sideboard. Doilies and pitchers on the shelves.

After we'd talked for a while Luca's mother told us we could look in the other room. I got up. We crossed the hall. She opened the door. The Tom and Jerry pillow was on the bed and another with the Union Jack. Computer and monitor on the desk. A model car on the mouse pad that pictured bowling pins knocked down by a strike. The small black plastic light attached to the closet door, a few centimeters from the bed, which Luca turned on to read and turned off before going to sleep. Some books on the shelves. *The Little Prince*. A dictionary. A big Mickey Mouse puppet on the wall. Next to it, also on the wall, was the only element that might enable someone who didn't know the story to comprehend the situation: a commemorative poster with a collage of photos in which Luca appeared at various moments of his life.

We returned to the living room. We sat around the table and started talking again. Signor Varani offered us a carob liqueur. The living room was at the back of the house. The view from the open windows was stupendous. We saw the countryside, the tall pines, the meadows. "So? How's this liqueur?" Soon the sun would set. The heat would give way to a placid summer evening. We were still chatting as the starry sky, taking possession of the scene, was revealed to our gazes by the complicated principles of rotation and revolution, the gigantic machine that gives birth to us and reduces us to dust.

Once you crossed the threshold of international airports, cities were all the same. London, Paris, New York. The differences dissolved in the windows of a clothing store. And now Rome, thought the Dutch tourist, ascending to the third level of Terminal 3.

The new space had been inaugurated a few months earlier. A large, light-filled pavilion whose shapes evoked a carefree world, without conflicts and differences. The first two levels devoted to shopping. Then an immense food court. The offerings ranged from Asian cuisine to Italian. There was the restaurant of a famous chef where you could get a quick but elegant meal. Farther on were the great couture boutiques. Order. Beauty. Italy as it would have been if the national genius had been handed over to a Scandinavian spirit to manage. Luckily it wasn't like that, thought the Dutch tourist. It never would be.

After the arrest, the cops had tried to scare him. They'd said that in jail the other prisoners would give him the treatment reserved for people like him. Nothing like that had happened. In the end they'd had to release him. A legal vacuum. If the minor was under ten, the crime was prosecuted automatically by law. Over fourteen the offense became prostitution of minors, provided the injured party pressed charges. Between ten and fourteen, however, a parent or guardian of the minor had to press charges—the minor, by himself, couldn't do it. He, of course, knew that. It was the boy who didn't know it, the thirteen-year-old who had reported him. He had arrived on a boat with other desperate people. Parents didn't exist. Guardians didn't exist. They had had to release the man.

The Dutch tourist sneezed, got a brioche and cappuccino. He looked out the enormous window that faced the runways. He heard his flight called.

The Thai Airways Airbus A330 rolled along the runway and in a moment had taken off. The plane flew over the Mediterranean for a few seconds. Then it made a semicircle and headed in the opposite direction. Before altitude made the underlying world indistinguishable, the man saw Rome again. He sneezed again. How strange. He suddenly had a bad sore throat. From the window he recognized the Colosseum. Anyone who had read a book in his life knew that that was the world's inheritance. They robbed you in the subway. They insulted you at the traffic lights. They fleeced you in the restaurants, they coughed in your face. But in the end the balance was positive. The city gave you much more than it asked in exchange.

The story told in this book is true.

Its reconstruction is the product of an extended work of documentation that includes legal proceedings along with reports, wiretap recordings, now definitive rulings, audio and video evidence, official statements, interviews. I've used this documentation to reconstruct the events, the versions of the people involved, the narrative of the protagonists. For some of the people involved in the story, but largely absent from the media, fictional names have been used out of discretion.

I would like to thank those who have helped me in the lengthy task of preparation. In particular thanks to Chiara Tagliaferri, the journalist Chiara Ingrosso, and all those who agreed to talk or provide material on this story.

This book is dedicated to Alessandro Leogrande (1977-2017) and Fabio Menga (1974-2018).